The Magic Collector

Books by Clayton Taylor Wood:

The Runic Series

Runic Awakening

Runic Revelation

Runic Vengeance

Runic Revolt

The Fate of Legends Series:

Hunter of Legends

Seeker of Legends

Destroyer of Legends

Magic of Havenwood Series:

The Magic Collector

The Lost Gemini

The Magic Collector

Book I in the Magic of Havenwood Series

Clayton Taylor Wood

Special thanks to my wife, an endless supply of inspiration and support. And to all our muses, who hide in the strangest of places, whispering magic into our ears.

Table of Contents

The Magic Collector

Prologue

year after his young son Xander's death, a painter set about to do something terrible.

He set his old wooden easel in the center of his studio, a good-sized room on the second floor of his home. A home once filled with love and a beautiful wife, with friends that visited almost daily. Now it was abandoned. Everyone else had moved on after Xander's death.

Everyone but him.

The painter gathered his paints and paintbrushes, mixing his colors carefully. Then he placed a large canvas on the easel, and got to work.

He outlined a shadowy head, then a body. A hand stretching out, reaching for him…even as it fell away, deeper into the canvas. Then deep, dark blue water that filled the entire canvas, save for the very bottom. On this he painted the edge of a wooden raft, slick with puddles of water.

And in the reflections of these puddles, he painted children running toward the edge of the raft, faces struck with desperation…and horror.

At the very surface of the water, around the shadowy figure reaching for him, he painted violent ripples that expanded outward. As if something had just plunged beneath the surface.

The painter stopped, the pain too unbearable to continue.

He went to the small window in his studio then, one overlooking a wide expanse of backyard. And beyond that, a lake. Moonlight splashed over the water in ghostly silver ripples, the sun having long since buried itself below the horizon. He lowered his chin to his chest, closing his eyes.

I'm sorry son.

Tears trickled down his cheeks, dripping onto his paint-smudged shirt. He turned back to the painting, walking up to it and stretching his hand out to the figure reaching for him. If he'd only been a minute earlier, he could have…

Stop it.

He took a deep breath in, centering himself. Then he put brush to canvas, forging onward.

He filled in the dark figure's details. An eight-year-old boy's bare chest, a pair of blue shorts. Skinny legs and bare feet. A head of short brown hair, large brown eyes.

Frightened eyes. Desperate, filled with terror…and hope.

The painter almost stopped again, his guts twisted with grief. More tears blurred his vision, and he wiped them away, pushing past his feelings. No…*using* them. He painted as if possessed, the story of the painting flowing from his heart and through his brush, so that it might find life on his canvas.

A mouth open in a silent scream, bubbles of air rising from it in a horrible torrent. Life-giving air leaving the boy, rising to the surface even as he sank deeper into the deadly lake.

The painter cried out then, a tortured sound that filled the studio. But still he painted, the strokes at times angry, then bitter. Loving, then guilty. Every stroke a memory, an emotion. Every layer of paint a layer of his soul.

And then, at long last, as the sky outside began to brighten, the sun promising to peek above the waters of the lake any moment now, the terrible deed was done.

The painter stood before his work, studying the painting carefully. His son Xander, reaching out to him, fingers seeming to leap off of the canvas. A painting so vibrant it almost seemed real.

He stared at his son's face, twisted with horror, desperate to be saved…and extended one hand toward his son's, reaching for the boy. His fingertips touched the canvas, pressing against it. He blinked in surprise, not expecting the resistance, and withdrew his hand.

It's not real.

He stared at the boy's face, that angelic face. A face burned into his memory. Trusting that his father would always be there, that if anything bad happened, daddy would save him. But daddy hadn't been there. Daddy hadn't saved him.

The painter's eyes went to the bottom right of the painting, at the surface of the raft. Then they dropped to the palette in his left hand…and to a fine-tipped paintbrush lying on the floor nearby.

He swallowed in a dry throat, his heart starting to race.

It's not real, he reminded himself.

But he found himself kneeling down, reaching for the paintbrush. His hands trembled as he stood, dipping the tip of the brush into the white splotch of paint on his palette.

He faced the canvas, his whole body quivering now, his heart hammering in his chest.

Taking a step forward, he leaned over, pressing the tip of the brush against the canvas. Before he could change his mind, he cried out, signing his name in quick, sure strokes, each letter perfectly executed.

A gentle breeze caressed him from behind.

He stood then, staring at the painting. And in that moment, he didn't care about the consequences. Didn't care about what might happen to him. He felt a sudden sense of peace…a feeling he hadn't felt since…

The painter smiled, reaching out to the painting again, his fingertips touching the canvas.

And passing right *through* it.

He felt a familiar warmth in his fingers, spreading to his hand as he plunged it into the painting. A warm, pulsing sensation, along with a subtle tingling, as if his hand had started to fall asleep. His wrist vanished into the painting, and then he felt his hand touch something warm and soft.

A palm.

He drew a sharp breath in, then pressed his own palm against it, marveling at the resistance. Then he hesitated, but only for a moment. Reaching in further, he went past the palm, feeling his fingers wrap around a small, bony wrist.

He closed his eyes, taking a deep breath in…and pulled.

3

Chapter 1

BAM!

Bella jerked upright with a start, her eyes snapping open. She realized she was sitting in her desk at school…and that a hand had slammed down on her algebra book, jolting her out of a particularly pleasant daydream. Bella stared at the hand, following it upward. An almost skeletal wrist poking out of a black sleeve. A scrawny neck. And the face of a dreadfully thin, middle-aged woman staring down at her, pale lips pursed in disapproval.

"*What* did I tell you about daydreaming in my class, Miss Brown?" the woman inquired. Bella stood up straighter, warmth spreading across her cheeks. Everyone in the class was staring at her…and a few were snickering.

"Sorry Mrs. Pittersworth," she mumbled. Mrs. Pittersworth lifted her hand from Bella's book, crossing her arms over her chest. She held Bella's gaze for a moment longer, then turned away, walking back to the front of the room. Bella let go of a breath she hadn't realized she'd been holding, wiping sweaty palms on her thighs. She felt the eyes of her classmates still on her, and pretended to ignore them, glancing at the clock on the wall.

She sighed, groaning inwardly.

For while her daydream had seemed to go on for hours – a silly fantasy involving a mushroom forest and a sparkling lake, with dragons flying in the air all around her – only five minutes had passed in the real world. And there were far too many more to go before the last class of the day was over.

Tick, tock.

Bella stared at the black hands of the clock on the wall as Mrs. Pittersworth droned on. The hands made no sound in real life, but in her imagination they rang loudly between each dreadful pause in their movements, celebrating every hard-earned step in the laborious passage of time.

Tick, tock.

Mrs. Pittersworth paced in front of the classroom, reciting almost verbatim from the textbook she held. But try as she might, Bella couldn't focus on what Mrs. Pittersworth was saying for more than a minute or so. She found her mind wandering again, and soon her eyelids grew heavy.

Focus, she scolded herself.

Bella sighed, opening her notebook. On the left page were various algebra problems, and on the right a half-finished sketch of a dragon standing next to a sixteen-year-old girl. The girl was Bella herself; slender, with chocolate-colored skin and long, curly black hair pulled back into a ponytail. Big brown eyes and arched eyebrows. Jeans and a loose sweater…the clothes Bella was wearing now. The dragon was one she'd drawn hundreds of times before, if not thousands. It was no ordinary dragon, the ones with pretty golden scales and elegant wings and such. No, this dragon had no scales whatsoever. Or much in the way of flesh for that matter. It was a skeletal dragon, pinpricks of ghostly light glimmering from deep within in its eye sockets. Bony wings spread outward magnificently from its back, skeletal fingers connected by inky-black skin. The dragon stood between the girl and a menacing figure; a tall man cast entirely in shadow, wielding a long, slender sword that glowed with an eerie light.

She gazed at the dragon – *her* dragon – for the moment forgetting the tortuous passage of time.

"Now, if you turn to page fifty-seven," Mrs. Pittersworth instructed, her voice practically quivering with anticipation, "…you'll find your very first quadratic equation!"

Bella glanced at her textbook, flipping to the appropriate page. Not because she was particularly interested in what it had to say, but because she didn't want to get caught not paying attention again. The last thing she needed was another day of detention. It was obvious that teachers knew how absolutely awful school was; the worst punishment of all was to give you more of it.

Tick, tock.

She turned to gaze out of the tall, narrow windows to her left. Stately trees stood in a sea of grass, their red and orange leaves fluttering in a slight breeze. The year was dying, its long, cheery days – and the freedom they'd brought – but a wistful memory now. Dark, dreary days were ahead, cold and devoid of life, with no end in sight.

Bella sighed again, returning her attention to her dragon. She picked up her pencil and started filling in a few details. Long bone-colored horns atop its head. Short spikes on each vertebra of its spine. Each finger and toe terminating in a deadly black claw. And, as always, a heart-shaped ruby amulet embedded within its long breastbone.

Bella hesitated, then drew a jagged crack in the center of the ruby, touching her chest with her other hand. She felt the same amulet there, resting against *her* breastbone.

"Bella?"

She barely heard her teacher, continuing to draw, finishing her dragon's tail. It was long and thin, curling around its feet.

"Bella!"

She jerked her head up, staring at Mrs. Pittersworth from across the room. Mrs. Pittersworth stared right back, her hands on her narrow hips. She did *not* look pleased.

"Are you doodling again?" her teacher snapped. Bella grimaced. There was no point in lying; Mrs. Pittersworth would march right up and snatch the notebook away to see for herself.

"Yes Mrs. Pittersworth," she mumbled.

"Show me," Pittersworth commanded, extending a hand. Bella sighed, grabbing her notebook and getting up from her desk, walking dejectedly to the front of the class. She heard snickering from her classmates.

"Here," she muttered, handing the notebook over. Mrs. Pittersworth studied the drawing, her lips pulled into a thin, disapproving line. Then she handed Bella the notebook, crossing her arms over her chest.

"Do you think you'll be able to make a living doodling *dragons*, Bella?"

More snickers from the back of the classroom.

6

"No Mrs. Pittersworth," Bella mumbled, lowering her gaze to her feet.

"Then I suggest you pay attention during class," her teacher counseled. "Look at me when I talk to you!"

Bella lifted her gaze reluctantly.

"How many times have I warned you Bella?" Mrs. Pittersworth demanded. "And still you don't listen. So now we'll be spending some quality time together at detention."

Bella nodded mutely, walking back to her desk and slumping back into it.

"Weirdo," someone whispered from behind.

Bella felt her cheeks grow warm, and did her best to ignore the eyes she knew were on her. She glanced at the clock, its hands seeming to move even slower than before.

Tick, tock.

She gave a heavy sigh, turning her attention to her algebra book and doing her best to listen to her teacher. Time stretched outward before her, a veritable infinity of drudgery. First school, then a job, forever a slave to the clock. Always waiting for something better. For a tiny sliver of freedom at the end of the day, where she could finally be herself…without anyone yelling or snickering at her for it.

She'd been so close, a mere twenty minutes away. But now there would be many more *ticks* and *tocks* before she was finally free of the clock.

* * *

Bella plodded up the spiral staircase toward the third floor of her apartment building, her overstuffed backpack threatening to pull her backward and send her tumbling down the stairs. A heavy sigh escaped her, the weight on her shoulders both literal and figurative. For though she had finally managed to escape that horrid prison they called high school, she was not truly free from its clutches. A monstrous amount of homework was waiting for her, cackling from its lair within the dark recesses of her backpack.

It offered a grim choice: a quick death by yanking her down the stairs with its awful weight, or the slow, painful disintegration of her soul.

7

She chose the latter, trudging along until she'd reached the third-floor landing. A dull brown door greeted her, the paint scuffed and peeling. Stepping up to it, she knocked precisely thirteen times, in the rhythm she'd long since memorized.

There was no answer.

She counted to herself, reaching thirty-three, then knocked again, seven times.

"Yes?" a deep, muffled voice inquired from beyond the door.

She recited the following passage:

"A dragon circle,
White and good,
Will one day rise
For Havenwood."

There was a *click* from beyond the door, followed by a *thunk*, then another series of *clicks*. The door swung open, revealing a short, narrow hallway beyond...guarded by an old man. He would've been tall if the weight of time hadn't bent his spine. Time had been similarly cruel to his short curly hair and haphazard beard, draining them of their color until they were stark white. He wore a ratty brown sweater and gray sweatpants that'd grown far too big for him...the same ones he'd worn yesterday, she noted with dismay. His dark brown skin was lined with wrinkles, only his eyes carrying the spark of life. They peered at her from behind golden spectacles, then past her to the stairwell beyond.

"You're late," he accused in a deep, rich baritone, the kind of voice that could fill a room and send chills down your spine. "Are you...?"

"I'm alone Grandpa," she confirmed wearily, pushing past him and into the hallway beyond. She kicked off her shoes, setting them neatly against the wall, then slid her backpack off, letting it fall to the floor with a *thump*. Grandpa shut the door quickly, re-engaging the ridiculous number of locks he'd installed on it.

"Did anyone follow you?" he asked, turning from the door and putting his hands on his hips. She sighed.

"No Grandpa."

"Did you see any police?" he pressed.

"*No* Grandpa," she repeated, rubbing her aching shoulders. "You met that friend of yours again, didn't you," she accused. He was always like this afterward.

"You're sure you didn't see any…"

"Grandpa!" Bella exclaimed exasperatedly. His shoulders slumped.

"Fine," he mumbled. He eyed her for a moment. "Caught doodling again?" he guessed.

"Yeah."

"Show me," he requested, holding out a hand. She sighed, kneeling down to rummage in her backpack. She found her notebook, handing it to him. Grandpa flipped to the proper page with a practiced hand, peering over his spectacles at it. "Hmm, it's good," he admitted.

"Mrs. Pittersworth didn't think so."

"Bah," Grandpa scoffed, giving her a look. "Only concern yourself with what people who *think* think," he counseled. "Believe me, they're few and far between."

Bella smiled at that. Grandpa had a low opinion of most people, Mrs. Pittersworth included. He often mused on how he'd spent the first part of his life trying to make friends…and the remainder trying to get rid of them. He must've done a good job, seeing as how he only had one friend left in this world…and Bella, of course. He could stand to have more, she knew. As it was, all he did was sit at his desk and write books that he wouldn't let anyone read. He left their tiny apartment a few times a year at most, even paying their downstairs neighbor to go grocery shopping for him. It was profoundly unhealthy if you asked her, but trying to get Grandpa to change was like smashing her head repeatedly against a brick wall: the only thing she got out of it was a splitting headache.

"Guess I'll be in the dining room," she sighed, grabbing her backpack by one strap and lugging it out of the narrow hallway and across the living room. "Did you eat today?"

"Doing what?" Grandpa inquired, ignoring her question. Which meant he hadn't.

"Grandpa," Bella scolded exasperatedly, stopping to glare at him. "You have to eat!"

"Doing *what?*" he repeated.

"Hard labor," Bella answered, continuing into their small dining room and tossing her backpack atop the old wooden table there. She began extracting her books.

"No no," Grandpa retorted, following her and grabbing her by the arm. "You can do that nonsense later. I want to show you something."

"Grandpa," she complained wearily. "I really need to get this done. And *you* need to eat something. I made you that chicken you like last night, remember?"

"Later, later," he insisted. "Come," he added, dragging her back into the living room. She sighed, allowing herself to be led toward one of the three small bedrooms in their little apartment. She spotted Grandpa's old wooden desk in the living room, set against the far wall. His notebooks were stacked haphazardly upon it, with framed drawings of mushrooms of all kinds displayed at the desk's edges, sketches Bella had drawn for him. She loved mushrooms, but not eating them. There was something magical about things that thrived in dark places.

She slowed, staring at the desk. There was something…*off* about it. She frowned, then realized what it was.

There was a painting hanging above it. A very large painting.

She stopped, studying it. Nearly as tall as the ceiling and a good three feet wide, it was of a graveyard bathed in ghostly moonlight. Tombstones rose from the dank earth like rotted teeth, and before these lay a body sprawled on its belly over the dirt. A naked body with dead eyes staring right at her.

"Oh god!" Bella gasped, bringing her hand to her mouth. "Grandpa!"

It *was* Grandpa…an eerie likeness of him, anyway. Grandpa followed her gaze, his eyes lighting up.

"Do you like it?" he inquired. "My friend painted it for me."

She didn't have to ask which friend, of course; he only had one. She'd never met the man, and strongly suspected she never would.

"He painted you dead in a graveyard," she stated. He nodded happily. "You sure he's your friend?" she pressed.

"Well, we did have a bit of a falling out years ago," Grandpa admitted, scratching his short beard. "He sort of ruined my life, actually. But he's doing his best to make it up to me."

"Huh."

"What do you think of it?" he pressed.

10

"I like everything except my naked dead Grandpa staring at me."

"I'll take that as a compliment."

"Tell me you didn't pose for this," she pleaded, eyeing him warily. He gave her a look that was far too innocent. "That's it, I'm shampooing the carpet," she grumbled.

"I laid on some towels," he reassured her. "And threw them in the wash," he added hastily.

"Just...why, Grandpa?"

"Well, my naughty bits were on them, you see, and I..."

"The *painting* Grandpa."

He chuckled, then regarded the painting for a quiet moment.

"It helps remind me of what's coming," he answered at last. "And that every beginning has an end...and every end a new beginning."

"There you go, being all mysterious again," Bella muttered. Grandpa was always saying things like that.

"I'm a writer," he replied matter-of-factly, as if that explained it. It was his excuse for just about everything he did.

"You're really going to keep that up there, aren't you?"

"Just be glad I wasn't on my back," Grandpa replied with a wicked grin, waggling his bushy eyebrows. She pretended to retch, and he laughed. "Come on sweetheart," he urged, pulling her toward one of the bedrooms again. "I want to show you something."

"I think I've seen enough," she retorted. But she let herself be led, and they entered the small spare bedroom Grandpa used as a storage room. To her surprise, it'd been cleaned out...and at the far end of the room stood a wooden easel, a fresh canvas sitting upon it.

She drew a sharp breath in, her eyes widening.

"Happy birthday sweetheart," he declared, gesturing at the easel. She just stared at it, her mouth agape. She closed it with an audible *click*.

"How...?"

"I had the neighbor get them," Grandpa explained.

"Grandpa, this..." Bella said, shaking her head. She gave him a big hug, wiping sudden moisture from her eyes. "Thank you Grandpa."

"You're welcome."

11

They disengaged, and she walked up to the easel, running her fingertips over the rough canvas. For the first time that day, she felt a burst of excitement. A spark of life. He'd gotten her *everything*…the easel and canvas, a palette, brushes, and boxes and boxes of paints.

"You always said you wanted to be a painter like your mother," Grandpa reminded her, gazing at the gifts with a satisfied smile. "And if you want to *be* something…"

"You have to *do* it," Bella recited.

"Right," he agreed. "I thought we'd start you off with acrylics."

"This is great," Bella murmured, shaking her head slowly. She turned to Grandpa then, her hands on her hips. "How much did it cost?"

"I've been saving," he stated rather defensively.

"I counted our money last week," she retorted. "We barely had enough for rent!"

"I've been saving," he insisted. "I put some cash away." Her eyebrows rose.

"You hid money from me?"

"I wanted it to be a surprise," he explained. "You only turn sixteen once you know."

"Is this why you haven't been eating?" she pressed. He grimaced, but held his ground.

"We can afford it," he insisted. "We *have* to afford it. Yes this cost a lot, but not following your dreams will cost you far more."

She sighed, dropping her hands to her sides. The thought that Grandpa had gone hungry, lying awake at night starving…and all for her…was heartbreaking. But it was clear that he was absolutely delighted with the result, his eyes twinkling with excitement. She gave a reluctant smile, and Grandpa beamed back at her. She stepped up to him, giving him another hug.

"Thanks Grandpa."

He gave her a squeeze, then pushed her away gently, gesturing at the canvas.

"Go on," he urged. "Try it out!"

She turned to the easel, stepping up to it. Then she hesitated. The pristine whiteness of the canvas was suddenly intimidating, a perfect emptiness that she could only ruin.

"I don't know…"

"Of course you don't," he agreed. "You've never painted before."

"Can you teach me?" she asked. He scoffed.

"I'm a writer, not a painter."

"But I don't know what to do," she pointed out.

"Well it's easy," he replied. "Squeeze some paint on this," he instructed, pointing to the wooden palette, "...then dip your brush in it. Then wipe your brush on the canvas."

Bella shot him a withering glare, crossing her arms over her chest.

"Thanks for the tip," she grumbled.

"Have fun!" he exclaimed, walking out of the small room and closing the door behind him. She stared at the door for a long moment, then turned to give similar treatment to the canvas.

Its perfect emptiness was vast, an unconquerable wasteland. She stepped up to it slowly, feeling overwhelmed. The thought of doing homework was suddenly far preferable, and she turned back to the door, opening it.

And found Grandpa standing there, arms crossed over his chest.

"What's wrong?" he demanded.

"I...don't know what to paint."

He relaxed visibly, a smile lighting his features.

"Ah, of course," he replied, leading her back to the easel. "Terrifying, isn't it?" he added, gesturing at the canvas. "A blank page is the artist's most dreaded enemy." He wrapped a bony arm around her shoulders. "I feel the same way when I'm writing."

"Really?"

"Oh yes," he confirmed. "That perfect blankness! Untouched. Pure!" He looked down at her with a conspiratorial smile, his eyes twinkling. "Ruin it."

She blinked, and his smile broadened.

"Go on," he urged.

"What?"

"Ruin it!" he cried, grabbing the package of paintbrushes and tearing one free from its window of plastic wrap. He grabbed a tube of acrylic, squirting it directly onto the brush, then presenting it to Bella.

"But..."

13

"No buts!" he retorted, shoving the brush into her hands. He pointed at the canvas. "Destroy!"

Bella hesitated, eyeing the canvas. Then she stepped forward, looming over it. She glanced back at Grandpa, who made violent slashing motions with one arm, as if conducting a mad orchestra. She smiled reluctantly, facing the canvas.

And brought the paintbrush down upon it, violating its perfection with an angry black gash.

"Ha!" Grandpa cried in triumph, beaming at Bella. She broke out into a bigger smile, eyeing her handiwork. The canvas was utterly ruined.

"*Now* you can paint," he declared.

"But...what if it's bad?"

"Oh, it *will* be," Grandpa answered matter-of-factly. He gestured to the right of the easel then, at an enormous number of canvases stacked on top of each other, forming a tower that threatened to touch the ceiling. He pointed to the top of it. "This one will be too," he added. Then he pointed to the canvas at the bottom of the stack. "But *this* one, ahhh...I can't wait to see it!"

Bella must have looked entirely unconvinced.

"You'll be terrible," he assured her. "Even your mother was at first. And she ended up being the second-best painter I ever met."

"But..."

"Just paint," he interjected. "When you're done, I promise I'll devour that delicious meal you made me." Then he turned about, leaving the room and shutting the door behind him again.

Bella sighed, trudging up to the easel, then glancing down at the tubes of acrylic paint set neatly in their packaging to her left. She knew full-well that Grandpa really *wouldn't* eat until she'd filled the canvas with paint. He'd clearly lost weight this month, and couldn't afford to lose much more. They were barely getting by on him selling his stories.

She sighed again, looking down at the paintbrush in her hand. Suddenly she felt silly wasting her time painting. There was a mountain of homework she still had to do, after all. She had to do well in school to have a chance at getting a good job...one that would let her take care of both of them. Mrs. Pittersworth had been right, of course; Bella would never make a living doodling.

But she couldn't *not* paint, not after what Grandpa had sacrificed to get this for her.

14

"Just paint, huh?" she mumbled to herself. She took a deep breath in, squaring her shoulders and focusing on the blighted canvas. "All right Bella, you can do this."

And with that, she got to work, proving herself utterly and horribly wrong.

Chapter 2

That day, Bella did a painting of an orchid she kept on her windowsill, attempting to transform the angry black gash she'd made into its stem.

It was a disaster.

Her colors were garish and grotesque, her lines far too thick. Every attempt to salvage the painting only made things worse, each stroke of her brush driving it further from her original vision. Her frustration mounting – and matched only by her despair – she'd finally thrown up her hands in surrender, fleeing the scene of the crime and slamming the door behind her to hide the evidence. To her relief, Grandpa took this as undeniable proof that she'd performed the task he'd given her, and he did not ask to witness the gruesome result. Holding up his end of the bargain, he'd devoured every last morsel of the meal she'd cooked for him.

She'd been so distressed by her utter failure that she'd almost given up on painting altogether...and would have if Grandpa hadn't threatened to go on another hunger strike. He'd insisted that she paint every day, no matter what. Even if she didn't feel like it. *Especially* if she didn't feel like it.

And so she did.

Days passed, each bringing yet another failure. But each was a smaller failure than the last, and the usual dread she experienced with each fresh canvas gradually dwindled, until that once-awful white void was simply an invitation to fill it. She began to experiment with mixing colors, and with brushes of different shapes and sizes. And while the results were hardly to her standards, they got closer bit-by-bit, until the thought of revealing them to another soul no longer filled her with terror.

Grandpa never asked to see the paintings, taking her at her word that she'd painted them. His only request was that he see the last painting, the one from the canvas at the bottom of the heap. Two weeks later, she found herself reaching for that very one.

It was then that she returned to her very first painting, still set against the wall, facing away from her in shame. She turned it around, staring at it for a while. Then, with a deep breath and squared shoulders, she retrieved the orchid from her bedroom that had inspired it, setting it on the windowsill next to the easel.

And she painted.

By the time the sun began to set on that Sunday afternoon, Bella set the final stroke of her brush upon the canvas, backing away from her painting and regarding it for a long moment. To her surprise, it was rather good. A fine orchid with sun-kissed purple and white petals that cast gentle shadows on the leaves below, supported by a slender, stately stem.

"Huh," she said, tapping her chin with her brush. Then she frowned, realizing she'd painted a purple blotch there. She set her brush down, exiting her little studio and crossing through the living room to go to the bathroom and wash it off. Grandpa was home, of course, sitting on his perennial perch at his desk.

"All done?" he inquired, looking up from his notebook. He still wrote his books longhand, refusing to use a computer.

"Yep," she called out as she passed, reaching the bathroom and washing her face. She emerged, stretching her stiff back. "Ooof."

"There's still time for one more," he stated.

"We're out of canvases," she replied...and instantly regretted it. Grandpa's eyebrows rose.

"Already?"

"Yeah," she admitted.

He stood from his chair with a grunt, gesturing at the door to her studio.

"Then I suppose it's time," he proclaimed. "Lead the way!"

Bella sighed, dutifully grabbing Grandpa's arm and leading him toward the studio.

"Should I cover my eyes?" he inquired.

"Definitely."

He did just that, allowing Bella to pull him into the studio. She brought him to stand before the easel.

"Okay," she declared. "You can look."

He dropped his hand, studying the painting for a long, silent moment. Then he leaned in close, peering at the brushstrokes while scratching his scraggly white beard. Bella chewed a fingernail nervously, the suspense threatening to drive her mad.

"Well?" she blurted out at last. Grandpa stood up as straight as he could, turning to face her.

"It's good," he proclaimed, breaking into a smile. "Well done, Bella!"

"You think so?" she asked, daring to hope. He shot her a look, and she smiled. Grandpa was a vicious critic, incapable of telling a lie for the sake of sparing someone's feelings. A trait Bella had inherited...and almost certainly the reason why they both had trouble keeping friends.

"Where's your first painting?" he inquired. She pointed to one of the paintings facing the wall. "May I see it?"

"I guess."

He retrieved the painting, turning it around and eyeing it critically. She looked over his shoulder, cringing at the sheer awfulness of it.

"It's pretty bad," she admitted.

"It's downright horrible," he countered, making a face.

"Gee, thanks."

"I'm getting a headache looking at it," he added, putting it down and making a point to have the business end face the wall.

"Ha ha," Bella grumbled. "You know what? I'm just going to throw it in the dumpster. And set it on fire."

"No no," he retorted. "Keep it. It's important to know where you started. That way you'll always be able to remind yourself of far you've come."

She nodded, and he gazed out of the small window at the far end of the room with a wistful smile.

"I remember my first book," he mused. "Nearly a year of hard work, slaving over my precious story! I was so proud of it." He turned to her with an impish grin. "I showed my brother, and he read it from start to finish. Do you know what he said?"

18

Bella shook her head.

"It's not good," he answered. He chuckled at the memory, putting a warm hand on Bella's shoulder. "He was right," he continued. "Though I hated to admit it. So I rewrote it. And rewrote it again, and again, and again. Eight times I wrote that book, until I was satisfied with it. Then I had your grandmother read it. You know what *she* said?"

"What?"

"It's not good," he repeated. He cackled then, his eyes lighting up at the memory. "So I wrote it again! And then it *was* good...or good enough, anyway. My point is, the only way to truly fail is to give up...and most people do."

"So keep painting," Bella translated. Grandpa nodded.

"If you want to *be* something..."

"You have to *do* it," she finished. She sighed then, looking around the room. "Guess I'm going to need more canvases."

"Already ordered," Grandpa declared with a proud smile. Bella gave him an exasperated look, and he put up his hands defensively. "We have the money," he insisted. "I'll have you know I managed to con someone into buying one of my short stories."

"You did?"

"I did," he confirmed. "Not for much mind you, but we'll have a roof over our heads and food in our bellies for another month."

She smiled at him, giving him a hug.

"I'm proud of you Grandpa."

He embraced her back, then pulled away, turning back to her most recent painting. He put his hands on his hips.

"I don't want you painting this stuff anymore," he declared.

"What stuff?" she asked, taken aback. He gestured at the painting.

"This stuff," he answered.

"Flowers?"

"Things you see," he corrected. "Things outside of you. I know painters who spend their whole lives painting like that. What a waste!"

Bella frowned at him.

"So...what do I paint? My internal organs?" The idea suddenly intrigued her.

"Why did you paint the flower?" he countered, ignoring her quip. Her frown deepened. She hated when he answered a question with a question, which he did far too often.

"It looked pretty," she answered with a shrug.

"Exactly!" he exclaimed. And that's all someone who looks at it will ever think. Hmm, that's pretty. I like the way it looks." He scoffed. "That's not art, it's decoration!"

"Okay…"

"If I wrote books that just said: 'Jack went home. Jack ate dinner. He went to bed. His bed was soft. He fell asleep…' Would anyone read it?"

"I don't know," she replied testily, her hands on her hips. "You've never let me read your books."

"No one would read it!" he answered. "Because I'd just be describing what happened. This, then this, then this. Boring!"

"What does that have to do with my flower?" she pressed.

"You're just describing the flower with paint," he explained. "Green stem, a few leaves, nice petals. A flower in bloom. Boring! You need to tell a *story*."

"With paint?"

"With paint," he confirmed. "And those stories aren't out there," he added, gesturing at the orchid on the windowsill. "They're in here," he continued, jabbing a finger at her chest. "Everyone is the main character of their own story…and the story we tell ourselves *about* ourselves guides everything we do. We can be the hero, the victim, or the villain…and the choice is ours."

"Okay…"

"Tell me, do you *really* care about flowers, Bella?" he asked.

"They're all right."

"They're *safe*," he corrected. "Painting pretty petals all day. Where's the risk? You need to paint things you're afraid of!"

"Like your cooking?"

"Ha!" he replied. "I mean things deep in your heart. Things that *matter* to you. Secrets you don't want anyone else to see. Things you don't want *you* to see. That's where real art comes from."

"Okay…"

"Those canvases," he added, gesturing at the canvases propped against the walls, "…are mirrors, Bella. They can show you who you are." He let go of her shoulder, crossing his arms over his frail chest and glaring down at her imperiously. "And you are *not* a dainty flower!"

She had to smile at that.

"Maybe a black one with thorns," she conceded.

"Indeed," Grandpa agreed with a rather rueful smile. He paused then, glancing at Bella's notebook on the floor beside the easel. He reached down to pick it up, flipping to the last page she'd drawn in and handing it to her. "Or perhaps you could paint this."

Bella glanced down at the notebook, seeing her latest sketch of her dragon there.

"I'm not ready for that," she protested. Grandpa frowned.

"Why not?"

"I'm not good enough," she answered.

"You mean you're not ready to," he corrected. "Well, at least promise me that you won't wait forever to *be* ready," he compromised. "Part of getting better is becoming comfortable with being uncomfortable."

"Alright," she agreed. "I promise."

"When I write, I'm like an archaeologist excavating an ancient subterranean tomb," he declared, pretending to grab a shovel and dig through the floor. "Finding priceless treasures buried deep within the earth! And those treasures are pieces of my heart and mind, lost to the ravages of time."

"Okay Grandpa," Bella said. Then she hesitated. "So what *should* I paint?"

"Something that makes you feel something," Grandpa answered. "If it makes *you* feel something, it will make others feel it. That's the magic of art, Bella. Throwaway art pleases the eye, good art changes people's minds, and great art...great art opens their hearts."

* * *

That evening, after cooking Grandpa his favorite meal – chicken and bell-peppers with roasted garlic and caramelized onion – they both got ready for sleep. Bella laid down in her bed, pulling her warm blanket up to her shoulders. Grandpa laid down atop the blanket next to her as he always did, telling her a story. It was the same ritual they'd gone through since...well, for as long as she could remember. He spun a fantastic tale right on the spot, somehow able to craft a different story every night. Extraordinary tales of a world of wondrous magic and vile monsters, valiant heroes and dastardly villains.

Grandpa had never let Bella read any of his books, but if they were anywhere near as good as his nightly tales, it was a wonder that he wasn't a world-famous author by now.

When the tale was done at last, he kissed Bella on the forehead.

"Goodnight sweetheart," he murmured, smiling down at her. She smiled back.

"Goodnight Grandpa."

He got up to leave, but Bella stopped him.

"Wait," she said. "You...you said Mom was the second-best painter you ever met?"

Grandpa laid back down, turning onto his side to face her.

"Oh yes," he replied. "She was magnificent."

"Tell me more about her," she urged. Grandpa hesitated, and she put a hand on his arm. "Please."

He sighed, lowering his gaze. Grandpa rarely talked about Mom, even when asked. He'd always deflected Bella's questions by saying he'd tell her when she was older, or that she'd learn soon enough. But "soon enough" had never been soon enough for her.

"All right," he decided, looking her in the eye. "What do you want to know?"

"What was she like?"

"She was a lot like you," he answered. "Same eyes, same smile." He smiled himself. "Her skin was darker, like mine. And her hair was a bit curlier."

"You're describing the flower," Bella accused. Grandpa frowned at her.

"Using my lessons against me, eh?" he groused. "Clever girl. I shouldn't teach you anything."

He sighed then, rolling onto his back and staring up at the ceiling. Moonlight cast its gentle silver rays on his dark skin, making his eyes glitter. He glanced at her nightstand then, spotting her notebook on it. And the drawing she'd done at school, of her and her dragon. He picked it up, gesturing at it.

"She had the heart of a dragon," he declared. "And your dragon has her heart," he added, pointing to the heart-shaped ruby embedded in its breastbone. He glanced down at the amulet Bella still wore around her neck, and Bella did as well, tracing the crack

22

in the middle with her finger. She had no pictures of her mother. Nothing else to remember her by.

The only thing her mother had left her was a broken heart.

"She *was* like a dragon," Grandpa mused. "Powerful and fierce. And always there to protect you, even in…"

He swallowed, putting the notebook back on the nightstand.

"Tell me her story," Bella insisted. Grandpa sighed again.

"I'll tell you *a* story," he decided.

He cleared his throat, then began.

"One day, your mother brought you to the college I was teaching at, at the time," he began. He'd been an English professor, Bella knew, before he'd been forced to retire. "You were only four then, such a cute little thing." He smiled at the memory. "You decided on the spot that your favorite place in the whole college was the great library. All the books on the shelves…you ran around, opening them up just to smell them and look at the pictures."

Bella listened intently, wishing she could remember. She still loved libraries, especially the city library a few blocks down the road, though she'd only been a few times. Back when Grandpa went out more.

"Your mother was strict with you, almost as bad as you are with me," he continued, giving her a wink. "She wanted to tie you down to the chair next to her while she and I talked. I told her to let you go and explore. That libraries were places of adventure and discovery!" He chuckled. "She said that there still had to be rules. She was very keen on rules, even though she was the very first to break them."

"Really?"

"Oh yes," he replied. "She had a rebel's heart and a mind that was quite the opposite. And the two fought constantly, like an old married couple."

Bella smiled at that.

"She sounds complicated," she admitted.

"Oh, you have *no* idea," he replied with a chuckle. "In any case, I told her that she'd made a terrible mistake bringing you to a library. Every book there had been written by people who loved to break rules. All the good books, anyway."

"What'd she say?"

"She said well, then it was a damn good thing you couldn't read."

They shared a chuckle, Grandpa's eyes twinkling at the memory.

"Your mother was something else," he mused. "I've never met anyone like her, other than you of course." He smiled then. "She could find beauty in the darkest dark, just like you."

"Did she...fit in?" Bella asked.

"Goodness no," Grandpa replied. "She *refused* to."

"So she was a weirdo?" she pressed. "Like me?"

"Most definitely."

Bella nodded, then fell silent, chewing at her lower lip. She hesitated, then looked Grandpa in the eye.

"How did she die?"

Grandpa stared back at her, his smile fading. He looked so miserable suddenly that Bella had the urge to take back her question, to tell him it was okay. That he didn't have to answer. But she held her ground, remaining silent. And that silence stretched out between them, growing bigger and louder with every passing second.

He rolled onto his back, staring at the ceiling. The few times she'd asked the question in the past, he'd avoided answering...and made it quite clear without saying it that she wasn't to ask the question again. But this time was different.

"She died the way she lived," he answered in a near-whisper. "Beautifully."

A lump formed in Bella's throat, and she swallowed past it, not daring to say anything. Grandpa turned to face her, tears wetting his cheeks.

"Your mother was a great artist," he murmured, reaching out to stroke her hair. "She painted with her heart," he added, his eyes dropping to the amulet Bella wore around her neck. "But of all the strange and wonderful things she brought to life," Grandpa continued, "...the greatest of them all was you."

Bella smiled, her own eyes brimming with moisture. Grandpa leaned in, kissing her on the forehead again, then pulling her head to his chest. She snuggled against his oversized sweater, letting it soak up the tears trickling down her cheeks. He held her for a while, and she closed her eyes, hearing the *lub-dub* of his heart beating in his chest.

At length he sighed, getting up from the bed and standing over her with a sad smile. Bella couldn't help but feel disappointed, knowing the story was over.

"Goodnight sweetheart," he murmured.

"Goodnight."

He walked around the bed, reaching the doorway and stepping through. He'd almost closed the door behind him when Bella stirred.

"Grandpa?" she asked.

"Yes?"

"Why did Mom have to die?"

Grandpa stood there for a long moment, a dark silhouette against the light from the living room beyond.

"She didn't have to," he replied at last.

And that was that.

Chapter 3

Weeks passed, the sun rising a little later and falling a little earlier each day. Autumn's chilly fingers swept through the neighborhood, sucking the life out of everything it touched. Grass yellowed and leaves turned dry and brown, falling from their lofty perches to form a crunchy carpet of corpses below. People combed their precious lawns with rakes, working feverishly to collect the leaves into big piles, bagging them and sending them far away as if they were radioactive. Jack-o-lanterns popped up on porches all over the neighborhood, their faces carved into wicked grins, seeming to relish the stark reality: the year was dying, the great cycle coming to a close once again.

It was Bella's favorite time of year.

By the last week of October, the first frost gripped the land, coating the streets and grass. A reminder that winter was coming, a Grim Reaper that would blanket the earth with its murderous snow, killing off an entire generation of plants and animals.

And so Bella found herself hopping down from her school bus on a chilly Friday afternoon, landing on the frosty sidewalk with a *thump*, her backpack bouncing painfully on her lower back. She escaped from the bus as quickly as she could, desperate to leave the school week far behind. Freedom beckoned, and she was eager to answer its call.

She made her way quickly down the sidewalk, leaving most of the other kids behind. No one tried to talk with her, and she didn't bother to talk to them. She was the weird girl, after all. The quiet girl that kept to herself, holed up in her apartment. Never going over friends' houses, always reading or doodling. She found the constant chatter of her classmates exhausting after a while, much preferring the quiet of the school library whenever she got the chance to go there. It was her one safe space outside of her apartment, a place where she could lose herself in books…in the minds of authors like Grandpa, who seemed so wise compared to kids her age…and most adults, for that matter.

Something unusual caught her attention as she walked; two police officers on the opposite side of the road, intercepting a few of the kids as they crossed the street. The officers started talking to the kids, gesturing at the bus.

Huh.

Bella promptly ignored them, keeping her head down and continuing forward. Her apartment building was only two blocks away. She spotted it in the distance, a narrow three-story building with faded yellow paint guarded by a rusty chain-link fence that was clearly not up to its task. It wasn't long before she reached it. The front gate opened with a loud screech, and she closed it behind her, climbing up the front steps to the porch. She unlocked the front door, propping it open with her foot and checking the mailbox labeled "Brown Family." Grandpa never checked the mail, of course; that would require leaving the apartment.

Bills, bills, and more bills.

She sighed, stepping inside the apartment and being sure to lock the door behind her. The same routine as always, one drilled into her from the moment they'd moved here nearly a decade ago. Up the spiral staircase she went, reaching the third floor and executing the usual ritual of knocks, followed by Grandpa's poem.

> "A dragon circle,
> White and good,
> Will one day rise…"

The door flung open before she could finish, and she jumped, nearly falling backward down the stairs. Grandpa burst out of the doorway, grabbing her arm and hauling her bodily into the apartment.

"Grandpa…!" she exclaimed. But he ignored her, slamming the door behind them and feverishly re-engaging the multitude of locks. She backed into the living room, staring at him with wide eyes. He finished, then whirled on her.

"Did they see you?" he asked. It was more a demand than a question. Bella shrank away from him; she'd never seen him like this.

"What?"

"Did they *see* you?" he repeated. She shrugged helplessly.

"Who?"

"Those men!" he answered. He pushed past her into the living room, hurrying to one of the windows and peering out. Bella slid her backpack off, walking to his side and following his gaze. He was looking at the two police officers she'd seen earlier. They were still talking to the children.

"The cops?" she asked. He scoffed.

"Cops," he muttered. "If they're cops then I'm one too, and so are you."

Bella frowned, putting a hand on Grandpa's shoulder.

"Grandpa, what's going on?"

He watched the police officers for a moment longer, then turned away from the window, running a hand through his curly white hair. It sprung haphazardly from his head, and Bella suddenly wondered when he'd washed it last. He looked frailer than ever, his skin hanging loosely over his bones. Grandpa noticed Bella watching him, and blinked.

"Hmm?"

"What's going on?" she repeated. "You're acting weird."

"I'm acting *weirdly*," he corrected automatically. Then he frowned. "Wait, no I'm not. Those aren't police officers Bella. They're bad people."

She arched an eyebrow.

"They're...it's complicated," he continued, walking to his desk and slumping into his chair. He sighed, shaking his head and staring off into space. "They're getting closer...we don't have much time."

"Much time for what?"

"For..." he began, then gestured at the apartment around them. "This."

"Grandpa, you're not making any sense."

"I know, I know," he replied with a grimace. "Thank the gods it's the weekend. That might just give us a few days. But I don't

28

think you should go to school anymore, not until they move on. *If they move on.*"

She stared at him uncomprehendingly, suddenly concerned for his well-being. He looked even more disheveled than usual, and his desk was awfully cluttered. Grandpa had always been a bit paranoid, what with the ridiculous number of locks on the door and refusing to leave the apartment, but it was clearly getting worse. Most of the time he was mostly normal, but sometimes there were times like this.

Not for the first time, she wondered whether or not he might be a bit…off.

He glanced at her, and it was clear that her expression mirrored her thoughts.

"I know this sounds crazy," he confessed, his shoulders slumping. "But I'm asking you to trust me. I know those men. From…a long time ago. They're dangerous, and you have to avoid them."

"Okay Grandpa, I will," she agreed. And she meant it. Not that she believed him, but she had no qualms about avoiding the police. He relaxed a bit.

"If they question you, give them a false name," he instructed. "And a false address. If they take you here…"

"Do the wrong knock," Bella finished, having heard this countless times before.

"Right."

"You're really going to pull me out of school?" Bella asked hopefully. Grandpa broke out into a smile.

"You'd like that, wouldn't you?" he replied. She nodded vigorously, and he chuckled. "Yes, I will. At least for a few days, until I know they're gone."

"Then I'll do anything you want," she decided with a smile.

He sighed, looking suddenly rather ashamed.

"Bella I…" he began, his voice cracking. "I'm not crazy."

Bella said nothing. There was nothing honest she could say without making him feel badly.

"I'm not," he insisted. "I know it seems like I am sometimes."

"Sometimes?" she inquired with an arch of her eyebrow. He gave a rueful smile back.

"I wasn't always like this," he insisted. "You should have seen me before all…this," he added wistfully, looking about the room. "Maybe one day you'll get to see me like I was."

"Okay Grandpa."

He got up from his chair, walking up to her and lowering himself awkwardly kneel before her. He took her by the hand, holding it in two of his own and looking up at her with such awful desperation that it was heartbreaking.

"I love you more than anything in this world," he declared, his eyes brimming with moisture. "You *are* my world, Bella. And I'm so proud of the woman you're becoming."

She nodded, feeling tremendously uncomfortable.

"Trust me for the next few days," he insisted. "That's all I ask."

"Okay Grandpa."

"Promise?" he pressed. She nodded.

"Promise."

He smiled, clearly relieved. For he knew it was exceedingly rare for Bella to make a promise, knowing how difficult they were to keep…and how easy it was to break them. When Bella made a promise, she kept it.

"Thank you sweetheart."

"Did you eat?" she asked, desperate to change the subject. She'd had enough drama for one day.

"A little," he answered. "I could use a bite, now that you mention it."

"I'll cook you something good," she promised, pulling away from him and walking toward the kitchen.

"Are you taking requests?" he inquired.

"If they're reasonable," she replied.

"How about your world-famous chili?"

She smiled, reaching the kitchen and grabbing a large pan. She set it on the stovetop with a *clang*, turning on the flame and opening the fridge to gather her ingredients.

"For you Grandpa," she declared, "…I'll do anything."

* * *

After their meal, Grandpa returned to his desk, slaving over whatever it was he happened to be writing. He insisted that Bella paint, seeing as how their downstairs neighbor had dropped off fresh armfuls of canvases earlier that day. The third shipment that month, in fact. Bella was getting quite proficient at finishing each painting, going through at least a canvas a day. The mere act of finishing – of seeing her work to its conclusion – had freed her from the fear of starting another project. For most of that fear was in doubting that she *could* finish anything.

Now she *knew* she could.

It was, she knew as she painted a fresh canvas utterly black, just as Grandpa had planned. Sure, he was a complete mess in most aspects of his life, but when it came to teaching he was second-to-none.

She stared at the now-black canvas, tapping her lower lip with her free hand. Her eyes went to the stack of paintings in the corner of her studio; her favorite paintings. Stepping up to them, she looked at each, trying to find some inspiration.

The first was of dull gray stone steps leading up to a pair of ornate double-doors. The rightmost doorknob was slick with crimson blood, and a chocolate-brown hand with long black fingernails faced the doors palm-first. A much larger hand made of dense fog smashed into the doors, forcing them slightly ajar…and exposing a pale golden light that peeked out from beyond.

The second painting was of a long, dark hallway facing the inside of those double-doors. A narrow, blood-red carpet led past long lines of white stone statues on either side, dense fog spilling across the corridor. The statues were of men in heavy armor, carrying swords whose sharp tips touched high above. And standing before the double-doors at the far end of the hallway, twin figures in thick black cloaks rose from the floor, their faces hidden in shadows throw by their hoods. Each wore silver metal gauntlets that emerged from their loose sleeves, clutching identical scythes. Scythes made of entirely of bones, wet blood staining their blades.

And between the two figures was a third. A tall man whose features were hidden entirely in shadow, wielding a long, glowing silver sword in his right hand.

Suddenly, she had an idea, and she went back to her inky-black canvas.

Bella mixed the various acrylic paints on her palette, making a light gold. Then, with a brush barely bigger than a pencil, she began to painstakingly recreate each link in a long chain, not even needing to glance at the necklace she wore that had inspired it. She'd long

31

since memorized its every detail. It'd been Mom's, after all. The very last thing her mother had given her before she'd died.

When she finished the golden amulet with the ruby heart in the center, she paused, then got some white and silver paint, making a thin, straight line to the right of the amulet.

A silver sword that glowed in the darkness.

She outlined a shadowy fist to hold the sword in a soft white glow, extending the glow upward to silhouette one side of an arm, then a shadowy face. Then she made bright rays of light shoot outward from that glowing silhouette, making them converge on the ruby.

A muffled voice came from beyond the closed door of her makeshift studio, and she stopped, straining her ears.

No, not a voice. Voices.

Bella set her brush down carefully, tiptoeing to the door and putting her ear against it. There were *definitely* two voices. Male voices, too muffled for her to make out what they were saying. But one of them was Grandpa's. She frowned, taken aback. Grandpa *never* had company over, not even the neighbors. When they brought him groceries, he made them wait outside the front door of the apartment.

She twisted the knob slowly, then cracked the door open.

The living room was empty, Grandpa's chair vacant.

Bella stepped out into the living room. It sounded like the voices were coming from the kitchen.

"Tomorrow?" she heard Grandpa hiss, his voice barely audible. There was a pause. "...not ready," she heard him say.

More muffled talking.

She hesitated, then creeped across the living room, making her way stealthily toward the kitchen.

A floorboard creaked under her foot.

The voices stopped immediately, and Bella cursed under her breath, sprinting toward the dining room, which led into the kitchen. She heard a loud *bang*, then muffled swearing. A moment later, she burst into the dining room, turning to look into the kitchen.

Grandpa was standing there by the stove, alone.

He startled, whirling around to stare at her with the guiltiest look she'd ever seen.

"What's going on?" she demanded. "Who was that?"

"Who was what?" Grandpa asked, far too innocently for her liking. He'd always been a terrible liar.

"I heard him," she insisted. "You two were talking."

Grandpa blanched, and he swallowed visibly.

"I was just, ah, talking to myself," he answered, giving her a weak smile. "Practicing different voices."

She stared at him for a long moment, then crossed her arms over her chest, shooting him a glare.

"You're lying to me," she accused.

"Bella…"

She stormed into the kitchen, having a look around. There was no one there but them…and the kitchen was a dead-end. No way out but the way she'd come in. She frowned, then began opening cupboard doors one-by-one, peering inside.

Nothing.

"See?" Grandpa said. "I told you."

"Uh huh," she grumbled. But of course he had to be telling the truth; there was no one else here. "What was that banging sound then?"

"I hit my head on the freezer door," he answered, rubbing the top of his head. "You surprised me."

"All right," she muttered. "Fine. So you were just talking to yourself."

"Yes."

"In different voices," she continued. He grimaced.

"Right."

"With the freezer door open while you were getting something from the fridge."

"I was hungry," he stated. She arched an eyebrow.

"We just ate."

"I wanted more of your delicious chili," he explained, smiling innocently at her. She rolled her eyes, but gave up, skulking out of the kitchen into the dining room. He followed behind her, grimacing and rubbing his chest. "You and your mother would've made fine interrogators," he grumbled. "You almost had me believing there *was* someone else here!"

"What's wrong?" she asked, glancing back at him. "Why are you holding your chest?"

"Just a little heartburn," he reassured. Still, he was clearly in pain, and his color looked a little off. She stopped, going to his side and putting a hand on his frail shoulder.

"Are you sure you're okay?"

"I'm fine," he insisted. "I love your chili, but just because you love something doesn't mean it has to love you back."

"Okay...well, I'll be painting," she replied, crossing into the living room.

"Wait," he stated. She felt a hand on her shoulder, and she stopped, turning to face him. "We...need to talk."

"What's wrong?" she asked.

"I know I said I was going to pull you out of school next week," he began. "But now I don't think it's such a good idea."

Bella crossed her arms over her chest.

"Why not?" she demanded.

"Those men don't know who you are yet," he explained. "If they did, they'd have gotten you. But if you don't show up next week, it might raise suspicion."

"Grandpa..."

"I know, I know," he interrupted. "Believe me, I understand how crazy this seems."

"Really crazy," she grumbled. "Like, certifiable."

"It's very important that you listen carefully to what I have to say," he insisted. He hesitated, his jawline rippling. "It could mean the difference between life and death."

Bella rolled her eyes.

"Oh come *on*," she groaned. "Seriously Grandpa?"

"Dead serious," he replied. And judging by his expression, he was. She had the sudden urge to sit down, and walked to the kitchen table to do just that. She rested her elbows on the table, rubbing her forehead with both hands.

"You're giving me a headache," she muttered. Then she sighed, looking up at him, still standing there in the living room. "Grandpa, do you think you might be a little...sick?"

"Sick? No," he replied. "I'm fine."

"Maybe you should go see a doctor," she suggested. It wasn't the first time she'd had the thought. As far as she knew, he hadn't seen a doctor since they'd moved here. He had to be in his late seventies, if not his eighties. To think that he might be developing dementia...it was heartbreaking.

"Bella, I'm *not* crazy."

"Then tell me what's really going on," she pleaded. Grandpa stared at her silently, then sighed, lowering his gaze to the floor. He turned to his desk, taking a small golden key from his pants-pocket and unlocking the bottom left drawer. He pulled it open, taking out a stack of papers, paperclips, and handfuls of pens. Then something else; a flat rectangular piece of wood. A false bottom.

"Grandpa, what are you...?" she began, but Grandpa ignored her, reaching into the drawer again and pulling out another key. This one was silver; he brought it to the bottom right drawer, unlocking it and lifting a small black safe from it. He brought this to Bella, setting it on the table before her.

"If anything happens to me, I want you to open this," he instructed. "Take what's inside and bring it to a safe place. Follow the instructions inside."

"But I don't know the combination," she protested, eyeing the safe's dial.

"Yes you do," he countered with a sly smile. "It's the same as the front door."

She frowned, mulling it over. Then her eyes widened. She put a hand to her mouth.

"Oh!"

"Thirteen knocks, thirty-three seconds, seven knocks," he recited.

"13-33-7," she replied. "Got it."

"I made sure you'd never be able to forget it," he revealed with a wink. And it was true; she'd been doing that little ritual since she was six.

"What's in this?" she asked. But Grandpa took the safe away, putting it back in the drawer and returning everything to its proper place. He handed her the golden key.

"Keep this on you always," he instructed. "And if something happens to me..."

"Open the safe, take what's inside and bring it to a safe place, follow the instructions," she recited.

"Good girl!" he exclaimed, grabbing her by the temples and leaning down to kiss her forehead. Bella tolerated this, crossing her arms over her chest and shaking her head at him.

"You're weird Grandpa," she proclaimed. "You know that?"

"Well of course I am," he replied with a smile. "I'm a writer."

"What's that got to do with it?"

"Have you ever met any other writers?" he inquired. She shook her head. "We're all a little weird. It's because we're *possessed*," he added, wiggling his fingers before her and making a scary face. Bella's eyebrows rose.

"Possessed?"

"We've all got stories and characters inside of us, clamoring to get out!" he exclaimed, spreading his arms out wide. Bella just looked at him, and he chuckled, putting a hand on her shoulder. "Now go paint, my little one."

She opened her mouth to protest.

"I promise you'll know everything soon enough, Bella," he interjected. "Every beginning has an end." He smiled. "So enjoy each adventure while you can."

Chapter 4

It was the peculiar habit of Time to plod along at a glacial pace during moments of pain and drudgery, and to speed up during the few fleeting moments of joy life offered. A most disagreeable thing, Time, bent on torturing everything that had the misfortune of being able to sense it.

So it was that the weekend neared its end far too quickly, and Bella found herself sitting at the dining room table that Sunday evening finishing up the homework she'd put off 'til then. When she was done, she set her backpack by the door wearily, announcing her decision to go to bed. Grandpa finished writing at his desk, then joined Bella in her room to spin one of his wild tales. When he was finished, he rolled onto his side, staring at her for a long moment.

"What?" she asked self-consciously.

"Bella, I'm...sorry," he apologized. She frowned.

"Why?"

"For all of this," he answered. "Keeping you in the house every day, not letting you go over your friends' houses. For...spending all my time writing."

"Grandpa..."

"I know you say you don't mind," he interjected, "...but I do. This isn't the life I wanted, and it's not the life I wanted for you."

Bella had the urge to say something, to contradict him, but held her tongue.

"I adore you more than anything in my life," he continued, putting a warm palm on her cheek. "And I love to write…I *have* to write, to escape this dreadful prison."

"Prison?"

"That's what this is," he replied. "This apartment. And if it weren't for you it would have swallowed me whole. After your mother died…" He stopped himself then, taking a deep breath in, then letting it out. "You rescue me from myself, Bella. You make this all worthwhile."

Bella smiled, having no choice but to gracefully accept this.

"Thanks Grandpa."

He smiled back, giving her a kiss on the forehead. Then he got up from the bed, walking stiffly to the door.

"Grandpa?"

"Yes?"

"Why don't we have any pictures of Mom?"

Grandpa sighed, reaching the door and pausing there. He seemed at a loss for words.

"It's…complicated, Bella," he answered at last. Bella was unsatisfied with the non-answer, but she left it alone, knowing that Grandpa wouldn't say anything more about the matter. He never did.

Grandpa stood by the door, his hand on the doorknob, gazing down at her for a long moment.

"Goodnight Bella," he said at last. "I love you more than anything in this world. Or any other world, for that matter."

"I love you too Grandpa."

And then he closed the door, leaving her alone in the darkness.

* * *

The next morning ushered in the start of another long school week, the sun having just peeked above the horizon by the time Bella left the apartment for her bus stop. A few minutes later, the bus arrived, traveling across town and depositing her and her fellow students at the front double-doors of the high school, a dull brick building that she soon found herself inside. The inside of the school was as ghastly as the outside, with stark white linoleum floors and gray lockers set against the walls. The only color was that which the students had added, with hand-drawn posters on the bulletin boards announcing the upcoming election of the next class president.

And so the day dripped along, each class separated by a five-minute frenzy to get to the next. Then lunch – leftover chili – and her study break.

Then came more classes, ending of course with Mrs. Pittersworth's algebra class. Bella resisted the urge to doodle, weighing it against the threat of more detention. Mrs. Pittersworth's eye was upon her, she knew, and the woman was downright vindictive. Bella succeeded in not doodling, but not quite in paying attention, and was relieved when the bell tolled to signal the end of the school day. She got up hurriedly, joining the mad dash to the door.

"Bella?" Mrs. Pittersworth called out. Bella grimaced, veering off toward her teacher's desk.

"Yes Mrs. Pittersworth?"

"You did better today," she declared approvingly. However, her expression rapidly returned to its natural state...like she'd just bitten into a lemon. "However, I'm *extremely* disappointed that your grandfather not only failed to come to the scheduled parent-teacher conference, but failed to re-schedule one as well."

"Oh."

"This is unacceptable," she continued. "It is of vital importance that your guardian be invested in your education. Regrettably, not showing up gives me the impression that he isn't." She put her hands on her narrow hips. "Now that can't be true, can it?"

Bella chose to be silent, knowing that Grandpa was, in fact, *not* invested in her education. At least not the one she was getting in school. He often said it was a fine way to train zombies, but not human beings...and mostly served to transform the latter into the former.

"Bring this letter home with you," Mrs. Pittersworth commanded, handing Bella a white envelope. "Give it to your grandfather and insist that he reads it."

"Yes Mrs. Pittersworth."

And with that, she was set free.

* * *

The air was ice-cold by the time Bella got off the school bus, the sun already dipping into the horizon. Darkness began its slow spread over the earth, blanketing the skeletal trees and houses. A far cry from those endless summer days Bella had enjoyed what seemed like only moments ago. She sighed, trudging down the sidewalk toward her apartment, passing the Jack-o-lanterns leering at her from the safety of their porches, their face lit with flickering fire. She kept her eyes on her feet, huddling against a frigid wind that assaulted her, whipping through her long curly hair. She shoved her hands in her coat pockets, feeling the envelope Mrs. Pittersworth had given her in the right one.

She hesitated, then pulled it out. Grandpa wouldn't care if she opened it. Probably.

Bella did just that, removing a folded piece of paper from within. It was a hand-written letter:

Mr. Brown,

Your daughter Bella is having continued difficulty with attention. I have taught countless children over the last twenty years, and many with her difficulties have benefited greatly from medication.

It is imperative that we set up a conference to discuss Bella's future. Please call me at your earliest convenience.

Sincerely,
Mrs. Pittersworth

Bella stopped in the middle of the sidewalk, reading, then re-reading the letter. She felt numb.

Her difficulties. Medication.

She blinked back sudden tears, stuffing the letter back into her pocket. A part of her wanted to tear it to shreds. But she knew full well that Mrs. Pittersworth was right.

She closed her eyes, taking a deep, steadying breath. She'd always known there was something wrong with her. It was why she didn't have many friends. She preferred the warmth and vibrancy of her imagination to real life…and for the life of her, she didn't know why.

40

Because real life can hurt you.

Bella swallowed past a lump in her throat, forcing herself to put one foot in front of the other. She suddenly dreaded showing Grandpa the letter, knowing full well she would. They shared everything, good and bad. A part of her hoped he'd tear it up himself, after going into one of his epic rants about her school.

But what if he didn't? What if he made her go to the doctor and start taking pills? The thought of having to take something that would change her brain – change who she *was* – was terrifying. As was the thought that who she was...wasn't enough.

Shoving the thought out of her mind, she focused on the gate to her apartment building ahead. She opened it with a loud *screech*, climbing up the steps to the front porch.

She heard the gate close...and footsteps approaching from behind.

Bella whirled around, her breath catching in her throat.

"Afternoon, Bella."

Two men were walking leisurely toward her. The police officers she'd seen questioning the kids last Friday.

She stood there, pressing her back against the front door.

"Hi," one greeted, mounting the steps and stopping before her on the porch. A very tall man with pale skin, short black hair peeking out from his cap. He extended a gloved hand. "I'm officer Stanwitz."

"And I'm officer Reynolds," the other officer greeted, staying at the bottom of the stairs. He was shorter than officer Stanwitz, with broad shoulders and olive skin. They both spoke in strange accents Bella had never heard before. She glanced at Stanwitz's hand, keeping her own hands stuffed in her pockets. She fingered the refurbished flip-phone in her left pants pocket. It was ancient but cheap, a gift from Grandpa a few years back...and only for use in emergencies.

"We just want to ask you a few questions," Stanwitz stated.

"Have I broken the law, officer?" she asked, as she'd been taught.

"Relax," officer Stanwitz soothed, stepping in a little closer. Too close. He loomed over Bella, smiling down at her with his thin lips, but not his eyes. His uniform smelled musty, and Bella shrank away from him. "We're just...investigating a few minor crimes we think one of your fellow students might have committed."

41

"Someone vandalized the principal's mailbox again," Reynolds explained.

"Don't know anything about that," she stated tersely. "Sorry." She turned to open the door, but officer Stanwitz grabbed the doorknob before she could, blocking her hand.

"See, now that's what everyone's been telling us," he replied. "They can't *all* be telling the truth, can they Bella?"

"I am," she retorted.

"Are you?" Stanwitz pressed, his dark eyes narrowing.

"Someone has to know what happened," Reynolds pointed out.

"Yeah," Bella replied. "Someone else."

Stanwitz smirked.

"Well that's funny," he stated. He twisted around, glancing at Reynolds, who was still at the bottom of the steps, blocking the only path out of the fenced-in front yard. "Isn't that funny Reynolds?"

"Hilarious," Reynolds muttered. "Let's just get this over with."

Stanwitz turned back to Bella, slamming his palm against the door beside her head and making her flinch.

"Wanna know why that's so funny?" he inquired. Bella just stared at him, her heart pounding in her chest. "The other students we questioned? They said *you* did it."

"You just said I didn't break the law," she retorted, trying to keep her voice calm.

"No, I told you to relax," Stanwitz corrected. He reached out and grabbed a lock of her hair, leaning in to smell it. "This is gonna be so much easier for you if you do."

She shrank away, then tried to slip past him, but he blocked her with one leg, smirking down at her.

"Where you think you're going, honey?"

"Let me go you creep," she ordered, reaching for the knob again. But his hand was still on it.

"Perpetrator used a rubber mallet to break the principal's mailbox," Stanwitz murmured, running the lock of hair against his lips, then letting go. "Guess we're gonna have to search your place to find it."

He turned the knob then, but it was locked.

"Open it," he ordered.

"Do you have a warrant?" Bella shot back.

He rolled his eyes, grabbing her by the shoulders and shoving her chest-first against the door, leaning his body against her backpack.

"Search her pockets," he told Reynolds.

She felt hands in her coat pockets, and Reynolds retrieved the letter, glancing at it, then tossing it aside. He shoved a hand into her right pants pocket.

"Hey!" she blurted out.

"Found it," Reynolds announced, handing the key to Stanwitz. Stanwitz smirked, unlocking the door, then opening it and shoving Bella through. She stumbled, barely managing to keep her balance with her backpack on.

"Resisting a police officer, tsk tsk," Stanwitz said, smirking at her. "Which floor Bella?"

"First," she lied.

"Check the mailboxes," Stanwitz told Reynolds, who nodded reluctantly, going back outside. Moments later he returned with an envelope in his hand.

"Letter addressed to the girl," he announced. "Third floor."

Stanwitz shook his head at Bella.

"Bet you thought that was *real* clever."

He grabbed her arm, hauling her upstairs. Reynolds followed close behind, and they climbed to the third-floor landing, stopping before the door. Stanwitz turned to Bella.

"After you," he prompted, gesturing at the door.

"You have the key, remember?" she shot back. He glanced at Reynolds, then smirked, slipping the key in the doorknob and turning it. Then he twisted the knob, pushing on the door.

It didn't budge.

Stanwitz tried again, then sighed, turning to Bella.

"Okay," he grumbled. "Open it."

"It's deadbolted," she pointed out. "I can't open it."

"Oh, right," Stanwitz replied, turning toward the door.

Then he spun around, punching Bella right in the gut.

Hard.

Bella lurched backward, striking the railing behind her, then falling to her side on the landing. She gasped for air, tears blurring her vision. Her stomach lurched, sour fluid filling the back of her throat.

She puked.

"Jesus Stanwitz," Reynolds blurted out. "Take it easy!"

"Bella Bella Bella," Stanwitz muttered, kneeling down beside the pool of vomit, looking at it with disgust. He grabbed a fistful of her hair, yanking her head backward and forcing her to look up at him. The sudden pain in her scalp made her eyes water. "You *need* to start cooperating honey."

She gasped for air, clenching her teeth against another wave of nausea. Then she reached inside her left pants pocket, finding her phone and flipping it open inside her pocket, feeling the buttons to orient herself, then dialing 9-1-1. She held her thumb over the speaker, glaring back at Stanwitz.

"You're not really cops, are you," she accused. Stanwitz smirked at her.

"Looks like we got a god-damn *genius* over here," he shot back. "Bravo Bella! You figured it out."

There was a *BAM!* as Reynolds kicked the door. The door held, and Reynolds stumbled backward, nearly colliding with Stanwitz.

"Damn thing must be made of metal," he grumbled.

"Door frame isn't," Stanwitz pointed out. "Hit it hard enough and it'll break through."

"You sure about that?" Reynolds retorted. "How about *you* give it a try."

"Quit wasting time," Stanwitz shot back. Reynolds glared at him, but readied himself again, lunging forward and kicking the door as hard as he could.

BAM!

There was a loud *crack*, part of the doorframe breaking free. But the door still held. Stanwitz smirked.

"See?" he told Reynolds. "Again."

Reynolds gathered himself for another round, then kicked.

BAM!

The doorframe shattered, the door flying open and ricocheting off the wall, slamming into officer Reynolds. He shoved it all the way open, striding into the hallway beyond and unholstering his pistol.

"Grandpa!" Bella screamed.

Stanwitz grabbed a fistful of her hair, dragging Bella across the floor toward the broken door. She cried out, reaching blindly for his wrist and grabbing it with both hands. He dragged her into the hallway of her apartment, the carpet there burning her side as she slid across it.

"Run Grandpa!" she screamed. "*Run!*"

"Shut up," Stanwitz growled, stopping to twist around and glare at her. He unholstered his pistol, shoving the cold hard metal against her forehead. He held it there for a moment, then turned around, dragging her into the living room.

And to Bella's horror, Grandpa was there, sitting in his favorite chair at his desk, his back to them.

Stanwitz let go of Bella, striding forward and aiming his pistol at Grandpa's back.

"Careful," Reynolds warned. "We don't know what he brought with him."

"Well well 'Mr. Brown,'" Stanwitz said. "Or should I say Mr. *Birch*," he added with a smirk, stopping a few feet behind Grandpa. "Been looking forward to this for a *long* time."

He paused, then cocked his head to the side. Grandpa didn't so much as move, sitting on his chair silently, his hands in his lap. Some of the framed drawings on his desk had fallen on the floor around him, the painting above his desk hanging askew.

"Proud till the end," Stanwitz mused. He circled around to the right, his gun aimed at Grandpa's head. "Must've been exhausting, knowing we were coming. Hiding for all those years in a book, just *waiting* for us to find you."

Still, Grandpa said nothing.

Stanwitz stared at him, then edged forward, stopping a foot from Grandpa.

"What's the matter Mr. Birch?" he inquired with a smirk. "Won't stoop to talk to one of *us*?"

Still no answer.

Stanwitz kicked Grandpa's chair, sending it toppling over. Grandpa fell to the carpet with a loud *thump*, sprawling out on his side. Bella gasped in horror.

"Grandpa!" she cried.

Stanwitz nudged Grandpa with his foot. Then he knelt down, putting two fingers to Grandpa's neck.

"What is it?" Reynolds asked. Stanwitz glared at him, then lowered his gaze, staring at Grandpa.

Then he cursed, standing up.

"I can't believe it," he muttered, shaking his head.

"What?" Reynolds repeated.

"Really?" Stanwitz stated. "After all these years we spent looking for your damn book. Ten *goddamn* years we looked for you, and you had to end up dead." He looked up at Reynolds. "Honestly, he's taking all the fun out of the job."

And then he fired three rounds into Grandpa's chest.

"*Grandpa!*" Bella screamed, scrambling to her feet. Stanwitz whirled around, pistol-whipping her in the temple. Her head snapped to the side, her skull exploding in pain.

She barely felt her face strike the carpet.

Reynolds swore, taking off his cap and running a hand through his hair.

"What do we do?"

Stanwitz sighed, turning to look at Grandpa, then Bella, his arms at his sides. He walked up to her then, his boots *thumping* on the floor until he was looming over her.

"We *could* have a little fun," he admitted, tapping his pistol against his thigh. Then he sighed, turning away from her. "You know what? I'm just not in the goddamn mood."

"Just grab the kid and go," Reynolds pressed.

"Oh, we'll go all right," Stanwitz replied, his thin lips curling into a smirk. "But I'm not up for babysitting right now."

He pointed his pistol right at Bella's head.

"Time for a family reunion, kid."

Bella screamed, throwing her hands in front of her face and rolling to one side.

"No!" Reynolds cried out, leaping at Stanwitz and shoving him to the side at the last minute.

BAM!

Stanwitz lurched backward, tripping over Grandpa's body and slamming into the desk, scattering notebooks everywhere.

Bella stared at him uncomprehendingly, then heard the thunderous sound of footsteps coming into the living room from behind her. She turned, seeing four police officers rushing toward her, their guns drawn.

"Drop your weapons *now!*" one shouted.

Stanwitz shoved Reynolds away, raising his pistol...and the cops opened fire.

BAM BAM BAM!

Stanwitz fell backward on top of Grandpa's desk, the rain of bullets striking him in the shoulders and chest. Reynolds cursed, bolting into the dining room.

"Go, go!" one of the cops ordered.

One officer ran after Reynolds, another checking on Stanwitz, who was lying next to Grandpa, blood soaking through his uniform. The third cop ran to Grandpa's side, rolling him onto his back. He checked his neck for a pulse, then swore, placing his hands over Grandpa's chest and starting CPR. He pushed so hard Bella heard a crunching sound.

Bella crawled up to Grandpa's other side, her lower lip quivering as she looked down at him. At his kind brown eyes, staring off into nothing. His head bobbing lifelessly with each *thump* of his chest.

His face as pale as Death.

She shook her head mutely, kneeling over him and cradling his head against hers. She sobbed, tears streamed down her cheeks, wetting his.

"No Grandpa, no," she moaned, rocking back and forth.

She felt a hand on her shoulder. One of the police officers was kneeling beside her.

"Are you hurt?" he asked.

She ignored him, continuing to rock back and forth, cradling Grandpa's head in her hands. She brought her lips to his ear.

"Don't go," she whispered. "It's me Grandpa, it's Bella."

"Aw kid," the cop muttered. "I'm real sorry."

The officer doing chest compressions looked up.

"I need a medic!" he yelled. Sweat was already beading up on his forehead, dripping into his eyes. The cop who'd ran into the dining room after Reynolds came back into the living room.

"He's gone," the other stated. "Not sure how. The kitchen's a dead-end, but the guy's nowhere."

"What do you mean he's *nowhere*?" the cop behind Bella retorted.

"I don't know, sir," he replied sheepishly. "He just, um…vanished."

"Jesus," the cop behind Bella muttered. "Call in more back-up. Search the whole damn apartment, every damn floor. And set a perimeter around the building. No one comes in or out without going through us."

"This one's dead," the cop checking Stanwitz notified. "No pulse."

"Call two ambulances then. And put on some gloves and do CPR."

The cops got to work, but to Bella they weren't there at all. It was only her and Grandpa, as it'd always been. As it was always supposed to be, until the end of time.

Grandpa, telling her stories of a better, more beautiful world. Bringing life and color into an existence that too often seemed to have none. A man larger than life, the only one who made it worth living.

But it was the peculiar habit of Time to plod along at a glacial pace during moments of pain and drudgery, and to speed up during the few fleeting moments of joy life offered. And there had been no greater joy in Bella's life than Grandpa.

So it was that, far too soon, Grandpa's time had run out.

Chapter 5

Like a candle flickering in the darkness, Grandpa had been Bella's guiding light. Warm and burning ever bright, he'd shown her the way through a world that often seemed cold and indifferent. But his flame had been snuffed out, and darkness seized the opportunity, rushing in to envelope Bella in its icy embrace.

Without Grandpa, Bella went numb.

The police had to drag her screaming away from his body when the paramedics arrived. The medics went through the motions of bringing Grandpa back to life, but soon ended their futile efforts. They declared him dead at the scene.

Time of death: 1515.

She was taken out of the apartment, where police were already surrounding the yard with yellow tape that said: POLICE SCENE DO NOT CROSS. The paramedics put her in an ambulance, bringing her to the local emergency room, where she waited for hours laying on a stiff gurney in a cold room. Eventually a doctor came to see her, asking her some rote-sounding questions, then touching her head and pressing on her neck and belly. He concluded that there was nothing seriously wrong with her, which was hardly surprising. The doctor had no instrument to evaluate the gaping wound in her soul, and no medicine that could have healed it.

Another half-hour later, a nurse came in to say she was going home.

Which was a lie.

A while later, a woman calling herself a social worker came in to talk with her, asking her if there were any relatives that could take her in. Any friends.

There were none, of course. She'd only had Grandpa.

A temporary court-appointed guardian was chosen, some lawyer. They called Bella's downstairs neighbors, who graciously agreed to take Bella in until a more permanent "solution" could be found. The police had an officer stationed in a cruiser in front of the apartment just in case Reynolds tried to return.

And through it all, Bella just sat there, feeling hollow. Like her heart had been carved out of her body, leaving her incapable of feeling anything.

That night, as she laid on her side on a blow-up mattress in her neighbor's spare bedroom, she stared at the wall for hours. She tried to cry – *wanted* to cry – but nothing came. All she felt was that awful numbness, as if she'd lost the ability to feel anything at all. And every time she closed her eyes, she saw Grandpa's eyes staring off into oblivion. The life that had oozed out of every pore in his body when he was alive, that had animated every gesture, every smile, was gone.

And it terrified her that, no matter how hard she tried, she couldn't imagine him any other way now.

* * *

Morning came, and the neighbors' kids went off to school while Bella stayed home. Their mother offered to take a day off from work to be with Bella, but Bella refused, saying she wanted to be by herself for a while. Everyone left, and she remained.

Alone.

She laid in bed fully clothed, still dressed in her clothes from yesterday. Bella huddled in her warm jacket, staring out of the window. She had no desire to eat breakfast. Or lunch. She felt no hunger. Other than a headache, she felt nothing at all. Not even sadness.

She *should* feel sad, but she didn't.

Time passed as it always did, but without anything to look forward to, time didn't matter anymore. Nothing mattered anymore.

Eventually she had to go to the bathroom, the call of nature the only thing that managed to get her out of bed. She answered the call, then walked back through the living room toward the spare bedroom, slowing as she did so.

There, nestled against one wall, was a desk.

Her mind went to her Grandpa's desk, that wooden monstrosity he'd slaved over. His voice, deep and earnest, seemed to whisper in her ear.

If something happens to me...

She reached under her shirt into her bra, pulling out what she'd put there for safekeeping.

A golden key.

For the first time since Grandpa died, Bella felt something.

She spun around, walking toward the front door of the apartment and opening it, making sure it was unlocked. Then she bounded up the spiraling staircase beyond, slowing as she reached the third-floor landing. The front door was still busted open, yellow police tape spanning the doorway.

She hesitated, peering beyond it and straining her ears. The coast seemed to be clear.

Bella took a deep breath in, then ducked under the police tape, stepping quietly into the hallway of her apartment. She moved stealthily into the living room, scanning it.

Empty.

It was bizarre, this emptiness. The apartment had never been empty before, not with Grandpa always being there. Death had taken him away, and now the apartment was just a place, not her home. A hollow series of rooms, like her soul.

She crept to Grandpa's desk, trying to ignore the bloodstains on the framed pictures of mushrooms atop it. Retrieving the golden key from her pocket, she unlocked the leftmost drawer. She emptied it, pulling out the false bottom and retrieving the silver key, which she used to open the right drawer. Then she pulled out the heavy black safe, setting it on the floor.

13-33-7.

Twisting the dial, she entered the combination, and the door swung open. She reached inside, feeling something there...something heavy. She pulled it out.

It was a book.

Take what's inside and bring it to a safe place, follow the instructions.

She heard footsteps coming up the stairs from behind.

Bella stuffed the book under her shirt, rushing back into the hallway. The footsteps were getting louder, and she heard voices echoing in the stairwell. They were clearly past the second-floor landing…and approaching quickly.

Her heart leapt into her throat.

The door to her bedroom was in the hallway; she bolted into her room, closing the door most of the way and peering through the crack between the door and the doorframe. She heard a man talking as he entered the hallway, and moments later a police officer passed by her door and into the living room, followed by a second person. Someone wearing a brown cloak with a hood over their head. The cloak was open in the front, exposing a colorful painted vest covering their chest.

"You sure there's no one here?" this person asked. It was a woman's voice.

"Just the cop outside we killed," the police officer replied. Fear gripped Bella, her breath catching in her throat.

It was Reynolds' voice.

"You should've notified me when you found Thaddeus," the cloaked woman scolded.

"You were away," Reynolds countered. "Stanwitz insisted on…"

"And now he's dead," the woman snapped. "Why didn't he wear protection?"

"He was in character for years," Reynold's explained. "He got lazy…and stupid. Idiot almost killed that girl."

"If he had, the boss-man would've killed him anyway," she replied.

"I still don't get why we have to hunt down that girl," Reynolds grumbled. "Or her stupid book."

"Neither do I," the woman admitted. "Be a good boy and check the bedrooms, love. Looks like someone already went through that desk."

Bella hid behind the door, hearing Reynolds pass by her room again. Luckily he went into Grandpa's room first, leaving the door half-open. The cloaked woman knelt before the empty safe with her back to Bella, peering inside of it. Then she stood, lifting her gaze to stare up at the painting above Grandpa's desk.

Bella steeled herself, then made her move.

She opened her door, slipping into the hallway as quietly as a mouse, then ducking under the police tape and tiptoeing down the stairs. She made not a sound, taking the stairwell past the second floor to the first, then bursting out of the front door, leaping down the steps and sprinting out of the front gate. She turned left down the sidewalk.

There was a police car at the curb, a single bullet hole in the windshield on the driver's side.

Bella jerked her gaze away, running as fast as she could for as long as she could. Until sweat poured from her skin, her lungs burning and legs threatening to give out underneath her. Only then did she slow to a walk, struggling to catch her breath. She glanced behind her, seeing empty streets as far as the eye could see.

Breathing a sigh of relief, she bent over and rested her hands just above her knees. She closed her eyes, feeling sweat drip from the tip of her nose.

Okay.

Bella took a deep breath in, then stood straight up, trying to get her bearings. She was on the corner of Arlington Street and Main Street; downtown was a short distance down Main Street, the city library only a few blocks away.

Bring it to a safe place.

She turned down Main street, passing City Hall on her left, then Summer Street. The library was on Summer Street, a squat, rectangular building with a small clock tower. It was just as she remembered it from two years ago; she turned left down the street, walking up to the double-doors at the library entrance and opening one, stepping inside.

The woman at the front desk glanced up at Bella, then returned to being hypnotized by her phone.

Bella made her way to the main area of the library, a rather plain room with gray patterned carpet and endless rows of bookshelves. She found herself drawn to one of the long rectangular tables sandwiched between the tall shelves of books, and sat down before it. Glancing around to make sure no one was watching, she retrieved the book she'd gotten from the safe, setting it on the table and studying it.

It was an old book, that was certain, and awfully thick. Its hard cover was a dull maroon, dark blocky letters embossed on its surface.

"The Chronicles of Collins Dansworth," it read. "By Belthazar Squib."

She was disappointed to find that it wasn't written by Grandpa, a part of her hoping she'd finally get to read one of his books. She didn't recognize this author's name at all. When she opened the book, she spotted a folded-up piece of paper between the cover and the first page. Unfolding it, she immediately recognized Grandpa's fine handwriting:

Dearest Bella,

I've left you all alone, and for that I may never forgive myself.

I ask you to trust me one last time, Bella. Read this book until you are lost in its pages. Then close it and find the answers to the mysteries you hold in your heart.

Remember that love is something you give, as I gave mine to you. Give it to your art and heal your heart.

A friend awaits.
~ Grandpa

Bella read, then re-read the letter, blinking away tears. Then she re-folded the letter, stuffing it in her pants pocket. She flipped past the introductory pages, reaching the prologue.

Collins Dansworth was an average boy to most. An average student, average at sports and school, with an average number of friends in an average neighborhood. Nothing about him stood out at all...which made the life he ended up living all the more outstanding.

The boy's name sounded awfully familiar. She wracked her brain, trying to think of how she knew it. There was no way she'd read this book before; she would have remembered that. Maybe there'd been someone at school with a similar name a few years back.

She read on, her chin propped in one hand, turning to the next page, the paper thick and stiff. Though the prose matched the paper, it wasn't long before the story exerted that strange power books had, to make the rest of the world fade away. It drew her deeper within itself, and before Bella knew it, the small part of her brain that remained within the real world alerted her that a considerable amount of time had passed.

She closed the book, rubbing her tired eyes and leaning back in her chair with a big yawn, stretching her arms up and to the sides. Then she opened her eyes.

And was struck by a terrible surprise.

Chapter 6

There had been a few times in Bella's life when she'd woken from a particularly vivid dream, one that'd felt so real that she'd found herself questioning whether she was returning to reality or escaping it. On each occasion, it'd taken a fair bit of time for her to accept that she'd truly awoken, and that what her eyes were telling her were not lies, but the truth.

This was one of those times.

The city library on Summer Street was rather plain, both inside and out. The floors were covered in a thin gray patterned carpet, the shelves made of pine and dark brown metal. There were a few old couches here and there, and a row of long rectangular tables sandwiched between the endless bookshelves. The most decorative thing about the library was the white statue of George Washington standing proudly on his pedestal near a small shallow pool in the middle of the main room. This library was where Bella had been.

But it was no longer where she was.

She found herself instead in a long, cathedral-like room of massive proportions, with dark, polished wooden floors, and walls that rose up a good fifty feet high on either side of her, not a single ray of light streaming through stained-glass windows of nearly equal height. The ceiling far above was arched, and decorated by elaborate paintings like the Sistine Chapel. The cheap rectangular table she'd been sitting at had been replaced by a dark wooden one, with elegant carvings inset on its polished surface. There were still long rows of bookshelves on either side of her, but they were now three times as tall, and made of the same rich wood as the table. And the books they held were not the simple paperbacks she'd seen earlier. No, these were all oversized hardcovers of impeccable quality, their spines richly designed and decorated with gold and silver. A few even looked to be studded with gemstones of various sizes and colors.

And in front of Bella sat a long row of tables identical to the one she found herself sitting at, arranged like pews in a church.

Bella closed her eyes, rubbing them vigorously, then opened them again.

No change.

She realized her jaw had gone slack, and shut her mouth with a loud *click*. Then she glanced down at the tabletop before her.

Grandpa's book was gone.

She looked down on either side of her chair, searching the floor around her, but the book was nowhere to be found.

"Got lost in a book?" a voice inquired from behind.

Bella jumped, twisting around in her chair. There, seated at the table behind her, was a man. He looked to be in his fifties, and was dressed in a formidably formal three-piece suit a shade lighter than black, with a deep purple dress shirt and fine silver tie. He had a short salt-and-pepper beard and a mustache that didn't quite qualify as a handlebar mustache, but got as close as one could without earning this designation. His well-groomed beard joined the extremely short hair at his temples, which in turn blossomed into the longer – and meticulously swept back – hair atop his head. His face was quite pale, with rather deep horizontal furrows in his forehead and much finer lines elsewhere. His eyebrows were full and fiercely angular, his eyes a piercing shade of green.

And they were staring right at her.

"What?" was all Bella could blurt out.

The man stood from his chair abruptly, walking around the table with an unnervingly quick stride and making his way toward her. He was shorter than Bella, but with broad shoulders, and carried a slender black cane in his left hand. But it was not the cane that caught Bella's eye; it was the hand.

And not the left hand, but the absence of the right.

For his right forearm terminated at the wrist, a fleshy stub that peeked out from his fine sleeve. And it was this that he thrust at her when he reached her side.

"My name is Gideon Myles," he introduced in a deep, crisp voice.

"Bella," Bella replied, hesitating for a split second, then shaking Gideon's…stump. It would have been rude not to do so.

"Oh I know who you are," he revealed. "Your grandfather told me all about you."

"You know him?" she asked.

"He hung my painting above his desk," Gideon revealed. Then he smirked. "Heard you weren't a fan."

Bella's eyes widened.

"You're his friend!" she exclaimed. He winked.

"The one and only."

"Where…am I?" she inquired, looking around.

"Someplace you shouldn't be," he answered. "Surrounded by people that want you dead." He pointed his cane at her chest. "And if you don't do exactly as I say precisely when I say it, they'll get what they want."

He turned about abruptly, striding quickly between the tables.

"Follow me," he ordered. "Stay at my left side, two steps behind. Say absolutely nothing unless I tell you to."

Bella hurried to catch up to him, following his instructions. Gideon led her past the rows of tables, toward a narrow hallway at the end of the room, which in turn terminated in a set of double-doors. Large paintings hung on the walls on either side, high enough up that she couldn't reach them, and each was encased in glass. One of the glass encasings closest to the door had shattered, though the painting beyond was still intact. A painting of a man in blood-red armor flying through the air, silhouetted against a starry night sky.

Her shoes *crunched* on the broken glass as Gideon reached the doors, opening one and stepping through. Bella followed behind him, passing into a long hallway beyond. This too had a dark, polished wooden floor and walls, upon which more paintings had been hung, protected by identical glass enclosures. Lanterns bolted to the walls at regular intervals glowed a pale, ghostly yellow.

"To my left!" Gideon reminded her, his cane *clacking* on the floor with every other step.

"Wha…" Bella began to ask, but Gideon raised his stump up sharply to his lips. Her mouth snapped shut, and she followed him down the hallway.

Suddenly Gideon stopped, blocking Bella's way with his cane. He cocked his head as if to listen, then he set his cane against the leftmost wall, retrieving a large, rolled-up piece of paper resembling canvas from within the recesses of his fine suit. He unrolled this, placing it against the wall, muttering something to himself.

It stuck to the wall, perfectly flat.

"Take off your coat and stand here," Gideon ordered, gesturing between himself and the paper with his stump. Bella hesitated, then did so, facing the paper. It was taller than she was. "Turn around," he ordered impatiently. Again, she obeyed, turning to face him.

He shoved her right into the wall…and then grabbed her arm, hauling her forward an instant later.

"Grab your coat," he ordered, leaving the paper on the wall and retrieving his cane. "Let's go."

Bella put her coat back on, then opened her mouth to ask him what on earth he'd just done all that for. He swung his cane at her face, stopping it a hair's width from her lips. She flinched, her mouth snapping shut…and he turned about, continuing quickly down the hall. Bella struggled to keep up, making sure to stay two steps behind him and to his left. The hallway made a right turn at the end, and Gideon turned down it, leading them down another hallway. This was shorter than the last, terminating in a single, black closed door.

One guarded by a bald man wearing red chainmail armor over his black leather shirt and pants, a fine-looking sword sheathed at his left hip.

Gideon slowed his pace instantly, breaking out into a warm, cheery smile.

"Afternoon!" he greeted, stopping before the guard and tucking his cane under his elbow, extending his left hand. The guard smiled back, shaking Gideon's hand briskly.

"Ah, if it isn't the good Painter himself!" he exclaimed. "Who's this?" he inquired, turning to Bella. Bella glanced at Gideon.

"My brother's niece," Gideon answered. "Lola Amesbury." He beamed down at Bella. "Lola, this fine gentleman is an official guardian of Blackthorne."

"Nice to meet you," the guard stated, reaching out to shake Bella's hand. She arched an eyebrow at Gideon.

"Go on," he urged. "He doesn't bite."

"Not unless you're food!" the guard joked rather lamely. Bella smiled dutifully at the terrible joke, shaking the man's hand.

"How do you like it?" the guard asked Bella. "The library, I mean."

"It's beautiful," she replied meekly, lowering her gaze.

"Sure is," the guard agreed. "Well, don't let me hold you," he added. "Just let me make it official and all that."

He took a small book from a pack at his waist, flipping through it. Then he frowned.

"No entry," he muttered, glancing up at Gideon. "One for you, but none for her."

"That's strange," Gideon replied with a frown of his own. "Are you sure?"

"Bet you my day's pay it was Cyrus," the guard grumbled. "Useless bastard is always forgetting stuff like this. Least complicated thing in the world, right? Greet a person, log it. And he still screws it up 'least once a week!"

"It's difficult to find quality people who'd agree to work here," Gideon ventured. The guard shot him a knowing look.

"Ain't that the truth," he agreed. "Still can't figure out why you've stayed here all this time. Everyone else is leaving. I'm sure you could've filed for a transfer by now."

"To be honest, I'm not sure either," Gideon admitted. Then he smirked, raising his right arm. "Guess you could say I'm stumped."

The guard burst out laughing.

"Good one!" he declared, slapping his knee. "Ah, that was good."

Bella glanced at Gideon, raising an eyebrow. It hadn't been *that* good.

"Well, all right then," the guard said. "Fear not my good man, I'll fix the record. Just show me her identification."

Gideon turned to Bella, gesturing at her right arm.

"Pull up your sleeve, Lola," he instructed. "Just like before."

She hesitated, then did so, pulling up the sleeve of her coat and exposing her bare forearm.

Her eyes widened.

For there, on the front of her forearm, was a large black tattoo. A complex series of shapes that fit together to form an intricate pattern that extended from the crease of her elbow all the way to her wrist.

The guard made a show of studying it, then nodded at Gideon. "Have a good night," he stated. "Nice to meet you Lola."

Bella smiled at him, and the guard opened the door for them, ushering them through. Yet another hallway greeted them, which took a right turn. Beyond was a long hallway with a dull red and gold rug on the floor and tall white statues standing on elegant golden pedestals set against either wall.

Bella's breath caught in her throat; it was identical to the hallway she'd painted over a week ago...except for the fact that every one of the statues was headless.

Gideon led Bella down this hallway, toward a set of large double-doors at the end of it. Another guard stood there holding a notebook, this one with short black hair and a meticulously-groomed beard. Gideon stopped before the guard, nodding briskly, then striking the butt of his cane rather sharply against the floor.

"Good day Baxter," Gideon greeted. "Taking an early leave today to spend some time with my brother's niece here."

Baxter said not a word, gesturing at Gideon's right arm. Gideon pulled his sleeve up, revealing a tattoo similar to Bella's on his stump. The guard scribbled something in his notebook, then nodded at Bella.

"Go on," Gideon urged.

Bella pulled up her right sleeve as before, displaying her tattoo to the guard. He peered down at it, then frowned, flipping through pages in his notebook. At length, he looked up at Bella.

"No record of her entry," he stated, eyeing her suspiciously. He closed his notebook, reaching for something that looked like a blowhorn at his left hip.

Gideon burst into action, swinging his cane in a vicious arc at the man's temple.

Thwack!

Baxter's head snapped to the side, and he literally flew sideways through the air, slamming into one of the statues and ricocheting off. The guard fell to the floor, looking for all the world like he was dead. Bella gasped.

"Oh my god!"

"Go!" Gideon cried, flinging open one of the doors and bursting through. Bella sprinted after him, passing through the doorway…

…and emerging from a great big gothic building onto a wide cobblestone path. The building had a black stone façade, thick vines with black thorns crawling up its surface, all the way to a row of glowering gargoyles leering at her from the rooftop some forty feet up. Beyond the gargoyles, the crescent moon glowed with a pale silver light, peeking out between dark gray clouds that obscured most of the night sky. To her sides were large stone buildings that looked like dormitories, and ahead, the cobblestone path cut through a huge, wide-open grassy courtyard.

Gideon sprinted forward over the cobblestone path, and Bella rushed to keep up with him. More of the headless statues flanked the path on either side, and ahead, the path led through a large, ornately carved stone archway…one guarded by two more guards.

"Hey!" one of the guards shouted, unsheathing their sword and charging up the path toward them. Gideon cursed, slamming the butt of his cane onto the street and rushing right at the guards.

"Stay behind me!" Gideon shouted…and then the guards were upon them.

The first guard swung their sword at Gideon, who intercepted the deadly blade with a vigorous swing of his cane. The sword flew out of the guard's hand, and Gideon thrust the butt of his cane into the man's groin.

The guard crumpled, falling to the ground and curling into the fetal position.

The second guard reached Gideon then, thrusting at his chest with a deadly-looking spear. Gideon dodged to the side, cracking the guard atop the head with a swing of his cane.

The guard dropped like a stone.

"Go, go!" Gideon shouted, rushing through the stone arch and sprinting down a gently-curving set of stone steps beyond. Bella followed just behind him, taking the steps down and to the right. They led to another stone arch at the bottom, with a narrow cobblestone path continuing onward from there. This path cut through a forest of tall, stately trees ahead. A forest almost completely obscured by a wall of thick white fog that hung in the air, swirling and churning as if it had a life of its own.

There was frantic shouting from behind, followed by the clamor of many feet rushing after them.

Gideon sprinted forward along the path, plunging into the swirling mist, Bella right behind him. The mist was so thick that she couldn't see more than a few feet ahead, and the oppressive mugginess made it difficult to breathe. She focused on keeping up with Gideon, knowing that if he got more than a few yards ahead of her, she'd lose him.

The shouting behind them grew louder, followed by the rhythmic *clopping* of what sounded like hooves.

Gideon cursed, skidding to a halt. Bella ran right into him, nearly knocking him over.

"To the side!" he hissed, guiding her to the left of the path. He swung his cane, striking one of the tree trunks, then stepped back onto the path, gripping his cane so tightly his knuckles turned white.

Thump-a-thump, thumpa-a-thump...

The hoofbeats grew louder, and Bella peered into the mist, but could barely see beyond her own nose. Gideon tensed, crouching down low.

Thump-a-thump, thump-a-thump...

A shadow appeared in the mist ahead, and Gideon leapt into the air...just as a huge stallion burst through the haze, galloping down the path! Its red-armored rider shouted, yanking back on the reins as he spotted Gideon and Bella.

Gideon swung his cane in mid-leap, striking the rider in the chest with a loud *thwack!*

The rider shot backward out of the saddle with ridiculous speed, vanishing into the mist.

The horse skid to a halt, rearing up on its hind legs. Gideon rushed up to its side, vaulting into the saddle in a single smooth motion. He tucked his cane into his armpit, grabbing the reins with one hand and turning the horse toward Bella. Then he lowered his cane to her.

"Grab it!" he commanded.

Bella did so, grabbing the shaft of his cane with both hands. He hauled her up, and she scrambled onto the horse's back in front of him. He scooted back out of the saddle, pulling her into it.

"Feet in the stirrups," he ordered. "Take the reins and turn the horse around!"

Bella grabbed the reins, but hesitated.

"How do I...?"

"Pull the right one," he instructed. "Don't yank, pull!" She did so, and the horse turned about, facing the way they'd been running. "Ha!" Gideon cried, kicking the horse's flanks with his heels. It bolted down the path, nearly throwing her off in the process. If Gideon hadn't been behind her, it would've done just that.

They galloped through the mist, the trees on either side of them tall shadows that zoomed by with terrifying speed. She resisted the urge to pull back on the reins, though every fiber of her being screamed at her to do it. Gideon leaned to the side, swinging his cane at one of the trees as they passed with a loud *thwack!*

Suddenly they burst out of the mist into the clear night air beyond, leaving the misty forest behind. A huge grassy field opened up before them, the cobblestone path continuing onward. It led forward, curving gently to the right, barely visible in the faint moonlight from above.

And behind them came the sound of more hoofbeats.

"Keep her steady," Gideon instructed...and promptly spun around, facing the horse's rear. He tucked his cane under his chin, stripping off his suit jacket.

"What are you doing?" she asked.

He ignored her, tearing at the inner lining of his jacket, then pulling out something that had been hidden within. A large, folded-up piece of thick paper, like canvas. She saw hints of color on one side, like a painting.

Beyond him, Bella saw three guards on horseback burst out of the fog, galloping down the path after them. One of them was carrying a bow; he took an arrow from the quiver on his back, nocking it and drawing back on the bowstring even as he galloped toward them.

"Left!" Gideon snapped.

The guard fired just as Bella yanked on the left rein. Her horse swerved sharply to the left, nearly throwing Gideon off its back, but the arrow zipped right by them.

The archer grabbed another arrow, even as the other two guards gained on them, closing the distance between them rapidly. The archer drew his bowstring, letting another arrow fly...just as Gideon finished retrieving the canvas, holding it before him. He muttered something, and the canvas unfolded itself, going perfectly flat, as if it'd been framed.

The arrow plunged right through it.

"Gideon!" she cried.

But to her surprise, there was no hole in the paper, and no arrow sticking out of Gideon's chest. The arrow was just…gone.

"Faster!" Gideon shouted. "Use your heels!"

Bella kicked the horse's flanks, but it didn't go any faster. She tried again, digging her heels into its sides, and it burst forward, matching the speed of the horses behind it. White foam dribbled from its mouth, its breath coming in rapid, noisy grunts.

The archer fired again, and again the arrow struck the painted side of the canvas Gideon held before him, vanishing from sight.

"Get on his sides!" one of the other guards shouted, retrieving a long spear from his horse's saddle-pack.

And then a blinding light assaulted Bella's eyes as a huge fireball shot outward from Gideon's canvas, engulfing the three soldiers!

Two of the soldiers burst through the flames, but the archer's horse fell, tumbling onto the street and sending the archer careening through the air. He struck the street head-first, flames licking at his body.

"*Painter!*" one of the surviving guards cried. He reached down to his saddle-pack, retrieving a white horn and bringing it to his lips. A wailing sound pierced the night air, echoing across the land.

And ahead, the path continued forward, sloping down toward a long, gently curving line of huge tents about a mile ahead. The tents were illuminated by tiny orange lights from countless torches. And beyond the line of tents was a massive, churning wall of gray fog over a hundred feet tall, beyond which nothing was visible. Standing between the tents and the fog wall were huge statues of giants that dwarfed the tents, placed at regular intervals behind them.

Behind Bella, the two remaining soldiers dropped back, and were soon left far behind.

Gideon twisted around, clutching the paper to his chest and peering over Bella's shoulder.

"Keep on the path," he ordered. "No matter what!"

Bella nodded, focusing on the path ahead. She leaned forward, the wind whipping through her hair as the horse sped through the night.

Thump-a-thump, thump-a-thump...

Another wailing sound came from far behind, a second blast from the soldier's horn. Shortly thereafter, Bella heard another horn...but this came from ahead. Guards swarmed out of the tents, some on getting on horseback, others rushing toward Bella and Gideon on foot.

Hundreds of guards.

"Incoming!" Bella warned.

Gideon lifted his legs, spinning around to face forward. He held out the painting he'd been holding, painted side facing away from her.

"Take this," he ordered. "Hold it by the edges. Don't let go!"

She obeyed, but the wind struck the paper as if it were a kite, nearly tearing it from her hands. She held on, surprised to find that it was rigid despite not having a frame.

"Face it forward!" he shouted, hooking the reins with his stump. She did so, and suddenly – inexplicably – the force of the wind against the paper vanished. There was shouting from ahead, and she peered around the paper to see more than a dozen guards on horseback rushing on either side of the path toward them. They were only a quarter-mile ahead, and closing in fast.

And far behind these guards, a literal army of men on foot charging after them.

"Steady," Gideon said, his lips inches from her right ear. He reached around her with his left hand, putting it on the surface of the canvas facing away from Bella.

The soldiers on horseback drew rapidly closer, their deadly spears and bows gleaming in the starlight.

Thump-a-thump, thump-a-thump...

They were only a hundred feet away now.

Ninety. Eighty.

"Steady..." Gideon repeated, his eyes locked on the approaching soldiers. A few of them raised their bows, nocking their arrows and pulling back on their bowstrings.

"Gideon!" Bella cried, gripping the canvas tightly, her heart leaping into her throat.

Gideon thrust his left hand outward.

A streak of pure silver light shot out of the canvas, zooming forward over the path toward the guards ahead. It coalesced into a large, glowing silver wolf that slammed into one of the guards, knocking them right off their horse.

"Holy…!" one of the other guards shouted.

The wolf kicked off the guard it'd struck, sailing through the air and slamming into another guard's horse, knocking it over. Then it dissolved into a beam of silver light, streaking toward a third guard, re-forming at the last minute to rake one of its claws across the man's face. The guard flew off his steed, slamming into the grassy field below.

The remaining horses squealed in terror, rearing up on their hind legs as the wolf streaked between them, dissolving into a beam of light and re-forming over and over as it took down their riders.

"Archers!" a voice cried. "Kill that thing!"

More men on horseback galloped toward Bella, some with bows in their hands. They fired at the glowing wolf, but it streaked out of the way, shooting leftward across the path in front of Bella's horse. It ran on the grass alongside her then, so large it nearly reached the horse's shoulder. The wolf matched pace with the horse, its silver glow fading. It glanced up at Gideon.

"Myko, take her!" Gideon ordered, reaching around Bella again to touch the other side of the canvas. He flung his hand outward at the approaching guards then, and a bolt of lightning shot out at one of them, striking him in the chest…and then zig-zagging to strike another, then another. Eight of them fell from their steeds, convulsing on the field below.

"Shoot the Painter!" one of the surviving guards cried.

"Get on Myko," Gideon shouted, taking the canvas from Bella and nudging her with his stump. "Lower yourself onto his back!"

Bella glanced down at the huge wolf galloping alongside them, then at Gideon.

"Are you serious?" she shot back.

"Go or die!" Gideon retorted.

Thump!

An arrow slammed into the saddlebag on her right, missing her leg by inches.

Bella swung her leg over the saddle, grabbing the horn-thing at the front and lowering herself along the horse's left side. The wolf's back was level with her butt; she swung her left leg over it, easing herself onto it.

"Hold on to his collar!" Gideon ordered.

Bella looked down, spotting a silver collar around the wolf's neck. She grabbed on to it, holding on for dear life. She could feel the wolf's powerful muscles working beneath her as it pulled away from the horse, veering leftward over the grassy field.

"I'll come for you Bella," Gideon promised as the wolf took her farther and farther away from him. Eventually she couldn't see him at all in the darkness, his horse's hoofbeats the only evidence that he was still there. Bella turned her gaze forward; the long line of tents was only a hundred yards away now, the wall of fog beyond it rising as high as the eye could see. She spotted one of the huge structures she'd seen earlier between the tents and the fog; it was a statue of a giant forty feet tall facing away from her, with a bald head and huge muscular arms and legs.

And as she watched, it began to move.

Bella's eyes widened.

Color spread over the statue, its skin turning from dull gray stone to flesh-colored. It twisted to face her, its head tilting down as its bulging eyes locked on her.

Then it raised its leg, stepping *over* the huge tents toward her, even as the army of guards approached, less than a hundred feet away now.

And the wolf was galloping right toward them, its ears flat against its head.

"Oh god," Bella cried, gripping the wolf's collar so hard her knuckles turned white. The wolf's thick fur began to glow a faint silver. "Turn around!" she ordered, pulling back on the collar. But the wolf ignored her...and the army of guards was only fifty feet away now, the ground quaking with every step the giant took behind them.

Thirty feet.

"Oh god oh god watch *out!*" Bella screamed as the first of the guards rushed right at her, raising his spear to throw it.

And then the wolf shot forward and upward in a burst of silver light!

Bella held on for dear life as the ground dropped out from underneath her, and they sailed over the army of guards, flying through the air with terrifying speed. The wolf glowed so brightly underneath her that it might as well have been made of light, leaving a long silver trail behind it.

They flew right over the guards, and suddenly the silver light diminished. They slowed rapidly, plummeting right toward the giant's monstrous head.

Bella screamed, her stomach flip-flopping as they fell.

The wolf burst forward and upward again, shooting in a straight line mere feet above the giant's bald head, passing it and sailing over the tents beyond. They shot past the tents altogether, plunging right into the swirling wall of fog ahead. The mist swallowed her whole, glowing silver with the wolf's light.

Then that light faded, and there was darkness.

Bella felt herself falling, her sweaty palms slipping free of the wolf's collar. She screamed, her heart leaping into her throat as she fell faster and faster.

She heard a *splash* from below, and then icy-cold fingers enveloped her, pulling her into the abyss.

Chapter 7

Bella's throat locked up as icy-cold wetness swallowed her whole, soaking through her clothes instantly and chilling her to the bone. Her body went rigid with shock, and she felt herself sinking.

Then her limbs came to life, and she kicked and clawed desperately through the darkness, until at last her head burst through the surface!

Bella took a deep breath in, nearly choking on the muggy air as she treaded water, her wet, heavy clothes threatening to pull her back under its surface. She looked around, but could see absolutely nothing. There was only darkness.

There were shouts from behind, and the *thump, thump* of massive feet striking the earth.

Getting closer.

Bella swam away from the sounds, her heart pounding as she made her way blindly forward. Her feet struck something below; it was the floor of whatever body of water she was in. It sloped upward gradually, and she switched from swimming to wading. Her shoes sank into the ground with each step; it had to be mud sucking at her feet.

A soft, hazy silver light appeared ahead and to the left, a beacon within the darkness.

"Hello?" Bella called out, feeling herself step out of the water. She clutched her arms to her chest, shivering violently. Even with the light, she could barely see past her own nose. The light ahead grew larger and brighter, and she walked toward it, her cold, wet clothes clinging to her with each step.

A wolf stepped through the haze, stopping a foot away from her, its fur glowing bright silver. It was as tall as she was, its head level with hers. And it had striking blue eyes that gazed back at her, seeming to peer into her very soul.

"M-myko?" she asked, her teeth chattering.

The wolf nodded.

There was more shouting from behind, and then a blood-curdling scream. Bella spun around, but could see nothing through the fog. Myko's ears went forward, his body going rigid. A low growl rumbled in his throat.

Then he leapt at Bella, biting her arm and yanking her violently backward!

Bella cried out, falling onto her back, and the huge wolf dragged her kicking and screaming through the muck, his jaws clamped down painfully on her upper arm.

The fog blasted toward them, a huge head slamming into the ground a few yards away…right where she'd been a second ago.

BOOM!

The ground quaked, a wave of muddy water slamming into Bella. She felt Myko let go of her arm, and she scrambled to her feet, wiping mud off her face and chest…and backpedaling away from the massive head before her. It was the giant she'd seen earlier; she caught a glimpse of its eyes staring vacantly outward, blood pouring from a large gash in its forehead. Its skin began to change color, turning stone-gray.

And then the fog spilled inward to fill the gap the giant's fall had left, swallowing the huge creature whole.

There was more shouting in the distance, followed by the sharp scream of a horse. Myko snorted, nudging Bella's shoulder with his nose. She flinched, then glanced at the wolf.

"Where's Gideon?" she asked.

Myko raised a rear leg, swiping it at his collar as if scratching an itch. Then he lifted a big front paw, swiping gently at Bella's left hand…and promptly turned away from her, backing up until he was right beside her. She hesitated, placing her hand on his collar.

"You want me to hold on?" she asked.

Myko gave a snorting nod.

Bella curled her fingers around his collar, and he promptly began to walk forward across the muddy terrain. With his silver light, she could tell that they were in some sort of marshy area, with narrow islands of muddy earth surrounded by pools of dark water. Still, the mist was so thick that it was hard to breathe, much less see. How Myko could tell where he was going, she had no idea.

There was a splash behind them, and Myko whirled around, yanking his collar out of her hands. In a flash of brilliant silver light, he was gone…leaving Bella alone in the darkness.

"Myko?" she hissed.

There was a sudden *yelp*, followed by silence.

Bella froze, a chill running down her spine. She heard another splash nearby, and then another. Getting louder. Coming toward her.

Then a silver glow appeared in the mist ahead, and moments later Myko returned, his jaws stained with blood. He snorted, stopping alongside Bella and scratching at his collar again. She hesitated, staring at the blood and feeling sick to her stomach. Myko scratched at his collar again, and Bella swallowed back a wave of nausea, grabbing the collar and letting the wolf lead her through the mist.

"Where are we going?" she asked. Myko said nothing, of course. She felt rather stupid, kicking herself for thinking the wolf could talk. But then again it could clearly understand her…at least a little…and communicate back in a way.

The great silver wolf led her through the haze, paws squelching in the mud underfoot. A great heat radiated from his body, for which Bella was grateful; she found herself pressing her side against him as they walked. If he minded, he certainly didn't show it. His fur was thick and surprisingly soft, and didn't smell like dog. In fact, it didn't smell like anything at all.

Myko slowed for a moment to sniff the ground, then continued forward.

At length they reached a large stone pillar, one so tall it vanished into the mists above. Thick brown vines crawled up its surface, wicked-looking black thorns protecting their stems. Myko stopped before this pillar, standing perfectly still save for his ears. They were erect, busily turning this way and that, as if searching for a telltale sound. Then they locked in place, and Myko turned his head slightly, staring off into the choking fog.

Bella heard a splash in the distance, followed by a muffled curse.

Moments later, a shadow appeared in the mist ahead, a vague blur that became sharper as it approached. Bella pressed closer to Myko's warm flank, gripping tufts of his fur tightly.

"Relax," a familiar voice called out. "It's me."

"Gideon!" Bella blurted out.

And it *was* Gideon; the man stopped before them, looking a complete mess. His suit jacket was missing, his silver tie askew. His dress pants and the lower half of his purple shirt were utterly soaked, and mud caked his fine dress shoes and his socks, water dripping from the rolled-up painting he held in his left hand. Blood oozed from a small cut on his left cheek…and dripped from the butt of his cane, which he'd tucked under one armpit.

"Well, that went better than I expected," he declared. "Then again, I expected us to die."

"Are you okay?" Bella asked.

"Just fine, thank you," he replied. "Might want to keep your voice down, by the way," he added. "There *is* a literal army looking for us."

Bella winced, realizing she'd spoken far too loudly.

"What was…all that?" she asked in a hushed tone. "Why is an army after us? What was that giant-thing? What the heck is going on?"

Gideon ignored her, setting the painting against the stone pillar, then handing his cane to Myko, who carried it in his mouth. Then Gideon used his one hand to straighten his tie and smooth out his shirt. After scraping his boots on the pillar to get the mud off, he retrieved the painting, shaking the water off of it and muttering something under his breath. The painting unrolled itself instantly, becoming completely flat, as if framed.

"Hold this up, would you?" Gideon requested. Bella stepped away from Myko, instantly missing the wolf's warmth. The painting was taller than Gideon himself, and a few feet wide. It was of a moonlit hilltop; lightning was frozen in mid-flash within clouds to the upper left, a four-sided lantern resting atop a wooden casket on the lower left. Objects littered the ground beside the casket, including a few arrows, a sword and two spears, as well as a few paintbrushes of various sizes, a palette, an easel, and jars of paint set out in neat rows. And a bronze fire pit sat to the right, a fire crackling merrily within.

"Go on," Gideon urged. "Hold it by the edge."

She did so, holding it with one hand. It was quite easy to do so, given how light it was. Gideon knelt down in the muck, reaching out with his lone left hand toward the lantern on the painting, his fingers brushing up against the canvas there.

They passed right through.

Bella's eyes widened, and she stared in disbelief as Gideon's entire hand plunged into the canvas. But instead of disappearing, his hand appeared on the *surface* of the painting, as if it too had been painted. He grabbed the lantern...and pulled it right out of the canvas.

After which it appeared entirely real.

"What?" Bella blurted out, staring at the lantern in disbelief. Gideon held it before him.

"Luminos," he murmured.

The lantern flared to life, bright rays of light piercing through the fog. The light cut through the mist like a knife, shoving it backward violently...and revealing the marshy landscape around them, clear as day. The light ended a good fifty feet away in all directions, somehow keeping the churning fog at bay. Muddy earth extended in all directions around them, along with countless small pools of mucky, turbid water. Plants like cattails pierced the surface of the pools, and huge waterlilies floated on top.

Gideon muttered something, and the painting promptly rolled itself up in Bella's hand.

"Switch," he instructed, handing her the lantern and taking the painting from her. "Alright Myko, let's get my portal and go," he prompted. Myko sniffed the ground, then walked forward across the mud, and Gideon followed him. Bella hesitated, then rushed to walk at his side. The wolf, she noted, was no longer glowing.

"They'll be sending more dogs soon," Gideon warned, glancing behind them. Myko snorted, the cane still between his jaws. "I know *you're* not worried," he told the wolf.

"What's going on?" she demanded. "Where are we? And why were all those people chasing us?"

"If you ask more than one question at a time," he replied, "...you'll give me a chance to avoid answering one of them."

"Fine," Bella grumbled. "Where are we?"

"Before I can tell you where you are," Gideon replied, "...you need to know where you've been."

Bella just stared at him, and he stopped, turning to face her.

"You, Bella, have been lost," he explained. "In a book."

Bella blinked.

"Huh?"

"You were lost in a book," he repeated.

"What do you mean I was lost in a book?"

"The world you and your grandfather lived in for the last decade was a fiction," Gideon declared. "Everyone you knew there – your teachers, your schoolmates – was a character in a book. Your apartment, the city. Everything."

Bella raised her eyebrows, crossing her arms over her chest.

"Really."

"This book was written by a man named Belthazar Squib," he continued, ignoring her doubting expression. Bella's eyes widened.

"The Chronicles of Collins Dansworth," she recalled. "That's the book Grandpa gave me!"

"Correct," Gideon confirmed. "This was the book you were lost in. And by lost," he added, "...I mean that you were *living* in."

"I was living in a...book," she stated.

"Right."

"But that's impossible!"

"So is pulling a lantern from a painting," Gideon pointed out. She glanced at his lantern, realizing he had a point. "You're not living in a book anymore," he explained. "In this world, the impossible is only the stroke of a brush...or a pen...away."

"So...my apartment, my school," she stated. "That wasn't real? My friends weren't real?" What few she'd had, anyway.

Gideon paused, glancing at the rolled-up painting in his hand. He muttered a word under his breath, and it unrolled itself immediately, displaying the same scene as before.

"Myko, go home," he ordered.

The big wolf snorted, then dashed toward the painting, leaping right at it...

...and went *into* it.

Bella stared at the painting, her mouth falling open. For there, standing atop the hill below the full moon, was Myko. Motionless on the canvas. Where once his hair had been as real as hers, now it was composed of innumerable fine brush strokes. He emitted a soft silver light that matched that of the moon, casting a faint glow on the ground beneath him.

"He's..."

"A painting," Gideon confirmed. "I painted him myself, actually."

"He's not real?"

"You tell me," Gideon replied. Supporting the back of the painting with his stump, he reached into the painted side with his left hand. Then he *pulled*...and Myko burst out of the painting, landing on the mud beside Bella.

The great wolf shook itself, then turned back to look at Gideon.

"Are you real, Myko?" Gideon inquired. Myko turned to Bella, stepping up to her and nudging her shoulder with his cool, wet nose...and pushing her back a step in the process. Gideon gave Bella a tight smile. "So there it is."

Bella hesitated, then put a hand on Myko's fur, feeling its softness under her fingertips. Its warmth.

"I painted Myko, but when I draw him out of the painting, he's as real as you are. Just like the lantern, and everything else I paint," Gideon explained. "My paintings are magical...and so was Belthazar Squib's book."

Bella took a deep breath in, letting it out slowly.

"So you're saying that, my entire life, I've been living in a book."

"In the world that the book's magic created, yes," he confirmed. "When Belthazar wrote his book, he made it so that anyone who read it – and became lost in its pages – would look up to find themselves living within its world."

"So everyone I've ever known was just a character in this guy's book?" Bella pressed. Gideon hesitated, then nodded. Bella felt fear grip her, and she swallowed past a sudden lump in her throat. "Even Grandpa?"

"No," Gideon corrected. "You and your Grandfather weren't part of the book."

Bella let out a breath she hadn't realized she'd been holding. She glanced at Myko, eyeing him critically. To think that the wolf had been *created*...and that her apartment, her school, even her friends and teachers had been mere characters in a book...was unbelievable.

No, it was impossible.

But if it *was* true, then her entire life – at least the life she could remember – had been a figment of someone else's imagination.

"I can't believe it," she muttered, shaking her head. "You're saying my whole life was just a book."

"Not all of it," Gideon countered. He gave her a warm smile. "Your grandfather wasn't," he added gently. "And believe me, what you two had in each other was as real as anything can be."

Bella smiled back, picturing Grandpa lying next to her in bed at night, telling one of his wonderful bedtime stories. Of him saying goodnight, silhouetted in her doorway, the light catching his gold-rimmed glasses just so.

And then she heard three gunshots, and saw Grandpa's eyes staring lifelessly through her as a police officer thumped on his chest.

Bella felt that horrible numbness return, the cold darkness that had surrounded her ever since the afternoon Grandpa died. That utter lack of feeling, so complete that she felt no sadness. Just…nothing. She should have cried right then – a normal person would have – but she didn't.

Maybe there was a lot more wrong with her than even Mrs. Pittersworth had thought.

"I know this is a lot to process," Gideon offered. "But we need to keep moving. The Collector's men – and things far, far worse – will be coming after us."

"The Collector?"

"The man who was hunting your grandfather," Gideon answered. "And the one who wants *you* dead."

He continued forward then, striding quickly over the marshy terrain, his dress shoes leaving wet footprints in the muck. Myko nudged her shoulder, then bolted ahead to lead the way through the fog. She sighed, following along as Myko, and the light from Gideon's magical lantern, guided her through the darkness.

But as it did, Bella couldn't stop thinking about how her life had been a mere fiction, words on a page. None of it mattered anymore. None of it had been real.

The most horrible thought of all was that, as much as she'd thought she'd loved Grandpa, her love too had been just a fiction. Just another part of the book she'd been lost in.

And now that she was in the real world, her love – like everything else in her life – was gone.

Chapter 8

For Simon, the dream came as it always did. Every night the same.

Sunlight streamed down from the mid-afternoon sky, birds chirping from their perches on the tall, yellow stone buildings of downtown Twin Spires. A huge city whose maze-like streets he'd long since memorized, at least the ones going from his school to his home. He found himself walking with his best friend Vin, laughing and joking while they strolled across the street, a few blocks from his house. At fifteen, Vin was a year older than Simon, and a little taller, with golden tanned skin and gentle brown eyes. He had short brown hair that fell in messy curls atop his head, and an easy smile.

"So I put a few drops of the stuff in his drink," Vin explained, grinning from ear-to-ear. "And made him crap his pants in class."

"Oh *man*," Simon exclaimed, laughing so hard he doubled over. He struggled to catch his breath. "You didn't!"

"Oh yes I did," Vin retorted proudly. "Shat all over his chair. It *stunk*. Cleared out the whole room."

Simon shook his head. Vin was always pulling pranks like that...and more often than not, he got away with it. Probably because he was the best-looking kid in his class, and charming, and just...perfect. Simon found himself staring into Vin's eyes for a little too long, and turned away abruptly, clearing his throat.

"Did he find out it was you?" he asked.

"Nah," Vin answered.

"What if he does?"

"Who cares?" Vin replied. "I can take him in a fight."

Which was true. Vin lived a little further downtown, in the rough part of the city. He wasn't afraid of a fight. And even if he didn't win – which he almost always did – he made damn sure the other kid never wanted to fight him again.

"You are pretty awesome," Simon agreed, glancing at Vin. Sunlight shone through Vin's hair, giving it a golden hue, and Simon found his gaze lingering again.

"What?" Vin asked.

"Huh?"

"Lost you there for a sec," Vin explained. Simon blinked, then lowered his gaze.

"Just...thinking," he mumbled. But he felt his cheeks grow warm, and turned away from Vin, gazing at the windows of the building to his left. He tried to come up with something to say, but he couldn't.

"You're weird sometimes, you know that?" Vin told him. Simon grimaced. He *did* know that.

Just stop it, he told himself, gritting his teeth. For two years he'd kept his feelings hidden, knowing damn well what would happen if anyone found out the truth. If they discovered his terrible secret. He'd played along for the last couple years, chiming in every time his friends gushed about girls. Girls were supposed to have a sort of magic, he knew. But he didn't feel it. *Couldn't* feel it, no matter how hard he tried.

He took a deep breath in, forcing himself to turn back to Vin with what he hoped was a natural-looking smile.

"Says the guy who poisons kids and makes them crap their pants," he replied. Vin nudged Simon playfully on the shoulder.

"You like it," he retorted.

"I do," Simon admitted. "I like you," he added without thinking. A bolt of fear shot through him, and he immediately cursed himself. But Vin just threw an arm around Simon's shoulders, pulling him close so their shoulders were touching as they walked.

"I like you too," he replied.

Simon smiled, glancing sidelong at Vin as they made their way further down the street. Simon's apartment was only two blocks away now. He stared at the building, feeling a sickly sensation in the pit of his stomach. The same feeling he got every time he got close to home.

Suddenly he wanted the walk to be much longer. Vin would have to go as soon as they reached Simon's house, after all…and Simon didn't want this moment to end. He enjoyed the feeling of Vin's side against his…and was suddenly acutely aware of the fact that their hips were touching.

Vin stopped suddenly, gesturing ahead at Simon's apartment building.

"Here we are," he declared. "The House of Simon." He turned to face Simon with another one of his easy smiles. "Until next time?"

Simon nodded, staring into Vin's eyes…and found his gaze dropping to his lips. Their faces were only inches away…and he was struck by the sudden, mad urge to kiss Vin.

And before he could stop himself, that's exactly what he did.

Their lips pressed together, soft and warm, and Simon felt a tingling sensation all over his body. The world seemed to drop away, and in that moment, there was nothing else.

A moment he'd dreamed about for two years now…but better than he'd ever imagined it could be.

Then Vin shoved him backward. Hard.

Simon lurched backward, falling onto his butt on the hard cobblestones.

"What the *hell*?" Vin blurted out, glaring at Simon. He wiped his mouth with his sleeve in disgust, backing away from Simon. "What's wrong with you?"

Simon stared up at Vin, the blood draining from his face.

"I was just…it was a joke," he stammered, picking himself up off the street. But Vin took another step back, holding out one hand to stop Simon.

"Keep the hell away from me," Vin ordered. "Damn *weirdo*."

And then he strode away quickly, spitting on the street as he left. Simon watched him go, his heart sinking.

Oh now you've done it, he wailed silently. *Stupid idiot!*

He stood there, watching Vin go, then lowered his gaze to his feet, his lower lip quivering. His vision blurred with moisture, and he wiped the tears away quickly, taking a deep, shuddering breath in.

Idiot idiot idiot!

This was it. Vin would never be his friend again…at best. At worst, he'd tell the whole school about Simon. About what Simon had done. His life was over.

Slowly, dejectedly, he made his way home.

When he reached the front door to the tall, narrow apartment building where he and his father lived, he went inside, climbing the stairs slowly to the second floor. He opened the door, walking into the living room…and found his father there in the small dining room adjacent to it, sitting at the table. He already had a beer in his hand…and two other empty bottles nearby.

"Hey," Simon muttered, trudging across the living room toward his bedroom door. His father's bleary eyes followed him.

"Stop," he ordered. His voice cut through Simon's misery like a knife. Simon froze, turning to face the man. He knew that tone…and knew what would happen if he disobeyed.

His father took a swig from his bottle, then slammed in on the tabletop, making Simon flinch. The man stood, swaying slightly, and glared at Simon. His cheeks were ruddy, but not with cheer.

"You're late," Dad accused.

"Streets were crowded," Simon replied.

"Oh yeah?" Dad said. He grabbed the beer, taking another swig, then lowering the bottle to his side. "Funny. Didn't look crowded to me."

Simon glanced past his father, to the window in the dining room, facing the street. It was open, a slight breeze ruffling the rose-colored curtains. Curtains Mom had put there years ago, before he was born. She'd been a Painter, unlike his father. He'd never known her, although Dad talked about her all the time. She'd died giving birth to Simon.

"I had to talk with the teacher," Simon lied.

"Shut up."

Simon's jaw snapped shut, a chill running down his spine. His father took a step toward him, pointing a finger at him.

"I saw what you did, Simon."

Simon's eyes widened, the blood draining from his face.

Dad stared at him silently, lowering his finger. He took another swig of his beer.

"Did you like it?" he asked.

Simon said nothing. Could say nothing.

"You did, didn't you," Dad muttered. Another swig. "Bet you *really* liked it."

Simon just stood there, frozen.

"Bad enough your mother died having you," Dad groused. "Leaving us in this *shithole*," he added, gesturing around the room. "And now…this," he continued, gesturing at Simon in disgust.

"Father…" Simon began, his voice cracking.

"Am I?" his father inquired, raising an eyebrow. "Because I *know* I didn't sire a god-damn *faggot*."

Simon swallowed past a lump in his throat, tears welling up in his eyes.

"Dad…"

His father drew the beer bottle back, then whipped it at Simon's head. It clipped him in the temple, smashing into the wall behind Simon and shattering into a thousand pieces.

His skull exploded in pain, his head snapping backward. The world went black for a moment, and he felt himself falling. His back struck the floor.

And then agony shot through his spine.

Simon cried out, his vision returning. He found himself lying on his back, staring up at the ceiling. Blood was pouring from his right temple…and shards of glass were strewn across the floor around him. And under him. The razor-sharp pieces jabbed into his back.

He moaned, trying to sit up.

His father stepped in his field of vision, stopping beside Simon and swaying as he glared down at him.

"You know what my daddy woulda done to me if he found out I was a faggot?" he inquired.

Simon froze, lying flat on the floor. Warm wetness spread across his back and buttocks…and he knew it wasn't beer. Or even urine. His whole body began to tremble uncontrollably.

"He would've beaten it outta me," his father growled.

Simon lay there, a mewling whimper coming from his throat. His father sneered.

"But you know what?" he spat. "You ain't worth it."

He spat on Simon, warm spittle striking Simon's cheek. He turned away then, walking back up to the kitchen table and eyeing the two empty beer bottles. Then he went into the kitchen, retrieving two more bottles and carrying them back to the table.

Still Simon waited, but his father just sat down, popping open a bottle and drinking the entire thing in one long gulp. He grunted, rolling onto his side and pushing himself up off the floor...and stifled a scream as a shard of glass sliced into his right forearm.

He froze, gritting his teeth against the pain.

Simon got up carefully, avoiding the rest of the glass, then got to his feet. Blood seeped from his right forearm. His head. And almost certainly from his back.

Then, without a word, he tiptoed to his room, closing the door behind him. He sat down on the edge of his bed.

And cried.

His shoulders heaved, awful choking sounds coming from his throat. He tried to hold them in, but he couldn't. They spilled out from him in wave after wave, until there were no tears left. Until he was spent.

Then the door swung open, and Simon flinched, wiping his eyes hurriedly. Dad stood there in the doorway, glaring down at him, an empty bottle hanging loosely from his right hand. His grip tightened around its neck, his knuckles going white.

"On second thought," he said, "I changed my mind."

* * *

Simon eyes snapped open, and he gasped, bolting upright.

He found himself sitting on a hard, rectangular slab of gray stone. The only piece of furniture in a small prison cell. Three stone walls and a fourth made of vertical metal bars. A commode sat in one corner, its stink filling the cell. There was no mattress to lie on, no pillow. No blanket to ward off the chill. And the short sleeves and thin fabric of his bright red prison uniform were hardly up to the task either.

Simon wiped the sweat from his forehead, forcing his breathing to slow.

Just the dream.

He gazed past the bars of the cell, seeing a section of narrow hallway running perpendicular to it, facing another gray stone wall. Of course, it hadn't been just a dream. It was the past. But though it'd been over a year ago, the past wasn't behind him; it stayed with him. Every morning the same.

He lowered his gaze, staring at his hands...and at the dozens of crisscrossing scars on his forearms. Then he found himself staring at what lay in the palm of his right hand.

A small fragment of pale porcelain.

Do it, it seemed to whisper in his mind. *The next time your guard comes.*

Simon squeezed his eyes shut, rocking back and forth at the edge of his cot, willing the voice to go away. He curled his fingers around the fragment of porcelain, as if doing so would silence it.

Do it, the voice urged. *Or die here like the rest of them.*

Simon shook his head, tears welling up in his eyes. They dripped down his cheeks, then fell to the stone floor below.

Do it!

"No!" Simon shouted, leaping to his feet. His voice echoed off the stone walls, then went silent. He stood there, cheeks damp, clutching the porcelain fragment so hard it bit into his palm. Uncurling his fingers, he saw blood there. Simon slumped back down on his stone cot, staring at the bloodied porcelain.

Then he gripped it between his fingertips, bringing its sharp edge to his left forearm...and sliding it straight across.

He winced at the sudden sharp pain, watching as a thin trail of blood welled up from his skin as he cut himself. A shallow wound, barely more than a scratch. But the pain soothed him. Focused him. And unlike everything else in his life, it was something he could control. It was the *only* thing he could control.

Because you're weak, the voice accused.

"Shut up," Simon whispered, gripping the fragment harder. He brought it a little higher up on his forearm, pressing it more firmly against his skin. There was a sudden pinch as it broke his flesh, and he drew in a sharp breath.

Don't cut yourself, the voice told him. *Cut them.*

Simon heard footsteps coming down the hallway, and sat bolt-upright on his cot, folding his arms over his lap and hiding the porcelain fragment. One of the prison guards strolled by a moment later, barely glancing Simon's way before continuing down the hallway. The guard vanished from sight, his footsteps slowly fading.

And Simon let out a breath he hadn't realized he'd been holding.

The voice in his head went mercifully silent, leaving Simon alone in his small jail cell. The last room he'd ever sleep in. For in two days, he'd be sentenced for his crimes. Painting without a license. Painting an unapproved Familiar.

And murder.

"It's not my fault," he whispered to himself, rocking back and forth again. "I didn't want to."

But he knew even as he said it that it *was* his fault. And he *had* wanted to, in the moment. That he was defective, screwed up. Someone even Vin...even his *father*...couldn't love. He *deserved* to die. To be strung up by the neck and hanged, as he surely would be in two days' time.

And now all he could do was wait.

Unless...

Simon's eyes went to the pulsing vessel at his wrist...and then to the fragment of porcelain. He swallowed in a dry throat, his heart *thumping* in his chest.

Don't.

Simon ignored the voice, bringing the fragment to his wrist, over the artery.

Don't!

The fragment flung out of his hands, slamming into the wall and ricocheting off. It fell to the floor...and slid all the way to the bars, stopping there.

Do it again and I'll leave, the voice warned.

"No!" Simon blurted out. "Don't leave me, please."

The fragment laid there by the bars, then flew right at Simon of its own accord, landing back in his hand.

Be patient, it soothed. *We'll survive.*

"How do you know that?" Simon whispered.

We always do.

Chapter 9

The Misty Marsh was so muggy it was gross, even with Gideon's magical lantern keeping the fog at bay. Bella's clothes remained perpetually damp, condensation beading like sweat on her skin. She wiped her eyes with the back of her sleeve for the umpteenth time as Myko led her and Gideon through the wall of fog surrounding them, the muck sucking at her shoes with every step. There was a rotten smell in the air, enough to make her queasy.

"So who's this Collector?" she asked. "And why was he after Grandpa?"

"The Collector is a very wealthy, very powerful man," Gideon answered. "And like all wealthy and powerful men, whatever he has is never enough."

Bella waited, but Gideon didn't elaborate.

"You didn't answer my second question," she accused. He smirked.

"Remember what I said about asking more than one question at a time?"

"Right," Bella grumbled.

"Ten years ago, your grandfather was teaching at Blackthorne, and you and your mother went to visit him," Gideon told her.

Bella frowned, recalling the story Grandpa had told her. Of how she'd gone to the college he'd taught at, visiting him in a huge library with Mom. How she'd run amok smelling the books.

"Then the Collector attacked Blackthorne," Gideon continued.

"Why?"

"He wanted to steal Blackthorne's treasure trove of paintings and books," Gideon explained. "You see, Blackthorne is part of the Pentad, a vast kingdom...of which your grandfather and I are citizens." Gideon sighed then. "Against all odds, the Collector succeeded."

"So he owns Blackthorne now?"

"Correct," Gideon confirmed. "Those were his guards that you met outside of the library, and his soldiers that tried to stop us from escaping into the Misty Marsh."

Bella looked around, guessing that the Misty Marsh was where they were right now. As apt a name as any, she supposed.

"And the two men you met – the ones you know as Stanwitz and Reynolds – were also the Collector's men," Gideon revealed. "They've spent the last decade hunting you down."

"That doesn't make any sense," Bella protested. "Why would anyone hunt *us* down? We're nobodies."

"Oh, on the contrary," Gideon retorted. "Your grandfather is Thaddeus Birch, the most famous author alive...and one of the greatest Writers to have ever lived."

Bella slowed, then stopped, staring at Gideon uncomprehendingly. First of all, Grandpa's last name was Brown, not Birch. And she couldn't possibly imagine him being anywhere *near* famous. Then again, Stanwitz *had* called Grandpa Mr. Birch, before he'd...

She pushed the thought away.

"I know it's hard to believe," Gideon stated. "But Thaddeus – your grandfather – was a great writer, even more powerful than the one who wrote the book you were lost in. You see, Writers have magic a bit like Painters do. Tell me...have you ever read a really good book and gotten lost in its pages? Or perhaps even felt that it was real?"

"Well yeah, I guess."

"Books here do that literally," he explained. "When the Collector attacked Blackthorne, your grandfather grabbed a book from a pile on one of the tables there...a book he knew very well. The Chronicles of Collins Dansworth, an old, boring classic. He read it with you, Bella. And when you read a magical book, and get lost in its pages, you vanish from this world and appear within the world of the book."

Bella frowned, processing this.

"So when I read the book again…"

"You reversed the magic, and left the book, returning to the library exactly where you'd been ten years before," Gideon finished. "Thaddeus did it to save you," he explained. "He hid you within that book for ten years, Bella. Even as the Collector sent teams of bounty hunters to search every book in that library for you."

"You mean Reynolds and Stanwitz."

"Among others," Gideon agreed. "They didn't get to your book for nearly a decade, but once they did, it was only a matter of time before they found you. Your grandfather knew that."

"That's why he never left the apartment," Bella realized. She felt woozy, and had the sudden urge to sit down. But there was nowhere to sit; she felt something soft brush up against her left side, and realized it was Myko. She leaned on the wolf a bit.

"It nearly drove him mad, staying in that apartment day after day," Gideon continued. "Year after year. Waiting for the Collector's men to close in on you two. At first he refused to even let you go to school, but eventually he relented. You needed as normal a life as possible."

"You visited him in the book then," she guessed. Gideon nodded.

"Thaddeus and I have been best friends for a very long time," he revealed. "Long before you were born, in fact. When I heard about the attack on Blackthorne, I traveled here and went undercover, working for the Collector." He sighed. "I spent nine years in that damn library, getting lost in book after book until I finally found yours…and your apartment."

"How come I never saw you?" Bella asked.

"We couldn't run the risk of the Collector's men finding you and interrogating you," Gideon answered. "If they had, you would have given away my identity."

"But you visited?"

"On occasion," he admitted. "Only when it was safe to do so, which was seldom. Most of the time I was under surveillance by the Collector's men. I couldn't risk leading them to the right book. It took me nearly nine years just to find it…and I prayed they never would."

Bella shook her head, thinking of poor Grandpa holed up in that awful apartment. Sitting at his desk day after day, alone while she was at school. Trapped in a prison of his own making.

Those aren't police officers Bella. They're bad people.

She swallowed past a lump in her throat, blinking moisture from her eyes.

I'm not crazy Bella.

But deep down inside, she'd thought he was. A little bit, anyway. And he'd been right all along. Suffering in silence, unable or unwilling to tell her the truth.

"Why didn't he tell me?" she asked. Gideon sighed, lowering his gaze.

"He wanted to, believe me," he answered. "But if he told you the truth, and the Collector's men got to you, they would've forced it from you. And you would've led them straight to Thaddeus."

"I wouldn't have told them," she retorted. He gave her a look.

"You'd like to think so," he replied. "But believe me, they have their ways."

Bella took a deep breath in, then let it out, trying to collect herself.

"So why were they after us?" she pressed.

"Your grandfather is the greatest Writer alive. As powerful as paintings are, books might be even more powerful. You see, when one person reads a book, its world becomes real to them. But if enough people read a book, and it is written with exceptional skill, its world becomes real to *everyone*."

"Huh?"

"When you read a regular magical book, you go into its world for a time, until you read it again. Then you come out. But when enough people read a book written by a very powerful Writer, everything in that book – its lands, its characters – becomes real in *this* world. Permanently."

"Wow."

"Your grandfather's books are some of the most popular and beloved of all time," Gideon explained. "And one of them created an entire kingdom in this world…a place called Havenwood."

Bella's eyes widened.

A dragon circle
White and good,

Will one day rise
For Havenwood.

The simple rhyme that opened the door to her happy place, a safe haven from an otherwise uncaring and colorless world.

A chill ran down Bella's spine.

"Havenwood is the one place the Collector can never conquer," Gideon continued. "And it was your mother's home. *Your* home. It's my job to bring you there...where you'll be safe."

Bella nodded mutely. It was just like Grandpa to hide so much meaning in a few words. The numbers to unlock their front door had been the combination to the safe that contained the book that had been the key to bringing her here...and Havenwood was the ultimate goal.

Havenwood meant *home.*

"The ability to create entire places and people in this world is a power the Collector would very much like to have," Gideon stated. "And a power that, if it worked against him, would be a grave threat indeed."

"So he was...scared of Grandpa?" Bella asked. It was ludicrous to imagine anyone being scared of the man, after all. He was a lovable, absent-minded teddy-bear. But Gideon nodded.

"Your grandfather was not a man to be trifled with."

Bella lowered her gaze as she walked, shaking her head.

"I thought I knew him," she murmured. "But I guess I didn't."

Gideon slowed, then stopped, turning to face her. He tucked his rolled-up painting in his armpit, then put a hand on her shoulder.

"You didn't know his past," he replied, "...but you knew his heart. He was every bit the man you thought he was...and more." He smiled. "Thaddeus Birch was not only the finest Writer alive, but also the finest human being I've ever met."

Bella nodded, swallowing past a sudden lump in her throat.

"Where are we going?" she asked, wanting nothing more than to change the subject.

"We're leaving the Misty Marsh," Gideon answered. "Then we'll need to brave Devil's Pass before we get to Havenwood."

"Devil's Pass?"

"You'll see," Gideon promised. The way he said it was a bit ominous for Bella's liking, but she didn't press the issue.

They walked in silence for a time, hopping over a few small puddles and splashing through the ones that were too wide and deep. Myko had no problem traversing these, of course; the few he couldn't leap over, he simply glow-dashed across.

"How does he do that?" Bella asked.

"He uses the power of moonlight," Gideon answered. "I painted Myko to absorb moonlight. He can use it to moon-dash in any direction in a perfectly straight line, like a ray of light. Or even bounce off of reflective surfaces like light can."

Bella thought back to how Myko had flown her over the giant statue…the one that had somehow come to life.

"Why not just ride him and have him fly us to Havenwood?"

"It would drain Myko too quickly," Gideon explained. "He can only hold so much moonlight."

"So why not paint him to have unlimited moonlight?" she pressed.

"Magic is like an unruly child," he declared. "It needs limits. And if you don't set those limits when you're painting, you'll live to regret it…if you live at all."

Bella frowned.

"What does that mean?"

"You'll see," he promised. Which meant it was the end of *that* discussion. Bella sighed, gazing at the dome of fog all around them. It swirled at the edges of the lantern's mysterious power, as if waiting for a chance to attack. She felt her mind going inevitably back to Grandpa, and cleared her throat, desperate to distract herself from her morbid thoughts.

"What is this place anyway?" she asked. "Why all the fog?"

"The Misty Marsh wasn't always like this," Gideon admitted. "We believe it was once the home of an ancient civilization, a city of huge stone temples and underground tunnels. Legend has it that they worshipped water, and that a great Painter among them created a magical chalice. When the Painter drew it out of the painting, the chalice began to fill with water. An endless supply of pure water."

"Huh."

"The people were overjoyed, and the chalice was set in a large underground temple somewhere in the ancient city. Night came, and everyone fell asleep. The next morning, the entire city was flooded."

"From the chalice," Bella guessed. Gideon nodded.

"They sent the Painter back into the temple to retrieve it, but it'd floated away through the underground tunnels that ran through the city. Scouts tried to find it, but no one could. And the water kept coming, until the city had to be abandoned."

"And then it made this marsh and all this fog," Bella reasoned.

"Correct."

"All because of one painter," she mused. "Wow."

Gideon stopped, and Bella stopped beside him. He turned to her, putting his stump on her shoulder.

"Wielding magic is a grave responsibility, Bella. One governed by three great laws…the first of which is the Law of Unintended Consequences."

Bella frowned.

"Huh?"

"The first thing any creator must learn is that there is magic in what they do. And magic is a great, wild power. A vicious beast that will turn on the careless in the blink of an eye." He grimaced then. "And believe me, the Law of Unintended Consequences doesn't give a damn about good intentions."

He turned away abruptly, continuing forward.

"Magic needs limits," he stated, waving his cane for emphasis. "If you don't set those limits when you're painting…"

"You'll live to regret it," Bella grumbled.

"If you live at all," he agreed.

They continued their journey in silence then, the squelching of their shoes and Myko's paws in the muck the only sounds. Bella found her mind wandering, processing everything that had happened since she'd sat down in the city library back on Summer Street. To think that everything she'd experienced since she was six – her whole life, almost – had been a fiction, mere words in a book…

It was too much to wrap her brain around, that none of it had been real.

Don't think of it as real and not real, she reminded herself, glancing at Myko. The wolf was plenty real, yet had been created. Magic had made him real, just as magic had made the book she and Grandpa had been lost in seem real. Her apartment had been real. Her classmates. Even Mrs. Pittersworth. But they weren't real like she was, or like Grandpa was.

They'd been made, not born.

Eventually Gideon led them to the ruins of a huge stone building, its great gray walls covered in a thin carpet of bright green moss and pale yellow lichen. They passed through a doorway into one of the few intact rooms, which was flooded with a foot's worth of water. They waded across to the very center of the rather large room, and Gideon muttered to himself. The painting he was holding unrolled, becoming flat. It showed the same scene as before, of course.

"See those arrows and that spear?" he asked. Bella nodded; they were scattered on the hilltop in the painting. "Take them out."

Bella hesitated.

"Me?"

"That's right," Gideon replied. "Come on, we haven't got all day."

She stepped up to the painting, staring at the arrows. Then she crouched down, holding a hand up to the painting's surface. She touched it gently with her fingertips, fully expecting them to press against the canvas.

But they passed right through.

She gasped, feeling a sudden warmth spread through her fingertips, followed by a powerful pulsing sensation. She jerked her hand away reflexively, looking up at Gideon. He smiled.

"Everyone does that the first time," he reassured. "Go on, it won't hurt you."

Bella returned her gaze to the painting, steeling herself, then dipping her fingers into it again…and again felt that warmth and pulsing. She plunged her whole hand in, then her wrist, seeing them transform into brushstrokes on the canvas.

"That's *weird*," she breathed, opening and closing her fingers, watching as they moved within the painting. They seemed sluggish though, moving only with great difficulty.

"Grab one of the arrows," Gideon instructed. She did so, reaching in up to her elbow. She felt a sudden tingling in her fingertips, and it spread to her hand.

"It's tingling," she stated.

"Hurry!" he urged.

She grabbed one of the arrows, feeling her hand close around its cool wooden shaft. Then she pulled it out. Sure enough, a very real arrow was in her hand, larger than it'd been in the painting. The warmth and pulsing sensation she'd felt earlier was gone.

"Toss it aside," Gideon instructed. "And the others."

"Why?" she asked. "You painted them, didn't you?"

"No. Those are the arrows those soldiers shot at me."

Bella frowned, looking down at the arrow. Then she remembered how one of the archers on horseback had shot at Gideon, the arrow plunging into Gideon's painting. She'd been amazed that it hadn't gone right through and impaled Gideon in the chest.

"You mean...?"

"Paintings are magic," Gideon replied. "Things can be drawn out of them...and can be trapped within them."

"Like Myko," she reasoned.

"And you, and me, and anything else but another painting," Gideon corrected. "You don't have to be painted to go into a painting. Once a painting is completed – and signed – it becomes a doorway into its own static world."

Bella stared at the painting, swallowing visibly.

"What if I fell into it?" she asked.

"You already did once," Gideon replied. Bella blinked.

"What?"

"In the library at Blackthorne," he clarified. "I had you stand in front of the canvas, remember?"

Bella's eyes widened.

"You pushed me!" she accused.

"Right into the painting," he agreed. He tapped her right arm with his stump. "Pull up your sleeve."

She did so, and saw the tattoo still there on her forearm.

"I painted that on you while you were in there," he explained. "Been practicing that little pattern for years now, let me tell you. Had to move quickly."

She ran her fingers over the tattoo, half-expecting it to smudge, but it didn't.

"Is it real?" she asked. "A real tattoo?"

"Of course."

"But...I was only in the painting for a split-second," she protested. "You pulled me right out!"

"A finished painting is a doorway into its own *static* world," Gideon repeated. "It's not like a book, where things are always happening. There's no time in a painting. Everything stands still. So, anything that goes in it stands still too."

Bella processed this.

"How long was I in there?" she asked.

"A few minutes. But if you'd been inside for a hundred years, it would have felt the same." He gestured at the painting with his stump then. "Go on then, get the other arrows. I don't want them cluttering my painting."

Bella took a step back, shaking her head.

"You get it," she retorted. "I'm not going *near* that thing."

"You'll have to get over that real quick if you ever want to become a Painter," Gideon shot back.

"Excuse me?"

"The only people who can pull things out of paintings are Painters," he explained. "So you were born with the gift."

She just stared at him.

"I've seen your paintings," he revealed. "You've got talent...as much as your mother did when I first started teaching her. If you ever want to be as good as she was, you'll need to get past your fear."

Bella's eyes widened, her mouth falling open.

"You taught my mom?"

"That's right," Gideon confirmed, squaring his shoulders proudly. "She was the second-best Painter I ever met."

"Who was the first?"

Gideon smirked.

"You're looking at him."

Bella felt her heart racing, a giddy sensation coming over her. *He'd* taught Mom how to paint!

"What was she like?" she asked breathlessly. "Was she nice? What did she paint?"

"I'll tell you," Gideon promised. "Just as soon as you get those damn arrows out of my painting."

Chapter 10

Bella did get Gideon's damn arrows out of the painting, all the while being terrified that she'd accidently trip and fall into it. Of course, Gideon could've pulled her right out, but the idea still frightened her. That she could quite literally become part of a painting, trapped forever in suspended animation. A fate like death…if no one ever drew her back out.

He'd rolled the painting back up, then said something to Myko that she didn't quite hear. The great wolf sniffed around, then dug furiously in the water, bringing up globs of mud. Then he thrust his head into the water, coming up with a black disc in his jaws. It was as thin as paper, and about the size of Bella's head.

"Take it," Gideon instructed Bella. Bella did so, grabbing it from Myko's mouth. It felt cool and slick, like glass. "Put it against the wall."

Bella sloshed over to one of the stone walls, setting the disc against it.

"Higher," he instructed. "Don't want to get my things wet."

She obeyed.

"Anulus!" Gideon exclaimed.

The disc melded with the wall…and started to grow. Bigger and bigger, until it was nearly as tall as she was. The bottom of it was a few inches above the water.

"Go on in," Gideon instructed, gesturing at the disc with his stump. Bella blinked.

"Huh?"

"Step through," he clarified.

Bella turned to the disc, staring at its utter blackness. Then she put a hand up to it. It passed right through, vanishing from sight. She withdrew her hand, glancing suspiciously at him.

"Is this another painting?" she asked. He arched an eyebrow.

"Is it?"

She thought it over. She couldn't see her hand past the disc, and there was no pulsing or warmth when she'd plunged her hand through. So no, it wasn't.

"Right," she muttered. Then she took a deep breath, stepping through the disc.

And gasped.

For she found herself in a room three times as big as her bedroom back home. The floors were made of warm red cherry, the walls painted off-white. There was a fireplace crackling merrily at the far wall, and a large built-in bookshelf set into the rightmost wall. And against the leftmost wall, a big, comfy-looking bed.

Gideon stepped through the black disc, now against one wall of the room. Water dripped from his pants onto the floor as he strode up to the bookshelf, his shoes leaving muddy tracks, to his obvious distaste. The bottom half of the bookshelf consisted of large drawers, the top a series of shelves with books atop them.

Gideon grabbed one of these books, pulling it out slightly. Then he pulled out another book in the same way.

The bookshelf spun in a quarter-circle, revealing a secret room beyond.

"Come on," he urged, stepping into the next room. Bella followed, finding herself in a large walk-in closet. There were various suits, shirts, and pants hung neatly on either wall, as well as an assortment of hats and what looked to be capes. And shoes. *Lots* of shoes. A door at the end of the closet was partially open, revealing what appeared to be a large studio. She caught a glimpse of an easel and a bag filled with rolled-up canvases.

Gideon retrieved a stack of neatly folded clothes at the far end of the closet, as well as a pair of tall boots.

"These are for you," he declared. "You change outside, I'll change in here. Let me know when you're decent."

Bella obeyed, relieved that Gideon had the decency to spin the bookshelf again from the inside to give her privacy. She was glad to be rid of her still-soaked and muddy clothes, and for the warmth of the fireplace. She stood in front of it for a while to dry her skin, then studied the outfit Gideon had given her: black leather pants, a black leather shirt, and a black hooded cloak that was ruby-red on the inner side. And tall black leather boots. There were unusually large holsters of sorts at her mid-thighs below either hip, and a beige, canvas-like material on her chest and belly. The same canvas-like material encircled her upper arms, forearms, and shins like bracers.

The outfit was just a bit too big for her.

"They don't fit," she called out. The bookshelf spun, and Gideon stepped into the room. He was dressed in a uniform that looked remarkably similar to hers, but with a long red cape and a black Victorian top hat...and instead of plain beige fabric at his chest, arms, and shins, his were little paintings of sorts. He wore a black glove on his left hand, and tucked in his armpit were a bunch of rolled-up paintings. He began stuffing a few of them into the holsters on either thigh.

"Well then," he declared. "That's better."

"These clothes don't fit," Bella repeated, gesturing at herself. Then, to her surprise, her outfit began to shrink, until it *did* fit...even her boots. Gideon smirked.

"They'll *always* fit," he countered. "I painted them to. They were your mother's, by the way.

Bella's eyes widened, and she stared down at her new outfit.

"She wore these?" she asked.

"Oh yes," Gideon confirmed. "When she was around your age, in fact. It was her Painter's uniform. It stores weapons and items for battle," he explained.

"Like those?" she asked, pointing at his chest-painting. There were several fireballs painted there, and a strange black orb with a red glow around it.

"Correct," he confirmed. "Here," he added, reaching into his chest-painting. He pulled out the black orb...and promptly shoved it into her chest. Bella took a step back, expecting to be pushed backward, but Gideon's hand went *into* her chest-painting, and he deposited the orb there, removing his hand. She stared at the orb, now stored within her uniform

"Wow," she murmured. Then she looked up at him. "What's it do?"

"Pray you never find out," he replied. "Come on."

And with that, he walked back to the black disc on the wall, stepping through and vanishing from sight. Bella hesitated, squatting down to search through the pockets of her old, muddy pants. She found Grandpa's folded-up letter there, and stuffed it into her pocket. Then she followed Gideon, finding herself back in the flooded ancient room, water lapping at her boots. But they were clearly waterproof, keeping her nice and dry.

"Anulus," Gideon said…and the disc shrank, falling off the wall. He caught it, handing it to Bella. Then he took off his hat, holding it upside-down with his stump; he took his cane from Myko, putting it right into his hat. It went all the way in, vanishing from sight. The remaining rolled-up paintings were next, somehow managing to fit right into the hat. Then he took the disc from Bella, repeating the process. That done, he placed the hat back on his head.

"Let's go," he stated, and trudged through the water toward the room's exit, Myko at his side.

"How did you do that?" Bella asked, splashing after them.

"Magic," he answered, patting the top of his hat.

"Did you paint that?" she pressed, hurrying up to walk beside him.

"Of course," he answered. "I painted just about everything I own."

"What was that room?" she pressed.

"My Conclave," Gideon replied. "Just about every Painter has one. You see, when I painted the disc, I made it a portal to a place I created," he explained. "I painted that room – the entire house, in fact – in the same painting as the disc."

"Wait, I thought you could only paint things and pull them out of their paintings," Bella protested. "You're saying if you paint a portal, it'll go to whatever you painted it to go to, and that place will just suddenly exist?"

"That's right," Gideon confirmed.

"Huh."

It was powerful magic indeed, that could not only create things and animals like Myko, but actual *places*. But then again, apparently so could books. She'd lived in one for most of her life, after all.

99

"The more creative you are," Gideon stated with a wink, "...the more powerful your magic will be."

They continued in silence for a while, trekking through the Misty Marsh in their new clothes. They reached another set of ruins, and Gideon led them between crumbling stone buildings. The terrain sloped upward a bit, the ground drier and harder under their feet.

Gideon stopped abruptly, turning to Bella.

"We should make camp," he declared. "This is as good a spot as any. I'll fetch the fire."

Gideon unrolled his painting, reaching in and grabbing the bronze fire pit with his gloved hand. He pulled it out, setting it on the ground. Fire danced within, but there was no wood fueling the flames. And no smoke came from the fire. More magic, Bella supposed. Nothing Gideon painted was merely ordinary, it seemed.

Gideon sat before the fire, and Myko laid beside him. Bella sat cross-legged on the other side of the fire pit, its warmth a stark contrast to the crisp night air. It was then that Bella remembered Gideon's promise.

"You said you'd tell me about my mom," she prompted.

"I did," he replied. "What do you want to know?"

"Everything," Bella answered immediately. Gideon chuckled.

"Let's start with something," he countered.

"You taught her how to paint?"

"Oh yes," he confirmed. "Let me start from the beginning. Your grandfather Thaddeus and I were old friends long before we decided to have children. I was his student, in fact...many, many years ago."

"But you're a Painter, not a Writer."

"As are you," Gideon pointed out. "And you were his student too."

"Fair point."

"He taught me the art of storytelling, which is the root of all magic. Then I finished my studies with some of the best Painters in the world. But I was young and craved adventure, so instead of becoming an academic like Thaddeus, I decided to become one of the Pentad's bounty hunters."

"Huh?"

"I did what Stanwitz and ah...Reynolds did," Gideon explained. "But I searched for rogue Painters and Writers and so forth, those who'd created illegal art and escaped the law by getting lost in a book or in this world. It was a well-paying job, and quite dangerous. Very attractive for a young man like me, at the time. And it just so happened that I was rather good at it."

"Huh."

"Thaddeus continued teaching at the palace in the capitol of the Pentad, writing his books. After a very long time, he met an Actress and settled down. And they had your mother."

Gideon paused, smiling at the memory.

"I was there when she was born," Gideon revealed. "She was lovely and stubborn, right from the get-go. Thaddeus desperately wanted her to become a Writer, but by the time she was seven, it was clear she was destined to be a Painter."

"So you started teaching her?"

"When she turned thirteen, yes," Gideon confirmed. "At first she was hesitant, unsure. Always doubting herself. And stubborn – gods she was stubborn! – but I worked with her every day. I made her tell stories with her art. And her art was unlike anything I'd ever seen."

"What was it like?"

Gideon sighed, lowering his gaze.

"Dark," he answered. "Disturbing. Beautiful." He glanced up at Bella across the fire, his green eyes seeming to glow in the firelight. "Like your mother."

Bella processed this.

"Grandpa said she was complicated," she recalled. Gideon burst out with a laugh.

"That," he replied, "…is an understatement."

"Why?" she pressed.

"I'll tell you another day," Gideon promised. When Bella's face fell, he smiled. "Don't worry, I'm not being evasive, I'm just exhausted. And by the looks of it, you are too. We'll talk more tomorrow."

"Promise?"

"Promise."

With that, Gideon took off his cape, setting it on the ground and laying atop it, facing away from the campfire and Bella. It wrapped itself around him, and promptly lifted off the ground, levitating a few inches above it. Bella stared, marveling at the magic, then laid down herself. Myko lowered his head to the ground, resting beside his master and creator.

Within moments, Gideon was snoring.

Bella gazed into the fire pit, enjoying the gentle crackling of the fire. But as tired as she was, she couldn't sleep. Her mind raced, overwhelmed with everything that had happened that day. To think that she'd woken up this morning in her bed…

No, not *her* bed. The neighbor's bed.

Reality came rushing back to her then. Stanwitz and Reynolds dragging her upstairs. Kicking down the door. Stanwitz shoving Grandpa out of his chair.

Three gunshots went off in Bella's head, and a vision of Grandpa's body lying there on the carpet. Eyes staring vacantly into nothing.

Dead.

That horrible numbness returned, draping over her like a lead blanket. So heavy that it was impossible to shrug off. She closed her eyes, willing herself to fall asleep, but Grandpa's dead eyes stared at her from beyond her eyelids.

She opened them, staring into the fire.

Minutes passed. Then what seemed like an hour. And still she couldn't sleep.

Bella tossed and turned, then sighed, rolling back onto her side and curling in the fetal position. She resigned herself to the terrible truth: she wasn't going to sleep tonight, and tomorrow was going to be very, very hard. Reaching down to her pocket, her fingers found Grandpa's letter; she brought it out, unfolding it.

Dearest Bella, it began.

She read the whole thing, then re-read it, a lump forming in her throat. Blinking back tears, she folded it, putting it back in her pocket. She sighed again, shifting her gaze from the fire…and saw Myko lying across from it, staring at her. She startled, staring back.

The great wolf stirred, standing up and walking toward her. He circled around behind her, then laid down, curling his body to press against her back. He was warm and soft, and she could feel his gentle breath on the back of her neck.

She nudged back a bit, pressing against him.

Time passed, and still she couldn't sleep.

"Myko?" she whispered.

There was no response; the wolf was clearly asleep.

102

She took a deep breath in, letting it out slowly.

"My Grandpa died yesterday," she whispered. The statement sent a chill down her spine, the first time she'd ever said those words. The first time she'd admitted the awful truth out loud.

She swallowed past a lump in her throat.

"I can't cry," she confessed, so quietly even she barely heard it.

Bella closed her eyes, gritting her teeth. A normal person would've cried. When someone you loved died, that's what you did. But she clearly wasn't normal. Or maybe the truth was even more terrible than she wanted to admit.

Maybe she hadn't loved Grandpa as much as she'd thought.

"What's wrong with me?" she whispered.

She felt Myko stir behind her, and then his great big paw draped over her, resting on her chest. It pulled her gently backward, pressing her spine firmly against him. She felt the slow, steady *lub-dub* of his heartbeat on her back.

The dam burst.

Tears welled up in Bella's eyes, dripping down her cheeks. Awful sobs burst out from deep within her, wracking her body. She cried, remembering Grandpa lying beside her at night, telling her stories. Remembering feeling his heart beating as he hugged her close, her head resting on his frail chest. His great big smiles, his endless exuberance.

She cried, unable to stop, terrified that Gideon might wake up and hear her. But he didn't. She cried until there was nothing left. Until exhaustion took over.

And then, when she was done, she closed her eyes, surrounded by the warmth and softness of the great silver wolf embracing her. Her mind began to wander, and at long last, she fell asleep.

Chapter 11

The day of Simon's judgement was upon him.

He'd woken up that morning in his cell, having slept fitfully on its unforgiving stone bed. After relieving himself in his commode, he'd sat cross-legged on the floor, watching as guards strolled by, clad in the gold and red uniforms of the Pentad. None of them paid him any mind. None of them cared. No one cared about anyone but themselves.

His father had taught him that.

Simon fiddled with the porcelain fragment absently, waiting. It was silent, as it often was. Like him, it rarely spoke. It rarely needed to.

Another guard passed by, then another.

Hours passed, and Simon grew antsy, standing up to pace back and forth in his cramped, narrow cell. He found himself staring down at his right forearm, at a small bulge in the front of it. A shard of glass from that fateful day. The day he relived over and over in his dreams. The only piece of glass he hadn't been able to get out after his father'd finished with him. It was a part of him now…and would be until his death.

And that, he realized, was only hours away now.

More footsteps echoed through the hallway, but they were different. Sharper. They rang out slowly, leisurely, getting progressively louder. A guard strode into view, but the footsteps weren't his.

"Hey," the guard called out, putting a hand on the hilt of his sword and staring off at something further down the hall. "Who're you?"

The footsteps drew closer, and then Simon heard a woman's voice sing.

Stop world
Rest for a while,
Time goes on
But yours is slowing.

You stop
But Time goes on,
An eternity in every
Second.

The guard froze, not so much as blinking. He just stood there as the woman continued to sing, her voice hauntingly beautiful. Simon blinked...or at least he tried to. His eyelids seemed frozen, moving so slowly that it was barely imperceptible. And try as he might, he couldn't move a muscle. His body simply wouldn't obey him.

And then she stepped into view.

The woman was tall and slender, wearing a tight silver dress that clung to her every curve, and silver high heels. Even her hair was silver, and perhaps six inches long, fashioned into several sharp spikes that shot straight upward. Her temples were shaved into complex curving patterns, her small ears sharply pointed. She had the most unusual silver eyes, and high, sharp cheekbones. And though she had the body of a young woman, something about the way she carried herself hinted at her being much older than she appeared.

She strolled right up to the guard, who still hadn't moved, stopping a foot away from him. Then she turned her head – still singing – her eyes lighting on Simon.

A chill ran through him, goosebumps rising on his arms.

Still she sang, locking eyes with Simon. She held his gaze, even as she reached for the guard's sword, drawing it free from its scabbard.

Then she slid the blade across the guard's throat.

No blood came from the wound, though it cut deep into his flesh. The guard just stood there, unmoving, even as the woman re-sheathed his sword, then took the keyring from his belt.

She stopped singing.

The guard slumped to the floor, blood spurting from his neck. Simon gasped, instantly regaining control of his body. He bolted to his feet, backpedaling to the rear wall of his cell.

The woman turned to face Simon, using the guard's key to unlock the door to Simon's cell. She pushed it open, the barred door swinging open with a *creak*.

"Hello Simon," she greeted in a silky-smooth voice. "My name is Miss Savage. I've come to rescue you."

Simon stood there, pressed against the wall, staring at her mutely.

"Come with me," she requested...and immediately turned, walking back the way she'd come, her heels ringing loudly on the stone floor with each step. Simon watched her go, then shifted his gaze to the guard lying on the floor in a pool of his own blood.

Listen to her or die.

Simon glanced down at the porcelain fragment in his hand, then took a deep breath in...and obeyed. He stepped out of his cell, carefully avoiding the blood around the guard, and rushed to catch up with the silver-haired woman. The hallway was long and straight...and ahead, another guard could be seen lying on the ground in a pool of blood. And beyond that, another. And another.

Miss Savage stopped suddenly, turning to face him.

"Look at me, Simon," She requested. He did so. She produced a purple crystalline key from a tiny pocket in the side of her dress, holding it out to him. "This is a very special key," she explained.

"Why are you doing this?" he asked, his voice cracking. "Why save me?"

"Because we need you, Simon."

"Need me?" he pressed.

"You're a Painter, aren't you?"

He nodded. He *was* a Painter, like his mother had been. He'd painted in secret ever since...since his father had passed.

106

That's one way to put it, the voice in his head remarked.

"I've seen your work," Miss Savage revealed. "My...employer is interested in hiring you."

"Your employer?"

"The Collector," she clarified.

Simon's eyes widened, and Miss Savage smirked.

"You've heard of him then," she noted. Simon nodded. Everyone had heard of the Collector.

"He's a criminal," he pointed out.

"So are you."

Simon grimaced.

"What does he want with me?" he pressed.

"See for yourself."

She held the key before her then, twisting it as if she'd put it in an invisible keyhole. A door made of shimmering purple light appeared in front of her. She opened it, revealing a rectangular doorway leading to a magnificent hallway. One with a white and gray marble floor, a red and gold carpet running over the middle of it. Paintings hung from the walls, along with elegant lanterns at regular intervals.

And at the end of this hallway was a huge, black stone door unlike any that Simon had ever seen. Twenty feet high and ten feet wide, it had a carving of a demon's face upon it, its awful mouth open in a silent roar.

"Step through and meet your destiny," Miss Savage told him, gesturing at the magical doorway.

Simon hesitated, staring at the opulent hallway beyond.

"My destiny?" he asked.

"Justice," she explained. "The Pentad rejected you, Simon. They couldn't control you, so they were going to destroy you. The Collector offers a way to fight back."

Still Simon hesitated.

Why should you trust her?

"Why should I trust you?" he asked.

"Because they tried to destroy me too," Miss Savage answered. Her eyes went to his arms, and the innumerable scars crisscrossing them. "We both have scars, Simon. The Pentad tried to destroy us, but they failed. We healed, and now we're stronger. The Collector is our weapon, Simon. And one day, very soon, we'll have our revenge."

She gestured at the doorway.

"You have a choice," she declared. "You can be the victim of your story...or the hero. What will you choose?"

Simon hesitated for a moment longer, then clenched his fists, feeling the sharp edges of porcelain fragment bite into his right palm.

You know what to do, it told him.

He took a deep breath in, then strode forward into the magical doorway. And on the day of his judgement, he was set free.

Chapter 12

The next day, Bella, Gideon, and Myko broke camp, allowing Myko – or more specifically, Myko's nose – to lead them through the foul, dank terrain of the Misty Marsh. Gideon's lantern kept the fog at bay, lighting the way. Apparently it was powered by sunlight, absorbing and storing the sun's rays much as Myko did with moonlight. The great wolf had, to Bella's relief, offered to carry her on his back, and she'd gladly agreed. He carried her without any evident difficulty whatsoever, his powerful muscles rippling beneath her. She was grateful for his support, and the good night's sleep she'd gotten the night before.

"I always wanted a dog," Bella mentioned to Gideon as they walked. "Grandpa said the apartment was too small for one."

"I know," Gideon replied with a smile. "A husky or a wolf, right?"

"How'd you know?"

"Thaddeus told me all about it," Gideon admitted. "He couldn't tell you of course, but it's because of Myko."

Myko snorted loudly in agreement.

"What do you mean?" Bella asked.

"You and Myko were best friends when you were growing up," he explained. "He slept with you since you were a baby, all the way up until you visited Blackthorne and didn't come back."

Myko gave a lone whine, and Gideon ruffled the wolf's head with his one hand. Bella grimaced.

"Sorry Myko," she apologized. "Guess I was too young to remember."

Myko *wuffed.*

"He says it's okay," Gideon translated.

Bella smiled, leaning down and giving the wolf a hug.

"Thanks Myko," she stated. "For everything."

The wolf didn't respond, and Bella glanced at Gideon.

"Does he…?"

"Oh, he understands everything," Gideon replied with a smile. "Just as well as you and I do. But like a good book or a good painting, he shows instead of telling."

"Grandpa used to say that all the time," Bella mused. "Show a story, don't tell it."

"That's the beauty of painting," Gideon revealed, arching an eyebrow rather dramatically. "You *have* to show instead of telling."

"I still don't get how to tell a story with a painting," Bella admitted.

"You will," he promised.

Myko froze suddenly, turning his head to look back the way they'd come. His ears perked up, a low growl rumbling in his throat.

"Dogs?" Gideon asked. Myko nodded. "Get off," Gideon ordered Bella. She dismounted, her boots sinking into the mud. Myko glowed bright silver, then shot into the fog at the edge of the magical lantern's sphere of influence, leaving a beam of pure moonlight in his wake.

There was barking, then squealing…then silence.

Myko stepped back out of the fog a moment later, blood staining his jaws and chest. He shot forward a few yards with another beam of light, and when he stopped before them, his coat was spotless once again.

"What were those?" Bella asked.

"Trail-hounds," Gideon answered. "They leave an invisible trail behind them when they're tracking something. If they find what they're looking for, the trail turns into a bright yellow light that hovers about the ground for a few hours." He turned to Myko. "Did they activate their trail?"

Myko nodded.

"Damn," Gideon cursed, turning about and walking forward quickly. "They'll lead the Collector's men right to us. Get back on Myko," he ordered. We have to get out of here before it's too late."

* * *

Myko set a brutal pace through the marsh, with Gideon following alongside the tireless wolf. Hours passed, although it was impossible to tell what time it was with the thick fog above their heads. They didn't even stop to eat, much to Bella's disappointment. At length, she noticed a slight silver glow around Myko, the only hint that the moon was out, and that the great wolf was attracting and absorbing its faintest of light.

Bella spotted a sudden upsloping of the terrain ahead, and Gideon held up a stump, stopping suddenly. Myko stopped dutifully beside his master.

"Dismount," Gideon ordered. Bella did so, standing at his side. "We're at the edge of the Misty Marsh," he warned. "The marsh is in a crater of a large, extinct volcano. There's only one path out of the crater, and that's through a town called Devil's Pass."

"Is it safe?" Bella asked.

"Quite the contrary," Gideon replied. "Devil's Pass was converted into a military base for the Collector's army after the fall of Blackthorne. It's managed to hold off the Pentad's armies for the last ten years."

"So we need to get past an army?" Bella pressed. Gideon nodded grimly.

"Unfortunately yes."

"And how are we going to do that?" she inquired.

"*We're* not," he countered. "You're going into my Conclave."

"What?"

"You're going into my Conclave," he repeated. "I'll carry you through Devil's Pass and let you out on the other side."

He set his lantern on the ground, then took off his hat, turning it upside-down and holding it with his stump. He reached in with his only hand, pulling out his cane and tucking it in his armpit. Then he retrieved the black disc that served as the portal to his Conclave, holding it out to her. She crossed her arms over her chest.

"I'm not going into your Conclave," she retorted.

"It's the safest way," Gideon insisted.

"And if you don't make it?" she pressed. "Then I'm stuck in your Conclave forever?"

"I'll make it."

111

"I'm not hiding away in some room wondering if you will," she insisted. "Waiting for the Collector's men to come through the portal and kill me. I'm staying out here," she declared. "I can help."

Gideon arched an eyebrow at her.

"Can you?"

She just glared at him.

Gideon held her gaze, then dropped the black disc onto the ground by Bella's feet.

"Anulus," he intoned...and the disc expanded right under her feet. She tried to take a step back, but it was too late. She fell right through the portal, landing on her belly on the wooden floor of the Conclave.

"Son of a..." she blurted out, jumping to her feet and lunging at the portal on the wall. But it shrank before her eyes, vanishing from sight. She slammed her palms on the wall. "Gideon!" she shouted. "Open up!"

But of course he couldn't hear her...and wouldn't have listened anyway.

She sighed, walking over to the big bed and sitting down on the edge. There was nothing she could do now but stare at the wall, waiting for the portal to open again, and hope that Gideon was the one who walked through to get her.

* * *

Gideon watched as Bella fell through the portal, then quickly knelt down before it.

"Anulus," he incanted.

The disc shrank immediately, and he picked it up, shoving it in his hat. Then he placed his hat atop his head, glancing at Myko.

"What?" he asked.

Myko whined, and Gideon sighed, unrolling a painting and gesturing at Myko to jump into it.

"Go on," he prompted. "You're too recognizable. Don't want the whole damn army coming down on us."

He felt Myko's hesitation through their magical bond, and the wolf's concern. Myko loathed the idea of leaving him. Of not being able to protect his master.

I'll be all right old friend, he reassured silently. Still Myko hesitated. *So will she,* he added. *I promise.*

112

Myko resisted for a moment longer, then walked up to Gideon, nudging his shoulder with a wet nose. Gideon chuckled, rubbing the wolf's head affectionately, then planting a kiss between Myko's ears. Myko snorted, giving Gideon a wet, slobbery kiss on the cheek.

"I know," Gideon murmured. "I love you too."

Myko *wuffed*, staring into Gideon's eyes earnestly.

"I'll tell her," he promised. Myko just stared. "I know, I feel bad about it too. We'll tell her the truth soon enough."

Still that silver-eyed stare.

"Go," he urged.

Myko snorted. But the wolf obeyed, leaping into the painting…and becoming one with it.

Gideon sighed, then rolled the painting back up, putting it back into his thigh-holster. Then, his cane in hand, he continued the long walk up the dirt slope. It wasn't long before the soggy earth grew firm under his feet. Gideon deactivated his lantern, and the fog quickly filled in all around him, thrusting him into darkness. He shoved the lantern into his chest-painting.

After a few minutes, he emerged from the omnipresent fog as if bursting through the surface of a great body of water. Moonlight shone down on him from high above, countless stars twinkling in an inky-black sky.

Gideon glanced back, seeing nothing but an endless sea of white, swirling fog behind him, bordered by a ring of rock hundreds of feet high extending as far as the eye could see. This was the crater of the long-extinct volcano, home of the ancient civilization that had created the Misty Marsh. He took a deep breath in, savoring the fresh air.

Ten years, he muttered to himself. Almost a decade in that miserable place, and he was free at last. *They* were free.

Almost.

He turned forward; ahead was a canyon maybe a hundred yards wide that cut through the lip of the crater, with rock walls looming on either side of it. And ahead within the canyon, he spotted more than a few lights piercing the darkness.

Devil's Pass, the only way into the Misty Marsh, and by extension, Blackthorne. And the only way out. He could risk flying, but…

He looked up.

There, floating thousands of feet above his head, was something...*huge*. A massive cloud of black and red flesh as large around as the crater itself, with countless huge eyeballs embedded in it. Eyeballs that darted constantly to and fro, as if searching the crater below. It was the Overseer, created by one of the Pentad's Writers a few centuries ago to protect Blackthorne from aerial assault. Anything that tried to fly in or out of the Misty Marsh – or Devil's Pass – would trigger it.

I'll walk, he decided.

Gideon did just that, making his way toward the lights in the distance. As his eyes adjusted to the darkness, he made out a tall wooden fence running from one wall of the canyon to the other ahead, with a gate in the center lit by several tall, flickering torches that cast long shadows of the two guards standing before it. Beyond the fence, he saw tall wooden buildings, dim lights shining out of a few of their windows. He strode right up to the guards at the gate, flashing an easy smile.

"Good evening, gentlemen," he greeted. The guards glanced at each other, then at Gideon.

"Evening," one of them replied. "Identification?"

Gideon pulled up his sleeve, showing his tattoo. The guard studied it, then nodded briskly. "Go on in," he stated. "Have a good night." The gate opened, revealing more guards on the other side.

"You as well," Gideon replied.

He stepped through the gate into the military base, and the guards closed the gate behind him. A narrow cobblestone street greeted him, with tall, narrow wooden buildings rising three to four stories high on either side. Lanterns bolted to the sides of the buildings illuminated the streets in a ghostly yellow glow. To his surprise, the base looked deserted...a far cry from when he'd seen it a decade ago, on his journey to Blackthorne. Of course, looks could be deceiving.

Gideon continued down the street at a leisurely pace...then froze.

The streetlights ahead were unlit, save for a lone lantern some thirty feet away cast a glowing circle on the cobblestones.

A dark figure stood within that circle.

The figure was clad in a dark brown cloak, a hood over its head, throwing its face into shadow. It wore a painted vest that covered its chest and abdomen, and had similar painted bracers on its forearms. A Painter's uniform.

Gideon gripped his cane tightly, waiting.

The figure strode forward, stopping a few yards away from him. It paused, then lifted its hands to its hood, drawing it backward...and revealing a woman's face. She had pale skin and long red hair that spilled out of her hood, draping over her shoulders. Her eyes were sky blue, a blood-red line of lipstick drawn in the middle of her lower lip.

She smirked.

"Well well well," she murmured. "Look what we have here."

"Kendra," Gideon greeted coolly.

"Alec," she replied. Her smirk broadened. "Or should I say...Gideon." She shook her head. "To think that the great Gideon Myles himself was hiding right under our noses all this time! Remarkable disguise, by the way."

"Thank you."

"Myko was a dead giveaway," Kendra continued. "Frankly, I'm disappointed you made the mistake of drawing him out."

"Mistake?"

"Now the Collector will know where you are," she explained. Gideon raised an eyebrow.

"And?"

Kendra eyed him for a moment, pursing her lips.

"You could join us, you know," she offered.

"I'll pass."

"The Collector offers us freedom, Gideon," Kendra pressed. "What did the Pentad ever do for us, hmm? A bunch of rich old men who can't even feel the Flow enslaving those of us who can."

"Kendra..."

"*We* have the talent," she insisted. *We* should have the power, not them! They're using you, Gideon. Like they used me. And Piper." She crossed her arms over her chest. "Look what they did to Thaddeus. Look what they did to your wife!"

Gideon grimaced.

"You don't have to remind me," he muttered. "I'm not doing this for them, Kendra."

"We worked well together before, Gideon," Kendra pressed. "You, me. Piper. Yero. Imagine what we could accomplish together!"

115

"Not under the Collector," Gideon retorted. "I know what he is, Kendra. He's not doing this for us."

"You don't know him like I do."

"Oh, I *sincerely* doubt that," Gideon countered.

"Come on Gideon," Kendra urged. "We can start a new age for artists! Think about it."

"I've thought about it, believe me," Gideon retorted. "Now if you'll excuse me, I'm going to leave now."

"Don't make me do this, Gideon," Kendra warned. "We were friends once. I still care about you."

"What about Thaddeus?" he shot back. "Did you care about him when you and your men were hunting him down?"

It was Kendra's turn to grimace.

"I'm sorry, Gideon. All we wanted was for Thaddeus to work with us," she insisted.

"Goodbye, Kendra."

Kendra stared at him for a long moment. Then her expression hardened.

"Where's the girl?" she asked.

"Don't know what you're talking about," Gideon lied.

"Oh, but I think you do," she pressed, folding her arms over her chest. "My guards told me you saved her from the book, Gideon."

"Like I said," he replied, "...I don't know what you're talking about."

"The Collector wants her," Kendra insisted. "And I'm not going to give up until I have her."

"Then I'm afraid you're going to be sorely disappointed," Gideon stated. Kendra stared at him, her jawline rippling.

"Fine," she muttered. "You leave me no choice."

Then she lifted one hand in the air, snapping her fingers.

The doors to the tall buildings around them opened, men spilling out onto the street behind Gideon...and behind Kendra. Men with crossbows leaned out of the windows all around them, aiming right at Gideon.

And all of the dead lanterns in the street ahead suddenly turned on, illuminating it fully. More soldiers filled the streets...along with more than a few hulking green Glargs. They were far taller than the soldiers around them, with massive, muscular chests and arms like tree trunks, and bald heads that shone dully in the lantern-light. As did the huge axes they held.

Gideon stood tall, looking around at the army of men and creatures around him, then turning back to Kendra.

"That's it?" he inquired. "I have to say I'm a little insulted."

"We're a bit short-staffed at the moment," Kendra apologized.

"Pity," Gideon stated. "Tell you what. I'll tie one arm behind my back to make it fair," he proposed, raising his stump.

"You even let us cut off your hand," Kendra mused. "Such dedication. And to think you were three months from earning it back."

"Shall we?" he inquired, arching an eyebrow. She smiled, bowing her head slightly.

"It would be an honor."

And before the words were out of her mouth, she reached into the painting at her chest, flinging a long, black spear at his head.

Gideon's cape unclasped itself from his neck, flying at the spear and intercepting it in mid-air...then unfurling with a loud *snap*, flinging the spear right back at Kendra.

She dodged out of the way in the nick of time, the spear's deadly point cutting a shallow line on her left cheek. Blood oozed from the wound, and she put a hand to it, then stared at her bloody fingertips.

"That was a warning," Gideon stated. "You only get one."

"Fire!" she ordered.

Crossbolts shot down from the windows all around Gideon. He reached into his chest-painting, retrieving his magical lantern and holding it before him.

"Eruptus!" he cried.

Light burst from the lantern, along with a rapidly expanding shockwave that flung the crossbow bolts backward in mid-air. Windows shattered, soldiers careening over the street. They fell to their backs on the cobblestones, their weapons flying from their hands. Kendra joined them, landing on her back twenty feet away with a *thump*.

Gideon bolted forward, shoving the lantern back into his chest-painting. He passed Kendra, sprinting toward the army of soldiers lying stunned on the street. He weaved between them, most still scrambling to get back on their feet. One of them reached for his ankle, but he dodged out of the way deftly.

117

Passing the small army of fallen soldiers, Gideon continued down the narrow street. He glanced back, spotting Kendra rolling onto her belly. The Painter flung something out of her chest-painting after him.

A golden cube.

It clattered on the street, bouncing and then rolling until it came to a stop.

Then it came alive.

Black, veiny tentacles snaked out of each of its four side-facets, extending outward twenty feet in all directions like grotesque legs. The cube lifted up, two more tentacles sprouting from its top and bottom facets, each arcing forward to form a "C" that hovered above the street.

Nightmare!

The cube charged at him, moving down the street with terrible speed!

A huge tentacle whipped at him, moving so quickly it was a blur. Gideon's cape flew upward to intercept, but the tentacle managed to knock his hat from his head...and pull it back to Kendra. Gideon cursed, tucking his cane in his armpit and flinging his left hand outward. His black glove flew right off his hand, hurtling after his hat.

But the tentacled monster called Nightmare slapped it away, giving the hat to Kendra. Gideon's glove flew back onto his hand, and he clenched his fist, glaring at the Painter.

Kendra smirked.

"Remember that job we did oh, thirty years ago?" she asked. "The one where we hid that hostage in your Conclave, and you stuck the portal in your hat?"

"Kendra..."

"My men already told me you left with the girl, Gideon," she interrupted. "Now where oh *where* could she be?" she added, arching an eyebrow at the hat.

Gideon's jawline rippled.

"We were friends once, Kendra," he stated. "But if you dare threaten her, make no mistake. I *will* kill you."

Kendra pulled out a small black disc, flashing him a smirk.

"Oops. Found it."

"Kendra..."

"Let's go say hello," she interjected. She tossed the disc onto the ground before her.

"No!" Gideon cried, lunging toward her.

"Anulus!" she incanted.

Chapter 13

Bella watched as the black portal in the wall of Gideon's Conclave appeared, rapidly expanding to full height. She sat on the edge of the bed, gripping the bedsheets tightly, and waited.

But no one came through.

"Gideon?" she asked.

Still nothing.

She hesitated, then slid off the side of the bed, stepping up to the portal.

"Hello?" she called out.

And then a black, veiny tentacle shot through the portal at her.

Bella screamed, turning to run. But the tentacle wrapped itself around her waist, yanking her back toward the portal...and through it. She found herself sailing upward into the air above a starlit cobblestone road, tall buildings looming on either side of her.

Below, she saw a woman in a Painter's uniform, standing beside a golden cube. One with black tentacles sprouting from each of its six sides, four acting as legs, and two as arms. And one of those arms was wrapped around *her*.

Bella struggled against the tentacle's terrible grip, but it was no use.

"Gideon!" she cried, spotting him sprinting toward the woman and the cube. He shoved his cane into his right forearm painting, then reached into his chest-painting, flinging a fireball at the cube-thing. A burst of heat struck her as the fireball passed below her, and it struck the cube dead-on.

And *exploded*.

The cube-monster flew backward, its grip around Bella loosening instantly. Her stomach lurched as she fell fifteen feet toward the street below…and felt her descent slow abruptly, her cloak billowing outward around her. Still, her boots struck the street with considerable force, and she fell backward, landing on her back on the hard cobblestones, her breath blasting from her lungs.

She saw a huge, bald creature step up to her…and watched in horror as it raised its huge axe over its head, bringing it right down on her!

Gideon thrust his hand outward, his black glove flying off and shooting toward her. It grabbed her ankle, then yanked her back toward Gideon right as the creature's axe fell.

The deadly blade struck the cobblestones with a loud *clang*, missing her by a fraction of a second.

"No!" she heard the woman shout. "Take her alive!"

Bella slid across the street, and Gideon's glove released her ankle, flying right back onto his hand. She slid to a stop before him, and he offered his hand, pulling her onto her feet.

"Hurry!" he prompted, running down the street. She obeyed, sprinting after him as fast as she could. The street ended ahead in a rock wall a good fifty feet tall, with several wooden platforms that appeared to be elevators hanging by thick ropes resting against it.

All of which were rising upward, leaving no way forward.

Bella heard shouting from behind, and glanced back, seeing dozens of soldiers rushing after them…led by the golden cube-monster.

And above it, its topmost tentacle wrapped around her waist, was the Painter-woman. Recognition dawned, goosebumps rising on Bella's arms. It was the same woman she'd seen in her apartment, the one who'd come with Reynolds the day after Grandpa died.

The Painter flung her hand outward, and a bolt of lightning shot outward, striking Bella's back.

Bella's body stiffened instantly, and she fell to the street, her limbs spasming uncontrollably. The pain was instantaneous, like hitting her funny bone, but all over her body. It vanished as quickly as it'd come, and she gasped, struggling to get to her feet.

Just as one of the cube's tentacles wrapped around her left arm.

Gideon's glove flew off of his hand toward one of the soldiers rushing after them, yanking their sword out of their hands, then flying back toward the cube. It chopped at the tentacle holding Bella, severing it.

Bella pulled the severed tentacle from her arm, rushing to Gideon's side. His glove returned to his hand, still holding the sword.

The remaining stump of the cube's tentacle retracted into the cube's facet...then immediately snaked out again. Completely whole.

"It healed!" Bella gasped in horror.

"Got that," Gideon muttered. "Come on!" he urged, turning and running toward the sheer cliff wall ahead.

"How are we..." Bella began.

"Run up the wall!" he ordered...and picked up speed, breaking ahead of her. He leapt at the wall, kicking out with one foot...and it stuck. He ran up the side of the wall, glancing back at Bella. "Come on!" he urged.

Bella leapt at the wall like Gideon had, her right boot striking its surface.

It stuck, and gravity *shifted*.

The wall became the floor suddenly, the street behind her an impossibly high wall. Nausea struck her, and she became so disoriented that she nearly fell. She resisted the urge to stop and cling to the wall, following behind Gideon as he ran toward the bottoms of the elevators at the top of the cliff.

A ball of fire struck the wall ahead of them, missing them by mere yards.

Bella looked backward – and upward – spotting the Painter, still in the cube-monster's clutches. It used its tentacles to start climbing up the cliffside after them, the veiny limbs somehow sticking to the sheer surface.

"Cut the ropes!" the Painter cried.

The elevator ahead of them broke free from its rope, plummeting toward them!

There was no time to dodge.

Gideon cursed, skidding to a halt and dropping his sword. He reached into his right forearm-painting, pulling his cane free from it and swinging it at the elevator right as it careened into them.

Thwack!

Bella cried out, throwing her arms in front of her face.

But there was no impact. No pain. There was nothing at all.

She lowered her arms, staring in disbelief at the bottom of the elevator platform. It'd stopped a foot from them.

Then it started to move toward them again.

Gideon swung his cane, striking the elevator again…and it exploded in a shower of wooden planks.

"Go!" he shouted, bursting forward. He reached the top of the wall, leaping off of it…and fell out of sight. Bella followed, but skid to a stop at the edge of the wall, peering down.

An infinite drop loomed before her, a vertical street with buildings sprouting from its side.

Oh god…

Bella glanced back, seeing the Painter and her cube-monster gaining on them rapidly.

Bella closed her eyes…and jumped.

The world *shifted* again, gravity pulling her sideways. She landed on her back on the street beyond, the impact knocking the wind out of her.

And behind her, the Painter and her tentacled monster reached the top of the wall, charging right at her!

Bella scrambled to her feet, spotting Gideon standing before her, propping up a large painting with his stump.

"Get Myko!" he cried.

Bella lunged for the painting, reaching in and feeling her hand close around Myko's collar. She yanked backward.

A streak of silver light burst out of the painting, shooting toward the Painter. Myko materialized right as he slammed into her, closing his jaws around her neck. She gave out a horrid, gurgling scream as she and Myko burst backward. They fell off the cliffside, taking the cube-monster with them.

"Clausus," Gideon incanted. Myko's painting rolled itself up, and he shoved it into his thigh-holster. Then he grabbed Bella's hand, pulling her forward down the street. "We're almost there!"

"But Myko…!" Bella countered.

A streak of light shot past them overhead, and Myko materialized, landing on the street before them and matching pace with Bella.

Dozens of soldiers rushed down the street toward them ahead, blocking the way out of Devil's Pass. Gideon skid to a halt, turning to Bella.

"The orb in your chest-painting, throw it up in the air!" he ordered, pointing to the orb he'd thrusted into her chest-painting. "Point your finger at it when it flies out, then aim your finger at those soldiers!"

"Uh…"

"Don't think, *do!*"

Still Bella hesitated. Gideon thrust his cane into her hands, then reached into her chest-painting himself, drawing out the orb and tossing it high into the air. He pointed at it, then lowered his hand to point at the oncoming group of soldiers.

The stone exploded into countless smaller pieces, each of which flashed bright red, shooting right at the enemy. The pieces grew larger as they fell, as big as basketballs. Then they struck the soldiers.

And *exploded.*

Men flew from the impact, flames engulfing them instantly. A burst of searing hot wind slammed into Bella and Gideon, forcing her to turn away. Screams echoed through the night air, mixed with the sound of windows shattering and falling stones clattering on the streets.

Bella turned forward.

Where the soldiers had been, shallow craters marred the street. Burning bodies littered the ground, some still moving, most not. And beyond, the nearest buildings were engulfed in flames.

"Come on," Gideon urged, striding forward.

Bella just stood there, staring at the carnage in horror.

"Come on," Gideon repeated, turning to face her. "Bella, we need to go. Now."

The last of the burning soldiers stopped moving, laying on the side of the street as he burned alive. Bella put a hand to her mouth, her vision blurring with moisture.

"Oh god," she whispered. Her legs wobbled, and she sank to her knees, staring at the bodies.

"Bella!" Gideon snapped. She turned to stare at him, hardly registering what he'd said. Gideon grimaced, glancing at Myko. "Take her," he ordered.

Myko nudged Bella with his cold, wet nose, and she flinched at the touch, turning to face the wolf. Gideon rushed to help her to her feet, then boosted her onto Myko's back. The wolf trotted forward, Gideon running at his side.

"Close your eyes Bella," Gideon urged, and she did so, feeling the heat of the flames as they passed through the devastation he'd wrought. A minute later, he had her open her eyes. They were past the burning buildings now. Ahead was a tall stone wall with a single portcullis guarded by several men.

Who took one look at the devastation around them, and fled.

"Almost there," Gideon reassured. "No, don't look back," he advised. "Keep your eyes forward. Always. It's the only way to stay sane."

They reached the open portcullis, passing through it. Beyond was a vast, wide-open rocky field…and ahead, a virtual city of tents stood a half-mile away, lit by countless torches. The tents were identical to the ones she'd seen at the edge of the fog in Blackthorne, but there were hundreds of them, if not thousands. Soldiers milled about outside the tents, some eating by campfires, others talking with each other.

"We'll have to go through," Gideon warned. "There's nothing but steep drops down the mountain on either side of this field."

Bella nodded mutely.

"Myko, you're up," he stated. He shoved his cane into his forearm-painting, then vaulted up on Myko's back behind Bella. The wolf held their weight with seeming ease, trotting forward across the field toward the tent city. As they approached, several soldiers turned their way. One of them pointed, and the others starting gesticulating wildly. More soldiers turned to look at them.

A *lot* more.

Bella felt Gideon's arm wrap around her waist, holding her tightly.

"Lean down and wrap your arms around Myko's neck," he instructed. "Hold on tight…and whatever you do, don't let go."

Myko broke out into a full-on gallop, barreling toward the tents and the nearest soldiers. A few of them had bows, and drew their arrows, aiming right at Myko.

"Wait for it," Gideon ordered, gripping Bella's waist tighter. She clung to Myko's furry neck as the wolf ran faster, the ground a blur beneath them.

The archers fired.

Arrows whizzed through the air at them, and Myko dodged to the left, two of them barely missing him. But a third slammed into his right hindquarter, burying into his flesh.

Myko yelped.

"Wait for it!" Gideon repeated. More arrows whizzed by, and Myko dodged again, running with a limp now. They were only a hundred yards from the tents now, and closing in fast. Soldiers swarmed out of the tents, rushing toward them with swords drawn.

"Gideon!" Bella warned.

Gideon leaned over, pressing his body against Bella's back...just as another volley of arrows flew at them. He grunted as one struck his right shoulder.

And Myko yelped as another arrow struck the wolf in the chest.

"Come on old boy!" Gideon cried. "Almost there!"

Myko dodged another volley, the army of soldiers swarming at them less than a hundred feet away now. Myko's breath rasped in his throat, blood-tinged froth spilling from the side of his mouth. Still he ran, barreling toward the enemy.

"Now!" Gideon cried.

Myko burst forward in a blaze of pure silver light, shooting forward and upward through the air. Bella clung desperately to his neck, feeling Gideon's weight threaten to yank her backward off the wolf. They sailed over the soldiers' heads, flying over the first of the tents.

And then the light faded, and Myko began to plummet toward the earth.

"Again!" Gideon shouted.

Myko moon-dashed a second time, then a third, leaving a trail of moonlight behind him as he flew them right over the tent city. They passed it completely, and Myko moon-dashed forward and slightly downward, landing on the ground a dozen yards away from the last of the tents. He galloped over the rocky terrain, leaving the tents – and the soldiers – behind.

"Woo!" Bella exclaimed, glancing back. "We did it!"

"Dodge!" Gideon cried.

Myko moon-dashed to the side, leaving a trail of silver behind him…just as a beam of blood-red light slammed into the ground where they'd been a split-second ago. The ground turned red-hot, the rock melting instantly.

"What the…!" Bella exclaimed.

"The Overseer saw us fly," Gideon explained, glancing backward and upward. His jawline rippled. "It's coming for us."

Bella followed his gaze, spotting a monstrous, many-eyed creature hovering in the sky above, like a huge, fleshy thundercloud. A few of the eyes were staring right at them…and as she watched, another beam of red light shot out of one of them. Myko moon-dashed out of the way, soaring a foot above the ground. He landed with a grunt, running at a full gallop.

And above, one of the eyeballs pulled free from its black, fleshy socket, flying down toward them.

"Uh…" Bella said, staring as the eye gained speed, zooming after them. "Gideon? One of the eyes…!"

"…is following us, I know," Gideon interjected. "We're lucky we only triggered one."

The ground sloped downward more sharply ahead, the rocky field narrowing considerably…and falling off to a steep drop on either side. It formed a winding – and treacherous – path down the mountain. Gideon let go of Bella, reaching for one of the paintings rolled up in his thigh-holster. "Apertus," he murmured…and the painting promptly unrolled itself. It was a very large painting, taller than Gideon himself, and portrayed a room cluttered with various objects.

He held the painting with his stump, then reached in, pulling out a large mirror.

"Steady Myko," he ordered, twisting around and holding the mirror so it faced the rapidly approaching eye. It was enormous, the eye. The size of a small house, with a blood-red iris.

Its pupil flashed bright red, and a beam of deadly light shot right at them!

Bella cried out, but the beam bounced off of the mirror, reflecting right back at the eye. It melted through its flesh, burning a deep hole there. Fluid gushed out of it, splattering the ground below.

The front of the eye crumpled inward as it deflated.

Myko followed the path as it wound ever downward, and the disembodied eyeball crash-landed behind them, rolling like a bowling ball after them.

"It's still coming!" Bella warned.

And then Myko turned left with the path, and the eyeball went straight, rolling right over the edge of the mountain.

Bella watched as it fell from sight, then glanced back the way they'd come. No more eyeballs were coming for them…and the soldiers were far behind. With the pace that Myko was setting, they would never catch up.

"And that," Gideon declared, "…was Devil's Pass."

Chapter 14

Simon shifted his weight on the long wooden bench he'd been sitting on for the last half-hour, his porcelain shard clutched in one fist. After his journey through the magical doorway with Miss Savage, she'd brought him past the demonic door in the hallway beyond, and into the large, opulent waiting room before the Collector's office. A large desk sat on the far left of the waiting room, but other than the desk and the bench, there was no other furniture. It was Miss Savage's desk, she'd told him; apparently she was the Collector's secretary of sorts. Miss Savage had stepped into her boss's office, closing the door behind her...and hadn't come out since.

They're up to something, the shard warned him. *Don't trust them.*

Simon nodded. He'd gone with Miss Savage to escape certain death, not because he trusted her. And he certainly couldn't trust a man like the Collector. A notorious terrorist, the man had done unspeakable things.

At least according to the Pentad.

They have our painting, the voice informed him. He felt a sudden burst of excitement...but it wasn't his. *I can feel it.*

Simon didn't reply. His entire portfolio had been taken by the Pentad's bounty hunters, the same men that'd tracked him down in the slums of the Twin Spires, after he'd been caught using painted weapons to protect himself from a few would-be muggers. How the Collector could've gotten ahold of any of his paintings was beyond him, but it had to be true.

It is, the shard assured him.

He felt the shard's eagerness, a sudden impatience that made him want to get up and start pacing. He resisted the urge, staying right where he was.

A moment later, the door to the Collector's office opened, and Miss Savage stepped out…with his brown leather portfolio in her hands.

"The Collector will see you now," she announced.

Simon stood from the bench, walking up to her. She offered him his portfolio, and he smiled, taking it. Then she stepped to the side, gesturing for him to continue through the doorway. He did so…and stopped in his tracks, his eyes widening.

The Collector's office was unlike anything he'd ever seen.

It was a magnificent room, thirty feet squared, with a golden, domed ceiling rising some twenty feet high. The floor was made of a beautiful dark cherry, as were the built-in multi-leveled shelves on either side-wall. Upon these shelves were countless objects – sculptures, books, various small paintings, musical instruments, gemstones – and above the shelves, various weapons and full suits of armor hung on the walls. Between these were large stained-glass windows, the glass so thick that little light streamed through. At the far end of the office was a single, closed door…and in the very center of the room sat an oversized, ornate wooden desk.

And seated behind the desk, in a gilded chair as ornate as any throne, was the Collector himself.

He was tall and slender, dressed in an exquisite, yet simple black suit. The jacket had five ebony buttons, and rose up like a turtleneck on his neck, but with a narrow rectangular notch cut out over his Adam's apple. The only color was provided by a blood-red folded handkerchief jutting out of a single pocket at the left breast. The suit's material shimmered slightly, as did the Collector's slicked-back hair. Curiously, the hair at his right temple was streaked with gray, the left pure black. And while the left side of his face was smooth, the right was lined with fine wrinkles. He had a broad, strong chin and fierce, perfectly symmetric eyebrows above his piercing green eyes…eyes that locked on Simon as he entered the room.

Simon froze, his breath catching in his throat. For the man was stunningly handsome, and possessed of an aura of power than was almost palpable.

"Come," the Collector greeted, gesturing at a chair in front of his desk with one black-gloved hand. His voice was buttery smooth, sending a chill down Simon's spine. "Sit."

Simon obeyed, walking up to the chair and sitting on it. He set his portfolio on his lap, folding his hands atop it.

"Thank you, Miss Savage," the Collector said. Miss Savage gave him a little smile, her gaze lingering on him. Then she curtsied, leaving the office and closing the door behind her.

He kept his eyes on Simon the entire time.

"You must be Simon," the Collector stated.

"Yes sir," Simon replied. His voice cracked, much to his horror. He was sixteen, but still mired in the awfulness of puberty. He felt his cheeks grow hot, and lowered his gaze.

"Miss Savage told me all about you," the Collector informed him. "You should be thankful she took an interest in you," he added. "I hear that today was supposed to end very differently for you."

"Yes sir," Simon confirmed. "Thank you for saving me, sir."

"Miss Savage told me yours was a life worth saving."

Simon lowered his gaze again, swallowing past a sudden lump in his throat.

"You're not used to hearing that," the Collector noted. Simon nodded mutely. The man leaned back in his chair, eyeing Simon for a long moment. "Do *you* believe you're worth saving?" he inquired.

Simon shrugged.

"Hmm," the Collector murmured. His gaze dropped to Simon's lap. "I'd like to see what you have in there, Simon."

"Uh…" Simon stammered, looking down at his own lap. He saw his portfolio there, and felt his cheeks flush again. "Yes sir," he added, bolting up from his chair and offering the portfolio. The Collector leaned forward to take it, then set it on his desk, unzipping it and opening it like a book. A stack of paintings was revealed…the very paintings for which Simon had been arrested. His life's work, painted in secret, in the dark alleys of the slums of the Twin Spires. Each painting had a wide cloth border framing the edges, to allow for easy handling, so one's thumbs wouldn't plunge through the canvas into the painting.

The Collector stared at the first painting for a long moment.

Simon picked under his fingernails, then wiped clammy hands on his pants. He was suddenly acutely aware of his shabby red prison uniform, of the stains and holes in the fabric. And the fact that he almost certainly smelled like the commode back in his prison cell.

The Collector flipped to the next painting, studying it silently.

Simon squirmed, watching the man's face. His expression remained utterly, maddeningly neutral, betraying nothing of what he was thinking. After a long, dreadful silence – and viewing a few more paintings – the Collector lifted his gaze to Simon.

"These are…dark."

Simon's cheeks flushed again.

"Sorry," he mumbled. "They're stupid, I know. I don't know why I painted them."

"Did you paint them for me, Simon?" the Collector inquired. Simon blinked.

"Uh, no. No sir."

"Who did you paint them for?" he pressed.

"For…me, sir."

The Collector flipped to the next painting, then the next.

"Do they please you?" he pressed. Simon hesitated.

"Yes sir."

The Collector lifted his gaze to Simon's.

"Then you have no reason to be ashamed," he counseled. "Never be ashamed of your story, Simon. These paintings are your truth."

Simon swallowed, then nodded.

"Thank you, sir."

The Collector got to the last painting…and froze. His eyes widened, his lips parting slightly. He stared at it for a long, long moment. So long that the silence became uncomfortable, and Simon longed to fill it. He dared not speak, however. Not without permission. Simon didn't know much about the Collector, but what he did know made him exceedingly careful to stay on the man's good side.

Minutes passed.

The Collector stood suddenly, grabbing the painting and walking around his desk. He dragged his chair across the floor, setting it beside Simon's, then sitting down. Their knees almost touched, and Simon resisted the urge to squirm in his seat. The Collector set the painting between them.

"Tell me about this," he requested.

Simon looked down at the painting. It was of a person…of sorts. One that bore a striking resemblance to Simon, with the same short, dirty-blond hair and blue eyes. The same tall, lanky, awkward body. But the figure's face had jagged cracks in it, and was deathly pale, as if its skin was made of shattered porcelain that had been glued back together. It held a broken glass bottle in one hand, the jagged end spattered with blood, and stood in a dark bedroom. Moonlight streamed through a single, shattered window, lighting upon a narrow cot. A stuffed teddy bear sat on the pillow, its head sewn crudely to its body with a length of shoelace. Broken glass littered the floor beside the bed, swimming in a large pool of blood.

And on the painted figure's forehead, a fragment of its porcelain skin was missing…in the exact shape of the one Simon held in his hand…revealing its hollow interior.

"I…" Simon stammered. He swallowed past a sudden lump in his throat. The Collector stared at him, waiting patiently. Simon took a deep, shuddering breath in. "I haven't had a good life."

The Collector frowned, considering this. He glanced down at the painting, then back up at Simon.

"Your father?" he guessed.

Simon lowered his gaze to his lap.

The Collector sighed, setting the painting on his desk. He eyed Simon silently for a long moment.

"It's a lie when they tell us they love us, isn't it," he murmured.

Simon looked up at the Collector, wiping his eyes with the back of his sleeve. He said nothing. Dared not say anything, for fear of shattering in front of this man.

The Collector gestured at the painting.

"Is that your Familiar?" he inquired.

"Yes."

"Have you drawn it out yet?" the Collector pressed. Simon hesitated.

"Once," he confessed.

"Once?"

Simon nodded. A vision of the porcelain figure came to him, of it standing in front of him, its bottle clutched in one hand. Of the blood spattered on that bottle…and a body lying in a pool of blood on the floor.

The Collector frowned at this, then stood, lifting the painting off the desk and handing it to Simon.

"I want you to draw him out, Simon," he stated. Simon's eyes widened, the blood draining from his face.

Do it, the shard told him. *Set me free.*

"It…I don't think that's a good idea," he countered.

"It'll be alright," the Collector reassured. "Nothing bad is going to happen."

"You don't understand," Simon insisted, instantly regretting the statement. But the Collector didn't seem offended. "I don't know what'll happen. It could be really, really bad."

"Simon, you're safe with me," the Collector reassured. His voice was soothing, and utterly confident. "I won't let it hurt you."

Simon stared at the Collector, swallowing in a dry throat.

"I'm not worried about…me," he clarified. The Collector smirked.

"Oh, I wouldn't worry about me," he replied. "I'm *very* hard to kill, Simon. Believe me. So many people have tried."

Simon hesitated. He'd heard the stories, of course. Everyone in the Pentad had. Of the Collector facing the armies protecting the great college of Blackthorne. And the Sentinels of the Forest of Giants. And so many other towns and cities.

Of what he'd done to them.

Do it, the shard insisted. It was practically quivering in his hand now. Simon took a deep breath in, squaring his shoulders.

"Okay," he decided at last.

And he reached into the painting with his left hand, his fingers passing through the canvas. He drew in a sharp breath, feeling a warm, pulsing sensation in his hand, as if it had its own heartbeat. He focused, grabbing the figure's arm, feeling his fingers wrap around the rough cloth of its shirt.

Then he closed his eyes, and gave it life.

Chapter 15

It was a good ten minutes before Gideon allowed Myko to slow his mad dash down the mountain, and Gideon and Bella dismounted, walking at a quick pace on either side of the wolf. To Bella's surprise, the arrows embedded in Myko's flank and chest were gone…and in fact, there was no evidence that he'd suffered any wounds at all. Bella gazed at the wolf in wonderment.

"How…?" she blurted out.

"Every time Myko moon-dashes, he heals," Gideon explained, patting the wolf's back. "As long as he has stored-up moonlight, he's safe."

"Thank goodness," Bella replied. "I thought he was going to…you know."

Myko gave her the wolf-equivalent of a smile, giving her a big wet kiss on the side of her face. She scrunched up her face, accepting this as gracefully as she could. Then she frowned, suddenly remembering the arrow sticking out of Gideon's shoulder. It'd penetrated all the way through, the wicked arrowhead protruding out the back. Blood stained his uniform there, and it was clearly causing him pain.

"Your shoulder!" she gasped.

"We'll take care of it at camp," he replied. "Which we should find a suitable place for soon. They'll have trail-hounds hunting us. We need to mask our scent."

Myko snorted, sniffing the ground, then veering off the path down the mountain. Within a few minutes, he led them to a shallow stream. Myko plunged right into it, then started wading upstream. Gideon joined him, forcing Bella to do the same. The water was a few inches taller than her waterproof boots, and absolutely frigid.

"Who *was* that woman?" Bella asked. "The Painter, I mean."

"That was Kendra," Gideon answered. "An old friend of mine. We used to work together, actually."

"That was your *friend?*" Bella pressed, staring at him in disbelief. Gideon shrugged, and Bella shook her head "Hate to meet one of your enemies," she grumbled.

"She's a bit lost, that's all," Gideon explained.

"She tried to kill us!" Bella protested.

"Even so."

It wasn't long before they discovered a waterfall at the source of the stream. Myko went right through it, vanishing beyond. Gideon hesitated, taking off his cape and holding it above his head. It shaped itself into an umbrella of sorts, and he passed through the waterfall, keeping relatively dry. Bella did the same with her cloak, and to her surprise it behaved similarly of its own accord, and she too went through.

Beyond, they found a cramped cave. Gideon retrieved the black disc he'd used before, placing it on the floor and activating it. They'd lowered themselves through the hole, finding themselves back in the familiar large room of the Conclave. The fireplace was still crackling away merrily, and Gideon took off his wet boots, setting them by the fire. Bella did the same.

"All right," Gideon stated, turning to her. "Pull it out."

Bella blinked.

"The arrow," he explained, gesturing at his wounded shoulder. "Break off the back end, then pull the front end out."

"I don't think we should," she warned. She knew enough to realize that doing so could cause serious – and even fatal – bleeding.

"Nonsense," he retorted. He went to the bookcase, pulling on a few books to unlock it. It rotated ninety degrees, and he stepped through into the closet. Bella and Myko joined him, reaching the door at the end of the large closet. Opening the door, she found a large studio beyond. Paintings were stacked against the walls, with a very large painting resting against the far wall. Gideon went to the easel, where a painting of an empty room stood. "Put this against the wall," he requested.

Bella lifted the canvas, setting it upright against the wall.

"Now pull out the arrow," he requested. "Then I'll take off my top and step into the painting. I'll need you to paint over the wound so it looks like my good shoulder."

"Excuse me?"

"If you paint my shoulder so it looks healed, when I step out, it will be," he explained.

Bella gave him an entirely unconvinced look.

"Go on," he urged, gesturing at the floor near the easel. There were paint canisters of all colors set on the floor, along with countless paintbrushes of all sizes and shapes sitting on a table to one side.

"You mean if I paint on you while you're in the painting, you'll...become what I paint?" she pressed.

"Sort of," he replied. "You can't change who I am, but you can change some of my physical characteristics. Like when I gave you that tattoo."

"So what I do will be permanent?"

"Relax," he soothed. "Take your time. If you screw up, I can always get re-painted later."

Bella must still not have looked convinced.

"You can do this," he insisted. "Or I can die of internal bleeding. Or infection. Your choice."

Bella sighed, doing as he instructed. She snapped the feathered end of the arrow off – making Gideon bite back a scream – then yanked the other end out. Blood spurted out of the wound instantly...and spectacularly. Gideon stripped off his shirt as quickly as possible, then stepped into the painting.

And became one.

Bella stared at the painting, now of a room with Gideon standing in it, facing away from her. He was life-size, of course, and his wounded shoulder had a bloody hole in it. She glanced at Myko, who licked her hand.

"You really think I can do it?" she asked.

Myko *wuffed*, stepping forward and giving her a big wet kiss on the nose and lips.

"Gah!" she blurted out, squeezing her eyes shut and taking a step back. Myko continued his assault, and she burst out laughing. "Okay, okay! I'll do it."

Myko gave a big smile, his tongue hanging from his mouth. Then he padded up to her side, circling around as dogs did, then laying down on the floor and nestling his chin between his outstretched front paws to watch her.

Bella wiped the slobber from her face, then gathered her paints. Studying the colors of Gideon's flesh, she did her best to match them on her palette. Then she dipped a fine-tipped paintbrush in the paint, facing the painting and taking a deep breath in.

"Here goes," she stated.

She got to work, painting over the wound, trying to match Gideon's good shoulder. At first the colors were a bit off, and she struggled to match them. After a few unsuccessful attempts, she finally got it. Not perfect, but darn close. An hour later, it was done.

She stepped back, eyeing her handiwork, then glancing at Myko. The wolf got to his feet, giving an affirmative "wurf."

Bella reached into the painting, pulling Gideon out.

"How'd it go?" he inquired. Bella studied the back of his shoulder. To her delight, it *was* healed...and the color was just a hint off, as if he had the faintest of birthmarks.

"Not bad," she admitted. Then she realized blood was pouring from the wound at the front of his shoulder. "Oh!"

"I'll back in this time," Gideon stated...and promptly backed into the painting. This time, he appeared facing her. With the proper colors already mixed, she made quick work of repairing his wound, and finished in half the time. She pulled him out, and he went back into the walk-in closet, studying her work.

"What do you think?" she asked.

"Not bad," he answered, running a hand over the now-intact skin. "Not bad at all." He turned to her with a smile. "Good job Bella."

Myko snorted in agreement.

"So wait," Bella said, eyeing the canvas he'd gone into. "How come my paintbrush didn't just go into the painting like you did?"

"Good question," Gideon replied. "No one knows, actually. Suffice it to say, if a Painter has the intention to paint on a live canvas, the brush will not go in."

"Huh."

"Let's warm up by the fire," he stated. "Then we'll get something to eat."

They went back to the fireplace, and she joined Myko in sitting before it. Myko curled up beside her, and she draped an arm across his warm fur, allowing herself to relax for the first time since…well, since Grandpa.

The thought was instantly depressing.

"Here's dinner," Gideon announced, unrolling a painting he'd retrieved from the studio. It was of a large dining room table filled to the brim with dishes of food, bowls of fruit and vegetables, and drinks of every kind. He drew out two plates of steaming chicken, sweet potatoes, and rice, along with glasses of water. Bella's stomach growled, and for the moment she forgot about Grandpa, devouring the food. Myko nudged her in mid-feast, and she handed him a piece of chicken, which he swallowed whole.

"He doesn't need to eat," Gideon revealed. "He lives on moonlight, after all. But he still likes to."

Myko *wuffed* his agreement, wolfing down another piece of chicken. Bella asked for seconds, and ended up giving half of it to the trusty wolf. Then she sighed, staring off into the fire.

"What now?" she asked.

"Now we sleep," Gideon answered. "You take the bed." Bella was about to protest when he held out one hand. "I insist. Tomorrow we'll reach the bottom of the mountain and make our way to the Forest of Giants."

With that, he put his uniform back on, eyeing the hole in the shoulder area.

"The Collector must have given his soldiers magic arrows," he muttered. "Regular arrows couldn't have penetrated my uniform. I'll fix it tomorrow."

Bella nodded, the image of the soldiers burning in the streets coming unbidden to her mind's eye. The sound of their screams. She felt a chill at the memory.

"What is it?" Gideon asked, frowning at Bella. "I lost you for a second there."

"The soldiers you…burned," she replied.

"You mean the soldiers I killed," he corrected. She nodded. "I didn't have much of a choice," he argued.

"Really?" she retorted. He grimaced.

"Bella…"

"There's always a choice," she insisted.

"They were coming after us, Bella. They wouldn't have hesitated to kill you, you know."

Bella lowered her gaze.

"I know, but…"

"I had to make a decision in the moment. I chose to kill instead of being killed," Gideon explained.

"But couldn't we have just had Myko fly us over them?" she countered.

"And trigger more of the Overseer's eyes?" he argued.

"Okay…but couldn't you have stopped them without killing them?" Bella insisted. "Like, blown them to the side or made them go to sleep?"

"I could have," Gideon admitted. "If I'd had a painting for it. But I didn't."

"But you had plenty of paintings that could kill people," she pointed out.

Gideon stared at her for a long moment, then sighed, lowering his gaze.

"You're right," he muttered. "If I'd prepared differently, I could have spared those men's' lives." He lifted his gaze then, staring into her eyes. "And then they would've killed the Pentad's men when the Pentad inevitably tries to recapture Blackthorne."

Bella blinked.

"The world isn't so simple, Bella," Gideon continued. "You show mercy to an enemy, there's no guarantee they'll return the favor. There are bad people out there, Bella. And they'll use your kindness against you."

He held her gaze for a moment longer, then turned away, putting on his cape and lying down on the floor beside the fire. With a word, the cape levitated him off the ground, forming a hammock of sorts.

"You're wrong," she told him.

"Goodnight Bella," Gideon grumbled. A moment later, he was already snoring.

Bella sighed, glancing at Myko, who was watching her quietly.

"He is," she insisted.

Myko just stared at her quietly with those striking silver eyes.

"I'm going to bed," she muttered.

She got into the bed, pulling the covers over her. The bed was quite comfortable, soft yet firm, and she had plenty of pillows to choose from. Myko stepped up to the side of the bed, giving Bella a rather hopeful look. She patted the bed beside her, and he jumped up, so large that he took up most of the king-sized bed. He gave her a wet kiss, then curled up beside her. His fur was soft, warm, and awfully comfortable, and she snuggled against him. The horrible images in her mind melted away, the screams of the dying soldiers fading. This is how it must have been when she was a little girl, sleeping with her loyal friend night after night. Snuggling up against him, surrounded by his luxurious silver fur. Myko made the badness go away.

With Myko, she was safe.

She heard the great silver wolf start to snore ever-so-softly, and ran her fingers through his fur, feeling her eyelids getting heavy. She closed them, a contented smile on her lips.

And it wasn't much longer before she too was asleep.

* * *

The next morning, Gideon repaired his uniform. It was remarkable watching him paint; he mixed his colors rapidly, then put brush to canvas with bold, sure strokes. In a fraction of the time it'd taken Bella to fix his shoulder, the uniform was whole again. He donned it, then led Bella and Myko through the black portal back into the cave behind the waterfall.

And with that, they resumed their journey, wading through the stream, then exiting to the right. Myko led them clear of the Collector's men, sniffing the air on occasion, then changing course slightly when needed. In this way, the wolf's keen nose brought them safely to the foot of the mountain. A dense forest encircled the base of the mountain, with a large clearing visible less than a mile ahead. And another city of tents erected within that clearing.

"It's alright," Gideon reassured, peering at the tents through a spyglass he'd drawn out of his forearm-painting. He put the spyglass away. "They're the Pentad's men. Looks like they're setting up for an assault."

"To take back Blackthorne?" Bella guessed. Gideon nodded.

"It appears that way."

Bella recalled their earlier conversation. If Gideon had let those soldiers in Devil's Pass live, they'd've ended up killing some of *these* men. She couldn't deny Gideon's logic.

But it still didn't feel right. There *had* to be another way.

"We'll have to go around them," he stated. "Come on."

"Why around?" Bella asked. Gideon grimaced.

"The Pentad and I had a…falling out years ago," he admitted. "Nothing that can't be fixed, but it'll be simpler if we just avoid them." He paused. "If they see us, let me do the talking. And act bored, like you can't be bothered."

"I'm a teenage girl," she quipped. "It's what we do."

Gideon led the way forward and leftward, staying a good mile away from the perimeter of the camp, and well within the safety of the trees. They were past the halfway point of the huge camp when Myko froze, his head whipping to the right.

A low growl rumbled in his chest.

"Damn," Gideon swore, pulling out his cane from his chest-painting. A small dog was bounding toward them…followed by a good dozen soldiers in silver armor so shiny that they were like mirrors.

"Painters!" one of them shouted as they rushed up to Gideon and Bella. "Two of 'em!"

More soldiers came, some with bows, others with crossbows. All aimed at them. Within moments, Bella, Gideon, and Myko were surrounded.

"Good morning gentlemen," Gideon greeted, smiling at the men as if they weren't shoving swords and spears in his face. "Who may I ask is leading this contingent?"

"Who's asking?" a soldier shot back.

"Gideon Myles."

The soldier gave Gideon a withering glare.

"Bullshit," he retorted. "You don't look anything like him. Hand over your paintings. Try taking anything outta them and you'll regret it."

"That won't be necessary," Gideon began…and then something flew over the soldiers' heads, careening right at Gideon at terrible speed. It was a sword over six feet long, with an inky-black blade and a golden hilt and crossguard.

Its wicked tip stopped mere feet from Gideon's face, hovering in the air before him.

The crowd of soldiers parted suddenly, allowing a man to step through. He was tall, his skin as black as night, and was utterly bald. In fact, he had no hair whatsoever. No eyebrows, no eyelashes. He wore a Painter's uniform much like Gideon's, with a gold and red cape. The soldiers gave the man a wide berth.

"We will decide what is necessary," he declared in a deep, powerful voice.

The man stopped before Bella and Gideon, studying them – and Myko – for a long moment. There was a sudden chill in the air, goosebumps rising on Bella's arms.

"Good morning Yero," Gideon greeted, holding out his left hand. "It's been a long time."

Yero stared expressionlessly at Gideon, then at his hand.

"Who," the man replied coolly, "...are you?"

"It's me old friend," Gideon answered. "Gideon Myles."

Yero's eyes narrowed, and he glanced at Myko, then back at Gideon.

"Is it now."

"I had my face re-painted," Gideon explained. "A disguise to get me into Blackthorne. I went undercover to save Thaddeus. He was lost in a…"

"Prove it," Yero demanded.

"Pardon?"

"Prove that you are Gideon Myles," Yero clarified. Gideon paused, then gestured at Myko.

"Do you think Myko would follow anyone else?" he inquired. Yero glanced at the great silver wolf. Myko snorted, then glowed bright silver, moon-dashing straight up into the air. He materialized a good fifty feet up, then moon-dashed to the ground, landing with a *thump* before the soldiers. Who all backed away rather quickly…and regarded Gideon with newfound respect…and if Bella wasn't mistaken, fear.

Yero's jawline rippled.

"You're a fool for coming here," he stated. "Old friend."

"Yero…" Gideon began.

"Or do you forget what you did?" Yero interrupted. "That you have a price on your head?"

"Mere allegations," Gideon countered. "You know me better than that, Yero."

"So I thought."

"You question my loyalty to the Pentad?" Gideon inquired, his tone suddenly sharp. Myko growled, his silver eyes fixed on the man. Yero glanced at Myko, then back at Gideon.

"Eighteen years," he muttered.

"Pardon?"

"Gideon Myles has been gone for eighteen years," Yero explained. "Left without a trace. Left us to fight against the armies of Epirus alone. Left us to fight the Collector ourselves."

"I…"

"Left his reputation," Yero interjected, "…in tatters."

Gideon squared his shoulders, glaring at the taller man.

"With all due respect," he snapped, "…if the Collector had gotten his hands on Thaddeus Birch, *we* wouldn't be having this argument right now. We'd be dead."

Yero frowned.

"Thaddeus is safe?" he asked. Gideon grimaced, glancing at Bella.

"The Collector no longer has access to him," he replied. Yero's jawline rippled, and he lowered his gaze, shaking his head slowly.

"This is a tragedy," he muttered. "No matter the Pentad's grievances with Thaddeus. He was a national treasure."

"Indeed," Gideon agreed. Yero turned to Bella then.

"And who is this?" he inquired. Gideon hesitated, but only for a moment.

"Bella Birch," he answered. Yero's eyes widened.

"She is…?"

"The daughter of Lucia Birch," Gideon confirmed.

Yero stared at Bella, making her feel uncomfortable. Myko pressed against her side, and she put a hand on the wolf's neck, refusing to make eye contact.

"Hey," she mumbled, as if it hurt.

"And Lucia?" Yero pressed.

"Murdered," Gideon answered. "By the Collector's hand."

Yero's eyes narrowed.

"Really."

"It's the truth," Gideon insisted. "She died protecting her daughter."

"In Blackthorne?"

"Yes."

"And how did Lucia Birch get to Blackthorne?" Yero pressed. Gideon shrugged.

"I don't know," he answered. "All I heard was that the Collector had taken Blackthorne, and I knew that Thaddeus was there. So I went to find him, and he told me the rest."

Yero crossed his arms over his chest.

"We will see," he stated. He paused for a moment then. "I thought you had abandoned us," he admitted. "Gone to live in Havenwood with all the other deserters," he added darkly. Gideon put his cane back into his chest-painting, then put his hand on Yero's shoulder. Surprisingly, the man accepted this.

"Never, old friend," he replied. Then he glanced at the black sword, still pointed at his face. "You may want to calm your Temper," he added. Yero smirked at that.

"To my side, Temper," he ordered. The sword drew back from Gideon, levitating at Yero's side with its blade pointed down. It was as tall as the Painter. "Clever, to switch back to your original face," Yero observed. "No one remembered it."

"I've grown rather fond of it actually."

"You weren't always," Yero reminded him. Gideon smirked.

"Can you blame me?"

"It has been too long, old friend," Yero admitted. "I miss our adventures."

"I don't know if I do," Gideon confessed. "I'm getting too old for bounty hunting."

"Walk into my canvas and I will restore your youth," Yero offered. He glanced down at Gideon's stump. "And your good hand."

"Maybe later," Gideon countered. "The Collector's men are still hunting for me. And so is Kendra, by the way. Myko slowed her down so we could escape."

Yero's expression darkened.

"Ah, she betrayed us too," he muttered, shaking his head. "You should have killed her, Myko."

The great black sword – Temper – seemed to quiver, the air around it becoming notably chillier. Yero gave it a grim smile, resting a hand on its hilt.

"You will get your chance, Temper," Yero promised. "We will reclaim Blackthorne soon."

"I'm surprised the Pentad hasn't already," Gideon admitted. Yero turned to him.

"The war with Epirus occupied us," he explained. "Now that Epirus has fallen, the Collector will be next."

"Well, I can provide valuable information about Blackthorne's defenses," Gideon offered. Yero nodded, putting an arm around Gideon's shoulders and gesturing further into the camp.

"Come then," he prompted. "General Craven will be happy to see you."

Chapter 16

General Craven was *not* happy to see Gideon.

Craven was the tallest man Bella had ever seen, easy over eight feet in height. He was built like a Greek statue of a long-dead warrior, with broad shoulders and heavily muscled limbs. He looked to be in his late forties, his short black hair graying at the temples. His skin was leathery from years of exposure to the elements, his huge hands heavily calloused. He wore a suit of gold and red armor, the official colors of the Pentad. His tent – the largest of all in the military base – was filled with the necessary furniture for his duties: a desk, a long table with many chairs upon which a large map had been placed, and stacks of paper. He didn't so much as offer a greeting when Yero brought her, Gideon, and Myko into his tent. He stood over the long table, glancing up from the large map there with slate gray eyes.

"General," Yero greeted. "I bring you Gideon Myles and Bella Birch, daughter of Lucia Birch."

"General Craven," Gideon stated, inclining his head slightly. He nudged Bella, who did her best to curtsy. General Craven walked around the long table, each footstep causing the ground to tremble a little. He stopped a few feet in front of Gideon, looming over the Painter.

"Gideon Myles," he murmured in a deep, hollow voice, staring down at the Painter with a stony expression. Gideon held out a hand, and Craven shook it. It was as if Gideon's hand were a baby's, so large was Craven's, and Gideon grimaced in pain at the general's formidable grip.

"Good to see you," Gideon stated, pulling his hand away and shaking it out.

"It shouldn't be," Craven replied. "There is a warrant for your arrest. One that is nearly two decades old."

Gideon grimaced.

"About that," he began, but Craven held out a hand.

"The judge will hear your testimony," he interjected. He turned to Yero. "Detain him."

Yero glanced at Gideon, whose gaze remained locked on Craven's.

"That," Gideon warned, "...would be *most* unwise."

"You have violated the law," Craven pointed out. "You will answer to it."

"Not today," Gideon retorted, crossing his arms over his chest. "And not anytime soon."

"This is not a negotiation," Craven shot back.

"Then be prepared to explain to the Pentad why your assault on Blackthorne failed," Gideon replied icily, reaching into his chest-painting. "Before it ever started."

Myko began to glow bright silver, his hackles rising.

Yero took a step back, the blood draining from his face. Even Temper backed away. General Craven stood his ground, staring down at Gideon.

"You think you can win this fight?" he asked.

"I know I can," Gideon answered instantly.

Yero took another step back, beads of sweat rising on his forehead. He glanced at Craven, swallowing visibly.

"General, I don't think now is the time," he stated. Craven ignored him.

"My orders are to reclaim Blackthorne," the general declared. "I will execute them. When I am done, I will return to the Pentad and tell them what happened today. You will regret threatening us, Gideon. You may not have committed a crime before, but you have now."

"Rest assured I'll deal with it," Gideon replied. "In my own time."

Craven turned to Bella, and she stared up at the massive man, wondering what Gideon had gotten her into...and what he'd gotten *himself* into.

"This is Lucia's daughter?" he inquired.

"It is," Gideon confirmed. "She and Thaddeus were lost in a book in Blackthorne, and the Collector's men were searching for them. I went undercover there for ten years and found them before the Collector did."

General Craven glanced at Bella, then back at Gideon.

"That is good news," he conceded. "Very good news. You should have notified the Pentad of your plan."

"I couldn't risk word getting out," Gideon answered. "If the Collector managed to get to Thaddeus..." He let the thought hang in the air.

"Granted," Craven replied. "So where *is* Thaddeus?"

Gideon glanced at Bella, then shook his head grimly. Craven's lips drew into a thin line.

"I see," he muttered. He turned to Bella. "My condolences," he added. "Your grandfather was a great man."

Bella nodded mutely, swallowing past a sudden lump in her throat. He'd been a great man even when she hadn't known he was a great man.

You should have seen me before all...this, he'd said.

Craven returned his gaze to Gideon.

"The Collector doesn't have him," he stated. "And for that we should all be grateful. May he rest in peace."

"Indeed," Gideon agreed.

"Is she trained?" Craven asked, nodding at Bella. Gideon shook his head.

"Of course not," he answered. "She doesn't have a license."

"That didn't stop her mother," Yero grumbled.

"We will take her back to the Pentad for processing," Craven decided. "We need all the Painters we can get."

"Is it that bad?" Gideon inquired. Craven sighed.

"It is," he confirmed. "The last ten years have been...difficult. The Collector took advantage of our war with Epirus, attacking Blackthorne and a few of our border cities while our armies were otherwise occupied."

"I assume Epirus was defeated."

149

"Yes," Craven confirmed. "But only three months ago. The war allowed the Collector to consolidate power. He doesn't have the manpower we do, but he has been stealing our Painters. Offering ridiculous amounts of land to bring Painters to his side. Promising them the ability to create without licenses or patrons." He shook his head. "Painters are flocking to him...and the Writers and Sculptors aren't far behind."

"And Actors?" Gideon asked.

"I'm sure he has a few posing as members of the nobility," Craven stated grimly. "No one's been caught yet. The Collector is careful. He's playing the long game."

"I see," Gideon muttered.

"I'm glad you're back," Craven confessed, putting a hand on Gideon's shoulder and smiling down at him. "I missed you, old friend. And I for one never believed the rumors about you."

"I missed you too."

"We could use you on the battlefield," Craven continued. "We're planning on taking back Blackthorne tomorrow."

"That...might not be a good idea," Gideon warned. "Kendra turned. She's with the Collector...and she recognized me. It won't be long before the Collector finds out...and apparently he's dead-set on apprehending Bella."

"Which means he will come here," Yero piped in, folding his arms over his chest.

"Unlikely," Craven countered. "Why would the Collector want an untrained girl?"

"I'm not sure," Gideon admitted. "But I'm taking Bella to Havenwood, where she'll be safe."

Craven's expression darkened.

"She's perfectly safe here," he argued. Gideon raised an eyebrow. "We need you, Gideon."

"And then what?" Gideon inquired. "You'll just arrest me afterward."

"Helping us will work in your favor in court," Craven pointed out. "I am willing to forgive your threat earlier. Remember that you are a servant of the Pentad, Gideon. And that I outrank you."

Gideon's jawline rippled, and he gazed up at the man.

"Make me."

General Craven stared down at Gideon, not even seeming to breathe.

150

"You've never defied me before, old friend," Craven stated at last, breaking the silence.

"I have my reasons," Gideon replied.

"Then I will not help you when your trial comes."

"Fair enough," Gideon agreed.

He took off his hat then, rummaging inside, then pulling out a very large rolled-up painting. He turned, handing it to Yero. Yero unrolled it partway, his eyes widening.

"Draw it out at the very start of the battle," Gideon advised.

Yero stared at the painting, swallowing visibly. He nodded.

"I will," the Painter replied. He looked up at General Craven. "He gives us Tartarus."

Craven's eyes widened.

"The Pentad has begged you for Tartarus for decades," he stated. "Why give it now?"

Gideon glanced at Bella again.

"Like I said, I have my reasons," he answered. "Use it with extreme caution, and only if absolutely necessary," he warned.

"I will," Yero promised. "Thank you, Gideon."

"Indeed," Craven agreed. "This is contribution enough. I will notify the Queen of your generosity personally."

Gideon gave a rueful smile at that.

"I imagine it'll soften the blow of my absence."

"It will," Craven agreed. "Somewhat. But I would still not wish to be you when you're forced to stand before the Queen."

Gideon grimaced, then cleared his throat.

"Well then, I'd better be off," he stated. "I could use two horses."

"Of course," Craven replied. "You'll return to the palace?"

"I will…when I'm done."

"It was good to see you," Craven declared, putting a huge hand on Gideon's shoulder. "For the Pentad," he added. Gideon gave a rueful smirk.

"Isn't everything?"

And with that, they left.

Chapter 17

The Glargs were big, humanoid beasts with large, gnarly feet and thick, muscular legs that led to a blocky waist. They had huge, muscular chests and backs, with arms as big around as a man's waist and powerful fists. Their heads were bald and ugly, with heavy eye ridges and deep-set red eyes. The peculiar man who'd painted the original Glargs centuries ago had chosen to make their skin a sickly yellow-green, like vomit.

Strong but dumb, the creations of a lesser Painter generations ago. Uninspired. But they were suitable in battle. A blunt instrument that was doggedly persistent and difficult to kill. And over the years, the few that had been painted had mated, as had numerous generations of their offspring, creating a large population of the beasts.

The Collector gazed down at the pieces of shattered white porcelain strewn across the packed dirt of the Testing area, a large outdoor arena consisting of boulders set in a closed ring. A Glarg stood before the mess, nearly seven feet tall, holding a big wooden club in one hand.

"Hmm," the Collector murmured, turning to Simon…and catching the boy looking at him. Simon jerked his gaze away quickly, his cheeks flushing bright pink, and turned to stare at the pieces of his own creation. A porcelain version of himself that had moved like a marionette, with awkward, jerky movements. As expressionless as a doll, its only weapon a small, blood-stained bottle. But if Simon was disappointed by his Familiar's quick loss to the Glarg, he didn't show it.

The Collector studied the boy carefully. Short blond hair. Pale skin, as if he'd never seen the sun. Deep brown eyes with dark circles underneath. He noted Simon's slouched posture. His quiet, sullen demeanor. A jagged scar on his left temple, and more on his forearms…along with a few relatively new cuts. Obviously self-inflicted. And this wasn't the first time he'd found Simon staring at him when the boy thought he wasn't looking. With an intensity that hinted at more than just awe, or hero-worship.

An odd one, this Painter.

Miss Savage had noticed it first, of course. She was the type of woman who turned men's heads, and adolescent boys were no different. But Simon had all but ignored her when she'd saved him, seeming immune to her charms.

Which hinted at less…conventional tastes.

This hardly bothered the Collector. Indeed, it could prove useful in handling the boy. After a long string of mediocre Painters, men and women with mediocre minds painting dull, lifeless creatures barely worth drawing out – cannon fodder for the Pentad's armies – the Collector had commanded Miss Savage to find someone different.

And Simon was certainly that.

He resisted the urge to reassure the boy, sensing that Simon was not disappointed. He had a difficult time reading Simon, which was unusual for him. Highly unusual.

He had to know more.

There was sudden movement, and the Collector turned to see the porcelain fragments sliding across the dirt. Slowly at first, then faster. Converging on each other. The pieces fit together like a living puzzle, and within moments Simon's strange doppelganger had reformed, carrying its bottle in one hand.

Interesting, the Collector thought, crossing his arms over his chest. He'd seen self-healing creatures before, of course. But this was certainly a novel way to do it.

The doppelganger turned to face the Glarg, who grunted, irritated by the unexpected return of its enemy.

The Glarg swung its big club, smashing it into the doppelganger's temple. The doppelganger's head exploded, the pieces flying to the side. The Glarg swung a second time, demolishing the thing's midsection.

The pieces fell to the dirt…and promptly reformed. Faster this time.

The Collector resisted the urge to comment, sensing that this was a time to observe. Simon's expression hadn't changed, other than a subtle flinch when the Glarg had attacked. It was clear the boy was sensitive; if this was all his creation was capable of, he would've already expressed his apologies.

The doppelganger faced the Glarg again, and again it was destroyed. But it reformed even faster now, its porcelain shards barely striking the ground before they flew back together. The Glarg growled, its eyes narrowing, clearly losing patience with the thing. It swung again, then again, obliterating the doppelganger. But Simon's creation reformed each time, its fragments barely separating now before flying back together. It stood there, facing the Glarg, its shoulders slumped, the bottle still in its right hand.

The Glarg took a step back, cocking its head at the doppelganger.

Then it swung again, but this time the doppelganger ducked, avoiding the blow…and then leapt into the air, bringing the glass bottle down on the Glarg's forehead with a loud *clunk*.

The Glarg blinked, taking a step back. The blow hadn't really hurt it – it had a phenomenally thick skull, both literally and figuratively – but it had taken it by surprise. The Glarg scowled, swinging at the doppelganger again. This time the blow struck true, but the doppelganger reformed before the swing was done, leaping up and smashing the bottle atop the Glarg's head again.

The bottle shattered, its jagged ends opening gaping wounds in the Glarg's forehead.

The Glarg *roared*.

It threw its club at the doppelganger, striking the thing in the chest. Its body shattered, then reformed almost instantly. The Glarg rushed forward, grabbing it by the throat and slamming its fist into the doppelganger's face, shattering it. The Glarg punched again and again as the doppelganger reformed, then grabbed its enemy by the arms, tearing them right off its body.

154

But the arms yanked right back in place…and the doppelganger swung its bottle at the beast's temple, slicing its ear and cheek.

The Glarg went ballistic.

It swung its arms in a blind fury, tearing into the doppelganger. But it was futile; the doppelganger recovered almost instantly each time it was attacked. It swung at the beast's head again and again, every blow opening another few gashes in its head and face. Blood poured from the wounds, staining the jagged edges of the bottle.

The Glarg stumbled backward, dazed…and before the Collector's eyes, the doppelganger's bottle came back together, whole once again.

The doppelganger swung that bottle at the Glarg's head over and over, each time hitting it harder, swinger the bottle faster. The Glarg backpedaled, but the doppelganger advanced, each blow striking true. The bottle broke again and again, but reformed faster each time, just like the doppelganger.

It was *part* of the doppelganger.

The Glarg fell backward, landing on its butt on the dirt, blood pouring down its neck and chest.

Still the doppelganger attacked, swinging that bottle like a madman, its right arm a blur. It struck the Glarg's temple so hard the beast flew onto its side on the dirt, its eyes staring vacantly outward.

But the doppelganger was not done.

It knelt over the Glarg, striking it over and over. Always to the head. A dozen times, then a hundred. Over and over until the Glarg's thick skull caved in. Until its face was bloodied mush.

A full minute passed until the doppelganger stopped its frenzied assault. It stood then, its broken bottle re-forming, blood staining its porcelain body. Its narrow shoulders heaved up and down as it stared silently at its tormentor, dead at last.

Then it turned about, calmly walking to Simon's side opposite the Collector and standing there silently. Its shoulders slumped forward like Simon's, its eyes downcast.

The Collector gazed at what remained of the fallen Glarg, then turned his head slightly, eyeing Simon. The boy was staring at the fallen beast, his face terribly pale.

The Collector glanced down at Simon's hands, noting that they were clenched into fists.

"You're hired," he declared.

155

Simon blinked, glancing at the Collector. He gave a weak smile of his own, but said nothing. The Collector turned away from the Glarg, walking Simon back toward a tall, dark castle in the distance. A castle with three spires, one far taller than the rest. Above the tallest spire, balanced perfectly on its point, was an identical tower. An upside-down tower that led to an upside-down castle that perfectly mirrored the one below. And above that, an upside-down mountain surrounded by an upside-down lake high, high in the sky...also mirroring the ones below.

Castle Under and Over, settled atop Mount Inversus. The Collector's homes.

"Is that all your Doppelganger does?" the Collector inquired. Simon blinked.

"Doppelganger?"

"Your Familiar," the Collector clarified.

"Sort of," Simon answered. "But I have an idea for something like it that might be...interesting."

The Collector raised an eyebrow.

"And that is?"

Simon hesitated, then told the Collector exactly what that idea was. The Collector listened, and for the first time in years, he felt goosebumps rise all over his body. He gazed down at Simon as they made their way toward his castles, regarding the strange, solemn boy with newfound appreciation.

This was no ordinary Painter.

It took mere seconds for him to come to this conclusion, and to realize that he couldn't just leave Simon under the tutelage of his senior Painters. No, this boy was different. Special.

This one he would have to manage himself.

"I believe I can help you," he told the boy as they walked. "Would you like to test your idea?"

"Yes sir," Simon answered.

"Good," the Collector declared.

They continued toward the castle, the Doppelganger following meekly behind its creator. When they reached the entrance, the Collector stopped, turning to face Simon.

"Tell me Simon," he stated. "Have you ever considered painting...bigger?"

* * *

156

Castle Under, the bottom of the two mirror-image castles that served as the Collector's home, was clearly grander than anything Simon had ever seen. The boy walked at the Collector's side, obviously admiring the castle's huge, ornate hallways, devouring the scenery with his eyes. Polished wooden floors with ornate designs carved into them. Huge paintings hanging high up on the walls with frames of solid gold, each encased in locked crystalline display cases. Statues of men and beasts alike in every corner of every room.

Every one of them magical, created by the Collector's army of Painters and Sculptors, or purchased from other collectors.

Or acquired through…other means.

The Collector studied Simon as they strode down one of these hallways, gesturing at a particularly large painting hanging on the wall a good twelve feet up as they walked. It was of a stormy sky over a barren landscape, countless lightning bolts striking the earth.

"That painting is titled 'Fulgur,'" he explained. "Lord Denton refused to part with it for any sum. So I stormed his castle and took it."

Simon nodded, admiring the sheer skill of the painting. The lightning bolts practically *hummed* on the canvas. A rare thing indeed, such power. A sign of a legendary Painter.

"Does that bother you?" the Collector inquired as they left the painting behind. "That I've acquired so much of my collection through force?"

"No sir," Simon answered.

"Why not, Simon?"

"The strong take from the weak," Simon reasoned. The Collector considered this.

"True," he conceded. "What do you think of that?"

"That I shouldn't be weak."

The Collector eyed Simon as they continued past the painting. The boy's shoulders were still hunched forward, his eyes downcast when not studying the paintings on the walls. The light from the lanterns on the walls cast dark shadows under his eyes.

"Were you weak, Simon?"

Simon froze, his eyes darting up to the Collector's. His throat bobbed up and down as he swallowed.

The Collector stopped beside him, turning to face the boy. Still, he kept silent, waiting for an answer. Knowing that the silence would grow more powerful with every passing second, until it was unbearable.

Silence always extracted truth from the weak.

But to his surprise, the boy did not speak.

The Collector waited a bit longer, then gestured for Simon to continue walking. The Collector studied the boy as they made their way down the hall, noting the scar on his left temple, and the crisscrossing scars on both forearms. He glanced back at the Doppelganger, still following behind Simon. At the cracks in its porcelain skin. And that bloodied bottle forever clutched in its right hand.

"Where are the other Painters?" Simon asked. The Collector sighed inwardly, seeing the sudden change in topic for what it was…a deflection. But he humored the boy, sensing that it would not be profitable to pry any further.

"Some are in my workshop," he answered. "Others are in Castle Over."

"The upside-down castle?"

"That's right," the Collector confirmed.

"I'd like to see it."

"The Painters who do have to earn it first," he explained. "If you work hard, one day you'll be promoted…and then you'll get to see Castle Over."

"Really?"

"Yes," the Collector replied. "In fact, I'll take you there myself."

"I'll work hard, I promise," Simon declared. The Collector smiled.

"I know you will, Simon."

The hallway turned left, and they walked silently for a while, until Simon glanced up at him.

"What happens there?" he asked. "In Castle Over. What do Painters do there?"

"They add to my collection," the Collector answered.

"Your collection?"

"Of paintings," he clarified. "I *am* the Collector, after all."

"So…is everything there upside-down? Or is gravity reversed, and everything feels normal when you're there?" Simon pressed.

"Be patient," the Collector counseled. "Prove yourself and you'll see soon enough."

"Yes sir."

The hallway ended at a closed door, and they stopped before it. The Collector retrieved a key from his pocket, handing it to Simon.

"Go on," he prompted.

Simon slipped the key into the door's lock, turning it. There was a *click*, and Simon turned the knob. The door swung open, revealing the room beyond.

His eyes widened.

A truly massive room lay beyond, one that took up most of the fourth story of the castle. The Collector gestured for Simon to continue forward, and Simon did so, stepping onto a small balcony beyond the doorway. A balcony standing three stories above the floor of the rectangular room below, with a spiral staircase leading downward to the right. The room had a huge floor made of gray stone, and each of its four walls was five stories high and over a hundred feet across, made of a rough white material.

"Come," the Collector prompted.

He led Simon down the spiral staircase to the floor below, walking up to the rightmost wall. There was a long wooden platform on the floor before the wall, one that extended from one end of the wall to the other. The Collector stepped up on this, and Simon followed, standing at his side.

"Going up," the Collector warned. "Elevare," he incanted.

The platform began to rise.

The Collector heard Simon draw in a sharp breath, watching as the floor dropped beneath them. It rose a good fifty feet before the Collector commanded it to stop. He gestured at the wall.

"Touch it," he prompted.

Simon hesitated, then walked up to the wall, putting a hand on it. His eyes widened.

"It's...!"

"Canvas, yes," the Collector confirmed. "I do hope it's large enough for you," he added with a little smirk. Simon gazed at the canvas-wall, running his fingers over it.

"Wow," he breathed.

"Rest assured that you'll be provided with plenty of paint," the Collector stated. "Enough for these canvases and many more."

"Is this where all the Painters paint?" Simon asked. The Collector shook his head.

"No Simon," he replied. "I don't want you painting with the other Painters. They're…not like you, Simon. They're mediocre. Assembly-line painters at best. They'll hate you because you're better than they are, and they'll pull you down to their level. You," he added, "…are special, Simon. You paint with your heart. You paint your truth. And I value the truth, Simon. More than you will ever know."

Simon frowned, staring at the massive studio.

"So all this…?"

"Is yours," the Collector confirmed.

"All of it?" Simon asked incredulously.

"Every last inch."

"I can't believe it," Simon admitted, shaking his head. "This…it's unbelievable."

"Believe it," the Collector replied. He gestured at the massive room. "Welcome to your studio, Simon. And welcome to your new home."

Chapter 18

Bella and Gideon left the military camp shortly after their talk with General Craven, saying their goodbyes to Yero, then taking two horses and riding away from the foot of the mountain. Myko had chosen to go back into his painting, leaving Bella and Gideon alone in their journey. Bella had never been on a horse before – other than during their harried escape from Blackthorne – and it took a bit of getting used to. But after a few hours, she'd relaxed into it. They took a wide, winding path through the forest beyond the camp, Gideon setting a pace that was quick, yet tolerable for horses and humans alike.

"What was that all about?" Bella asked. "Back there in the camp?"

"It's…complicated," Gideon answered.

"Why did they want to arrest you?" she pressed.

"Because they think I broke the law," he replied. Bella raised an eyebrow at him.

"Did you?"

He gave a rueful smirk.

"If I hadn't, you wouldn't be here," he answered.

"You still haven't answered my question."

Gideon sighed.

"Your mother was a criminal," he confessed.

Bella blinked.

"She dabbled in forbidden magic," he continued. "Painted things the Pentad didn't approve. And she got involved with a group of…controversial people."

"What's that supposed to mean?" Bella inquired.

"Let's just say that the Pentad sent bounty hunters to arrest her," Gideon answered. "And Thaddeus and I helped her…avoid them. The Pentad doesn't have real proof that I helped her, but they suspect I did, and apparently they have some circumstantial evidence."

"Oh."

"I'm supposed to turn myself in," he continued.

"Will you?"

"I don't know," he admitted. "I spent most of my life fighting for the Pentad. The Pentad *is* my life. Or at least it was."

He fell silent then, and Bella sensed that he'd said all that he was going to say about that. They rode onward for a while, until Gideon had them stop for a quick lunch, tying the horses to a nearby tree and pulling some food from one of his paintings. Then Gideon retrieved his black disc from his hat, opening the portal to his Conclave.

"Let's go," he prompted, and promptly lowered himself into the portal. Bella followed, finding herself back in the Conclave's main room. Gideon led her through the rotating bookshelf and closet to his studio. "All right," he declared, gesturing at the easel in the room. "Paint."

"Huh?"

"Paint," Gideon repeated. "You've been out of the habit for the last few days."

"Is this really a good time?"

"If you wait for the perfect time to create, you'll wait forever," Gideon retorted. "If you want to *be* something…"

"*Do* it," Bella grumbled. "You sound like Grandpa."

"He was my teacher, remember?"

"But you're a Painter."

"The concepts of creation – of magic – are similar across all disciplines," Gideon explained. "There are five main practitioners of magic: Writers, Painters, Sculptors, Musicians, and Actors."

"Wait, so it's not just Writers and Painters?"

"Not at all," Gideon replied. "Why do you think they call it the 'magical arts?'"

Bella had to smile at that.

"All right, you got me," she conceded.

"Sculptors make things out of clay or stone, or even metal. When done properly, these can come to life. Like that giant that attacked you at Blackthorne."

Bella nodded, recalling the giant Myko had moon-dashed over. It'd seemed like a statue before it'd come to life.

"That's not the only statue you've seen," Gideon continued. "Remember General Craven?"

Bella's eyes widened.

"He's...?"

"A statue," Gideon confirmed. "Sculpted of a single slab of pure, indestructible Invictium by a master Sculptor during the reign of the very first king of the Pentad. Craven is over a thousand years old...a statue come to life."

"Wow."

"Musicians can manipulate emotions with their instruments and voices," Gideon continued. "They can turn a crowd angry, or violent, or happy, or sleepy. Legend has it that there were once Musicians so powerful that they could even manipulate the world itself. A fiction, I assure you; no Musician alive can do that."

"And Actors?"

"Actors can manipulate emotions to a lesser extent," Gideon answered. "But their main power is that they can become someone else entirely. If they feel the Flow, they can change appearance to look and sound like someone else."

"Wait," Bella interrupted. "What's the Flow?"

"The Flow is when magic is summoned to go into whatever we're creating," Gideon answered. He raised one eyebrow. "Tell me, have you ever started painting, or even been bathing, and felt a sudden burst of inspiration? A realization of what you want to do, seemingly from nowhere?"

"Well sure."

"That's the Flow," Gideon declared. "You could only feel it slightly while you were lost in a book, but now that you're free, you'll feel it far more strongly. It is – quite literally – magic being summoned by the act of creation, guiding your mind and your hand."

"Like my muse," Bella translated.

"Another term for the same thing," Gideon agreed. "Most people wait for the Flow to come before they create. But the Flow is summoned largely *by* creation. You have to start painting – or writing, or acting, or playing music – to summon it."

"That's why Grandpa had me paint every day," Bella realized.

"Correct," Gideon confirmed. "And you needed the practice...and you still do." He gestured at the easel again. "So paint."

"What should I...?"

"What would your grandfather say?" Gideon interjected. Bella grimaced.

"Just paint," she answered. Gideon arched an eyebrow, and she sighed. "Paint what makes me feel something," she added.

"And tell a story," Gideon agreed. "All good art tells a story...music, paintings, acting, sculpture. Magic lives in stories, Bella. Show me one of yours."

And so she did.

* * *

Bella finished her painting, one of an eerie glob of green glowing goo spilling out of the eye socket of a half-buried skull. A gruesome scene, but one her muse – or rather, the Flow – had compelled her to create. That intense, giddy feeling of the Flow was indeed stronger here, and felt every bit like magic. When she'd finished, Gideon studied her work, his chin in one hand.

"A mystery," he murmured, seemingly in approval. "What is it?"

"A man who died in battle," Bella explained rather sheepishly. "His spirit lived on, turning into green goo. It's emerging from his skull."

"I see," Gideon replied. "Why?"

"Huh?"

"Why is his spirit living on? Why is it emerging from his skull?"

Bella frowned, considering this. Then her muse struck once again.

"He hates violence," she answered. "He died terribly and wants to stop others from killing each other."

Gideon glanced at Bella, a mysterious smile curling his lips.

"Go on," he prompted.

164

"He's turned into this green ectoplasm," she continued, more excitedly now.

"Ecto-what?"

"Goo," she clarified. "It's going to grow...he'll feed on hatred and anger and fear and pain. And when he sees people trying to kill each other, he'll trap them inside him and suck out all their anger, so they don't want to fight anymore!"

Gideon's smile broadened, and he put a hand on Bella's shoulder.

"*That's* a story," he declared. Then he gestured at the painting. "But you haven't told it yet."

Bella glanced at the painting, realizing he was right. Right now, the painting was merely an origin story.

"How do I do it?" she asked. She desperately wanted to tell the story now. She *had* to tell it.

"He's a warrior," Gideon explained. "Paint signs of a battlefield around him. Perhaps a helmet on or next to his skull. He regrets violence...make him have a reason why. Perhaps a locket with a painting of his wife or child nearby. And you have to show him absorbing the negative emotions around him and him growing because of it. And how he makes people peaceful."

"Hmm," Bella murmured, eyeing the painting with sudden doubt. "That's a lot."

"It is," Gideon agreed. "And that's what separates a competent Painter from a great Painter...the way they tell their stories. The better the story, the more powerful the magic."

Bella nodded, feeling suddenly rather overwhelmed.

"You can do it," Gideon encouraged. "And you *should* do it."

"Okay," Bella decided, reaching for her paintbrush. He stopped her.

"Tomorrow," he corrected. "Now we ride."

* * *

They left the disc-world, returning to reality. Every day from then on was the same. They traveled when there was daylight, stopping for lunch and dinner. And after each meal, they painted for an hour or so. Each time, Bella would paint a new iteration of the story she'd come up with, taking Gideon's suggestions and adding more to the painting. And each time, Gideon would critique the result, offering far more specific advice than Grandpa had. About color and lighting, about framing a scene. About drawing the eye naturally to each detail on the page, making it tell the story in the order she wanted.

And the next day, she'd set yesterday's painting aside, and start all over again.

The canvases she chose became larger and larger, until she was painting on canvases so large she needed a stepstool to complete them. The Flow came in bits and spurts, and she soon found herself daydreaming about her painting. The long rides between sessions allowed her mind to wander, and ideas would spring forth unbidden soon after. She kept a small notebook on her that Gideon had provided, jotting down each idea excitedly as it came.

Each night, they'd make camp. Gideon would release Myko then, allowing the great wolf to absorb a little moonlight before they all went into the Conclave. Myko slept with Bella every night in Gideon's bed in the Conclave, her warm, snuggly nightly guardian.

So it was that, five days later, they broke free from the forest, entering a wide grassy meadow filled with flowers of every color. Bees buzzed from plant to plant, busily collecting their nectar. Magnificent trees grew nearby, perhaps the tallest trees she'd ever seen, with thick trunks shooting straight upward, and a round canopy of bright red leaves. And in the far distance, a truly giant mountain loomed.

"Wow," Bella breathed, taking it all in.

"Behold," Gideon declared, gesturing with his stump. "The Forest of Giants!"

Bella glanced back, spotting the smaller mountain they'd come from many miles away, its crater obscured by mist. Then she turned forward.

"We're going through here?" she asked.

"No," Gideon answered. "We're only passing around it. Havenwood is fifty miles northeast of here."

"Oh."

They continued forward toward the trees ahead. They were only a hundred feet away...or so it seemed. For even after a few minutes, they hadn't gotten any closer. Bella commented on it.

"That's because they're still a few miles away," Gideon revealed.

"But..."

"Look," he interrupted, pointing ahead. The grass seemed to grow a bit taller, each blade triple the size of the grass behind them. Indeed, even the flowers were bigger, with petals as big as her hand. After another few minutes of travel, the grass was taller than she was, each blade as thick as her waist. They walked between the blades, in a veritable forest of grass.

Even the particles of dirt were larger, as big as her fist.

"The Forest of Giants," Gideon explained. "…is not a misnomer."

A shadow passed overhead, and Bella looked up, seeing a huge bee buzzing above them, landing on a flower to their left. A huge flower, well over twenty feet tall.

"Whoa!" she cried, clinging tightly to her horse's reins. She liked bees from far away, but the closer she got, the less she appreciated them. Especially bees with stingers over a foot long. Gideon chuckled.

"If you don't bother Nature, Nature won't bother you," he advised. "Most of the time."

"Are there real giants here?" she asked. "Like, giant people?"

"There were," he answered. "There's an ancient city on the mountain ahead. Buildings larger than any you could imagine. But they're abandoned. No one knows where the giants went, or why they left. Or if any still live."

"Huh."

Gideon glanced back at Bella, a bemused smile on his face.

"You were asking about the power of books," he stated. "Well, you may find this hard to believe, but all of this was created by a book."

"Really? How?"

"Books are their own worlds," Gideon explained. "If you get lost in them, you're transported into their world. A copy of the book comes with you into that world, while the real book remains here in the original world. If you read that copy while you're lost in a book, you're transported out."

"Yeah, you told me that already."

"So if you get lost in a book, the book becomes real to you," Gideon continued, ignoring her quip. "But if enough people read a book and get lost in it…if the world of the book becomes real to enough people…then the book's world appears somewhere here, in the original world."

167

"Like Havenwood," she recalled.

"That's right," Gideon replied. "Your home."

"Mom lived there?"

"She did," Gideon confirmed. "Her house is still there. It's your house now, actually. And her paintings are yours too."

Bella's eyes widened.

"I get to see her paintings?" she blurted out. Grandpa had always raved about Mom's paintings, saying how odd and beautiful they were. Much like her mother.

"Of course," Gideon replied with a smile. "And her studio."

"Well what are we waiting for?" Bella exclaimed, kicking her horse's flanks with her heels. "Let's go!"

"Hold your horses!" Gideon called out after her. "Or your horse, rather," he added, catching up with her. "We still have a ways to go."

Bella pulled back on her reins reluctantly, settling in to their usual pace. Still, she felt awfully excited.

"What was she like?" she asked. "You still haven't really told me."

"Lucia Birch was…different," Gideon answered. "Unlike any other woman I'd ever met. Very…complicated."

"That's what Grandpa said."

"Well, he was right," Gideon confirmed. "Your mother was difficult to know. I'm not even sure she quite knew herself…not completely. She was many different people in one person, you might say."

"How so?"

"Well, her paintings will tell you better than I ever could," Gideon answered. "Paintings, like any other piece of art, tell more about the artist than you might imagine. Your paintings will tell *your* story, Bella…just as your mother's tell hers."

"Grandpa never talked about my dad," Bella noted. Gideon raised an eyebrow at this.

"Oh really?"

"Never," Bella confirmed.

"I find that hard to believe," Gideon admitted. "But so be it. You do take after your mother."

"But not my dad?"

"That remains to be seen," Gideon replied.

"Did you know him?"

"Quite well," Gideon answered. "They both lived in Havenwood. That's where you were born, in fact."

"Tell me more about Havenwood," Bella requested. Gideon paused, gazing at the horizon. Then he sighed.

"Havenwood is a wonderful place," he declared. "Quite literally a haven for those that practice the magical arts. Painters, Writers, Sculptors, Musicians, and Actors all working together to hone their craft." He gave a rueful smile. "A bit of an artist's utopia, if you will."

"You make it sound like that's a bad thing."

"It is and it isn't," he replied. "It's just that…well, most artists go to Havenwood to have the freedom to create whatever they wish, free from the constraints of the Pentad's strict rules. So they get to create whatever they want…but very few get to see it."

"Why not?"

"Any works coming out of Havenwood will never be published," Gideon explained. "They'll be confiscated by the Pentad and either destroyed or taken for the Pentad's purposes."

"Why?"

"I'll explain in a moment," he reassured. "In any case, Havenwood is a small kingdom on a mountain called Dragon's Peak," he continued. "Castle Havenwood is on the top of the mountain, and the rest of the buildings are on its sides or at its base. It's surrounded by a very unusual forest," he added. Bella arched an eyebrow. "You'll see," he promised.

"Is there a king or something?" Bella inquired.

"Oh no," he answered. "There are no rulers. No formal hierarchy. Only artists being artists. Of course, the most experienced artists are deferred to, but there's no government per se."

"Sounds nice."

"Oh it is," Gideon agreed. "Your grandfather insisted he didn't mean for Havenwood to become what it is, he was only saying that to appease the Pentad. You see, the Queen isn't very happy with Havenwood."

"Why not?"

"Well, the Pentad – by necessity – sets limits on artists. Particularly Painters and Writers. You can't paint without a license, and you can't just paint anything you want. You have to get permission from the government first."

"Really?"

"Well, think of it," Gideon continued. "What if a Painter decided to paint a terrible creature that massacred people? Or an army to take over the Pentad?"

"Ah," Bella murmured. "Right."

"Art is extraordinarily powerful," he explained. "The ability to create is not without consequences. But in Havenwood, artists have utter freedom. That's very attractive for Painters and other artists, especially younger artists that can't afford a license or don't have much of an audience for their work. So they flock to Havenwood."

"So that means fewer artists for the Pentad," she reasoned. Gideon nodded.

"Right."

"Do you like it there?" she asked. Gideon paused, then sighed.

"I used to," he admitted. "I spent some of the best years of my life in Havenwood."

She waited for him to elaborate, but he didn't. And his expression told her that she shouldn't push the issue. They rode in silence for nearly an hour, then stopped for lunch. Gideon chose a small clearing in the forest of ridiculously large grass around them, retrieving his disc from his hat and opening the portal to the Conclave.

"Come on then," he declared. "Time to paint!"

Chapter 19

Piper stood just beyond the closed portcullis outside of the entrance to Devil's Pass, picking at his fingernails as he gazed down the narrow path that snaked down the mountain ahead. A treacherous route called Harm's Way, an apt name as any. For on either side of the narrow path was a sheer drop over a hundred feet to the rocky terrain below…and any anyone attempting to fly to save themselves from a fall would incite the wrath of the Overseer.

He watched as a vast army of silver-armored soldiers made their way slowly up Harm's Way, heading right toward him. The army was still miles away, but the writing was most certainly on the wall.

"I still think you should run," he insisted, turning to Kendra. She stood beside him, arms crossed over her chest.

"Not yet," she countered. "I have a job to do, remember?"

"Is this really necessary?" Piper pressed. "I mean, we're giving up Blackthorne anyway. Why not just leave with me and let the Pentad take it? Why put yourself in harm's way?"

Kendra gave him a look.

"You just can't help yourself with those terrible puns, can you?" she replied.

"All I'm saying is…"

"The Collector asked me to do this," Kendra interjected. "So I'm doing it."

"You do *everything* he says," he grumbled.

"He's my boss."

"So was the Pentad," he retorted. She ignored the comment, gazing off at the approaching army. Piper grit his teeth, suddenly annoyed at her. He hated when she ignored him...something she'd been doing more and more frequently. Things had gotten...tense between them. It hadn't always been this way.

He sighed, kicking a pebble across the rocky ground.

"Now now baby," Kendra soothed. "Have a little faith."

"The only person I have faith in is you, love," Piper retorted. "Everyone else just wants to use me."

Kendra arched an eyebrow.

"Who says I don't want to use you?" she shot back, giving him a little smile. He smiled back.

"That's different," he replied. "And is that a promise?"

"Mmm...maybe."

"You *are* vicious," he quipped. But as soon as he said it, the mood shattered. She *had* become vicious, more and more every year. He'd watched as she – and Stanwitz, and most of the others – had transformed over the last fifteen years, becoming colder. More violent. Marching in step to the Collector's every command.

Piper lowered his gaze, staring at the wedding band on his left ring finger. Remembering when Kendra had been softer. Kinder.

Warmer.

She still was warm to him, at least most of the time. But in the times she wasn't, he barely recognized her. Theirs was a love story gone wrong...and he had no idea how to fix it.

"Stanwitz woulda shot that girl if I hadn't stopped him," Piper told her.

"And then we'd have brought her body to the Collector," Kendra pointed out. "He said he preferred she be alive, but it wasn't necessary."

Piper shot her a glare.

"Really?"

"What?" she asked. He shook his head, turning away from her. "Tell me baby," she pleaded. "Please."

"It's just..." He turned to face her. "Sometimes I worry about you."

"You *always* worry about me."

"Yeah, well I remember a time when you would've felt differently about shooting a little girl in the head," Piper muttered.

Kendra put a hand on his cheek, leaning in to kiss him. But he turned his head away, and she sighed.

"Honey, I was *kidding*," she insisted.

"Were you?"

"I was," she insisted. "I promise."

"Right."

"Honey…" she began, but he cut her off.

"I'm telling you, the Collector is changing us," he told her.

"Us?"

"You," he corrected.

"Come on baby, don't be like that," she insisted, turning to face him. She leaned in, wrapping her arms around him and kissing him gently on the lips. He found himself embracing her back, losing himself in her kiss. It felt the same as it had the first time they'd kissed; her love was still as magical as she was.

She pulled back then, giving him a little smile, then ruffling his hair.

"You're so *cute*," she teased. "Never stop being you, Piper."

"You first."

"Mmm hmm. I know you'll always be there if I stray too far," she replied, caressing his cheek. "You're my heart, baby."

"Damn right," he agreed. "You remember my vow at our wedding, right?"

"Of course," she answered. "But say it again…I like it when you say it."

He grinned.

"Where you go, I go," he declared.

She gave him another kiss, then turned to face the approaching army. She reached into her Painter's uniform, pulling out a spyglass and peering through it.

"This is a fool's errand," Piper muttered, shifting his weight from one foot to the other. But he stayed where he was, watching the Pentad's army as it slowly ascended Harm's Way. They were only two miles away or so now, and approaching quickly. The Collector's army, in contrast, had disbanded, their virtual city of tents taken down. Kendra lifted her spyglass, peering through it. A lone man led the charge, followed by cavalry and foot soldiers in silver armor polished to a mirror shine.

Kendra lowered her spyglass.

"Ah, they're serious now," she mused. "They brought Craven."

"Craven?" Piper blurted out in alarm. A chill went through him. The legendary Craven approached. Piper had never seen him in battle, but he'd heard the stories. Everyone had.

He had every right to be afraid.

"And Yero," she noted, peering through the spyglass again.

"We need to leave," Piper stated tersely. "Now."

"You first," Kendra countered. "Your job is to run away, dear," she added with a vicious little smile, putting a hand on his cheek. "And you're *so* good at that."

"Ha ha," he grumbled. "I'm not worried about *me*."

"Aww baby," she murmured, stepping closer to him. He wrapped his arms around her waist, pulling her in and kissing her. She resisted, but only for a moment. Then she pushed him back a little. "You really do care, don't you?"

"You know I do," he replied.

"Scurry along to the Underground with the rest of them, love," Kendra prompted. "I'll join you soon."

"That a promise?"

"Of course baby," she murmured, leaning in for another kiss. He kissed her back, then pulled away.

"So we just leave the Glargs to die?"

"That's the plan," she confirmed.

"And we call *them* monsters."

"The Collector is wise," she replied. "Besides, they're just Glargs."

"Oh yeah?" he shot back. "So what if the Collector's 'wisdom' tells him we're next on the chopping block?"

"Then my brave, dashing husband will save me," Kendra answered with a little smile, her eyes twinkling. Piper couldn't help but smile back.

"Damn right I will," he agreed. "Where you go, I go…even if it kills me."

* * *

Kendra leaned in to kiss Piper one last time, then pushed him away toward the portcullis. He was roguishly handsome, with short black hair and a neatly trimmed goatee. Clad in a silky golden shirt and pants, he was a far cry from that dull character 'Reynolds' he'd played when he'd been hunting down Thaddeus. Piper was utterly charming when he wanted to be. In fact, as one of the better Actors of his generation, he was *anything* he wanted to be. A fact that had certainly kept their relationship from getting stale.

"See you soon, my love," she said. "Now go cower away in a deep, dark tunnel while the woman gets things done."

Piper stood up straight, saluting sharply...and promptly morphed. His face broadened, his jawline becoming square, his eyes turning slate gray. His eyebrows thickened, his hair shortening until it was less than an inch long. His arms and legs became remarkably muscular, veins bulging out of his skin. And he grew at least a few inches taller, looming over her now.

"As you wish," he stated, his voice deep and gravely.

"Oh, and fetch me General Mattox on the way," she added, admiring his new body. She ran her fingers over one huge bicep. "And save this character for later."

"Yes ma'am."

He turned then, stepping through the open portcullis. It closed behind him, leaving her alone outside of Devil's Pass.

Moments later, the portcullis opened again, and General Mattox stepped through. He was tall and well-built, with short, graying hair...and the leader of what remained of the army protecting Blackthorne. With Thaddeus dead and Gideon on the run, there was little point in wasting resources protecting the college. After all, the most valuable books and paintings had already been taken to Mount Inversus.

"You sent for me, Painter?" Mattox inquired.

"It's time," she announced. "Send the Glargs, I'll deal with the Pentad's army."

"Yes Painter," the general replied crisply.

"When they breach the wall, keep the Glargs focused on their Painter," she instructed. "I need him distracted."

"Yes Painter."

"Retreat to the Underground before the Pentad reaches Blackthorne. Make sure no one sees you escaping. That is all."

The general bowed, then left through the portcullis, closing it behind him.

Kendra sighed, closing her eyes and taking a deep breath in to clear her head. Then she opened them, focusing on the army, now not even a mile from where she stood. She fingered the rolled-up paintings in the thigh-holsters of her Painter's uniform, considering her options. She could use wind to knock the soldiers off the sides of the path; if they flew to save themselves, it would trigger the Overseer. Or she could set the path on fire, or create a blockade.

But there was Yero to contend with.

She smiled, remembering when they'd worked together, Yero and her. Bounty hunters for the Pentad, along with Gideon and Piper.

How times change, she mused.

After years of working together, Kendra knew most of Yero's tricks…but he also knew most of hers. Which would make this a most interesting confrontation. Still, she only had to slow him, not stop him.

The Pentad's soldiers were only a half-mile away now.

Wind it is, she decided.

She withdrew a painting from her thigh-holster, opening it. It was a painting of a falcon with sky-blue feathers; she drew it out, and it held on to her forearm, cocking its head at her. She whispered a command, and it leapt from her arm, flying upward and to the left. Higher and farther it went, until it was flanking the oncoming army. Then it dove toward the frontmost line of soldiers, spreading its wings wide, then bringing them forward in front of it in one powerful movement.

A gust of wind slammed into the army, tearing at the soldiers. There was shouting, and archers shot their arrows at the falcon. But the arrows flew backward harmlessly in the wind.

A beam of blood-red light shot down from the heavens suddenly, missing the falcon by a mere yard. Kendra looked up, spotting one of the Overseer's eyes tracking the bird.

Come on Temper, she thought.

Almost as if on cue, a black sword shot upward, flying toward the falcon, the wind not so much as slowing it. Kendra smiled.

So predictable, she mused.

Kendra's falcon darted away from Yero's magical sword, flying back toward her. Temper flew right after it, the two magical creatures zooming toward her, dodging two more of the Overseer's deadly attacks. She waited, watching as they drew ever closer. One hundred feet away now.

Fifty.

Her falcon reached her, Temper right behind it...and Kendra lifted her painting, facing it outward at them. The falcon went right into the painting...but Temper veered away at the last second, zooming past her.

Kendra spun around, watching as Temper reversed direction, boomeranging right back at her. She reached into her painting again, unleashing a flock of crows within. They burst from the canvas, flying toward the Pentad's army.

Temper changed course, flying past her to chase the flock of crows. But the birds flew high into the air, spreading outward from each other as they made their way toward the approaching army. Dozens of the Overseer's eyes locked on them, beams of light shooting down from the heavens, scorching the earth below. A few struck true, killing the crows instantly...and triggering their hidden power.

They *exploded.*

Fire rained down from their corpses, falling on the soldiers and sticking to their armor. The surviving crows dive-bombed the army, triggering the Overseer to shoot beam after beam at them. Some struck, making the crows explode...and sending nearby soldiers flying off Harm's Way. Others missed, the beams striking the soldiers below.

And a few birds exploded near Temper, sending the magical blade hurtling madly away.

The line of soldiers stopped, raising their shields above their heads. Shields polished to a mirror shine. More beams of light shot down from the Overseer, but the shields reflected them.

Clever, Kendra thought.

The crows that remained continued to dive-bomb the soldiers, smashing into them or into the ground nearby. They exploded on impact, sending more soldiers careening off the path. Some flew back onto the path, clad in magic boots that gave them the power of flight. But this triggered the Overseer.

Dozens of huge eyeballs detached from the flying monster, descending rapidly toward the approaching army.

"Archers!" she heard one of the soldiers cry. They were not even a quarter mile away now, rushing up Harm's Way toward her. And behind them, she spotted General Craven. Far taller than a normal man, dressed in his legendary gold and red armor, wielding a huge golden shield. It was Aganon, a shield as old as Craven, and immensely powerful.

It was enough to give her goosebumps.

Kendra reached into her chest-painting, then flung her hand outward. A black sphere shot forward and upward into the air over the soldiers, exploding in a flash of purple light. A hole opened up in the heavens above the Pentad's army, and dozens of flaming meteors shot downward from it, smashing into the men and exploding on impact.

Craven lifted Aganon above his head.

A massive shield of pure golden light extended from Aganon, in the same shape as the actual shield, covering the entire front line of the army. The meteors collided with it in explosion after fiery explosion, but the energy shield protected the soldiers beneath it, rendering Kendra's meteor strike harmless. She smiled, shaking her head.

Marvelous.

The meteors triggered more of the Overseer's eyeballs to descend, their beams of red light smashing into Craven's energy shield. They too were no match for the power of Aganon. In fact, the attacks seemed to increase the energy shield's power, making it glow brighter with every strike.

Craven marched calmly forward, holding his shield over his head, his eyes locked on Kendra's.

Damn that's sexy, she mused.

She heard the sound of footsteps behind her, and then a stream of Glargs rushed through the portcullis, charging at the approaching soldiers.

Who promptly retreated, leaving Craven at the front of the line.

The first of the Glargs reached the general, ramming their shoulder into the man…and promptly ricocheted off, falling off the edge of Harm's Way.

Another Glarg attacked, swinging their huge axe at Craven, who blocked the edge of the blade with his forearm. The axe bounced off, and Craven slammed his fist on top of the Glarg's head.

Its skull crumpled.

Craven tilted Aganon downward a little, the energy shield extending from it resting on the ground ahead. Then he broke out into a run, the edge of the energy shield smashing into the oncoming Glargs like a massive plow. They careened off the edge of Harm's Way, screaming as they all fell to their deaths.

And leaving Kendra alone by the front gate of Devil's Pass.

Kendra reached into her chest-painting, drawing out the golden cube that served as the six-sided portal for Nightmare, her Familiar...and her most formidable weapon. Black tentacles sprung out from each of the cube's facets, and it stood upon four of them.

Bring me to safety, Kendra thought.

One of Nightmare's tentacles wrapped around her thighs and waist, lifting her off the ground. The creature climbed up over the tall wall guarding Devil's Pass then, going right over it. Nightmare broke out into a run, its long legs moving far faster than any horse could, carrying her quickly through the city. Devil's Pass was deserted, its inhabitants having already escaped through the Underground.

Only the booby-traps remained, created and placed by Kendra herself.

Nightmare stepped over these expertly, knowing their location despite never having seen them before. The creature was connected to Kendra, able to share her thoughts...and vice-versa. It knew what she knew. Every elite Painter had a Familiar, a powerful creature bonded to their mind and soul.

And Nightmare was powerful indeed.

It took her to the edge of the cliffside, where elevators served to bring people down to the lower half of Devil's Pass. Nightmare leapt right off, plummeting to the ground far below. Its legs struck the cobblestone street, bending to absorb the impact. Then it continued down the street, past the buildings on either side, toward the wall bordering the opposite side of the city.

Nightmare climbed right over the wall, charging toward the swirling ocean of mist that filled the huge crater that was home to the Misty Marsh.

Then it leapt into the mist, carrying Kendra through the choking fog, toward the Underground...and the love of her life.

Chapter 20

hereas Gideon usually allowed Bella no more than an hour or two of painting time each afternoon, the day before they were to reach Havenwood, he made it quite clear that she had as much time as she needed to complete her work. And that she was not to leave his studio in the Conclave until she did just that.

Bella was more than happy to oblige.

For painting was her favorite part of the day, the one time her mind was so completely occupied that – for a moment – she stopped thinking about Grandpa. She still cried some nights, with Myko's soft fur absorbing her tears. But while it was still hard beginning each day with the realization that he was gone, she found herself able to feel again…thanks to Myko's silent support.

She still hadn't gathered the courage to talk to Gideon about it, though.

So it was that Bella found herself in Gideon's studio, minutes turning into hours as she painted on her largest canvas yet. It had to be at least eight feet wide and four feet tall by her estimate, larger than anything she'd ever attempted. And as Grandpa had taught her, she filled it entirely.

Within minutes of putting brush to canvas, she felt that wondrous giddy sensation of the Flow. And after painting so many iterations of the same theme – and days of obsessing over every last detail of how to tell the story – her brushstrokes came rapidly and confidently.

After nearly four hours, she was done.

Bella stood back from the canvas then, studying her work. A skull half-buried in the blood-soaked earth of a battlefield, wearing a soldier's helmet. A big mass of green goo oozed from the skull's eye socket, crawling over the ground. In the distance, men battled, corpses burning as fire rained down upon many of them. In the foreground, the ooze had enveloped several soldiers, trapping them within it. Other soldiers were trying to attack it, but tendrils of ooze wrapped around their weapons and their ankles, drawing them in. Those that had been captured had clearly lost their will to fight, while those still free fought in vain to destroy the goo.

And their negative emotions – fear, anger, hatred – were sucked into the ooze, portrayed by faint black mist drawn out of their bodies.

When she was done, Bella summoned Gideon, who entered the studio…and gasped.

"No!" he shouted, whirling to face Bella. He glared at her, his expression furious.

"What?" she asked, taking a step backward.

"You must *never* paint humans," he commanded, gesturing at the soldiers stuck in the ooze.

"Why…"

"Never," he repeated. She stared at him mutely, and he took a deep breath in, collecting himself. "It is forbidden," he explained, clearly trying to keep his voice calm…and barely succeeding.

"I didn't know," she protested.

"I know," he replied. "I'm sorry," he added. "I should have told you."

"Why can't I paint people?"

"It's illegal," he answered. "Highly illegal. The first rule of painting is that you can't paint people."

"Why not?"

"What would happen if you drew out one of them?" he inquired. Bella paused, glancing at the soldiers in the painting. The blood drained from her face. "That's right," he continued. "It is forbidden to create people, Bella. We're not gods."

"Sorry," she nearly whispered. She felt moisture welling up in her eyes, and blinked it away. Gideon sighed.

"No, *I'm* sorry," he countered. "I shouldn't have reacted so…strongly. It's easy to fix. Just make them into goblins, or some such."

Bella nodded, turning back to the canvas. She mixed some paints, then repainted the soldiers, making their faces dark green, and rather monstrous. She gave them horns, and thin tails, with cloven feet. Gideon watched as she worked, staying silent throughout. When she was done, she turned to glance at him. He was smiling.

"You're getting better," he noted. "That took no time at all."

"Thanks," she mumbled. "You're still a jerk though."

"You're not the first person to tell me that," Gideon admitted ruefully. He got closer, studying the painting, rubbing his chin while he did so. Then he turned to Bella. "It's your best painting yet," he declared. "But there's one thing missing."

"What's that?"

"Whenever you create a creature, it's best to give it some relationship with you," Gideon explained. "It needs to be sympathetic to you, or else it won't have any reason to help you or protect you."

"Oh," she replied. She hadn't thought about that.

"The last thing you want is to draw out something you painted, then have it attack you," he continued. "You need to give it a connection to you."

Bella nodded, eyeing the half-buried skull. Suddenly she had an idea…the Flow directing her once again. She grabbed a tiny brush, mixing some paint quickly to make a golden color. Then she painted a small locket next to the skull, one that hinged open to reveal a tiny portrait. And she painted her own face there. After years of drawing herself standing next to her dragon at school, she had no trouble at all with it. Within a half hour, she was done.

And through it all, Gideon stood watching her work. He gave a low whistle when she finished, shaking his head.

"My my," he stated. "You know, some students take years to figure out how to do that."

"Do what?" she asked.

"What you just did," he explained. "How to create a relationship with their paintings." He gestured at the painting then. "Is it done?"

Bella paused, staring at the paint for a long moment. Then she nodded.

"I think so."

"Then sign it," Gideon ordered. "That will complete the painting."

"Doesn't it need to dry first?"

"The paint is magical," he replied. "It will dry instantly once you sign your name."

She did as he requested, signing her name at the bottom right of the painting. The second she finished, she felt a slight breeze from behind.

"What was that?" she asked.

"Air going into the canvas," Gideon answered. "All right, care to do the honors?"

"Huh?"

"Draw it out," he clarified, gesturing at the green ooze. She blinked.

"Now?"

"Well of course," he replied. "Once you sign a painting, it seals the magic in. Unsigned canvases are 'dead' canvases. Now it's a 'live' canvas...one you can reach into. Go on."

Bella turned to stare at the ooze, chewing on a fingernail. She glanced back at Gideon, who was waiting patiently, then returned her gaze to her painting.

She took a deep breath in, closed her eyes, and plunged her hand into the canvas!

There was an immediate warm, pulsing sensation in her hand, and something else...a rubbery surface that dented under the pressure of her touch. She grabbed onto it, pulling it toward her.

There was a wet *plop*, followed by surprised shouting.

Bella opened her eyes, backpedaling away from the canvas. There, on the floor beside her feet, was a green, translucent blob half as tall as she was, and nearly as wide and long as the canvas it'd been painted on.

And stuck within it were the goblins she'd painted.

Bella gasped, rushing to Gideon's side and staring wide-eyed at the beasts. They struggled mightily, trying to free themselves of the blob.

"Gideon!" she cried.

Gideon reached into his forearm-painting, retrieving his cane and banging it sharply against the floor. Then he strode up to the nearest goblin, striking it in the chest so hard that it flew backward…right into the painting. He gave the other goblins equal treatment, and within moments every one of the creatures was back in the painting, shocked expressions on their faces as they hung suspended in the air above the painted battlefield.

"What's the first law of Painting?" Gideon inquired, giving Bella a rueful smirk.

"The Law of Unintended Consequences," she recited.

"Very good."

They both turned their attention to the blob then. Its surface was like firm gelatin, still wobbling with the vibrations from the goblins' violent evictions.

Then it oozed rapidly toward Bella, its frontmost section lifting up and striking her chest!

Bella gasped, jerking backward, but the blob wrapped around her chest and back, encircling her completely. Bella struggled against it, but it was no use…she was trapped!

"Gideon!" she cried.

And then she felt the blob squeeze her gently, once, then again. It unwrapped itself from her then, settling before her.

"I think it just hugged you," Gideon offered. Bella hesitated, then smiled, relief coursing through her.

"I think you're right," she agreed. She leaned in then, putting her arms around the front of the big blob and giving it a squeeze. Once again, it returned the gesture, then let her go. "Aww," she murmured, beaming down at it. "That's awfully sweet."

The surface of the blob jiggled a bit.

"I think it's happy," Bella guessed. Gideon nodded.

"It's not an *it* at all," he reminded her. "What's his name?"

Bella blinked, putting a hand to her mouth.

"Oh," she blurted out. "Right." She frowned at the blob, wracking her brain. "Um…I don't know. How about…Goo?"

Gideon's eyebrows rose.

"Goo?" he repeated. Bella grimaced. It was a bit too literal, but it certainly fit.

"Yes," she decided. "I'll call you Goo," she told the blob. "That is, if it's okay with you," she added hastily.

The blob jiggled again.

"Goo it is," Gideon murmured. "Well then," he added, walking up to Goo and extending a hand. "I'm Gideon Myles, Bella's…friend. A pleasure to meet you, Goo."

Goo extended a long, arm-width tendril, wrapping it around Gideon's hand and wrist. They shook, and Goo sucked the…well, goo…back into himself. Gideon turned to Bella with a rather proud smile.

"Well done Bella," he congratulated. "You are now officially a Painter!"

Bella smiled…and noticed small bumps rise up all over Goo's body.

"Aww," she cooed. "He has goosebumps!"

"He's proud of you too, I suppose," Gideon agreed. He placed his cane back in his forearm-painting, clearing his throat. "Well then," he declared. "Let's get Goo back in his painting. Havenwood awaits!"

Chapter 21

The Collector leaned his elbows on the top of his desk, staring at the books stacked upon it. He'd sat down to read them after leaving Simon and returning to his office ten minutes earlier, but found his mind stubbornly resisting the task. He forced himself to pick up the topmost book, focusing on it. The letters were slightly blurry to his right eye; he held the book further away, and the image sharpened.

An irritating reminder of what that damn Necromancer had done to him.

It was also a reminder of why it was of vital importance that he read these particular books. He'd taken great risks to acquire them, and at extraordinary expense.

The Collector scanned the book titles: "On Necromancy." "The Restorative Arts." "Book of Healing." "Codex of Curses."

He paused at the last one, his jawline rippling.

His eyes went to his right hand, hidden within a black glove. It'd been quite a while since he'd removed it; he found himself suddenly – and morbidly – curious.

Stop wasting time, he scolded himself.

But after a moment's hesitation, he pulled the glove off…and drew in a sharp breath.

The skin of his right hand was deeply wrinkled, liver spots scattered across its surface. It was thin, like an old man's, and slightly translucent, purple veins visible beneath. His wrist and forearm were less so, the wrinkles gradually fading the further up his arm he looked. The joints of his hand were stiff and painful, with hard, bony knobs on his knuckles.

The Collector reached up with this hand, touching the right side of his face. Feeling the fine wrinkles there. Wrinkles that had appeared years ago, long before their time.

A reminder that his time was running out.

There was a knock on the door.

"Come in," the Collector called out, hastily pulling on his glove. The door to his office opened, and Miss Savage stepped through. Tall and slender, with long legs and arms, and short, spikey silver hair, she was striking indeed. Her silver eyes and sharp, high cheekbones had not been painted; it was her natural appearance. Or had been, untold centuries ago. For Miss Savage was quite old. Ancient, in fact…nearly as old as the Pentad itself.

A woman who'd risen from the humblest of beginnings to become something spectacular. A queen in beggar's clothing…which was exactly as she preferred.

"Collector," she greeted, giving a slight curtsey. She wore a tight silver dress that matched her eyes exactly. A striking outfit a performer on stage might wear. Appropriate, given the nature of Miss Savage's considerable talents.

"How goes the evacuation?" he inquired. She stopped before his desk, gazing down at him.

"Almost complete," she answered. "Blackthorne has been gutted. Devil's Pass is working with a skeleton crew."

"And the Pentad's army?" he pressed.

"Preparing to invade."

"Good," the Collector murmured.

"They've assembled an impressive force," Miss Savage informed him. "Rumor has it they've tapped Craven."

"My my," the Collector replied, raising his eyebrows. "We're moving up in the world, aren't we."

"Naturally."

"Make sure to delay them," he instructed. "Keep the Pentad's eyes on Blackthorne while we…replace Lord Gustofson and Governor Cranston." The two highest-ranking officials of the Twin Spires, they were in charge of a large portion of the western part of the Pentad's forces. Two Actors were set to replace them…and to initiate policies that would significantly weaken the Pentad's defenses over the coming months and years.

"It will be done, Collector," Miss Savage confirmed. She did something she rarely did then; she hesitated.

"What is it?" he inquired.

"News from Blackthorne," she revealed. "Thaddeus was found by our bounty hunters. He's dead."

The Collector's expression didn't change.

"I see."

"The girl was with him," she continued. She hesitated for a moment. "She escaped."

His jawline rippled.

"Escaped where?" he demanded.

"Past Devil's Pass," Miss Savage answered.

The Collector swore, slamming his fist on his desk. He closed his eyes for a moment, taking a deep breath in to collect himself. That girl was the daughter of Lucia Birch…and might be the only person alive who had any clue how her mother had cursed him. It was a long shot – a very long shot – but it was all he had.

"I want her found," he demanded. "Spare no expense."

"It's gotten…complicated," Miss Savage warned. "One of the Painters we hired to work in the great library appears to have been an undercover agent for the last ten years. For the Pentad."

"And?"

"It was Gideon," she revealed.

The Collector felt a chill run down his spine, and forced himself to keep his expression neutral.

"Ah," he muttered.

"It may prove difficult to stop him," she pressed. "He's extraordinarily dangerous." He barely heard her, lowering his gaze to stare at the books on his desk.

Gideon Myles!

He took this in, accepting it. The truth was the truth. And no matter how terrible that truth was, it was still better than a lie.

Lies destroyed people, killing them slowly, long after they were told. They were a cancer that ate away at both the liar and the recipient of the lie. The truth was a surgeon, cutting the cancer from its host. It hurt once, allowing for healing…but the scar forever remained.

"Let Gideon go."

"Excuse me?"

"Let him go," he repeated.

Miss Savage put her hands on her hips.

"He has the girl," she countered. "That girl might be the only way we'll be able to cure you without having you go into a painting."

"I know," he replied. Just as she knew that returning to a painting is something he would never do again.

"Are you sure you're thinking clearly about this?" she pressed.

"Don't question me," he snapped, glaring at her. She didn't react – didn't so much as a blink – just continuing to stare at him. He grimaced, rubbing his face with his hands. "I apologize," he muttered. "Your question was valid."

"I know what Gideon does to you," Miss Savage replied. Her tone was gentle…a rarity for her. She put a hand on his. His left hand, the one he kept ungloved. Her touch was warm and soft.

"Yes, well," he grumbled. "Gideon will run away like he always does. He'll just hole up in Havenwood like he did the last time…and the girl will go with him. We'll know exactly where to find them when the time comes."

"Are you sure?"

"Quite," the Collector answered. "Is that all?" he inquired a bit too abruptly, slipping his hand out from beneath hers. She leaned forward, grabbing his hand again and holding it tightly.

"No."

He hesitated, feeling a flash of irritation at her brazenness.

"I'm not in the mood," he muttered. She gave a little smirk, stepping around the desk to stand at his left side. She pulled his hand to the small of her back, then slid it a little lower, arching an eyebrow. As if daring him to stop her.

He didn't.

"I can get you in any mood I want," she purred.

He found himself standing up, pulling her to him by her waist. A waist so tiny that his hands nearly wrapped all the way around it.

"It's not you," he stated. A poor apology, but all she would get. She smiled at him, grabbing the back of his head and pulling him into her. Their lips crushed together, and she kissed him brutally, finishing by biting his lower lip – hard – and letting him go.

"Is it ever?" she inquired, a little smirk curling her lips. He broke out into a rueful grin.

189

"Never."

She leaned in, her lips brushing against his ear.

"Tell me you love me," she murmured. He grimaced, pushing her away a little.

"You know I…"

"Just say it," she interrupted.

"You know what I am," he insisted, pulling away a little more.

"A copy?" she replied. "I don't care."

"A counterfeit," he corrected. She smiled, running a hand through his hair.

"You're real to me."

He hesitated.

"You know I love you," he conceded. "But you shouldn't love me." He said it without self-pity, only as a statement of fact. She gave that little smile of hers, then pulled away a little. Arched an eyebrow, her gaze drifting downward.

"I do what I want," she murmured. "And I want you." She glanced up at him, arching an eyebrow. "Any requests?" she inquired. He glanced down at the books on his desk.

"I could use an inspiring tune."

Her smile faded.

"As you wish, Collector," she murmured. "Let me get a drink of water first." She turned away then, walking out of his office and closing the door behind her.

The Collector watched her go, smoothing his hair back. Collecting himself. He sat back down at his desk, his gaze drawn to a huge painting hanging above the door to his office. A stunning creation…a painting of the surface of a lake, with the edge of a wooden raft visible at the bottom, as if looking down at the water from the raft. He stared at the water, peering below the surface, into the empty depths of the water. So detailed that it almost seemed real.

Almost.

He felt the affection he had for Miss Savage fade, replaced by an all-too-familiar bitterness. It was why he kept the painting there, always in his line of sight. A necessary reminder of what was real…and what wasn't.

Of the great lie of his existence.

The Collector looked down at his desk, forcing himself to focus on the books before him. Written by authors who had studied the forbidden art of necromancy...and the secret, nearly impenetrable world of those who practiced that art.

There was a knock on the door, snapping him out of his reverie. "Yes?" he called out.

The door opened, and Miss Savage returned, walking to her usual chair in the corner of the room and standing before it. She lifted her right hand up to the ceiling, extending her thumb and first two fingers, each of which had a silver ring. Then she drew her arm down...and a violin bow appeared between her fingertips. Sitting down on her chair, she set the bow against her left shoulder, and her magical violin appeared there, out of thin air.

A gift from when she'd been a slave for the Pentad.

She began to play.

The music tread softly at first, gently easing into the Collector's consciousness. Long, beautiful notes, mournful but sweet. He felt them first only with his ears, but as Miss Savage's eyes closed, as her body began to sway with the music, he felt it in his mind, and in his heart.

Sweet and sad, like memories of better times. Memories of his childhood. Much of it a lie, but still...

He resisted the music's pull, and almost brought his hands to his ears and ordered Miss Savage to stop. Not for the first time, he wondered how much her music was manipulating him...and how long its effects could last.

Trust her.

He closed his eyes, letting her music wash over him. Letting it take him on its journey. Allowing it to tell him its story. *His* story.

It compelled him to remember.

* * *

In the beginning there was pain.

It slammed into the back of his head, shooting through his skull. Cold wetness enveloped him, swallowing him whole. His head slipped under, his vision going black.

Then a hand grabbed him by the wrist.

He felt himself being pulled then, not upward but *forward*. Light assaulted his eyeballs, and he squeezed his eyes shut, feeling himself being pulled out of the water. He landed with a *thump* on something

191

hard. A wooden floor. His clothes were soaking wet, water dripping from him to form a pool around him.

He gasped, drawing air into his lungs, and opened his eyes.

And found himself in a medium-sized room. He instantly recognized it as Dad's studio on the second floor of their home on the lake.

The lake...

"Oh god," he heard a voice say.

He got to his feet, his bare feet almost slipping on the slick floorboards. To his surprise, Dad was there, standing before him. Smiling at him.

But something was terribly wrong.

Dad looked *old*. His skin was wrinkled, his hair stark white and thinning. His clothes were torn and spattered with paint, and tears were streaming down his cheeks.

And he reeked of alcohol.

"Oh god," Dad blurted out, grabbing him and pulling him in to a tight embrace. "Oh god oh god."

"Dad? What's wrong?" he asked, pushing away. He glanced back...and realized that he was standing a foot from a painting leaning against the wall. A painting of a raft on a lake, looking down at the water. The center of the painting was pure deep blue, an empty abyss. "Dad, what happened?"

"You...got hurt," Dad answered. "Don't you remember?"

He struggled to remember, but everything was hazy. Suddenly he couldn't remember how he'd gotten here, or what'd happened before. Or much of anything. Just vague memories of Mom and Dad, and of the lake.

And nothing else.

"What's wrong with me?" he demanded, panic rising within him. "Why can't I remember?"

"Shhh, it's okay son," Dad soothed, reaching in to hug him. "You're okay now. You're with me."

He hesitated, then relaxed, giving in to his father's embrace. All the while not noticing the bottles of paint clustered around an empty easel in the center of the studio, and the paintbrushes littering the floor.

Or the still-wet paint of his father's signature at the bottom-right corner of the painting he'd been pulled from.

The Collector opened his eyes, emerging from the memory.

Miss Savage's music continued, visions of his childhood flashing before his mind's eye. Of a gurgling stream and autumn leaves covering the ground. Running through that colorful patchwork, laughing. Chasing his father around the meadow.

Not your father. Not your memories.

This was the childhood he'd been given. One manufactured, not lived.

Lie after lie after lie.

He was about to tell Miss Savage to stop when the rhythm changed, the notes coming faster now. He felt his mind match pace with it, his focus shifting from his childhood to the present. The Collector relaxed, grateful for the reprieve.

His thoughts quickened.

The melody grew more complex, Miss Savage's bow drawing up and down madly, the fingers of her left hand dancing over the strings. His mind matched that frenetic pace, and he opened his eyes, focusing on the books on his desk. He picked up the first one, opening it and starting to read. His eyes darted over each page, and he finished each in seconds, memorizing them instantly.

Faster and faster she played.

The Collector flipped through page after page, finishing the first book, then the second. Then the third and fourth. When he was done, he leaned back in his chair, staring up at the ceiling, his thoughts racing.

Necromancy. Curses. Regeneration.

He'd tried every method of healing money could buy, which was just about everything…and nothing had worked. Not the ring of regeneration, a cocktail of healing potions, or various other powerful artifacts.

Which meant that Lucia's curse wasn't a simple aging spell. It had to be something more. Something devious.

If he couldn't heal, then the life that had been taken from him was no longer a part of him. It could not be returned. The curse must have made *this* – his withered flesh – his new normal. Of course, if he went into a painting, he could be healed…

His gaze lifted to the painting hanging above his office door, of the raft on the lake.

Never again.

He grimaced, lowering his gaze and wracking his brain. Lucia had been a Necromancer, a member of a mysterious, secretive cult. No one knew where they came from, or who led them. Their magic was as mysterious as they were, the few books written on the subject already in his possession. And yet they'd offered little information on Lucia's curse…and none on how to cure it.

Round and round his mind went, whirling with possibilities. Thoughts moving at incredible speed, propelled by Miss Savage's music.

But as usual, in the end, he came up with nothing.

"Stop," he ordered.

The music ended.

Miss Savage opened her eyes, glancing at the Collector. His thoughts slowed, becoming more indistinct. More distractible. He sighed in frustration.

"Thank you Miss Savage," he murmured. "That will be all."

"No luck?" she inquired.

"Not yet," he answered.

"Would you like another song?" she inquired.

"No," he answered. "Thank you."

She curtseyed, then left the office, closing the door behind her. The Collector sighed, rubbing his eyes wearily. He felt suddenly exhausted, spent by her music. Leaning back in his chair, his eyes went to the painting above the door to his office. A constant reminder of why he did what he did. Of how important his calling was.

I may not be real, he thought. *But my actions are.*

He studied the painting, taking in every detail. Details he'd long since memorized. Then he sighed, lowering his gaze to his desk.

Gideon Myles, he mused.

To think that Gideon had spent ten years in Blackthorne trying to save his old friend Thaddeus. To think that he'd let them cut off his hand…the standard price of employment for unvetted Painters wanting to join the Collector's service.

"So dedicated," he muttered.

Gideon had always been loyal, to a fault. That dedication extended to everything…which was precisely why Gideon would never be a threat to him. The fool was living a lie. A lie he'd go to his deathbed believing. A lie he'd told the Collector so many years ago, one the Collector had believed. Gideon was a fantastic liar…one of the best.

The greatest liars always lied to themselves first.

Oh, he'd let Gideon live all right. For now. And as the foolish Painter went from one self-imposed prison to another, the Collector would continue to consolidate his power. It wouldn't be long now before he'd have the resources to annihilate the Pentad.

But Gideon's little stunt required a change in plans. He would deal with the Pentad soon enough, but first he needed to retrieve that girl.

The Pentad would fall, but now Havenwood would have to come first.

Chapter 22

It was mid-morning by the time Bella and Gideon found themselves riding up the gentle, winding slope of a large hill a few miles outside of the Forest of Giants. Bella was relieved at the return to a normal scale of things. Grass was once again mere inches tall, pebbles no longer as large as boulders. Bees shrank, ants were once again more liable to be stepped on by her than the other way around. A curious novelty, the Forest of Giants, but hardly a place for humans. At least *this* human.

They rode mostly in silence, for which Bella was grateful. She'd become accustomed to long periods of silence living with Grandpa, and found the constant chatter some seemed to require – particularly her classmates – quickly tiring. The silence gave her time to think.

And for the most part, she thought about Grandpa.

Bella spent hours reminiscing about all the good times they had together. Of Grandpa's easy smile and hearty laugh. Of him lying next to her at night, telling his wonderful bedtime stories. She'd never met anyone more *alive* than him, and found herself profoundly grateful for having been given the chance to know him.

But at this particular moment, as she and Gideon left the Forest of Giants far behind, she found herself pondering Goo.

Gideon had made her store Goo in a different painting than he'd been created in. Apparently it prevented anyone from determining how he'd been made, keeping his creation a trade secret. Gideon did that for all of his creations, putting them in different paintings after they were drawn out. Even Myko's painting – the one with the moon in the distance – wasn't the one he'd been painted on originally.

It was still beyond belief that she'd *created* Goo.

For it was clear to her that Goo was very much alive, a creature with thoughts and feelings. To think that she could make a life…it was sobering indeed. An incredible responsibility. Not quite as monumental as having a child, but similar. The Pentad's strict rules, requiring licenses and government approval for each painting, seemed more reasonable now. It didn't take much imagination for her to see how a Painter could abuse their power.

"Bella," Gideon stated, riding alongside her. She broke free from her reverie, focusing on him. It was clearly not the first time he'd said it.

"Hmm?"

"We're almost there," he notified. He pointed to the top of the hill, which was only a hundred feet away or so. "Come on," he urged, kicking his horse's flanks and pulling ahead of her. She matched his speed, and within moments they made it to the top of the hill.

And were treated a magnificent view.

The hill sloped downward ahead, to a forest over a thousand feet below. This forest extended for miles, and out of it rose a mountain a few miles away. A quite unusual mountain, in that it was cone-shaped, corkscrewing upward into the sky. Fine white buildings seemed to cover every square inch of the mountain, with a marvelous white castle standing on its peak. The castle had three towers, each taller than the one before, and capped with brilliant silver peaks.

The second most peculiar thing about it was what lay at the foot of the corkscrewing mountain: a veritable forest of giant mushrooms. They had to be well over a hundred feet tall, with huge caps of various colors. The *most* peculiar thing was what surrounded the mushroom forest *and* the mountain.

A huge, white…thing.

Bella frowned, staring at it. It almost looked like a massive white snake over a mile long, completely encircling the base of the mountain.

"What *is* that?" she asked, turning to Gideon. Gideon smiled, gesturing at the mountain in the distance.

"That," he proclaimed, "...is Havenwood!"

Bella frowned, turning back to the scene before her. Then she pointed at the white snake-thing.

"No, I mean the thing around it," she clarified. "At the base of the mountain."

Gideon chuckled, his green eyes twinkling.

"That," he declared, "...is the White Dragon."

Bella blinked.

Gideon smirked, retrieving his spyglass and handing it to her. She peered through, following the long white body of the thing, spotting huge scales on its surface. Then she froze, drawing in a sharp breath.

For there, as plain as day, was the magnificent, horned head of a dragon.

She stared at the creature, countless times larger than even the castle at the top of the mountain.

A dragon circle
White and good...

A chill ran down her spine.

"Oh my god," she breathed, lowering the spyglass. She barely noticed it slipping out of her hand. "Oh my *god*."

"That's what people usually say," Gideon agreed, a look of bemusement on his face. She stared at the White Dragon a moment longer, then turned to him.

"It's huge!" she exclaimed.

"The largest dragon ever recorded," Gideon agreed. "Your grandfather's finest creation...other than your mother, that is."

"He *made* that?"

"Of course," Gideon confirmed. "He made all of it. The mountain, the town, the castle, the dragon...even the mushroom forest."

"He made all that," she repeated. "With a book."

"That's right."

Bella didn't say anything. *Couldn't* say anything. For the first time in her life, she understood what it felt to be rendered speechless. To think that Grandpa, a kindly, frail old man, had created *that*...

She found herself swelling with sudden pride, tears brimming in her eyes.

I always knew you were special, she thought with a smile. Even without magic, his stories had been magical. *He'd* been magical. And there, before her very eyes, his magic lived on. Like Grandpa's final bedtime story for Bella…a story she could quite literally call home.

"Come on," Gideon prompted, nudging his horse forward and down the hill. "I've been waiting ten years for this. It's time to bring you home!"

* * *

They reached the bottom of the hill quickly, riding their horses through the forest beyond. Gideon led them at a faster pace than before, clearly eager to reach their destination. It was a little over an hour before the forest opened up suddenly, revealing a huge grassy meadow…and the truly massive tail of the White Dragon. It formed a curving wall ahead, easily a hundred feet high, if not higher. Its shimmering white scales were simply massive, seeming to glow as they reflected the sunlight from the blue sky above.

Gideon took them rightward, following the curving tail, bringing them gradually closer to it. For the dragon was still a good half-mile away.

"Incredible," Bella breathed. She found herself unable to wrap her brain around just how large the thing was. "Does it have wings?" she asked.

"Oh yes," Gideon confirmed. "You can't see them from here, of course. He's curled up around Havenwood, with his tail slightly overlapping his head. We're heading toward the tip of his tail now."

"It's a he?"

"According to Thaddeus," Gideon replied. He gave a little smirk. "I'm not about to check."

"What's his name?" Bella pressed. She noted that the tail-wall was getting a bit shorter as they rode, the tail slowly tapering off. It was only fifty feet high now.

"He's the White Dragon," Gideon answered. "I don't believe Thaddeus ever gave him an actual name."

They rode ever forward and rightward, the tapering tail only a hundred feet away now. Bella spotted a much larger structure beyond it…one hundreds of feet tall and wider than any structure she'd ever seen.

The head of the White Dragon.

A chill ran down her spine, goosebumps rising on her arms. Its eyes were closed, two long, golden horns curving backward from its head. A few curved, sharp white teeth protruded from its closed maw, each many times taller than a man. Its huge nostrils were like endless pits, and as she watched, they flared outward slowly. Moments later, she felt a strong, warm breeze flow around her.

"Is it…awake?" she asked.

"Who knows?" Gideon replied. "I've only seen it rise once." He chuckled. "That was the first – and last – time that anyone tried to attack Havenwood."

"It defended Havenwood?" Bella asked.

"The White Dragon is Havenwood's guardian," Gideon explained. "I daresay it's an effective one. Not even the Collector would dare threaten the kingdom. Or the Pentad, for that matter."

Bella nodded. It was hard to imagine anyone even *thinking* about taking on the White Dragon, much less being successful in the attempt.

"The dragon also ensures that only those that practice the magical arts can pass into the kingdom of Havenwood," Gideon continued. Bella frowned.

"Regular people can't get in?"

"That's right," Gideon confirmed. "If you can't feel the Flow, you can't get in."

They were close to the end of the tail now, which overlapped a bit with the end of the dragon's nose. There was a ten-foot-wide gap between them, with the tail on the left and the head on the right. It was the only path into the great dragon circle. Gideon led them toward it.

"There are people that can't feel the Flow?" Bella inquired. She hadn't even considered the possibility.

"The vast majority of people can't," Gideon explained. "It's hereditary. If either of a person's parents can feel the Flow, their children will be able to. Otherwise…no."

"But our horses can't feel the Flow," Bella pointed out. "And Myko and Goo are in paintings, and…"

"It only applies to humans," Gideon clarified.

They reached the path between the overlapping dragon's tail and its head, and Gideon led them through it, Bella riding behind him. She felt the sudden blast of its the warm, moist breath as it breathed out of its massive nostrils. Her horse spooked a bit underneath her.

"Whoa," Bella blurted out, patting her horse.

"It's smelling us," Gideon called out from ahead.

Bella glanced up at the dragon's eyes as they rode, relieved that they were still closed. She must have passed whatever test it had given her, for she was allowed through without incident.

Then, having passed through the dragon circle, white and good, they arrived at last in Havenwood.

* * *

The first thing Bella noticed were the mushrooms.

They seemed to grow everywhere, little ones scattered around the wide cobblestone path Gideon and Bella rode on. These had short white stalks and cute little caps in an amazing variety of colors. Some had polka dots on them, others swirling designs. They were no taller than a few inches, and grew so densely she couldn't see the soil below them.

Mushrooms further back from the winding path grew as tall as bushes, and even farther back, as tall as trees. These larger mushrooms had caps that hung over the path, providing shade from the sun. There were other plants – some grass and flowers, and the occasional shrub – but for the most part, fungus dominated the landscape. The tree-like mushrooms grew so densely that Bella couldn't see past them; as a result, the path was a rather intimate space, each winding turn creating a sense of mystery as to what lay ahead.

"Quite a lot of mushrooms," Bella noted.

"Thaddeus was very fond of them."

"Why?" she asked.

"I suppose because they're a bit strange," Gideon answered. Bella smiled ruefully at that.

"It runs in the family."

"Hmm?"

"Being strange," Bella clarified. "I never felt…normal."

"Well then, you'll fit right in here," Gideon replied. "Havenwood is for people who can't fit in...or won't."

Bella gave a weak smile, remembering the letter Mrs. Pittersworth had written, about how she couldn't focus. About how something was wrong with her, and she needed to be on medication. She relayed the story to Gideon.

"Nonsense," Gideon retorted. "You couldn't concentrate because you didn't care."

"Well, not about algebra," she admitted.

"I daresay if you took a hundred adults and put them in school for seven hours straight, lecturing about things they didn't particularly care about, they'd all have trouble paying attention," Gideon declared. "Children don't learn by sitting and listening for hours, they learn by *doing*. By trying and failing and learning. You know what that's called?"

"Um..."

"It's called playing," Gideon stated. "And it's the most serious thing that children do."

"Oh," Bella murmured. "Guess I never thought of it that way."

"Adults make the mistake of thinking that play is frivolous," Gideon explained. "And that work must be arduous." He arched an eyebrow. "Is painting work or play for you, Bella?"

"Both?"

He smirked.

"Granted. Yet you see the power of art," Gideon declared, gesturing all around him.

"So you think Mrs. Pittersworth was wrong?" she asked hopefully. Gideon snorted.

"Only listen to what people who *think* think," he declared.

"That's what Grandpa said."

"We learned from the very best," Gideon replied with a wink.

The path wound to the left, then opened up abruptly ahead, reaching the end of the mushroom forest. Beyond, the path continued, curving to the right around a lake with crystal-clear water. A large waterfall fed this lake, cascading downward from a gushing stream near the top of the mountain upon which Havenwood had been built.

Or rather, written.

Bella pulled back on her horse's reins, stopping on the path. She followed the path with her gaze as it wound up the mountain, corkscrewing up to the very top. Beautiful buildings of every imaginable style were clustered on the sides of the mountain, some made of wood, others stone, or brick, and even one made entirely of what appeared to be crystals. Heck, she even spotted one made out of scales, and one that had been built out of a large, hollowed-out mushroom.

And on the very top of the mountain, a stately white castle, with the waterfall starting from a stream just below it.

"Wow," Bella breathed.

"Wow indeed," Gideon agreed, having stopped beside her.

"Is it named Dragon's Peak because of the White Dragon?" she inquired.

"You'll see," he replied. "Come on," he prompted, riding forward along the path.

They continued onward, the lake to their left, the curving wall of the mushroom forest to their right. The path began to slope upward, spiraling gently up the mountain. A dense cluster of buildings was ahead, flanking the path…and there was a man sitting on the front porch of the nearest one. He was tall and slouched and dreadfully thin, with long, messy black hair. He couldn't have been over twenty years old.

"Gideon?" the man exclaimed, standing bolt upright. "Is that you?"

"Hello Connor," Gideon greeted, waving at the man. Connor stood up like there'd been a spring under him, hopping down the porch stairs and rushing up to Gideon.

"Gideon!" he cried. "I thought you were…you know."

"Dead?" Gideon inquired.

"Well, I mean," Connor stammered.

"It took longer than I expected," Gideon replied, "…but I found what I was looking for." He gestured at Bella. "I believe she was a little shorter when you saw her last."

Connor turned to stare at Bella, looking suddenly bashful.

"Is that…?"

"Bella Birch," Gideon declared. Connor's eyes went wide.

"Bella Birch!" he exclaimed. "I can't believe it!"

"She was lost in a book all these years," Gideon told him. "She doesn't remember anything," he added. Connor frowned.

"Anything?"

203

"Not her mother or her father," Gideon confirmed. "Or any of this," he added, gesturing at their surroundings. "I'll fill her in on the details in due time."

"Got it," Connor replied. He broke out into a smile at Bella. "Sure is nice to see you," he added. "I'm Connor, by the way."

"Nice to meet you Connor," Bella stated, smiling at the man. "How do you two know each other?"

"Oh, everyone knows everyone in Havenwood," Gideon answered. "We're all one big happy family."

"Sure are," Connor agreed.

"Yes, well, it's good to see you Connor. We'll catch up later."

"Oh, right, of course," Connor replied. "See you!"

And with that, the man hopped back up the porch stairs, sitting back down. Gideon led Bella further up the path, feeling Connor's eyes on them as they walked.

"That was…"

"Awkward?" Gideon inquired. Bella broke out into a guilty smile.

"Little bit."

"Get used to it," Gideon warned. "There's a lot of awkward here. Havenwood is a haven for artists, and creative types tend to have…creative personalities."

"You don't," Bella pointed out.

"I'm from a different time," Gideon explained. "Most of these kids are just that…kids. Connor's in his twenties. We'll see how he is in a few hundred years."

"Wait, what?" Bella blurted out, pulling on her horse's reins and stopping in her tracks. Gideon stopped beside her. "A few *hundred* years?"

"Well yes," Gideon replied. "I for example am four hundred and sixty-two years old."

Bella stared at him blankly, and Gideon smirked, arching an eyebrow at her.

"Tell me…what do you suppose might happen if I were to step into a painting – like I did when you healed me – but instead of covering a wound, you were to smooth my wrinkles and return the color to my hair?"

Bella's mouth dropped open.

"That's right," he replied, answering his own question. "Writers can create worlds, Actors can become someone else. But Painters...they can make you immortal."

Gideon started up the path again, leaving Bella to sit there in her saddle and gawk at him. She snapped out of it, prompting her steed to hurry to his side, then matching pace with him. She stared at him incredulously.

"You're four hundred years old?" she pressed.

"Four hundred and sixty-two," he corrected.

"But..." she began. "You said Grandpa was your teacher!"

"That he was."

"But..."

"Nine-hundred and twenty-three," Gideon interrupted. "If you must know."

Bella swallowed with some difficulty.

"I don't believe it."

Gideon shrugged.

"Fine," he replied. "Come on," he added as they passed more houses. Doors opened as they did so, people rubbernecking from their porches. There were more than a few gasps, and many cried Gideon's name. Gideon waved politely to them all, telling them he was terribly busy but would chat later, and that he was quite fine, thank you very much. He didn't bother to introduce Bella, for which she was grateful. In fact, he hurried them right along. Eventually they passed the cluster of houses, and they continued up the mountain, dozens of eyeballs glued to their backs.

"All right then," Gideon declared, clearly relieved. "Only a few more neighborhoods to go."

"Until what?" Bella inquired.

"Until we get to your mother's house," he replied. He paused then, his expression turning grave. "I...haven't been entirely honest with you Bella. When we get to your mother's house, there's something I need to tell you...and to show you."

Chapter 23

Gideon withdrew into himself as he and Bella rode up the great mountain of Havenwood, not saying much of anything as they passed neighborhood after neighborhood. He waved at people as rode by, receiving a robust – and welcoming – reception each time. It was almost as if Gideon was a celebrity of sorts. She noted that he didn't really introduce her anymore, however. In fact, he insisted she hide her face in her hooded cloak to speed things along, telling people she was his newest apprentice. Which was true enough, Bella supposed.

In this way, they made it nearly to the top of the mountain, the cobblestone path leading up to the castle ahead. Gideon took a fork in the path, one that led leftward, straight across the side of the mountain...and toward the source of the waterfall feeding the lake far below. This, Bella saw, was a wide stream flowing from the mouth of a cave. The stream crossed a long, flat ledge of stone, then fell off the edge of this abruptly, forming the waterfall. A wide stone bridge crossed the stream. Upstream was a sheer rock wall some fifty feet high, and the mouth of the cave was quite literally that; a mouth of a dragon carved into the rock wall. It all looked terribly familiar, but Bella couldn't have said why.

"That is the Everstream," Gideon declared. "A continuous flow of fresh water created by the fossilized remains of a water dragon that died centuries ago. In Thaddeus's book, anyway," he added.

"Like the chalice in the Misty Marsh?" Bella inquired.

"That's undoubtedly what inspired Thaddeus," Gideon replied. "But he learned from their mistake. He made the water dragon have two heads...one that drank excess water from Lake Fenestra – that's its name – and another that spewed new, fresh water. The total volume of water in the lake never changes...and as you can see, there's no flooding or mist."

"Clever."

"Indeed," Gideon agreed. "The more creative you are..."

"The stronger your magic," Bella recalled. "Right."

Gideon gestured upstream at the mouth of the cave.

"Follow me," he prompted, and promptly turned off the path, following the rightmost edge of the stream toward the mouth of the cave. Bella nudged her horse to follow, and they soon reached it. The carved stone dragon mouth was easily twenty feet wide and half as tall, with sharp stone teeth protruding from its ceiling. There was a narrow stone walkway beside the stream that continued into the cave. Gideon dismounted, gesturing for Bella to follow his lead.

"Come on," he prompted. "We're getting close."

"Mom's studio is in a cave?" Bella inquired, dismounting as well. She glanced about dubiously. It was dark and dank, sunlight not daring to venture too far inside the cave.

Gideon pulled his lantern from his chest-painting.

"Luminos," he murmured.

The lantern did its thing, sending a warm, comfortable light throughout the entrance of the cave. It was a long, wide tunnel, one with fossilized vertebrae at the top of the ceiling. It looked for all the world that it was the *inside* of the long-dead water dragon's body.

"Wow," she breathed, taking it all in.

The stone walkway continued along the right side of the cave, the stream flowing to their left. Gideon strode forward, leading her deeper into the dragon-cave. Bella hesitated.

"What about the horses?" she asked.

"Leave them," he counseled. "They'll be fine."

"What if we need them later?"

"Put them in a painting then," he answered.

Bella retrieved the biggest rolled-up painting from her thigh-holster that she could find, and did just that, opening it and ushering each horse through. It must not have been the first time they'd been stored thus, as they walked right into the painting without a fuss. That done, Bella rolled the painting back up, following Gideon further into the cave.

They soon left daylight behind, the cave swallowing them whole. It began to slope downward, curving to the right. Strangely, water flowed *up* the stream, in the opposite direction they were walking…and against gravity. The sound of rushing water reverberated through the cave, growing louder the deeper they went. The air turned damp and cool, but not at all musty.

The cave spiraled into the earth for quite some distance, then suddenly opened up, the ceiling now so high up that it was barely visible. The vertebrae were larger here, and now there were long, thick ribs arching downward to form walls on either side. Looking back, Bella saw that they'd come to a convergence; a second tunnel – complete with vertebrae on the ceiling – plunged downward to the left of the one they'd come through.

"We're in the body now," Gideon stated. He gestured at the second tunnel. "That leads to the other head of the water dragon," he explained. "It goes all the way to the bottom of Lake Fenestra."

A second stream of water flowed *up* this tunnel, joining the first in a turbulent, foaming collision in the center of the cavern…or rather, the dragon's body.

"Come," Gideon prompted, continuing down the sloping cavern of the dragon's body. There was no stream ahead, only a huge breastbone on the floor of the cavern, with massive ribs converging on it. Bella followed quietly, taking it all in.

Minutes passed, and the cave gradually became smaller, the ceiling now only a few feet above their heads. It sloped more severely here, curving sharply to the right in what Bella strongly suspected were spirals deep into the mountain.

"We're near at end of the tail," Gideon noted. And indeed they were; the vertebrae at the ceiling stopped ahead. But the cave continued past this, forming a long, narrow tunnel. Gideon led her through this; at the end of the tunnel, some fifty feet ahead, was a pale white light. Gideon shut off his lantern, handing it to Bella. "Put this in your chest-painting," he requested. She gave him a questioning look, but did as he asked. Now the light at the end of the tunnel was the only thing guiding them.

Gideon stepped into that light, and Bella joined him.

Her eyes widened.

208

The tunnel opened up into a large cavern, the ceiling a good sixty feet above their heads. Pitch-black stalactites hung from the ceiling, water dripping from their tips. Small mushrooms grew in dense clusters at the edges of the cave, each glowing a pale white. Among these were larger green and blue mushrooms that also glowed, though not as brightly as their paler brethren.

And there, in the center of the cave, was a very large building.

It was not so much a building as it was an estate. Wrought of wood and stone in various shades of black and gray, it was one of the most impressive buildings Bella had ever seen. It was broad, perhaps two hundred feet wide, its two-story entrance flanked by twin towers three stories tall. Their roofs were sharply sloped, coming to a vicious-looking point a few feet below the ceiling of the cave. Tall, stately windows stared outward at Bella at regular intervals, the mushrooms growing nearby casting the dark glass in a pale white light.

A black, wrought-iron fence surrounded the estate, each of its tall posts terminating in a vicious-looking spike. It was guarded by an ornate iron gate directly ahead, with twin doors that were closed. Beyond this, a bloodstone path led to the front door of the estate. Or rather, a closed portcullis made of crisscrossing black metal slats.

Goosebumps rose on Bella's flesh, another feeling of déjà vu coming over her. She stopped before the gate, staring at the house beyond, and Gideon stopped beside her. He gazed at the building ahead, putting his hand on the gate.

"Here we are," he announced, turning to Bella with a wistful expression. "Welcome home, Bella."

Bella frowned at him.

"This...?"

"Was where you were born," Gideon confirmed. "Where you spent the first few years of your life, before going to Blackthorne." He pulled on one door of the gate, and it swung open, creaking creepily as it did so. He gestured at the entrance ahead. "Go on."

Bella started down the bloodstone path, then realized that Gideon wasn't following her. She glanced back at him questioningly.

"You go on alone," he urged, handing her his lantern. "I'll stay here."

"But..."

"Here, take Myko with you," he interrupted. He retrieved Myko's painting, drawing the big wolf out. Myko looked around, taking in his surroundings. It had to be quite disorienting to vanish into a painting, then a split-second later find oneself in a totally different place. Myko took it in stride, stepping up to Bella's side and licking her cheek. "Go on now," Gideon prompted.

Bella took a deep breath in, then nodded, continuing down the path until she reached the entrance. Five stone steps led up to the portcullis, which was closed. She looked around, searching for a doorbell, or a knocker, or...something. But there was nothing. She glanced back at Gideon again, but he just stood there by the gate.

Then a white mist spilled through the holes between the metal slats of the portcullis, flowing over her feet. It collected around her, so thick that she couldn't see her boots. A chill ran down her spine, the hair on her neck standing on end.

And then the mist withdrew back through the portcullis, and there was a loud *thunk*.

The portcullis lifted.

Bella paused, glancing one more time at Gideon. Then she stepped through the portcullis, Myko following behind her. Beyond was a short, narrow hallway, which ended in a set of wooden double-doors. The same white mist covered the floor entirely, making the floor impossible to see. It came all the way up to her knees, swirling around her.

She stepped through the mist to the double-doors, reaching for a doorknob. But the mist rose upward as a giant hand, shoving the doors open before she could, then falling back to the floor and flowing into the room beyond.

Bella saw a large foyer with a wide staircase at the far end, one that split into stairs going left and right up to the second floor. A red carpet ran down the middle of the stairs like a bloody waterfall. Lanterns were bolted to the walls at regular intervals, but no emitted no light. There was a large fountain in the center of the room, with a broad stone bowl at its base and a tall, dark bronze statue of a woman standing upon it. She was quite beautiful, with long legs and arms, and long hair in tight curls pulled back into a ponytail that sprang outward from the back of her head. Her full lips were slightly parted, her eyes glaring forward sternly...seemingly right at Bella. In her right hand was a golden sword, its tip pointed downward.

The mist crawled over the floor, wrapping around the base of the statue. It lifted up into the bowl, filling it, then sent pale tendrils up the body of the statue. The mist poured into its mouth and eyes, until there was no mist left.

Then the lanterns on the walls lit up, casting the room in a pale white light.

Bella paused, looking around. She spotted two broad doorways, one diagonally to her left, the other to the right. The golden statue moved suddenly, twisting its torso and lifting its golden sword to point to the leftmost doorway.

Bella took a step back from the statue, swallowing in a dry throat. Mist poured from its eyes and mouth, spilling down to the bowl of the fountain, then flowing to the floor. It spread across the floor, flowing through the leftmost doorway into the room beyond.

Bella stared at it, feeling entirely ill-at-ease. She glanced at Myko.

"Protect me, Myko," she pleaded. Myko *wuffed* in what she could only assume was the affirmative. She took a deep breath in, then followed the mist into the hallway beyond.

And froze in the doorway.

For there, at the other end of a long, narrow corridor, was a huge black boar, easily four times Myko's size. But there was something terribly wrong with it. Its flesh was torn off on the left side of its face and neck, its skull and spine visible beneath. More flesh was missing from its chest and flanks, its muscle and ribs glistening in the dull lamp-light. And it had no flesh on its tail whatsoever.

The boar's massive head turned toward her, its ears swiveling forward. It stared at her with empty eye sockets, dark fluid dripping from them. Then it lowered its head, its long, sharp tusks pointed right at her.

The boar charged!

"Myko!" Bella cried.

Myko pushed through the doorway past her, lunging between her and the charging boar. He shot forward, moon-phasing to the boar's right, then phasing a second time, slamming into the boar's side. It stumbled into the side-wall, losing its balance and tumbling to the floor a few yards from Bella.

Bella backpedaled rapidly, her heart pounding.

The boar snorted, scrambling to its feet. But Myko stood over it, baring his fangs and growling menacingly.

The boar sniffed at Myko, then lowered its head to the floor meekly.

Bella hesitated, then walked up to Myko, patting his furry back. "Thanks Myko."

The boar's ears perked up, and it glanced at Bella, then at Myko…and began wagging its skeletal tail. The boar got to its feet, nudging Myko with its huge nose, then stepping up to Bella and doing the same. Bella hesitated, then put a hand on its nose.

Huh, she thought.

She pet the boar's head, scratching behind its one intact ear, to its obvious delight. The mist flowed across the floor around it, continuing to the other end of the long hallway. Bella hesitated, then stepped around the boar, following the mist to the end of the hallway…and a stairway leading upward. The mist led her up it, and Myko climbed up the steps behind her as she made her way to the second floor.

Bella found herself in a small room, a closed black coffin in the center of it. There were no doors, nor was there any other furniture. Only a painting on each wall, and a lighting fixture on the ceiling, casting a pale light on the coffin below.

The mist swirled around the base of the coffin, staying there.

Bella walked up to the coffin, running her fingers over it. It had a pleasant, velvety texture, and a single golden circle surrounding a golden triangle embossed into center of the lid. She paused, looking about the room.

What now?

She turned to the paintings on the walls, studying them. Each was quite large, taking up most of the wall. One was of a blood-red moon overlooking a massive city, one with tall, dark buildings hidden in shadow. Another was of a very different city, one lit by the afternoon sun, with two huge towers in the very center of the city rising into the sky like upside-down vampire fangs.

The mist had guided her thus far, bringing her to this room. And now it was staying around the coffin. Which meant that the coffin was what it wanted her to see. Or maybe…

She found some metal latches on the sides of the coffin, and unlatched them one-by-one. Then she glanced at Myko, feeling suddenly uneasy.

"Get ready, Myko," she warned.

Then she gripped the lid of the coffin, swinging it open.

To her profound relief, it was empty.

The mist flowed into the coffin, vanishing into the blackness within. Bella waited, but that was it. Nothing happened.

"Huh," she muttered. "Wonder what…"

Something rose from within the coffin. A huge, nightmarish skull covered in a thin layer of glistening black flesh. One supported by a broad, fleshy neck that extended from the depths of the coffin.

The mouth opened wider – impossibly wide, larger than Bella herself – a long, moist tongue extending outward toward her. Bella backed away quickly.

"Myko!" she cried.

The foul creature wailed, an awful sound so deep and powerful that it made Bella's bones vibrate. A blast of putrid air struck Bella, making her gag…and Myko backed away from the thing, lowering himself to the floor.

The black tongue shot outward, striking Bella in the face, then wrapping around her neck.

"Help!" she cried, grabbing the tongue and trying desperately to pry it free from her. But it was far too slick, her hands slipping off of it.

The tongue pulled her forward, retracting into that terrible, gaping maw.

Another wail burst from the creature, sending a fresh wave of terror through Bella. She braced her feet against the side of the coffin, pushing against it even as the tongue continued to retract, drawing her closer to the creature's mouth. But it was no use; the tongue was too powerful, and it pulled her head right into its maw. Its breath was ice-cold, and reeked of death.

"Myko!" she croaked, feeling the thing's grip around her neck tighten. "Gideon!"

Then, even as the creature lowered itself back into the coffin, it pulled her all the way into its mouth. That black flesh closed all around her, surrounding her in cold, wet darkness.

And then Bella felt herself rotating to the left, just before the void claimed her.

* * *

At first there was only darkness.

Bella felt something hard underneath her, and realized she was lying on her back. There was no light whatsoever; she couldn't even see her own nose. She sat up...and promptly smacked her forehead into something hard directly above.

That smarted.

She rubbed her forehead, then reached upward with both hands, feeling a firm, flat, but velvety under her palms, only a few inches above.

"Hello?" she called out.

There was no answer.

She felt panic rise within her, and stifled it, closing her eyes and taking a steadying breath.

Stay calm, she commanded herself. *Think.*

She focused on her breathing, concentrating on the air coming in through her nose, then letting it out through her mouth. After a few breaths, she had an idea.

The lantern!

She reached into her chest-painting, feeling a familiar warm, pulsing feeling. Her fingers wrapped around something metallic, and she drew it out.

"Luminos," she whispered.

The lantern flared to life.

Bella found herself inside a box lined with plush gold velvet. No, not a box, she realized; a coffin. She steeled herself against another wave of panic, setting the lantern between her legs, then pushing harder on the lid of the coffin. It swung open soundlessly, revealing a black stone ceiling above. Stone mortared together with what appeared to be bones.

Human bones.

She hesitated, then sat up slowly, grabbing the lantern and holding it before her. A small room greeted her, one shaped much like the coffin she was sitting in. The walls and floor were made of the same black stone – and bones – as the ceiling. A closed wooden door stood at the foot of the coffin-like room, and directly above this was a hideous carving on the wall. One identical to the skull-like monster that had swallowed her up only moments before, only ivory-colored instead of black.

To her relief, it didn't move.

Bella got out of the golden coffin, walking to the door and putting her hand on the knob. She turned it, then pulled the door open.

Beyond, she saw a small room. But in stark contrast to the black stone and bones of the previous room, this room had a warm, red-brown wooden floor and off-white walls. A long table surrounded by chairs dominated the center of the room, with quite a few framed pictures on each of the room's four walls. There was a closed door on the other end of the room, with small windows on the leftmost wall.

How did I get here?

Bella stood up, making her way to the nearest drawing. It was a sketch, done in charcoal. Of a beautiful woman that looked just like the statue on the fountain, kissing a young girl on the forehead. A girl that was perhaps four years old, with slightly lighter skin, and more relaxed curls.

A girl that was most definitely Bella.

She stared at the drawing, her mouth falling open. For there, before her, was the very first picture she'd ever seen of her mother.

Bella reached out, pressing her fingertips on the glass protecting the sketch, running her fingertips over her mother's likeness. She looked to the bottom right corner, where the artist had signed their name in flowing, intricate cursive:

Lucia M. Birch

"Mom," she whispered, her vision blurring with moisture. She blinked it away, smiling at the sketch. Then she turned to the next framed picture. This was a painting done in oil, of her and Mom. Of Bella sitting on a stool watching her mother paint. It was remarkably detailed, the colors vibrant and sure. The kind of painting Bella could only dream of creating, so far beyond her ability that it was humbling to behold.

The next one was a painting of Bella plucking a glowing mushroom from the dirt, staring at it with utter fascination. Unsigned, of course. Bella could only imagine what would happen if it'd been signed, and a younger version of herself had been drawn out.

Almost *all* of the sketches and paintings were of Bella, she realized. Of her and Mom, of her alone, or with…

Bella frowned as she reached the far end of the room, staring at a sketch mounted at the head of the long table. It was of Bella, sitting between Mom and a man. A man with short black hair and a thick, wild black mustache and beard, wearing a Painter's uniform.

Bella swallowed, staring at the picture silently. Then she moved to the rightmost wall, studying the sketches there. More scenes of Bella and Mom, but each with this man. And one of Mom and the man alone, standing beneath an archway, kissing.

"She liked to draw too," a voice behind her stated. "Just like you."

Bella whirled around, her heart leaping into her throat. There, standing in the doorway to the room she'd just come from, was Gideon.

"Holy crap," she blurted out, her heart pounding in her chest. "You scared me!"

"My apologies."

"Where are we?" she asked, looking around. Her eye went to one of the small windows, and she stepped up to it, peering out. Rolling black hills spread out as far as she could see, leafless, twisted trees dotting the landscape. A blood-red moon hung low in the sky, angry black clouds blotting out the stars. "Is this Mom's Conclave?" she guessed.

"Something like that," Gideon answered.

"What was that...thing? The one that came out of the coffin?"

"That was Death," Gideon replied.

"Death?"

"The personification of death," he clarified. "The gatekeeper to this...place," he added. "Your mother was very fond of death. And dying, and decay. She thought they were underappreciated...a part of the natural order of things, a beautiful cycle of life and death and eventual rebirth."

Bella absorbed this, then turned back to the sketch of Mom and the man kissing.

"Is that...my dad?" she asked. Gideon nodded.

"A picture of him, yes."

"He was a Painter," she noted.

"Yes."

"What happened to him?" Bella pressed. Gideon sighed.

"That's a long story, Bella," he replied. "You see, he was a great Painter. They both were, he and your mother. But he did something terrible long before he met her. Something unforgivable…a crime that, had anyone discovered it, would have gotten him hanged."

Bella just stared at him.

"He kept this a secret, Bella. A secret he never told anyone…until he met your mother. She forgave him. She loved him despite what he'd done, and they came here, to Havenwood. And they had you here, on your mother's thirty-third birthday." Gideon smiled. "This is where you were born, Bella…here, in this place," he added, gesturing with one hand.

"But what happened to him?" Bella pressed.

"He stayed in Havenwood when you and your mother went to visit Thaddeus in Blackthorne," Gideon explained. "He had a painting he'd wanted to finish, and classes to teach. You and your mother left, and the rest…well, you know."

"I don't," she countered. "All I know is that my mother died in Blackthorne."

"Yes," Gideon confirmed. "She did."

"How?"

"The Collector attacked Blackthorne," he answered. "Personally. He tried to capture Thaddeus, and your mother stopped him."

A chill ran down Bella's spine, a vision of the man with the glowing silver sword coming to her.

"He's the man in black," she realized. "The one I painted back in the apartment."

"That's right."

"He killed Mom, didn't he."

Gideon swallowed visibly, nodding once.

"He did."

Bella stood there, feeling numb.

"Your mother gave you something of hers when the Collector attacked," Gideon continued. "An amulet with a ruby heart. Your mother called it *her* heart, Bella. It has powerful magic, that I know. But she never told me what that magic was."

Bella's hand went to the amulet she wore around her neck. She pulled it free from under her uniform, running a finger across the crack in the center of the ruby.

"The Collector attacked you and your mother, and from what Thaddeus told me, the amulet saved your life," Gideon revealed.

"Mom sacrificed herself...to save me," Bella realized. Gideon nodded, and Bella felt tears well up, dripping down her cheeks. She stood there clutching her amulet, remembering what Grandpa had told her.

She died the way she lived, he'd said. *Beautifully.*

And all that Bella had been left with, while hiding in the dreadful world of that book with Grandpa, was this broken heart.

"I'm sorry, Bella," Gideon murmured.

Bella shook her head mutely, tears streaming down her cheeks. To think that Mom had died for her...

She lowered herself to sit on the floor, hugging her knees to her chest.

"I can't," she whispered, gritting her teeth. "I can't take this."

Gideon came to her side, kneeling before her and putting a hand on her shoulder. She felt him staring at her, and suddenly she wanted nothing more than for him to leave. To leave her here in her Mom's house, in the bowels of the earth.

Alone.

If Gideon had said anything – anything at all – she *would* have asked him to leave. But he remained silent, staying at her side. At length her tears dwindled, and she wiped her eyes and cheeks with the back of her sleeve, turning to look at him. His face was paler than usual, his eyes downcast.

"Thank you," she whispered. "For telling me."

Gideon hesitated, his jawline rippling.

"I'm not done," he confessed. Her eyebrows drew together, and he drew in a deep breath, then turned to look into her eyes. "Before I came to Blackthorne to save you and Thaddeus, I had my face painted, back to the way it originally looked."

"What?"

"When I became a bounty hunter, I had to hide my identity," Gideon explained. "I had my face painted to change the way I looked every few years so I could go undercover to find my targets. But when I went to Blackthorne, I had my face painted back to my original face. A face that no one had seen in centuries."

"Okay..."

He stood then, his knees popping loudly, and gazed down at her.

218

"The last face I had before I went to Blackthorne," he continued, "...was this one."

And he turned, pointing to the sketch nearest them, at the man kissing Mom under the archway.

Chapter 24

Piper leaned against the uneven rock wall of a tunnel deep below the earth's surface, staring at a wooden door set into the wall opposite him. A deep purple light shone from the narrow gap between the door and the wall, evidence of the door's magical nature. It was one of the Doorways of the Underground, a vast network of secret tunnels rediscovered by the Collector...and known only to the Collector's most senior employees. Written by an ancient Writer called Persnickity Gibbons, the Underground was created as a way for the Writer to travel the world quickly, each door leading to a specific location in the real world.

Piper sighed, fidgeting with his wedding band. It'd been well over and hour, and Kendra still hadn't come through the Doorway. Which meant that she'd either been successful in slowing the Pentad's army down, or...

"Quit being paranoid," he told himself. "She's fine."

Still, he found himself having the urge to pace, and gave into it. Back and forth, stopping occasionally to eye the door, then resuming his pacing.

Minutes passed, his brain torturing him with visions of Kendra's body in various states of being murdered. He tried to ignore them, but with every minute that passed, his anxiety grew.

"Come on love," he pleaded. "Come back to me."

He tried to derail the bad thoughts, picturing the first time they'd met. Back at the palace at the Pentad. He'd been a bounty hunter fresh out of a particularly nasty divorce, assigned to the same team as Gideon and Yero. And she'd been the team's newest recruit. Brash, cocky, and sexy as hell.

He'd been instantly smitten.

And though he'd only been a few months free from a divorce that had torn a hole in his heart, so awful that it made him take a vow of celibacy – which for him was a considerable sacrifice – he'd broken that vow soon afterward, and replaced it with one he'd found far more pleasant to keep.

Piper smiled at the memory, realizing he'd stopped pacing...and heard the creaking of a door opening on rusty hinges.

He froze, half-expecting it to be one of the Pentad's men. Or even General Craven himself. But to his immense relief, it was not.

"Kendra!" he exclaimed, rushing up to her and giving her a big hug. He lifted her up, spinning her around, then set her down and kissed her.

"Mmm," she said, pulling away from him after a moment. "Hey baby," she murmured with a smile. "Aww, you were worried, weren't you."

"Terribly," he agreed, setting her down. He kissed her again, relishing it. Kissing her never got old. It was like the first time, every time. He'd never met anyone like that...and knew damn well he never would again.

"My sweet husband," she mused, giving him one of her mysterious smiles. "I confess, I waited a few extra minutes just to make you worry a little longer."

"Ass," he grumbled, knowing she wasn't kidding...and that she knew damn well how bad his thoughts could get. "How'd it go?"

"As expected," she answered. "I trust the evacuation went well?"

"Thanks to you," he replied. "Come on love, let's go home."

They held hands, walking down the long, dark tunnels of the Underground. The only source of light came from the Doorways on the side-walls, casting the tunnels in an eerie purple hue. Each door had strange symbols carved along its perimeter, supposedly marking the coordinates of the location in the real world it would bring them to. But they had a long way to go before they reached the door that would bring them home.

To Castle Under, on the peak of Mount Inversus.

The Doorway to Mount Inversus opened up to a small cave at the shore of Lake Inversus, a massive body of water, in the center of which was the formidable mountain after which the lake had been named. Piper's gaze drew upward, following the mountain to its peak...and Castle Under. Balanced on the tip of its tallest tower was the inverted Castle Over, and an upside-down mountain...and lake.

It was as if there was a giant mirror in the sky...a scene that never failed to fill Piper with awe.

"You're up, love," he prompted.

"My mother warned me not to marry an Actor," she mused with a little smirk. "She said I'd end up having to do all the *real* work."

"I'll do plenty when we get home," Piper shot back. She arched an eyebrow.

"Promise?"

She retrieved Nightmare from her chest-painting, and it came to life, six black tentacles emerging from its golden cube. It wrapped a tentacle around Kendra and Piper, then strode forward across the water, its legs growing longer as it went. Within minutes, they reached the shore of Mount Inversus, and Nightmare climbed right up the mountain with ease, quickly reaching the top. No one tried to stop them, and in fact it seemed for all the world that the mountain wasn't guarded at all. But Piper knew that was hardly the case.

There were eyes watching their every move.

Nightmare brought them all the way to the magnificent entrance to Castle Under, setting them down and returning to Kendra's chest-painting. There were two guards at the front entrance, creatures in black cloaks with deep hoods that hid their faces in shadow. They wore silver gauntlets that emerged from their loose sleeves, and each carried a huge black scythe.

The Twin Reapers.

Piper felt a chill run down his spine as he stopped before them. The Reapers were ancient, freed from their painting by the Collector decades ago. No one knew exactly what they were capable of, except maybe the Collector himself. But anyone who drew near was filled with a sense of impending doom.

To his relief, the Twin Reapers stepped aside, allowing him and Kendra through.

They stepped into the magnificent foyer of the castle, a massive room spanning three stories. White marble floors, marble stairways, huge marble columns decorated with golden inscriptions. Enormous chandeliers hanging from the ceiling, their countless diamonds sparkling in magical light.

It was awe-inspiring, the entrance to the great Castle Under. And that, Piper knew better than most, was exactly the point. For he was an Actor, and evoking emotion was his trade. The story this castle told was one of sheer power. Wealth beyond comprehension.

The stories most people told the world about themselves – through their clothes, their actions, and their possessions – were fake. Lies and aggrandizements to fool others into believing that they were more important than they really were. A game as old as time, in the never-ending race to the top. But the story the Collector told with this castle was the truth.

And that, more than anything, was how the man had earned Piper's grudging respect…and to a much larger extent, Kendra's. But unlike Kendra, Piper didn't trust the guy. No one got that rich without doing it at the expense of a whole lot of people.

One of the many guards standing at attention in the foyer led Piper and Kendra up one of the broad staircases to the third floor, then down a maze-like series of corridors to another staircase leading up to the fifth. Through locked door after locked door, past literally hundreds of guards…some of them human, many not.

Eventually they made it to *the* door.

The Demon Gate.

It was at the end of a long, narrow hallway, a red and gold carpet running across the white and gray marble floor. Paintings hung from the walls, far too high up to reach. And the door…well, it was no ordinary door. It had been painted by a master Painter long ago, a huge door wrought of black stone. Twenty feet high, ten feet wide, and over a foot thick, it was truly massive. Its face was literally that…a monstrous face carved into the stone, of a demon with horns atop its head and a gaping mouth open in a silent roar, exposing long, deadly fangs. And its eyes were closed.

But as Kendra and Piper approached, they opened.

The door's glowing red eyes stared at them, making Piper's skin crawl.

223

"WHO APPROACHES?" the Demon Gate growled. Its mouth did not move, and no sound came from it. The voice was in Piper's mind. The door knew damn well who they were, but procedure had to be followed.

"Kendra and Piper," Kendra answered.

"WHAT IS YOUR INTENT?"

"To meet with the Collector," Kendra replied. "We come from Blackthorne to…"

"ENTER," the door commanded.

Its mouth opened wider then, so large that a man could step into it. Beyond was pure blackness. Kendra stepped right into it, vanishing from sight. Piper grimaced, steeling himself and following her into the thing's mouth.

He passed through the darkness, knowing full-well that the door was reading his mind. Stealing his thoughts. If he'd carried any intent to harm the Collector, the Demon Gate's mouth would not bring him to the room beyond.

It would bring him someplace *far* less pleasant.

To Piper's relief, he found himself in the waiting room to the Collector's office. Miss Savage was seated behind a desk to one side of the office door; she glanced up at them as they approached.

"The Collector will see your shortly," she announced.

Piper and Kendra sat down on the bench opposite the office door, glancing at each other. Piper put a hand on Kendra's knee, and she put her hand on top of his, squeezing it and flashing him a smile. He smiled back, knowing exactly what she was thinking.

This was her chance. If the Collector was pleased with her performance at Blackthorne – over fifteen years of hard work – she would finally get her promotion.

"The Collector will see you now," Miss Savage announced, nodding at Kendra. Kendra gave Piper's hand one last squeeze, then stood up from the bench. Miss Savage opened the door to the Collector's office, and Kendra stepped inside, the door closing behind her.

"You may leave," Miss Savage declared, her silver eyes on Piper. He frowned, then stood, knowing the statement had been an order, not a suggestion. He glanced one more time at the door to the Collector's office, then made his way back into the hallway he'd come through. The Demon Gate was nowhere to be found; it was a one-sided door. He strolled down the hallway, whistling a cheerful tune.

But in his heart, he was anything but at ease. For it seemed to him that for every step Kendra took toward the Collector, she was one step further from him.

Chapter 25

Bella stood beside the long, rectangular table in her mother's Conclave, staring at Gideon, her mouth agape.

"You're my father?" she blurted out at last.

"Yes," Gideon confirmed. "I am."

She tried to process this, but her mind was as numb as the rest of her. She heard a *clunk*, and looked down, realizing she'd dropped his lantern onto the floor. Gideon was still staring at her silently when she lifted her gaze, his face looking terribly pale in the lantern light.

"I..." she began, but the words caught in her throat. She cleared it, swallowing visibly. "You're my father."

He nodded.

Her lower lip quivered, and she clenched her fists, her whole body trembling.

"Why didn't you tell me?" she demanded angrily. "All this time you knew, and you didn't tell me?"

"I..."

"How could you *do* that?" she yelled, stomping up to him and shoving him backward. He stumbled, catching himself.

"Bella, I can explain," he insisted. She put her hands on her hips, glaring at him. "I had to keep it a secret," he told her. "If the Pentad finds out I had a child with your mother, it'll prove that I helped her escape their bounty hunters. That I aided a wanted criminal."

"And?"

"And I'll go to jail…or be executed."

"I wouldn't have told them," Bella retorted.

"I couldn't take that risk."

"Right."

He sighed, lowering his gaze to the floor.

"And…I was ashamed to tell you," he confessed. He blinked rapidly, his jawline rippling. "I wanted to, believe me. Bella, I…" he began, then choked up. He drew a breath in, then let it out. "I wasn't there to protect you. If I'd been there, if I'd gone with you, your mother would still be alive."

"That doesn't mean you killed her."

"She was a wanted criminal, Bella. If the Pentad had found her…" He swallowed visibly. "I should have gone with you, but I didn't."

"But you didn't mean to…"

"It doesn't matter," he interrupted. "I wasn't there, and your mother died because of it. My wife…" he added, his voice cracking. "My wife died because of *me*. And you lost your childhood because I wasn't there for you."

"Gideon…"

"I've spent the last ten years in Blackthorne," he continued, "…trying desperately to save you. Terrified that I might fail, and that you might be killed…or worse. And terrified that I *would* save you. That you'd finally find out what I'd done. How I'd failed you."

"So you just pretended I wasn't your daughter."

"I was planning on telling you," he insisted. "It's just…I needed to focus on getting you home. On making sure that you were safe first. And I knew it was a lot for you, Bella. Learning that you grew up in a book. That your whole world was an illusion."

Bella crossed her arms over her chest, glaring at him.

"That sounds like an excuse," she shot back. "And not a good one." He grimaced.

"Bella," he stated. "I've…lived in fear of this moment for ten years. I've been terrified of telling you the truth. So I put it off as long as I could. It might be an excuse," he added hastily, "…but it's the truth."

Bella lowered her arms to her sides, then sighed.

227

"I get it," she muttered. "But you should have told me."

"But if the Pentad had found out who…"

"Save it," she interrupted.

"You're right," he conceded. "I should have." He sighed as well, his shoulders slumping. He looked absolutely miserable. Bella hesitated, then stepped forward, leaning in and embracing him. He tensed up for a moment, then relaxed, wrapping his arms around her in turn.

They held each other for a long while.

At length Bella drew back, wiping moisture from her eyes, and Gideon did the same, giving her a bitter smile.

"I'm sorry Bella," he murmured. "For everything."

"You should be," she agreed…and promptly punched him in the shoulder. "Don't keep things from me anymore," she ordered.

He grimaced, rubbing his shoulder.

"I…don't know if I can promise you that," he admitted.

"What?"

"There are some things I can't tell you right now," he confessed. Bella crossed her arms over her chest, glaring at him. "I will, eventually," he added hastily. "It's just that, well, now isn't the time."

"Gideon…"

"I will tell you," he insisted. "You just have to be patient."

Bella sighed.

"Fine," she muttered.

"I can tell you one thing," he offered. "I was married once before. Long before your mother and I met, of course. We had a child together, a boy. His name was Xander."

"I have a brother?"

"Ah…let me tell the story," Gideon answered. "Xander was a good boy. A sweet, gentle heart, much like you, Bella." He smiled at the memory. "A very thoughtful boy, and maybe a bit too serious. I think he got that from me."

"Definitely."

"When Xander was eight, he had an…accident. It was his birthday, and he was with a few friends, taking turns running and jumping off a raft in the middle of a lake. When it was his turn, he slipped…and hit the back of his head on the edge of the raft. He got knocked out, and went right under the surface. They tried to save him, but…"

He took a deep breath in, letting it out slowly.

"I'd planned on being with him that day, but the Pentad had a job for me. And when the Pentad calls...well, I didn't have the option of ignoring them. So I wasn't there when my son needed me the most."

"Oh Gideon," Bella murmured, putting a hand on his shoulder.

"If I'd been there, I could have saved him, or put him in a painting and healed him, but..." He shook his head miserably. "My wife was devastated. She couldn't face me. Every time she looked at me, she saw Xander. She blamed herself for his death, and the Pentad for pulling me away. And she blamed me for not being there. So she left me, and told me she never wanted to see me again."

He sighed, his shoulders slumping.

"I spent a year alone, Bella. I was...in a bad place. I missed Xander terribly. I kept thinking that, if only I had been there, I could have saved him. If I had been there, he'd still be alive."

"Gideon..."

"I never forgave myself for what happened," Gideon continued. "After you were born, I became...well, overprotective would be an understatement. So when you and your mother went to Blackthorne, I insisted on coming. Your mother refused to let me. She said I needed to stay in Havenwood, so that I could trust that things would be okay even if I wasn't there."

He shook his head, staring at his feet, his eyes glistening with moisture.

"So I didn't come," he concluded. He lifted his gaze to meet hers. "And here we are."

Bella leaned in to embrace him again, and they stood there for a long while, neither of them saying anything. There was nothing *to* say. Bella closed her eyes, feeling Gideon's warmth, and thought of Grandpa. How Grandpa had been the only constant in her world, her source of warmth and hope. She'd lost him, just as Gideon had lost his son and both of his wives. And now they only had each other.

At length, Gideon separated from her, clearing his throat and smoothing the wrinkles in his uniform. He gazed at Bella, whose eyes were downcast.

"What's wrong?" he asked.

"I miss Grandpa," she admitted.

"Ah, right," he replied. He cleared his throat again, looking profoundly guilty. "Bella, I told you I needed to tell you something, and I have," he stated. "But I also promised to show you something."

"Huh?"

"Let's go back outside," he prompted. "Then I'll show you."

* * *

They left the Conclave through the golden coffin, appearing in the black coffin in Mom's mansion. Myko hopped back into his painting, and Gideon showed her to her old bedroom on the second floor before they headed outside.

That done, Gideon led her downstairs, the mist she'd seen earlier following behind them. They went back to the room with the statue, the mist flowing back through its nose and mouth, vanishing within.

"What is that?" she asked. "The mist I mean."

"Animus," he replied. "Your mother's Familiar."

"Her what?"

"Every elite Painter has – or should have – a Familiar," Gideon explained. "Something they've painted that is connected to them. I, for example, have Myko."

"What do you mean by 'connected?'" Bella inquired.

"Well, sort of a psychic connection, if you will," Gideon answered. "I can sense Myko's thoughts, and Myko can sense mine." He arched an eyebrow at Bella. "How do you think I was able to find you two in the fog after you escaped Blackthorne?"

"Oh," Bella murmured. "I hadn't even thought of that." She frowned. "So you can sense Myko's thoughts?"

"In a way," Gideon confirmed. "I can sense his emotions, what he's feeling. And I can sense where he is. His thoughts aren't like yours or mine...he doesn't use our language to think. He thinks in smells, sounds, pictures and actions, mostly."

"Huh."

"Animus was your mother's Familiar," Gideon continued. "She's very special, actually."

"She?"

"Animus is a she, yes," he confirmed. "After your mother died, Animus was devastated. It's a terrible thing to lose someone you were so connected to." Bella lowered her gaze, thinking of Grandpa. And of Mom.

"I know," she mumbled.

"Animus is very powerful," Gideon stated. "She can inhabit inanimate objects and use them as her body, if you will. This entire house was designed with Animus in mind. Almost everything within it can be possessed by Animus, and has special properties when she does so."

"Like that thing in the coffin?" Bella inquired.

"No, Death is…something else," he corrected. "But everything else here was designed by your mother."

"I wish I remembered her," Bella murmured.

"This house will show you who she was," Gideon promised. "It's *your* house now, Bella. Your home." He paused. "*Our* home."

They stepped through the open portcullis, the mist – Animus – staying inside the house. Gideon led Bella along the bloodstone path to the gate, stepping through and closing it behind them.

"So," Bella stated. "You wanted to show me something?"

"Let's get outside first."

They made their way up the spiraling tunnel, reaching the literal mouth of the cave, then walking alongside the stream to the very edge. The great waterfall fell to their right, Lake Fenestra and the White Dragon visible far, far below. From here, Bella could see the hill they'd climbed to get here, and a vast forest beyond.

"All right then," Gideon declared.

He took off his top hat, turning it upside-down and handing it to Bella. "Hold this." She did so, and he reached inside with his hand, retrieving a large, rolled-up painting. "Apertus," he murmured. The painting unrolled itself, revealing a familiar scene. The very first painting of Gideon's Bella had seen.

A full moon gleaming down on a hill overlooking a starry night sky, heat lightning flashing within clouds to the upper left. A few paintbrushes of various sizes littered the ground, as well as a palette, an easel, and jars of paint set out in neat rows. A bronze fire pit to the right, a fire crackling merrily within. And to the left, a simple wooden casket.

"Hold this up," Gideon requested, gesturing at the painting with his stump. Bella got behind the big painting, holding it up, and Gideon stepped in front of it. He reached in then, drawing something out. It was the coffin; he slid it all the way out with more than a little difficulty, his face reddening with the effort. "Clausus," he muttered, and the painting rolled itself back up. He put it back in his hat.

"What's this?" Bella asked, gesturing at the coffin. Gideon hesitated.

"There's no good way to explain this," he replied. "You'll have to open it and see for yourself."

Bella raised an eyebrow at him, then stepped up to the coffin. There were latches on one side; she started unlatching them one-by-one.

"Might want to hurry," Gideon advised.

Bella glanced at him questioningly, but followed his advice, finishing up and curling her fingers under the lid of the coffin. She pulled it open, peering within.

And jerked away with a gasp, her eyes wide with horror.

For there, lying in the coffin, was Grandpa's corpse.

Chapter 26

Bella gasped in horror, recoiling from the open coffin, her hand going to her mouth.

"Oh my god!" she cried, turning away from the gruesome scene. Her grandfather, lying dead in a casket. She closed her eyes, fighting back a wave of nausea.

"Bella…" Gideon stated.

"Close it," she blurted out. "Put it away!"

"Bella, just…"

"Please," she insisted. "I…"

"Bella!" Gideon nearly shouted.

Her mouth snapped shut, and she opened her eyes, glancing sidelong at Gideon. He gestured at the casket.

"Look," he prompted. She was about to reply when he held up his stump. "Trust me."

She reluctantly obeyed, returning her gaze to the casket.

And froze.

For Grandpa was no longer laying within it. He was sitting up, looking right at her.

"Ah!" he exclaimed, breaking out into a relieved smile. "Sorry, I must have fallen asleep. Hello, sweetheart." He turned to Gideon then. "I trust everything went smoothly?"

And then the world began to spin around her, and Bella promptly fainted.

* * *

"Bella?" a deep voice called out.

She felt a hand slap her cheek gently, and she opened her eyes, finding herself lying on the ground beside the gurgling stream near the top of Havenwood. Gideon was standing over her...and so was Grandpa. Grandpa, wearing his old, ratty brown sweater, his eyes twinkling from behind his golden-rimmed glasses.

"There you are," he declared, kneeling before her. He stood up, his knees popping. "She has returned to us at last!"

Bella blinked. Gideon offered his stump, and she took it, sitting up. She stared at Gideon, then at Grandpa, hardly believing her eyes.

"You're dead!" she exclaimed. Grandpa raised his eyebrows, looking down at himself.

"I am?"

"I saw you," she insisted. "They shot you. You didn't have a pulse!"

Grandpa turned to Gideon, giving him a look.

"You didn't *tell* her?" he blurted out incredulously. "Gideon!"

"I couldn't," Gideon protested. "Not until we were safely in Havenwood."

"Which we are," Grandpa pointed out. "You should have warned her first!"

"I thought it'd be best to show her instead of telling her," Gideon insisted. Grandpa gave him a withering glare.

"Sometimes it's better to tell than to show," he retorted. Then he turned to Bella, his expression softening. He leaned in, embracing her gently.

And she just stood there, dazed.

"I'm sorry Bella," he murmured in her ear. "I can only imagine how hard this was for you." She hesitated, then pushed him away.

"I saw you die," she accused.

"I assure you, I'm most certainly alive," Grandpa replied. He gazed out over the edge of the waterfall, taking a deep breath in and smiling. "Perhaps more so now than I've been in years."

"But..."

"The me you saw didn't die," Grandpa explained, facing her. "He was never alive in the first place."

234

Bella just stared blankly at him.

"Tell me Bella," Grandpa continued. "Do you recall a certain…morbid gift my friend gave me a few weeks before my, ah, passing?"

Bella frowned.

"You mean the painting?" she replied, making a face.

"That's the one," Grandpa confirmed. "And that's the face she made when she first saw it," he added, winking at Gideon. Who chuckled.

"A good likeness, wouldn't you say?" Gideon piped in.

"A dead ringer," Grandpa agreed with a mischievous grin.

"Wait a sec," Bella blurted out, jumping to her feet. "You're saying…"

"Mmm hmm," Grandpa replied.

"Yep," Gideon agreed.

"The painting!" she exclaimed. "It was magic!"

"It was a live painting, yes," Gideon confirmed. "I painted it weeks ago, for the very purpose you witnessed."

"To fake Grandpa's death," Bella realized.

"That's right," Gideon confirmed. "The day Stanwitz and Reynolds came for you, I overheard their plan to apprehend Thaddeus while working in the library at Blackthorne. I had a copy of the book, and got lost in it before they did. I drew your grandfather's likeness out of that portrait, dressed it in his clothes, and we sat it in his chair."

Bella's eyes widened, her jaw dropping.

"I grabbed my copy of the book, returning to this world with your father," Grandpa explained. "He'd already painted this coffin," he added, gesturing at the open casket. "I laid in it, and he closed it, put it in the painting, and carried me all the way here."

"Without the Collector – or the Pentad – knowing any better," Gideon concluded. "All part of our master plan."

"But…why?" Bella blurted out. Grandpa frowned.

"Why what?"

"Why didn't you tell me?" she pressed. "I thought you were dead, Grandpa!" Her vision blurred, and she wiped tears from her eyes, glaring at Grandpa. "How could you *do* that to me?"

"It broke my heart, knowing what you'd go through," Grandpa confessed, lowering his gaze. "I'm sorry, Bella."

"No," Bella retorted, taking a step back from him. "No, you can't just say you're sorry, not after that. Sorry doesn't cut it."

"We had to, Bella," Gideon interjected. "We didn't have a choice."

"Bull," she retorted, turning on him. "There's *always* a choice."

"You're right," Grandpa interjected, lifting his gaze to meet hers. "There is. And I chose to deceive you Bella. I chose to break your heart…and mine." He stood up taller, squaring his shoulders. "And I would do it again."

She stared at him incredulously. Part of her wanted to turn around and storm out of there. And another desperately yearned to leap into his arms and never let him go.

"Do you know who I am?" Grandpa inquired.

"Thaddeus Birch," Bella replied. "A Writer."

Grandpa took a step closer to her, reaching out and gripping her shoulders. His expression turned grim, his voice powerful and commanding.

"A dragon circle,
White and good,
Will one day rise
For Havenwood."

Bella swallowed, a chill running through her.

"The first sentence of the last book I wrote," Grandpa declared, eyeing her sternly over his glasses. "Words create worlds, Bella. For most Writers, these worlds live within the minds of their readers, and their readers live for a time within these worlds. But in *my* hands," he added, gesturing at the White Dragon far below, "…words become reality."

He leaned in, his nose inches from hers.

"Imagine what I would do if the Collector took you," he stated. "If he threatened to torture or kill you. Imagine what terrible things I would do for him just to save you."

The blood drained from Bella's face, and Grandpa pulled away from her, letting go of her shoulders.

"Sometimes the right thing to do feels like the wrong thing to do," he declared. "And the converse is also true."

Bella lowered her gaze.

"Okay Grandpa." she mumbled.

"Besides," he continued with a sudden, wry smile, "...if I told you the truth, you'd have thought me mad. Well, madder than you already suspected I was."

Bella had to smile reluctantly at that. It was true, after all.

"We couldn't risk you becoming so concerned about my mental health that you'd try to get me some 'help,'" Grandpa continued. "I suspect you were close to doing just that before my, ah, untimely death."

"True," she admitted. "I thought you were losing it."

"Oh, but I was!" Grandpa replied. "Trapped in that dreadful book for all those years, in that dingy apartment!" He gave her a rueful smile, his eyes getting moist. "You were the only thing that made it worthwhile Bella. Every time I thought about ending it, I recoiled in horror at the thought of ending my time with you."

Bella smiled back, stepping forward and wrapping her arms around him. Grandpa kissed her on the forehead, then pulled her close. She closed her eyes, hearing the steady *lub-dub* of his heart beating in his chest.

Her lower lip quivered, tears streaming down her cheeks.

"Oh Grandpa," she murmured, squeezing him tighter.

"Every night, after tucking you in and telling you a story, I sat at my desk and stared up at that painting," Grandpa murmured. "For weeks, it reminded me of what was coming."

He pushed her away gently, running a hand through her hair.

"Every beginning has an end, Bella," he stated. "And every end a new beginning."

Bella smiled despite herself.

"There you go, being all mysterious again," she accused. Grandpa winked.

"I'm a Writer," he replied matter-of-factly. "It's what we do."

* * *

The sun had swung all the way overhead, beginning its slow descent through the afternoon sky by the time Bella, Gideon, and Grandpa reached the great white castle at the very top of Dragon's Peak. Grandpa had insisted on showing it to Bella, and, having never been to Havenwood himself, was eager to see it. There was no wall or gate blocking their access to the castle. Indeed, the winding cobblestone road led right up to the castle entrance.

This, Bella quickly realized, was no ordinary castle.

It had the typical trappings of a fairytale castle, with tall towers reaching high into the sky, a sparkling blue moat surrounding it, and a tall, arched entrance with an open golden portcullis. There was an arched bridge spanning the moat, complete with grand white statues of men and women in various dynamic-looking poses. And the castle itself was made of pure white stone that gleamed in the sunlight.

But that's where the cliché ended…and the unusual began.

For although the main portion of the castle had its foundation on the stone of Dragon's Peak, much of it was supported on huge mushroom caps at various elevations below this. Long, elegant skybridges connected each of these to the main part of the castle. And while the castle had plenty of windows, it also had many window-shaped paintings where windows would've been expected to be. What's more, there appeared to be parts of the castle that were hovering in the air, connected by skybridges and supported by nothing more.

It was all quite fantastic, and Bella found herself having to remember to close her mouth on several occasions. Gideon clearly noticed her expression.

"Amazing, isn't it?" he said.

"You created all this with a book?" Bella breathed, glancing at Grandpa. Grandpa chuckled.

"Never underestimate the power of a story," he advised. "Stories are the language of minds and hearts…and Havenwood is a story from when my heart and mind were young."

"Huh?"

"A haven from the most powerful and insidious force of all," Grandpa explained. "Public opinion."

"I didn't miss your riddles," she grumbled. Grandpa smiled, stopping in the middle of the bridge crossing the moat.

"Have you ever felt…strange, Bella?"

Bella glanced at Gideon, then back at Grandpa. She nodded.

"Hmm," Grandpa murmured, scratching his beard. "Why?"

"Because I don't fit in," she answered.

"Go on."

"I like drawing creepy things like bone dragons," she continued. "I'm not…normal."

"But why?" Grandpa pressed. Bella shrugged.

"How should I know?"

"Ah ha!" Grandpa exclaimed, his eyes brightening. "And there it is. *That* is the right question!" He leaned in closer, arching an eyebrow dramatically. "And I've already told you the answer."

Bella crossed her arms, giving him an annoyed look. Grandpa chuckled turning to Gideon.

"She looks just like her mother there, doesn't she?" he said. Gideon nodded.

"I used to dread those glares," Gideon mused.

"Art!" Grandpa cried, lifting his arms to the heavens. He beamed down at Bella. "That is the answer. The 'how.'"

"Art is how I'll know why I'm not normal," Bella stated. "That doesn't even make sense!"

"Tell me, when you draw a sketch, or paint a painting, do you want someone to watch you do it?"

"No."

"How do you feel right before you show it to someone for the first time?" Grandpa pressed.

"Like I want to crawl into a hole and die," Bella confessed.

"Why?"

"Because it's...personal," she answered.

"It'd better be," Grandpa agreed. "All great art is. Your art is *you*, Bella. Pieces of your heart and mind..."

"...lost to the ravages of time," Bella recited. "Right."

"You *do* listen," he proclaimed, not without a hint of pride.

"I listen to everything you say," Bella replied.

"Well that's mildly terrifying."

"She certainly doesn't get that from her mother," Gideon interjected with a smirk. Grandpa ignored the comment, clearing his throat.

"You see Bella, people have this awful compulsion to fit in," he continued. "The Terrible Force of Public Opinion," he added, clearly capitalizing the words, "...compels us to be less like ourselves and more like everyone else. We lose bits and pieces of our souls, and bury them deep within ourselves. Art is excavation, Bella. Art is self-discovery!"

"So I don't fit in because...I'm not like everyone else."

"Because you're too yourself," Grandpa corrected. "And neither your classmates, nor Mrs. Pittersworth, would accept you until you conformed. Until you sat in your chair all day like a good little zombie, dutifully pretending to care about things that have no meaning to you."

"That's why he didn't want you to go to school," Gideon piped in. "But there is value in fitting in, Thaddeus. And in developing discipline."

"Water has value in proper portions, and when put in its proper place. But too much is poison, and in the wrong place we call it drowning."

Gideon smirked.

"I'm not going to even *try* to win a battle of words with you," he stated. "But I think we're boring my poor daughter. Care to see the castle, Bella?"

"I'd love to," Bella replied. "Um...Dad," she added.

"You said that like it felt weird," Gideon noted.

"It *did* feel weird," she admitted. "Would you be offended if I accidentally called you Gideon once and a while?"

"Not at all," he replied with a smile. He offered his arm, and Bella hooked hers in his, continuing across the bridge to the other side of the moat. There were colorful fish darting about in the water, which was crystal-clear. Bella turned her gaze forward, seeing the entrance to the castle ahead. There were no guards, nor people, really. Everything seemed...empty.

"Where is everyone?" she inquired.

"Inside," Grandpa answered. "We'll have to make an appearance, I'm afraid. After that, we'll get down to business."

"What business?" Bella pressed. Grandpa gave her a mischievous grin.

"The Collector hunted us for ten years," he replied. "I think it's about time we repaid the favor!"

Chapter 27

Piper sat at the edge of his bed in his small room in the eastern wing of Castle Under, watching as Kendra smoothed non-existent wrinkles from the silky black cloak she'd been given. The Cloak of Ascension, the official garment worn by those who had earned the right to ascend to the great upside-down castle in the sky. Kendra's work at Blackthorne – fifteen years of faithful service – had finally paid off. She smiled at him, giving him a little twirl.

"What do you think?" she asked.

"It's a robe," he answered.

"Come on," she complained. "I worked hard for this, Piper."

"I know, I know," Piper conceded. "I'm happy for you hon."

"Are you?"

"I mean, I'm happy *you're* happy," he clarified. "It's just…you know what I think about all this crap," he added, gesturing at the robe. The cloak, rather.

"Pomp and circumstance?" she inquired, arching an eyebrow.

"Where I come from we call it 'bullshit,'" he groused.

"Well now, usually *I'm* the killjoy," she mused. "Honey, I think I'm rubbing off on you."

He gave her a wicked grin.

"I'm all for that," he told her. She rolled her eyes.

"Later."

"That a promise?" he pressed, standing up from the bed and sauntering toward her. He used his best swagger, reaching up to cup the sides of her face in his hands.

"Depends on what character you'll be playing," she replied with a smile of her own. He leaned in, kissing her gently.

"I was thinking of playing myself," he admitted.

"Oh," she mumbled, lowering her gaze.

"Really? Wow."

She broke out into a smirk, lifting her gaze to his.

"You're not the only one who can act, you know," she teased. "If you're you, I'm in."

"If you're in, it'll only be a matter of time 'til I am," he quipped with a mischievous grin. She ignored him, leaning in to kiss him again. Piper savored the moment. It was, for that brief moment, like old times. But eventually Kendra pulled away, giving him an apologetic look.

"I gotta go," she told him. "Don't want to keep the Collector waiting."

"Alright."

"See you soon," she promised.

And with that, she gave him one last kiss, then left.

* * *

Kendra followed the Collector as he guided her ever forward and upward through the maze-like corridors of the Castle Under, the marble floors cool under her bare feet. She felt rather naked in the silky black cloak he'd given her to wear, though it covered her from the neck down. It was all she'd been allowed to wear, the thin fabric unable to hold back the slight chill in the air. But she hardly minded. After all, the Cloak of Ascension was the mantle of those who had earned the right to work within the mysterious halls of the Castle Over, the upside-down castle. And after so many years, she'd finally joined their hallowed ranks.

It gave her goosebumps.

She smiled to herself, staring at the Collector's back as he led her up yet another flight of stairs. He strode with utter confidence, wearing his usual black suit. She'd never seen him wear anything else, she realized. It had to be magical; not for the first time, she wondered what power it held.

The Collector was a mystery, and Kendra *adored* mysteries.

No one knew much about him. He was as opaque as his suit, never talking about himself. He revealed not a trace of weakness, not to his allies or his enemies. He spoke little, preferring to communicate through his actions.

And his actions were legendary.

Kendra had a crush on the Collector, of course. Who wouldn't, after all? A harmless crush – she had never strayed from her husband, and couldn't imagine doing so – but Piper's abilities as an Actor made for a tempting scenario. Not that she'd gathered the courage to make the request.

Yet.

The Collector slowed, then stopped, having reached the Demon Gate. The only way to the inverted castle was through the Collector's office...and the only way to his office was through the huge black stone door.

Its eyes opened, its great mouth opening without question.

"After you," the Collector stated, gesturing her to step through.

She did so, having no fear of the door. The truly loyal had nothing to fear. Passing through, she found herself in the familiar waiting room, Miss Savage in her perennial spot behind the desk there.

"Miss Savage," Kendra greeted, inclining her head. The woman gave a little smile, nodding back.

"Kendra," she replied. "Congratulations on your promotion."

"Thank you," Kendra stated. The Collector continued forward, opening the door to his office and ushering Kendra through. They stepped around his large desk, continuing to a door on the opposite end. This was locked; the Collector produced a large key, inserting it into the lock and turning it 90 degrees.

There was a *click*.

The Collector pulled the door open, gesturing for Kendra to step through. She did so, finding a spiral staircase corkscrewing up a huge tower beyond. She craned her neck, looking up; the stairs led upward as far as the eye could see. This, she realized, had to be the tallest tower of Castle Under. The tower that led to the very top of the castle...and to Castle Over.

She glanced back at the Collector, and he gestured for her to lead them upward. So began the long climb up the tower, the stairs spiraling ever upward and rightward. Long after her thighs and buttocks had started to burn, they reached the very top of the stairs…but not of the tower.

For there, extending as far upward as she could see, was another spiraling staircase. One entirely disconnected from the first…a perfect mirror-image. There was only a horizontal bar set a good six feet up near the edge of the stairs they were on…and a drop to the stairs below beyond.

The Collector pushed past Kendra, then reached up to grab the bar with both hands.

"Step back," he ordered.

She did so, and he began to swing like a gymnast, back, then forward, then back again, each time gaining momentum and height. He swung forward again…and kept rotating until he was upside-down.

And dropped onto the landing of the staircase above.

Kendra stared up at the Collector, standing upside-down on the upside-down staircase. She realized they must have reached the top of Castle Under…and the very bottom of Castle Over. The mirror-image castle had reverse-gravity, and the bar the Collector had swung on had to be right in the middle of the two.

She stared up at the long, spiraling staircase above, then at the sheer drop below. Without her Painter's uniform, she felt uncharacteristically vulnerable. If her grip slipped, or she tripped…

"Trust me," the Collector insisted, giving her a reassuring smile.

Kendra gave a weak smile back, taking a breath in, then jumping upward and grabbing the bar. It felt slippery in her sweaty palms, and she gripped it so hard her knuckles turned white. She began to swing, backward, then forward, picking up momentum.

And as she reached the border between castles – on the backswing – she felt the world *shift*.

She cried out, holding on to the bar with a death-grip as she continued to swing backward around the bar. Within moments, she came to a stop, the staircase she'd been on above her, and this new gravity pulling her down to the landing the Collector stood on.

"You can let go now," the Collector instructed, unable to hold back a smirk.

Kendra hesitated, not at all trusting that she wouldn't "fall" upward the minute she let go. But she obeyed, and sure enough, she dropped to land at his side.

"Ladies first," he prompted, gesturing for her to continue down this new stairwell. The idea that she was really going *up* them was disorienting. Round and round they went, spiraling downward until they reached the bottom of the great tower. This led to a room identical to the Collector's office, at least in its dimensions. The furnishings were different, however. The desk was larger, with books stacked upon it. And there were more books on tall shelves lining the walls.

"You second office?" Kendra inquired.

"My study," he corrected.

He led her through it, to a room identical to the waiting room in Castle Under. Then down a great long hall. Every corridor, every door exactly the same as it was below. But the hallways were utterly deserted. There were no guards at the doors, no Painters milling about the premises. No paintings on the walls.

Nothing.

The Collector was silent as they walked, and Kendra felt increasingly uneasy with it.

"Thank you for the promotion," she said.

"You earned it."

"I didn't know if I would get it," she admitted. The Collector gave her a questioning look. "After Gideon managed to escape," she explained. "I'm sorry I…"

"Of course he escaped," the Collector interjected. "He's the great Gideon Myles."

Kendra grimaced.

"Yes, well," she grumbled. "Something's been bothering me about what happened back in Blackthorne. It's probably nothing, but…"

"Go on."

"When Stanwitz and Piper found Thaddeus, he was already dead," she explained.

"He was old, or he committed suicide," the Collector reasoned. "To avoid working for me, of course."

"Maybe," she stated. "But the girl seemed to know not to trust Piper and Stanwitz. That worries me."

"She was probably taught not to trust anyone."

"Yes, but there was something at the scene that was…odd," she confessed. "I went to Thaddeus's apartment the day after he was found dead. There was a painting hung above his desk."

"And?"

"It was a live painting," she revealed.

The Collector stopped in his tracks, turning to face her.

"Really," he murmured. "Tell me about it."

"A graveyard scene," she told him. "Set at night-time. Some tombstones…and a lot of empty space in the foreground in front of them."

"You think something was drawn out," the Collector guessed. She nodded.

"The more I think about it, the more convinced I am. Thaddeus was clever, and Gideon managed to hide in plain sight in Blackthorne for almost ten years."

"You think he painted it?"

"He could have," she answered. "It wasn't his style, but he's smart enough – and good enough – to change it up."

"What are you thinking?" the Collector pressed.

"Well, when Piper found Thaddeus's body, it was already cold," she stated. "But not at all stiff. And it didn't smell."

The Collector's eyes narrowed.

"You think the body was painted," he realized. She hesitated, then nodded.

"It's possible."

"Which would mean that Thaddeus Birch is still alive," the Collector reasoned. He stood there, staring off into space, his fists clenching, then unclenching. Kendra lowered her gaze.

"I'm sorry," she muttered. "I…"

"You've done well," he interjected, turning to her. He put a hand on her shoulder. "You've done very, very well. Thank you, Kendra."

She nodded silently.

"You've more than earned your promotion," he declared, giving her a rare smile. "Come," he added, continuing forward. "I want to show you something."

He led her through the maze-like castle, every hallway and room as empty as the ones that had come before. Eventually they came to a narrow hallway, one with windows on the right and left. Kendra looked out of them, seeing a lake far below. She gazed upward, seeing another lake. A reminder that she was upside-down.

She felt butterflies flit around in her stomach.

246

The Collector led her to a narrow wooden door. It was quite plain, without a doorknob or handle. The only adornment was a human skull embedded into its center, level with the Collector's head. The skull's eye sockets were twin voids, its mouth open in an eternal scream.

"Here we are," he announced, stopping before the door. Kendra arched an eyebrow, eyeing the skull.

"Charming," she replied.

"Death is nothing to fear," he counseled. "I've learned that from paintings."

"Excuse me?"

"When you send your Familiar into a canvas, it ceases to be," he explained. "It doesn't think, or feel. It's as if the world pauses."

"And?"

"I imagine that is what death is like," the Collector mused. "Like the time before you were born. Nothingness." He eyed Kendra with his striking green eyes. "Does your Familiar fear the canvas?"

"Why would he?"

"Because it's like death," he answered. "One day, he won't be drawn out again. Each time could be his last."

Kendra had never considered this.

"Cheery thought," she grumbled.

"To be in a painting is to die," the Collector declared. "To be drawn out is to be given life." He turned to gaze at the skull in the door. "Death is nothing to fear for those who've been in the canvas. They've already experienced it."

Kendra stared at him, waiting for him to continue. It was rare that the Collector spoke, much less at length. But he said nothing more. Instead, he leaned forward, pressing his forehead against the skull's.

A dull red light appeared in each of its eye-sockets, and the door swung open.

The Collector turned to Kendra, gesturing for her to step through. She did so, passing him and going through the doorway into the room beyond.

She found herself standing on a white marble balcony. It overlooked a room of indeterminable proportions. For the room was shrouded in darkness, a single light from a lantern on the wall above the door the only illumination. The balcony was semi-circular, barely six feet long and wide. And there were no railings.

The Collector stepped onto the balcony beside her.

"What…" she began.

And then the Collector snapped his fingers, and the room was instantly bathed in a golden light.

Kendra gasped.

The balcony overlooked a room of considerable size, a large cylindrical room whose cone-shaped ceiling came to a sharp peak fifty feet above their heads. She glanced down over the edge of the balcony, and drew in a sharp breath. For the room was not a room at all, she realized; it was one of the castle's huge towers, and they were near the top of it. The floor was hundreds of feet below.

And hung upon the walls of the tower, from top to bottom and all the way around, were paintings.

These were of uniform size, and spaced at regular intervals on the curved walls of the circular tower. Each with ornate frames, and some depicting empty rooms, or barren landscapes. But most of them were paintings.

Of *people*.

Kendra stared at the paintings. Hundreds, if not thousands of them, hanging in this monstrous room. A gallery unlike any she'd ever seen.

"What is this?" she breathed, her eyes going from painting to painting. The Collector smiled.

"My collection," he answered.

"But these paintings," she protested, "…they're of…"

"People?" he inquired, raising an eyebrow at her. She nodded. "Does that bother you, Kendra?"

She swallowed, staring at the paintings. Painting people was illegal, the greatest sin a Painter could commit. Not just in the Pentad, but everywhere…in any country she could think of. To have *one* painting of a person was sacrilege, but to have *hundreds*…

"Why?" was all she could manage.

The Collector turned to gaze at the gallery.

"Why not?" he countered.

Kendra swallowed in a dry throat, choosing her words carefully. She dared not offend the Collector…and this was most certainly a test. A test of her loyalty. Of her dedication to him.

"Most laws forbid it," she reasoned. "You of course are your own authority, and can do what you like."

The Collector smirked.

"True," he replied. "And true." He gestured at the gallery. "This is power, Kendra."

"Yes sir."

"No man would let me do this," he continued. "No government would allow it. They would use their power to stop me…just as they use their power to stop you Painters from painting whatever you choose."

Kendra nodded. The Collector offered that freedom. More freedom, anyway. That was why so many came to work for him. Why *she* came to work for him.

"Did I ask for permission, Kendra?" he inquired.

"No sir."

"The weak ask," he stated. "The powerful take."

"But this…" Kendra said, gesturing at the paintings. "To what end?"

The Collector sighed, clasping his hands behind his back and lifting his gaze to the ceiling.

"Musicians tug at the strings of our hearts," he mused. "Actors play at being others for a while. Writers create worlds to get lost in. But Sculptors and Painters create *life*."

Kendra said nothing, waiting for him to continue.

"When a Sculptor creates a person, they're still a sculpture. The sculpture knows this. It can turn to stone, or whatever its original substance was. It has no memories of what came before. It knows it was created."

He paused, lowering his gaze to stare at the paintings ahead of them.

"When a *Painter* creates life, however, it is indistinguishable from other life. It can have memories or feelings given to it with a stroke of a brush. It can believe that it's real…that it was never really a painting."

He went silent.

Kendra waited for a while, but he did not continue. She fidgeted, the silence growing more and more awkward with every passing second.

"And?" she asked at last.

"That is true power," the Collector declared. "To create life." He sighed. "But it is something I cannot do." He grimaced. "I'm not a Painter, after all."

"But you have us," Kendra countered. "You have Painters to do it for you."

The Collector smiled, putting a hand on her upper back, between her shoulder blades. His touch was warm, and surprising. For as far as Kendra knew, the Collector never touched anyone.

"I do," he agreed.

"So…" Kendra stated, gazing at the countless paintings before them. "What are you going to do with all of these people?"

The Collector's smile faded.

"They're not people," he declared. Kendra blinked.

"What?"

"They're Painters."

And then the Collector shoved her forward.

Kendra cried out, stumbling toward the edge of the balcony. She fell forward, her belly striking the edge, her upper body dangling off. She felt herself sliding off, and scrambled to grab onto the balcony. But her fingers slid on the slick marble, and she fell head-first off of it.

She screamed.

Paintings whizzed past her in a dizzying blur, wind howling in her ears as she plummeted toward the floor of the tower far below. She reached for her chest, for the chest-painting that should have been there, but of course she wasn't wearing her Painter's uniform. She called out for Nightmare, her faithful Familiar, but he was stuck in a painting…and it was far too late.

The floor rose up to meet her, so quickly that she barely had time to think. To process that these were the last seconds of her life.

And the last thing she saw before struck the floor were a grid of paintings laying upon it…directly beneath her.

Then, after a life spanning one hundred years, there was oblivion.

Chapter 28

The White Castle of Havenwood was filled with grand rooms and hallways, each with a unique name etched into fine golden plaques on the doors leading to them. And they were as unique as their names, these spaces. The grand foyer had a white marble floor, huge fluted stone columns thirty feet tall supporting intricately carved arches that held up a grand, equally impressive wooden ceiling. Tall, narrow mirrors went from the floor to the ceiling on the walls to either side, giving the illusion that the room was even larger than it was. A wide stairway with a red runner led downward in the middle of the room, with two stairways going up on either side of it. Two twelve-foot-tall statues of dragon-people hybrids with their great wings spread wide flanked a set of huge wooden double-doors directly opposite the entrance.

"This," Grandpa declared, told them as they stopped to admire the view, "…is the Hall of Dragonkind!"

Bella spun in a slow circle, taking it all in.

"It's beautiful," she breathed. And it was. Everywhere she looked, there was art. In the statues, the carvings on the columns and arches, and even the ceiling. Patterns inset into the marble floor. Even the golden designs stitched into the red runners going up and down the stairwells. She suspected she could spend days studying this one room, and still not catch all the little details.

"Isn't it?" Grandpa agreed. "It's just like I wrote it," he mused, looking around with the same expression as Bella.

"I forget you've never actually seen it," Gideon said. Bella frowned at that.

"What do you mean?" she asked.

"Oh, I've never been here," Grandpa explained. "The Queen wasn't too keen on the idea."

"For fear of him not wanting to leave," Gideon clarified. Grandpa nodded absently. Then he glanced at Gideon and Bella, and looked down at himself.

"Well now I feel underdressed," he confessed, grimacing at his ratty clothes. "Do you have anything for me, Gideon?"

"Of course," Gideon replied. "I have one of your old suits in my Conclave."

He retrieved the black disc from his top hat, setting it against one wall and activating it. Grandpa stepped into the Conclave, and minutes later he returned.

"Grandpa!" Bella exclaimed.

For he was now dressed in a fine white suit, with a black dress shirt and tie. His hair, normally haphazardly springing from his head in tight curls, was now neatly arranged, and he held a leather-bound notebook in one hand and a golden pen in the other. He stuffed these into the pockets in his suit jacket, then noted Bella's slack jaw.

"You like?" he inquired, striking a heroic pose.

Bella nodded, realizing that she was grinning stupidly. Unlike his clothes at home, which had become far too big for him, this suit fit perfectly. He looked imposingly handsome…like a man of means and distinction.

"Shall we be off?" he inquired, offering his arm to Bella. She hooked her arm in his, and in Gideon's, and the two men walked her to the double-doors ahead. These opened up into a grand hallway, which led to another room, simply labeled: The Studio.

And that, Bella found, was where the people were.

The Studio was a massive room with three levels, filled to bursting with men and women painting and sculpting. The middle of the room was open, giving a spectacular view of the domed ceiling high above…a ceiling upon which a sprawling mural had been painted, like the Sistine Chapel. Some of the artists were talking amongst themselves, or critiquing each other's work, but most seemed to keep to themselves, thoroughly engrossed in their work.

But when a few noticed Grandpa, Gideon, and Bella enter the room, there was a gasp…followed by more noticing, and more gasps, until every last person on the first floor – and some on the second and third – were staring at them.

"Thaddeus Birch!" a woman cried. A few others echoed his name, and Gideon's. The artists all abandoned their work, rushing to standing before the three…and forming a crowd of formidable proportions.

"Ah, hello," Grandpa greeted, smiling at them. Gideon let go of Bella's arm, tipping his top hat. The crowd burst into excited murmuring, then outright applause. Grandpa took a rather embarrassed bow, which made the applause even louder. It carried on for quite a while, and even after it was done, the assembled artists still whispered excitedly to each other, a few even stepping up to shake Grandpa's hand. This led to a line forming for *everyone* to shake his hand, which Grandpa did with his customary warmth and grace.

Bella could only stare, hardly recognizing him. She thought back to what he'd said, after she'd thought him crazy for being paranoid about Reynolds and Stanwitz.

Maybe one day you'll get to see me like I was.

Her eyes became moist, and she wiped them with the back of her sleeve. Which, given that her forearms were painted, plunged her face into that painting. She jerked her head back, blinking at the strange, pulsing sensation she'd experienced.

"This may be a while," Gideon warned, leaning toward Bella. "We can explore a bit if you like."

"Love to," she agreed. "Is that okay, Grandpa?" she asked, tapping on his shoulder. He turned to her.

"Hmm?"

"Gideon wanted to show me around."

"Oh yes," Grandpa agreed. "This may be a while."

Gideon led her through the crowd, and while many of the Painters and Sculptors in line reached out to welcome Gideon back, most were so focused on Grandpa that they didn't really notice.

This allowed Gideon to show Bella around the room. There were all sorts of paintings, of a huge variety of things. Some of the artists seemed obsessed with painting food, while others painted spectacular clothes. Still others painted animals, and a few painted more fantastical things, such as goblin-like creatures, fairies, and the like. But for some reason, Bella found herself drawn to the food…probably because she hadn't eaten in a while.

"Havenwood has its own food supply," Gideon stated, noticing the direction of her gaze. "The huge mushrooms in the mushroom forest have big caps that explode on occasion, sending big spores falling all over the kingdom. They're quite tasty, actually."

"Ew," Bella replied, making a face.

"It does get old eating them after a while," Gideon agreed. "Luckily we have a few Painters that love painting food."

"And the clothes?" she asked, gesturing at a painting filling with dresses of various kinds.

"Havenwood has Painters interested in all sorts of different things," Gideon replied. "No one wants for anything, I assure you. Anything material, that is."

"You said there's no king or queen?" Bella inquired.

"Not here," he answered. "It…takes a little explaining. Come, let me show you."

Gideon led her out of The Studio and back into the Hall of Dragonkind, stopping before the rightmost dragon statue.

"This is King Draco of the Dragonkind," he explained, gesturing at the statue. "And this is Queen Vecta. They are the rulers of Havenwood…and of all the Dragonkind."

"The Dragonkind?"

"Dragon people," Gideon explained. "The rightful citizens of Havenwood."

"But…" Bella replied, looking about the empty room. "Where are they?" Gideon smiled, gesturing at the wall to the left.

"See for yourself."

Bella frowned, but walked dutifully up to the wall. It had wooden panels, with floor-to-ceiling mirrors spaced at regular intervals. She glanced at Gideon.

"I don't get it," she admitted.

"It takes a bit of reflection before you figure it out," Gideon admitted.

Bella raised an eyebrow, turning back to face the wall. She glanced at the mirror, then blinked, leaning in closer.

And gasped.

For while the room was utterly empty save for themselves, in the mirror's reflection, she saw a bustling crowd of people. Well, sort-of-people. They had bodies like people, but with elegant dragon-wings, and fine scales instead of skin.

And in the reflection, she spotted a young girl-dragon-person leaning in, staring through the mirror right back at her.

"Oh!" Bella gasped, taking a step back. Gideon chuckled.

"The Dragonkind live in the Plane of Reflection," he explained. They live in Havenwood's reflection."

"There was a girl," Bella stated. "She was staring right at me!"

"We can only see them in reflections," Gideon replied. "And they can only see us that way. We live in two different planes of existence.

"So they're really…there?"

"Oh yes," Gideon confirmed. "They exist. I've spent quite a few days studying them. A fascinating culture."

"But they can't ever come here?"

"Not to my knowledge," Gideon confirmed. "The Pentad never would have approved Thaddeus's book if he'd created a race of creatures that could potentially threaten them. So Thaddeus, genius that he is, made them live in the Plane of Reflection."

Bella frowned.

"The Pentad had to approve his book?"

"All of them," Gideon replied. "The Pentad controls all art forms. Any that could represent a threat to the kingdom are rejected. That includes music, sculptures, paintings, and especially books from Writers as powerful as Thaddeus."

"What about acting?" Bella inquired. "Isn't that one of the five magic arts?"

"You have a good memory," Gideon stated approvingly. "Yes it is. It is forbidden to emulate a government official, or a physician, and so forth. And acting without a license is a criminal offense."

Bella nodded, peering into the mirror again. The Dragonkind girl had moved on, but the crowd of Dragonkind remained.

"All created by a book," she murmured, shaking her head.

"Your grandfather is a truly gifted man."

"I know," she agreed. "His bedtime stories were epic. I always wondered why he wasn't a more successful writer."

"And now you know."

She turned away from the mirror, facing Gideon.

"So…something's been bothering me," she confessed. "When you saved Grandpa, and pulled his lookalike from the painting to trick Stanwitz and Reynolds into thinking he was dead…why didn't you get me?"

"Pardon?"

"You could've saved me then," she reasoned. "And pulled me out of the book."

"That was the plan," Gideon replied. "After your grandfather pulled out his 'corpse,' we both read our copies of the book to return to the library at Blackthorne. I put Thaddeus in the coffin and stored him in the painting, but I was caught by some of the guards and had to…dispose of them."

"You killed them?"

"No, I tossed them into some paintings," he corrected. Bella frowned, recalling the painting with the broken glass case she'd seen, the one with the guard appearing to fly backward through the air.

"Oh."

"I searched for the book afterward, but it wasn't where I'd left it. The bounty hunters must have taken it somewhere else before they'd gotten lost in the book. I looked for it everywhere…but didn't find it until the next day, when Reynolds and Kendra came to the library and got lost in it. I followed after them. Followed you, actually, to the library. I saw you open the book, and returned to Blackthorne right before you did."

"Thanks for trying," she said.

"You're welcome."

"So…now what do we do?" she asked, looking around.

"Well, we *could* go back to The Studio and mingle with Thaddeus's adoring fans," Gideon stated. "But I'm not much for crowds, to be honest."

"Me neither," Bella confessed.

"And I've just escaped one," a voice called out from behind. They turned, seeing none other than Grandpa approaching them.

"Thaddeus," Gideon greeted. "I was just showing Bella the Plane of Reflection, and the Dragonkind."

"Ah yes," Grandpa stated. "A perfect segue into our next item of business. Come on, let's go to lunch and we'll talk about it."

"Ooo, I'm starving," Bella replied, her stomach grumbling.

"Naturally," Grandpa quipped. "You're an artist."

"And what exactly is our next item of business?" Gideon inquired. Grandpa gave him a mischievous grin.

256

"Why revenge, of course."

$$* * *$$

Revenge, it appeared, was a dish best-served cold.

Literally, in fact. For Gideon and Bella filled Grandpa in on everything that'd happened while he was stuck in the painting…and what had occurred over the last ten years with the Collector and the Pentad. They did so over a dessert of fine chocolate and vanilla ice cream, after a wonderful lunch. Grandpa had taken them to one of the restaurants in Havenwood's popular downtown district, a small establishment called The Painted Feast. Quite literally downtown, as it was down the mountain a ways. The restaurant itself was quite unusual. The "chef" was actually a Painter, and would take requests from patrons, then paint their meals in real time, drawing them out to be consumed. Bella had chosen a meal of chicken with caramelized onions and peppers, as had Grandpa.

It was, she found, absolutely scrumptious.

After scarfing up their meals, everyone finished their desserts, and they left the restaurant, taking a leisurely stroll back home. It was then that Grandpa took the opportunity to let them in on his plan.

"The Collector is consolidating power," he began. "And I suspect the Pentad will not act with sufficient urgency to defeat him."

"The Pentad has far more resources," Gideon pointed out.

"Then why haven't they defeated him?" Grandpa inquired.

"He wasn't considered much of a threat until he took Blackthorne," Gideon answered. "And the Pentad was preoccupied with winning their war with Epirus."

"That's all well and good," Grandpa replied. "But even if General Craven managed to secure Blackthorne, the damage is already done."

"How so?" Gideon inquired.

"You say the Collector was cataloging the various magic items in the paintings in Blackthorne," Grandpa answered. "And in the books there. Why do you suppose he was doing that?"

"To find weapons for his army," Gideon replied.

"Did he ever ship those items out of Blackthorne?"

"Not to my knowledge," Gideon answered. "He had plenty of paintings taken out of the library, but I assume it was for organization purposes. The Pentad's army sat at the base of the mountain for years…"

"…to prevent the Collector from establishing a route to bring those paintings and books back to him, yes," Grandpa finished. "And yet the Collector never attempted to destroy that army. Never used all of Blackthorne's wonderful paintings against the Pentad."

"What are you saying?" Gideon asked.

"The Collector had to know that, even if he took Blackthorne, the Pentad would ensure it was useless to him. But he still took it."

"Perhaps to get to you," Gideon proposed.

"Ha!" Grandpa scoffed. "Unlikely. How many bounty hunters did he send after me?" Gideon grimaced.

"Not many," he conceded.

"So he had to be after Blackthorne's resources," Grandpa deduced. "And if he knew he wouldn't be able to get those resources down the mountain and through the Pentad's army…"

"…then he must have found another way to ship them," Gideon realized, his eyes widening. "A magical path in and out of Blackthorne."

"Precisely," Grandpa stated with a smile.

"But the only path to Blackthorne was the magic hallway leading to Centrum," Gideon protested. Bella frowned.

"Centrum?"

"The capitol city of the Pentad," Gideon explained. "The Pentad destroyed that hallway to stop the Collector and his armies from getting to the palace."

"True," Grandpa agreed.

"And Blackthorne has magic that prevents anyone else from making another path to it," Gideon continued.

"I know," Grandpa agreed. "I wrote it myself."

"What do you mean by 'path?'" Bella inquired.

"Writers can create magical links between places in this world," Grandpa explained. "For example, I wrote that there was a hallway in the armory in Centrum that leads to a hallway in Blackthorne…even though they're nearly a thousand miles apart."

"Oh."

"I also wrote that no new links to Blackthorne could be created. Very powerful magic indeed…and no other Writer alive could

258

break that magic. Which means the Collector must have discovered a path that already existed."

Gideon frowned at this, rubbing his chin thoughtfully.

"If he did," he replied, "...then all of those books and paintings he had taken out of the library..."

"...are currently in his possession," Grandpa confirmed.

"Which means the Pentad is in deep trouble," Gideon realized.

"I don't get it," Bella interjected. They both turned to her. "Why didn't the Pentad just take Blackthorne back years ago? Why wait until now to do it?"

"Because they were...otherwise occupied," Gideon answered. "At the time, the Pentad was at war with another country...the great nation of Epirus."

"Oh, right," Bella remembered. General Craven had mentioned something about that.

"Divide and conqueror," Grandpa piped in.

"And they *did* try at first, with smaller forces," Gideon continued. "But the Collector himself was there at the time, and defeated them." He sighed. "It took ten years for the Pentad to win their war with Epirus, so they would have the ability to send Craven himself to lead the charge against Blackthorne."

"And the Collector must have known that the war was nearly won," Grandpa opined. "So of course he would have prepared for the full force of the Pentad's armies."

"By draining Blackthorne of its most valuable resources, then allowing it to be retaken," Gideon deduced. "But even *if* the Collector has all the power of Blackthorne, he still doesn't stand a chance against the full might of the Pentad's military."

"If they can find him," Grandpa countered.

"No one knows where he is?" Bella asked. Grandpa and Gideon shook their heads. "Oh."

"I tried to figure out his location myself, while I was undercover," Gideon revealed. "Apparently only his highest-ranking generals and Painters know where he is." His eyes widened then. "Like Kendra," he realized, snapping his fingers. "If Craven managed to capture her..."

"...then the Pentad might get the location from her," Grandpa concluded.

"If so, the Pentad will simply send its armies to defeat him," Gideon pointed out. "Which means *we* don't need to do anything."

"Except we do," Grandpa retorted. Gideon frowned, clearly not understanding. "If the Pentad takes the Collector alive, that could be…problematic for you, Gideon."

The color drained from Gideon's face.

"Ah," he muttered.

"What?" Bella asked. "Why?"

Grandpa glanced at Gideon.

"I take it that means you haven't told her," Grandpa deduced. They'd reached the mouth of the Water Dragon cave by then, and Bella stopped, turning to eye Gideon suspiciously. Both men stopped with her.

"Told me what?" she pressed.

Grandpa gave Gideon a look, and Gideon grimaced.

"I don't think this is the time," he countered.

"You know very well the damage secrets can do," Grandpa scolded. "You've let this one rot inside of you for far too long, Gideon. It's time you told Bella the truth."

"Thaddeus…"

Grandpa crossed his arms over his chest, glaring at Gideon.

"If you don't tell her," he declared, "…I'll tell her myself."

Gideon sighed, his shoulders slumping. Then he turned to Bella.

"Remember the story I told you about my son Xander?" he asked.

"The one who died," she recalled.

"That's right," Gideon confirmed. "My wife left me. My son was dead. I…was not in a good place."

He swallowed visibly, then cleared his throat.

"I stayed in the house Xander had been born in. I kept his room just as it was the day he died. But…I went through dark times, Bella. I fell apart. Started…drinking."

He rubbed his hands together, taking a deep breath in.

"And then I did the only thing I knew how to do to express myself," he continued. "I wanted to preserve my memory of Xander, the way I remembered him being. So I…painted him."

Bella blinked.

"I thought…"

"It's illegal, yes," Gideon interjected. "I had every intention of destroying the painting after it was done. All I wanted to do was express myself, to tell make sense of how he died. But when I saw him there on the canvas, looking so real…reaching out for help, pleading for me to save him…well…"

"You signed the painting," she realized with a gasp. "You drew him out!"

Gideon nodded.

"At first it was wonderful," he confessed. "It was like Xander was back from the dead, like he'd never died at all. He was *exactly* like Xander, in every way. It was…uncanny." He sighed. "I treated him like my son. I told him he *was* my son. That he'd just suffered a head injury, and that's why he couldn't remember things."

Bella put a hand to her mouth, her eyes widening further.

"But as he grew older, he began to question me. He tried to paint, but he couldn't feel the Flow. He demanded to know why. I told him it was because of his injury, but he didn't believe me. And one day, he found his painting."

"Oh god," Bella breathed.

"He was furious," Gideon continued bitterly. "He called me a liar. And he was right, Bella. I *was* a liar. I told him he was Xander, and he believed it. So when he found out his whole life was a lie, he…left."

"What happened?" she asked.

"Well, I didn't hear from him for a long, long time," Gideon confessed. "Decades, in fact. I met your mother, and we settled down in Havenwood and had you."

He closed his eyes, rubbing his face wearily. Then he lifted his gaze to Bella.

"And then I heard that a man in a black suit, wielding a glowing silver blade had attacked Blackthorne. The same suit and sword I'd made for…the boy I'd painted, so that nothing could harm him again."

Bella gasped in horror.

"You're saying you…"

"Made the Collector, yes," Gideon confirmed. "I created the man who murdered your mother. The man who hunted you and Thaddeus down." His eyes grew moist, his lower lip trembling. "Your mother died because I couldn't let go of my son. She died because of me."

Chapter 29

Piper sat on the bench in the waiting room before the Collector's office, his right knee bouncing up and down rapidly. He chewed at his lip, staring at the door, then glancing at Miss Savage, who was doing some paperwork at her desk. The Collector had been making him wait for nearly an hour...just like he had two days ago. He'd ended up not seeing Piper...and they'd rescheduled to today.

"How long is this gonna take?" he asked her. She glanced up from her work.

"Be patient," she replied. "The Collector is a busy man."

"That's what you said the last time," he retorted. She didn't respond, continuing her paperwork. Piper sat there for a moment longer, then stood up, pacing back and forth in front of the bench.

"It's been an hour," he insisted.

"The Collector is still in Castle Over," she explained.

"So is my wife," Piper replied. "And I haven't seen her in five days!"

"I'm sure she's busy too," Miss Savage reassured.

Piper grimaced, continuing to pace. He hadn't seen Kendra since she'd been promoted five days ago. And it'd been *years* since they'd been apart for that long. Kendra had to know how much he missed her.

"I just want to see her," Piper grumbled. "Even if it's just for lunch."

"I understand," Miss Savage replied. She paused then. "Would a little music help while you wait?"

"No, I don't want any damn music," Piper shot back. The last thing he wanted was some Musician to mess with his head. "I want my damn wife."

"You have to be patient," she insisted. "Please sit down."

Piper glared at her, but did as he was told, plopping himself down on the bench and putting his hands between his knees. He fidgeted, eyeing Miss Savage suspiciously. There was something *off* about her. Why a Musician of her caliber would settle for being the Collector's secretary was beyond him.

If Kendra were here, she would've told him he was just being paranoid.

Of course I am, he grumbled to himself. *Look who I'm dealing with.*

"Can you check?" he pressed.

Miss Savage sighed, pushing her chair back from her desk, then standing and walking to the Collector's door. She knocked, and moments later, cracked open the door.

Then shut it.

"He's still not back from Castle Over," she declared, giving him an apologetic look. "I'm afraid he has another appointment soon. You'll have to reschedule."

"Reschedule?" Piper blurted out incredulously, bolting up from his seat. "I've been…"

"…very patient, yes," Miss Savage interjected. She walked back to her desk, sitting down. "I have an appointment available next week, at six o'clock in the evening. Would that work for you?"

Piper stared at her, his fists clenched at his sides. He took a deep breath in, opening his hands and giving her the least sincere smile he could manage.

"That would be just lovely," he muttered.

"Would you like me to…" she began, but Piper was already storming out of the waiting room. She watched him go, then stood again, walking to the Collector's door and opening it. She stepped through into his office, seeing him at his desk.

"The Actor is going to be a problem," she warned. The Collector didn't even glance up at her.

"Then solve him," he replied.

＊ ＊ ＊

The Collector made his way through the labyrinth-like halls of Castle Under, the heels of his magical boots *clicking* on the marble floors. He'd received word that Simon had completed his painting…a feat he still didn't fully believe was possible in such a short period of time. Still, he found himself contemplating Kendra's last conversation with him more than what Simon may or may not have painted.

Thaddeus Birch may be alive.

No, not may be. *Was.*

It all made perfect sense. Gideon was far too clever to allow Thaddeus to die of old age within the book. The Painter could easily have placed Thaddeus in a canvas, touched up his features, and made him younger again. No, Thaddeus could *not* have died of old age. It was foolish to think so.

Thaddeus Birch is alive!

The thought filled him with unease.

He had no doubt that the legendary Writer was already in Havenwood, with Gideon and the girl. And like a fool he'd let Gideon go, thinking Gideon was helpless against him.

Gideon was, but Thaddeus most certainly was not.

The Writer was dangerous. Lethal. Armed with ink and paper, he could topple the Collector with a single manuscript. The Pentad would see to its distribution. Every pair of eyeballs that could read in the vast kingdom would be commanded to do so.

You're a fool, he told himself.

For the first time in years, the Collector knew fear.

He tried to push his worries aside, to focus on the task at hand as he made his way to Simon's huge studio. After meeting with the boy, he would have to go back to his office and make use of Miss Savage's talents. He would need all the inspiration she could muster to think his way out of this.

No one knows where you live, he reminded himself. And the Pentad – and Thaddeus – couldn't fight what they couldn't find. But he rejected the thought immediately, knowing that Thaddeus could create something that would locate him.

He made it to the studio at last, passing through the doorway into the massive room beyond. Simon was standing there a few stories below, all of the lights in the room dimmed, cloaking the walls in darkness. The Collector made his way down to the boy's side.

"Good afternoon Simon," he greeted. Then he lifted his gaze to the wall before them. It was shrouded in darkness, like the rest of the room. A canvas larger than any the Collector had ever seen. Five stories high and a hundred feet across, it was impossible to imagine a Painter being able to fill it in a year, much less in a month.

But Simon was no ordinary Painter.

"Good morning sir," Simon replied. "Ready?"

The Collector nodded.

Simon reached into his pants pocket, pulling out a small crystal sphere. With a word, it lit up…and so did the rest of the lanterns in the studio.

The Collector blinked…and then his eyes widened.

The boy had filled every last inch of the canvas with paint, working day and night like a man possessed, barely eating. He looked gaunt, even more so than he had when the Collector had first met him. But there was a brightness in his eyes that the Collector had never seen before. And the boy's shoulders were set back a little more, his back straighter. And the painting!

It was glorious.

It was all the Collector could do to stop himself from gaping at Simon's creation. To maintain the illusion of calmness, of nonchalance. But as he gazed at the boy's work, he found himself experiencing an emotion he hadn't felt in a long, long time.

Awe.

It was, like Simon's previous work, filled with strange humanoid creatures with skin that looked like it had been shattered and glued back together. But these creatures had black skin, not porcelain, and red-hot flames flickered in their eye-sockets. And there were literally thousands of them, an army of pitch-black warriors with clawed hands and feet. They sprinted across a barren, rocky landscape, some of them in the process of breaking apart in pieces – like the Doppelganger had – and others having done so completely. Millions of black fragments rose through the air, coalescing into a truly enormous creature, one that took up more than half of the gigantic canvas.

A still-forming creature made of millions of tiny fragments of the black soldiers, a nightmarish beast resembling them. But it was far more muscular, and had a rather long neck and massive jaws with sharp teeth. It lunged forward on all fours...or rather, all eights. For it had three pairs of arms, its giant hands armed with razor-sharp claws...and flames burst from its eye-sockets and its gaping maw, an inner fire that gave it life.

Dust and rocks flew from the violence of its passage, the very earth below it torn to shreds by its power.

The Collector stared at it for a long moment, saying nothing. Taking it all in.

And Simon stood at his side, his eyes wide and dark, gleaming in the light of the magical lanterns all around the room.

The magnificent creature seemed to leap from the page, the paint practically jumping off the canvas. The sign of a masterwork, of a painting so powerful, so imbued with the Flow that it could barely be contained.

A painting that screamed to be released. That demanded to be given life.

Goosebumps rose on the Collector's skin, and he was glad for his fine black suit, so that Simon would not witness them. He collected himself, then turned to Simon, allowing himself to smile.

"Well done Simon," he congratulated. "A most impressive work."

"Thank you sir," Simon replied. The boy looked up to him, a rare smile on his pale lips. The Collector noted the boy's arms...and the lack of fresh cuts on his forearms. Something within Simon had changed. Allowed to be himself, he was finally starting to heal.

A process the Collector knew all-too-well.

His own adolescence came back to him. The dark years after leaving his father. After he'd learned the horrible truth about himself. It'd taken him years to heal. To accept the truth about who and what he was. And in accepting it, he'd given himself permission to be happy. To be wholly himself, without apology. Without guilt.

He returned his gaze to Simon's painting, admiring the boy's work.

"What do you call it, Simon?" he inquired.

"Legion," Simon answered.

"I want you to draw it out, Simon," the Collector stated. "And then we'll have dinner."

Simon blinked.

266

"We?"

"Yes Simon," the Collector confirmed. "Just you and me. My chef will make you a meal the likes of which you've never experienced."

"Thank you sir," Simon murmured, lowering his gaze. The Collector paused, resisting the sudden urge to put a hand on the boy's frail shoulder. A paternalistic urge that both surprised and irked him.

An urge he couldn't afford to entertain.

"I'd say you've earned it," he stated, turning to gaze at the painting once more.

Legion, he thought. A good name.

And that, he knew as he marveled at the sheer act of creation before him, was an understatement. And while any other Painter would have considered a mere dinner with him to be a measly compensation for such an enormously valuable work of art, the Collector suspected that, for Simon, it would be more than enough.

"Draw it out Simon," he repeated, a smile curling his lips. "I have something very special in mind for it."

Chapter 30

The walk down the long, winding tunnel to Mom's estate was a troubled one. Neither Gideon nor Grandpa said a thing as they walked, and neither did Bella. She stared at her feet, following numbly behind the two men as the led her deep into the bowels of Dragon's Peak. By the time they reached the front gate of the estate, Bella's mind was still reeling from the story Gideon had told her. Without a word, she walked through the lobby, up the stairs, and went into her bedroom, closing – and locking – her door.

She curled up on her bed then, staring at the wall.

Bella half-expected one of the men to come and knock on her door, but they didn't.

Your mother died because of me.

She closed her eyes, burying her face in her pillow, and wept.

* * *

Bella didn't come out of her bedroom for hours, escaping into the merciful embrace of sleep. She was awoken some time later by a strange scratching at her door. At first she was alarmed, until she saw a hint of a big, furry paw slide under the door. She got up, unlocking the door and cracking it open.

It was Myko, of course.

The great silver wolf nuzzled her with his wet nose, then hopped on the bed, laying down in a "C" shape. Bella couldn't help but smile, and laid down in the bed, letting herself be the little spoon. He draped one soft, heavy paw over her side, burying his head her in curly hair.

And just laid there with her.

For some reason, this made Bella cry all over again, ugly sobs wracking her body. Around anyone else, she would have felt ashamed, but with Myko it was okay. With Myko, *everything* was okay.

And when she was done – when no more tears would come – she stroked his great big paw, feeling his warmth all around her.

"Is this what we used to do?" she asked. "When I was little?"

Myko *wuffed*.

Bella smiled, then swallowed past a sudden lump in her throat.

"I'm sorry I didn't remember you."

He gave her a little squeeze with his paw.

"Is…Gideon a good guy?" she asked. Another squeeze. "You're not just saying that 'cause he made you, right?"

Myko snorted, blowing her hair askew. She smiled, brushing curling strands of it away from her face.

"So my step-brother is dead, his painting killed my mother, my mother was a fugitive making illegal paintings for the black market, both my parents are basically criminals, and my thousand-year-old-Grandpa knew it all along and never told me."

No response from Myko.

"Anything else I should know, Myko?" she asked, turning around to look at him. He gave her a big old kiss, slobbering all over her cheek. She squealed, then laughed, kissing him on the nose.

"I love you too Myko."

He got up then, shaking as if he'd just gotten out of a pond, then hopping off the bed and landing with a loud *thump* on the floor. He went to the door then, turning about and staring at her.

Another *wuff*.

Bella took a deep breath in, then slid off the bed.

"Okay Myko."

He led her downstairs, and they went into the lobby, which was deserted. She paused, her eyes drawn to the golden statue holding the sword, standing on its pedestal. It looked a lot like her, but older. And more muscular, and fierce.

"Is that her?" she asked.

Myko nodded.

She heard footsteps approaching, and Gideon and Grandpa came through the front entrance of the mansion, stopping when they spotted her. They both stared at her, saying nothing.

"Hey," she muttered.

"Hey," they both said in unison.

"What else are you hiding from me?" she demanded. Gideon shook his head.

"No more secrets," he answered. "Anything else you want to know, we'll tell you."

"Promise?"

"Promise."

She stared at him for a long moment, her fists clenched at her sides.

"I'm angry with you," she confessed. "I'm *pissed*." She turned to Grandpa. "At both of you."

Grandpa blinked in confusion.

"You both knew the truth," she accused. "You *both* kept this from me." Grandpa opened his mouth to respond, but Bella cut him off. "I don't care what your reasons were. I don't care if they were good reasons. You kept things from me, and I'm allowed to be upset about it."

"You are," Gideon agreed.

Bella put her hands on her hips, glaring at both of them.

"No more dark secrets," she ordered. "No more lies."

Both men nodded, looking absolutely miserable. Bella sighed, stepping forward and hugging Grandpa.

"You're lucky I love you so much," she grumbled. He chuckled, giving her a squeeze back.

"Everything I did, I did for you, sweetheart," he promised. She smiled, pulling back from him.

"I know, Grandpa."

She turned to Gideon then, her smile fading.

"And you," she groused. "Come here."

He paused, then approached her cautiously. She opened her arms, stepping in and embracing him. He stiffened, then relaxed, embracing her back.

"You suck," she whispered in his ear.

She gave him a squeeze, then disengaged from him.

"I suppose I deserve that," he admitted.

"You both suck," she stated. "But you also spent ten years trying to save me." She sighed, turning to Grandpa. "You were the best grandpa I could've ever asked for," she stated. Then she turned to Gideon. "And you risked your life for me, and saved *my* life."

Both men stood there, saying nothing.

"No more secrets," she insisted. "If we're going to be a family, we need to be honest with each other from now on. Even if it hurts." She paused. "*Especially* if it hurts."

Gideon nodded.

"Alright Bella," he agreed.

"You have my word," Grandpa declared.

"We have to make this right," Bella stated. "We can't let the Collector get away with this."

"He can't hurt us now," Gideon countered. "We're safe in Havenwood."

"But other people aren't," she retorted. "And if he did this to us, he'll do it to others."

"Bella…" Gideon began.

"You can stop him Gideon," she insisted. "You're powerful enough to do it."

"The Pentad will take care of it," Gideon argued.

"Perhaps," Grandpa countered. "Perhaps not. But I for one won't wait for the Pentad to find and defeat the Collector."

"Why not?" Gideon asked.

"Because if you let other people clean up the mess you made, you'll carry that guilt with you for the rest of your life," Grandpa declared. "The only way for you to heal your heart is to set things right yourself…with my help, of course. Otherwise you'll continue telling yourself the same old story."

"What story?" Gideon asked.

"That you're the villain and your son's the victim," Grandpa answered. "And that villains don't deserve to be heroes."

Gideon grimaced, crossing his arms over his chest.

"And how do you plan on helping?" he pressed. Grandpa gave a mischievous smile, his eyes twinkling.

"I," he replied, "…am going to write a book."

271

After a robust dinner – drawn out from a few paintings in Mom's kitchen storeroom – everyone went straight for one of the living rooms on the first floor, and Grandpa plopped himself down on a U-shaped couch before a fireplace there, letting out a big sigh.

"I don't know about you," he said wearily, "…but I could use a nap."

"I second that," Gideon agreed.

"Third," Bella piped in.

"Oh ho, not you," Grandpa retorted. "You've still got your youth, young lady. You shouldn't be napping…you should be painting."

Bella sighed, her shoulders slumping.

"Grandpa…"

"Go on," Grandpa urged, waving her away. "Go paint while us old men nap." He stretched his arms out then, closing his eyes. And in moments, he was fast asleep.

"I've always envied your family's ability to sleep," Gideon mused.

"Yeah," she grumbled. "Grandpa said Mom was the same way."

"Oh, she was a glorious napper."

"Can I look around the mansion for a little bit?" she inquired.

"Go ahead," he replied. "Feel free to explore. I'll find you after I get a few things from my Conclave for Thaddeus."

Bella nodded. Grandpa had requested a desk, pens, and paper for the book he intended on writing. A sequel to the one that'd created Havenwood. As it turned out, Grandpa had been spending all those years slaving over his notebooks in the apartment coming up with ideas for this newest book, among others. It turned out that, just as you couldn't put a painting inside of a painting, you also couldn't write a magical book within a magical book. Grandpa had to wait until he'd been freed before he could write the sequel.

Gideon retrieved the black disc from his top hat, following her into the lobby of the mansion, then placing the disc on the wall and activating the portal. He stepped through, vanishing from sight.

"All right," she stated, looking around. She spotted Animus hovering nearby. "So…where should I go first?" she asked it.

Animus was all-too eager to lead Bella on a tour through the mansion, flowing from room to room. While Castle Havenwood was bright and cheerful, filled with whimsy and bustling with activity, Mom's house was dark and mysterious…and best of all, quiet. Bella felt quite at home there, in the rooms cast in pale lantern-light, the paintings on the walls ranging from the bizarre to the downright frightening. Animus showed her around each room, even floating up to various items of interest to draw Bella's attention to them.

The place was a mega-mansion, with more rooms than she could count. Bedrooms and dining rooms, kitchens and bathrooms. Cleverly, toilets had paintings at the bottom instead of water, and one's business simply passed through into the canvas. No muss, no fuss, no smell…as she soon discovered. Just crappy paintings.

There was even what appeared to be a large armory, with suits of armor and swords and such stored in paintings stacked against the walls. There were paintings everywhere, actually. Hanging on the walls, stacked on shelves, stuffed in closets. And they were all magnificent. Weird, dark, and often ugly…and wonderful.

There were paintings of corpses and zombies and ghouls, ghosts and dark beings made of shadow that could only move *within* shadows. There were tentacled things and things with claws, oozes and goo, guts and rot. Everything that any respectable person would avoid, Mom had painted. Every one of humanity's fears manifested on canvas for Bella to discover.

When at last Gideon emerged from his Conclave and found her, Bella was studying one of the paintings in the armory, of a pale creature with the head and torso of a man and the body of a pale maggot. Like a twisted centaur.

"What do you think?" he inquired, stopping at her side.

"She was strange," Bella replied. "Like me."

"That she was," Gideon agreed.

Bella put the painting back with the others stacked against the wall, then turned to face him.

"Why did she live…here?" she asked.

"You mean why didn't she live with the others outside?" Gideon inquired. Bella nodded. "That's…complicated," Gideon admitted. "You see, not everyone appreciated your mother's work."

"Mine neither," she admitted, thinking back to the skeletal dragon she'd drawn so many times at school.

"Unfortunately the Pentad was one of them," Gideon continued. "I started teaching your mother when she was thirteen, in a studio near the palace. She was talented, and she painted like...this," Gideon explained, gesturing at the paintings. "She was licensed, of course...she was Thaddeus's daughter, after all...but she kept wanting to paint paintings that the Pentad refused to allow."

"Like these," Bella guessed.

"Right. And your mother, well, to say she was stubborn is a gross understatement," Gideon continued. "She refused to listen to the Pentad – and me – and painted what she wanted in secret. In a Conclave she'd created without anyone knowing."

"What happened?"

"Well, your mother and Thaddeus had a falling out," Gideon continued. "She...well, let's just say she made friends with people your grandfather didn't approve of. They argued, and she left."

"She ran away from home?"

"She did," Gideon confirmed. "She ended up living in a city called the Twin Spires with these...friends for ten or so years. Painted for them, actually. Illegal paintings that she sold on the black market. It made her a lot of money, money she used to buy her estate. But eventually the Pentad discovered her paintings, and...well..."

"Well what?" Bella pressed.

"The Pentad got a warrant for her arrest. They interrogated Thaddeus to find out where she was, but Thaddeus didn't know. They thought he was trying to obstruct their investigation, but he was too valuable to the Pentad to prosecute, so they forced him to stay in Blackthorne, in a sort of house-arrest. That's how the Collector knew Thaddeus was there."

"Oh my god..."

"Then the Pentad sent bounty hunters to find your mother and take her in for sentencing."

"Sentencing?"

"For...hanging," Gideon clarified with a grimace. Bella's eyes widened, and she put a hand to her mouth.

"They *hang* people? For painting things?"

"Or cut their hands off," Gideon confirmed, showing her the stump of his right hand.

"Is that what they did to you?"

"Not the Pentad," Gideon replied. "The Collector's men. I was hired to retrieve useful objects from paintings and catalog their properties, not to paint. If I wanted to work for them, I had to agree to have my dominant hand amputated."

"But I've seen you paint perfectly with your left hand," she pointed out. He winked.

"I'm ambidextrous."

"Ah."

"They didn't want me to paint while I was there, of course. Not until I completed ten years of loyal service. Protection against double-agents, you see. Only Kendra was allowed to paint there."

"So you let them paint your hand off?" Bella asked.

"Ah, no," he replied ruefully. "They did it the old-fashioned way."

Bella's eyes widened in horror.

"You had your hand cut off for…"

"For you," he confirmed. "And for your grandfather, yes."

Bella swallowed with some difficulty.

"Thank you," she mumbled.

"You're my daughter."

She leaned in, giving him a hug. Then she pulled away.

"You should get someone here to paint it back on," she stated, gesturing at his stump. He grimaced.

"Ah, no," he replied. "That's quite alright."

"But…"

"It…reminds me of my mistakes," he explained. "With your mother gone, I can never be whole again."

"Gideon…"

"But enough talking," he interrupted. "It's time we took your painting to the next level. Come on," he added. "…time to paint!"

Chapter 31

Long after the sun had gone to bed beneath the horizon, plunging the world into darkness and lulling the denizens of the Castle Under to sleep, Piper laid awake in his own bed, staring up at the ceiling. It was a large bed, fit for two. And until Kendra had gotten her promotion, vanishing in Castle Over without a trace, two had always occupied it.

He rolled onto his side, staring out of the small window of his small room on the second floor of the castle. There was only blackness beyond, the stars hidden behind a thick carpet of gray clouds. To the right of the window was an old wooden door leading to the long hallway of the living quarters, the eastern wing of the castle that was devoted to housing the Collector's artists.

Piper rolled onto his back again, reaching up to pick at his lip. *Where the hell is she?*

Other Painters had been promoted. Plenty of them. Usually after having been with the Collector for years. After creating lots of paintings for the man. Then they were taken upstairs to the mirrored castle in the sky.

And now that Piper thought about it, he'd never seen a single one of them again.

Promoted Painters weren't allowed to work with the Painters in Castle Under, of course. They were probably working on secret projects, ones the Collector didn't want those of questionable loyalty to know about. It made sense to segregate them, but Kendra would never agree to be separated from Piper for so long.

It didn't make any sense.

Piper sighed, fidgeting in bed. That awful corner of his mind, the one that always assumed the worst – kicked into gear, a paranoid voice that whispered terrifying thoughts in his ear.

She's dead, it told him. *They all are.*

He squeezed his eyes shut, willing the dark thoughts to go away. *He killed them all.*

"Shut up," he muttered to himself, rolling onto his side again, this time away from the window. He closed his eyes, willing himself to go to sleep…and knowing that in doing so, he was virtually guaranteed not to. Then he heard a *creak.*

Piper's eyes snapped open.

He heard another *creak*, this time lasting much longer than the first. As if a door had been cracked open, then swung open all the way after someone had peered through.

Piper's heart pounded in his chest, and he closed his eyes, straining his ears. He heard nothing more, but knew damn well that didn't mean anything. Whoever was in his room – if there *was* someone in his room – could be wearing magical boots that made no sound. Or they could be levitating above the floor.

There's no one here, he told himself. *It's just your imagination.*

He felt a presence in the room, imagined dark eyes staring at him from the door.

He killed them all, the dark thoughts whispered. *And now he's going to kill you.*

Piper opened his eyes, forcing himself to imagine the Collector strangling his wife to death. Her eyes wide with horror, her face beet-red and swollen. Imagined what he'd do to the man if he got the chance.

Rage boiled within him as he played out his revenge, visions of extraordinary violence coming to him. He bit his own tongue, the pain magnifying his anger, the sudden taste of blood feeding it.

In his mind, he rammed the heel of his boot in the Collector's face. Over and over and…

His body swelled, muscles growing as he transformed, as he became Vengeance, the incarnation of his desire. A character he'd created long ago, when he was a child. Before he'd even realized what he was. Larger and taller he grew, until his legs threatened to dangle off the bed, even with his knees tucked to his chest.

And even as he grew, he rolled off the bed…and saw a man dressed in a black uniform and mask standing in front of him, holding a gleaming dagger. The would-be-assassin lunged at him, plunging the blade into Vengeance's belly.

The pain was hot and immediate, the dagger cutting through skin and muscle, lacerating his intestines. A blade almost certainly coated with lethal poison.

Vengeance roared, shoving the assassin backward into the stone wall. So hard the stone cracked.

The man bounced off the wall like it was a trampoline, and Vengeance swung one massive fist at the man's nose.

Bones crunched under his knuckles.

The would-be killer flew back into the wall again, his skull ricocheting off the stone. Vengeance roared, ramming the man with his muscled shoulder and pinning him against the wall. Then he grabbed the man by the temples, lifting him off the floor.

And smashed the assassin's head into the wall. Over and over again.

Then, long after the assassin had drawn his last breath, Vengeance threw him to the floor. Vengeance's shoulders heaved as he stared down at the body, imagining himself stomping on the assassin's face until it was nothing but bloody pulp. But a sudden, burning pain in his abdomen distracted him.

He looked down, seeing the dagger still jutting out of his lower belly.

Damn.

He felt the rage trickling away, and swore, gripping the handle of the blade and closing his eyes.

And yanking it out.

"Ahh, f…" he swore, the dagger falling from his hands and clattering on the floor. He bit back a scream, hot blood pouring from the wound. The burning pain intensified, spreading rapidly outward from the wound.

The poison!

Pain spread across his belly, as if hot oil were being poured on his skin. Spreading through his body to kill him. He doubled over, sweat pouring from him.

And then, as his rage left him, so did Vengeance.

278

The room seemed to expand around him as he shrank, his head no longer threatening to scrape against the tall ceiling. His arms lost their huge muscles, and his golden uniform once again appeared around him.

He was Piper once more.

Piper blinked, eyeing the body, then his bloody knuckles. The memory of being Vengeance was vague, as it always was. As all of his characters' memories were. But he remembered the wound Vengeance had sustained. A fatal one.

He lifted his shirt, the wound in his belly gone…and the pain gone with it. For Vengeance had been the one stabbed, not him. But if he changed into the character again, Vengeance would most certainly die…and Piper would never be able to play him again.

"Well then," he muttered, turning away from the body and running shaky hands through his hair. This was almost certainly not the only assassin who'd been sent to take him out. The Collector had to know how hard it could be to kill a good Actor…especially one as uniquely trained as Piper.

"Sometimes the paranoia is right, babe," he muttered. Which meant that the love of his life was already dead…or was trapped somewhere in the Castle Over. And there was only one person in this world he knew of that was powerful enough to help save her.

He focused, willing his feelings to fade. A chill ran through him, and he felt himself growing again. A black cloak appeared around him, his hands and forearms vanishing within silver gauntlets. There had to be many more assassins out there, waiting for him to emerge from his room.

But he doubted any of them would have the balls to face a Reaper.

Chapter 32

avenwood was everything an artist could ever want, a magical, cheery place filled with endless nooks and crannies to explore, each revealing small treasures that delighted the senses. There were small parks with sparkling fountains hidden within the great mushroom forest. Buildings that ran up Dragon's Peak in a vast, interconnected network, allowing one to scale nearly the entire mountain without ever once having to walk the spiraling path.

Most of these buildings were uninhabited, for Havenwood had only been created a few decades ago, populated by artists who had decided to make the pilgrimage to a place where they were free to create what they wished. And all a creation of the curious and ancient mind of Thaddeus Birch.

But for all of Havenwood's whimsy, Bella found herself happiest when she returned to the quiet solitude of her mother's subterranean estate, deep within the bowels of Dragon's Peak. It was a preference that made her feel rather guilty, preferring being alone over the company of other artists. But after a lifetime holed up in her apartment with Grandpa, she found the solitude comforting.

She'd also set up one of the larger rooms in her mother's mansion as her own personal studio, moving all the furniture out. It was just down the hall from Grandpa's new office, conveniently enough. Gideon had made her paint her own painting supplies, including an easel, an enormous quantity of paint, brushes, and even canvases. Magical canvases that rolled and unrolled themselves like Gideon's.

She'd spent the last few days sketching different ideas for paintings while Grandpa wrote and Gideon did…well, whatever Gideon was doing. Her father spent most of his time out and about in Havenwood on the surface, only occasionally returning to the darkness to check in with her.

This morning she'd run out of ideas of what to draw, so she threw up her hands and drew what she always did when she didn't know what else to do. A sketch of her dragon.

It came to her effortlessly, even at a much larger scale than her notebook back at school. A fierce dragon standing by her side, one bony hand clutching her shoulder. Great wings spread wide, its eyes glowing with an inner fire.

No, not *its* eyes. *Her* eyes. For her dragon was definitely a girl.

When Bella finished her sketch, she stood back, eyeing it critically. It was, she knew, her best version of her dragon yet. At three feet wide and five feet tall, this canvas allowed for far more detail than her algebra notebook.

"Hello Bella," she heard from behind.

She turned, spotting Gideon entering the room. He smiled at her, then eyed the sketch.

"Ah, Bella's dragon!" he proclaimed, studying her work. "Thaddeus told me all about it."

"Really?" Bella replied. She hardly expected Grandpa to mention her doodles.

"Of course," Gideon replied. "It's good," he opined. "At least the dragon is."

"Thanks."

"I wouldn't paint yourself in it though," he cautioned. "Remember what I told you about painting humans." She'd included herself in the sketch, after all.

"I wasn't going to paint any of it," she replied rather defensively. "I was just playing around."

"Why not paint the dragon?" he inquired.

She blinked, taken aback.

"Because."

"That's not an answer," Gideon countered. Bella folded her arms over her chest.

"Is too."

"Not a good one," he pressed.

"Because I don't want to," she answered, arching an eyebrow, as if daring him to challenge her. He smirked.

"You draw it an awful lot for someone who doesn't want to paint it," he pointed out. "Why?"

Bella shrugged.

"I like dragons," she answered.

"Ones with heart-shaped rubies in their breastbones?" he pressed. She grimaced.

"Yes. So?"

"When someone draws or paints the same thing over and over again, it means something, Bella," Gideon explained.

"Like what?"

"That's for *you* to answer," he replied. "The way we artists always do," he added, gesturing at the canvas. Bella shook her head.

"I'm not ready for that."

"Why not?" he inquired.

"I'm not good enough."

"Hmm," Gideon murmured. "And how would *you* know?"

Bella glared at him.

"Fine," Gideon replied. "Just asking."

"Uh huh."

"So this is what having a teenage daughter is like," Gideon grumbled. "Your mother warned me about this." Bella gave him a withering look.

"Are you trying to tell me I'm difficult?"

"Um…"

"I'm messing with you," Bella said, smirking at him. "You do have a lot to learn though."

"I missed out on a lot," Gideon agreed. He lowered his gaze. "Too much," he added.

"Gideon…"

"I couldn't reveal myself to you," he interrupted. "If I had, and the Collector's men had gotten to you…" He sighed. "But I wanted to, Bella. Believe me. More than anything in the world."

"I know."

"I don't think you do," he countered gently. "How many nights I spent in that damn library, waiting for those bounty hunters to leave the book there so I could get lost in it…" He sighed. "It took me nine years to find your book, Bella. And for over a year I…"

"I get it," she interjected, stepping forward and grabbing his hand in both of her own. He lifted his gaze, his eyes moist. Looking absolutely miserable. "I forgive you."

"It's not that simple," Gideon protested.

"It is for me," she retorted. "You cut off your hand for me...Dad. You risked your life for me, and for Grandpa."

Gideon took a deep, shuddering breath in, tears dripping down his cheeks.

"It wasn't enough."

"It is for me," she countered.

"Not for your mother, it wasn't," he countered. His eyes hardened then, his jawline rippling.

"Gideon..."

"I should never have listened to her," he insisted. "I knew better, Bella. Every inch of me screamed to go with you, to..."

"Dad!" Bella blurted out. His jaw shut with a *click*. "Shut up," she ordered.

He did.

"Give me a hug," she commanded. He paused, then complied, wrapping his arms around her. She did the same, and they held each other for a long, quiet moment. At length, they separated.

"Thank you," she stated. "For being there for me, even when I didn't know."

He smiled.

"You're welcome, Bella," he replied. He cleared his throat then, glancing at the canvas. "So about that dragon..."

"Not painting it."

"Right," Gideon muttered. "Then what *are* you going to paint? Not this, I hope," he added, gesturing at a canvas propped up against the wall. It was a sketch of a mushroom man growing out of a log.

"It's not *that* bad," she insisted.

"I beg to differ," Gideon retorted. "Keep in mind that I'm over four hundred years old...and widely considered to be the best Painter alive."

"Your humility is staggering," she grumbled.

"Paint something that matters to you, Bella," he insisted. "That's all I ask."

Bella sighed, staring at the canvas. Then she looked about the small studio, trying to find some inspiration. The mushroom sketch *was* pretty lame, she had to admit. But what else could she paint? She wracked her brain, trying to come up with something.

Then she was struck with an idea.

"I don't need to paint a painting," she declared. Gideon blinked.

"Excuse me?"

"I mean I don't need to paint on a canvas," she clarified. "What if I paint on clothes?"

Gideon raised an eyebrow.

"This uniform is okay," she stated, gesturing at her Painter's uniform. "But it only has panels for paintings. What if I made an entire suit that was painted. Like, *all* of it?"

"Tell me more."

"Well, my suit helps me draw out paintings in battle," Bella explained. "But it also protects me, right? Because if someone stabbed me in the chest with a sword, let's say, it would just enter the painting, right?"

"Right."

"So if I had an entire *suit* that was painted – made out of a single piece of painted cloth – it would protect me from *any* attack, right?"

"In theory," Gideon conceded. "But it could make interacting with your environment difficult."

"How so?"

"Well, if I had to grab your arm to pull you away from something, my hand would just pass into your uniform," he explained. "And your hands and feet would still need to be unpainted, and your head. They'd still be vulnerable."

"Unless I had a hood," she countered.

"Granted," he replied. "But how would you put it on? And take it off?"

Bella frowned, thinking it through. She hadn't thought of that.

"Don't stop," he urged. "Keep thinking."

"Well…what if I made it like the canvases?" she proposed. "And I could just say a command word and make it put itself on and off me?"

"Then anyone could say the word and take it off of you," Gideon countered.

"Hmm," she replied. "Well, can't Myko read your thoughts?"

"Yes."

"Why not make the cloak read my thoughts then?" she asked. "I could command it to cloak and uncloak me with a thought."

"Yes, but you should only have one thing connected to your mind," Gideon pointed out. "Your Familiar. Otherwise it gets…complicated."

"So I'd have to make the cloak my Familiar," she stated.

"Right."

She frowned. That certainly wasn't the Familiar she'd imagined herself having. Not that she'd imagined herself having one.

"Okay," she replied. "What if…I make a Familiar that's painted?"

"Aren't they all?"

"A Familiar with a body that I can paint on," she clarified. "And then I could pull painted things from it, like I can from canvases I paint."

"I suppose it would work," he conceded, his eyebrows knitting together. "But why?"

"Because then I could wear my Familiar," she reasoned. "And communicate with it telepathically to take it on and off."

"So it would be able to protect you, and you could draw out painted things from it," Gideon finished. "Interesting." He began to pace, considering this. "But why not just have a Familiar and a Painter's uniform?" he inquired. "How is this any better?"

"Because I can have both," Bella answered. "And store twice as many paintings. And the fact that my Familiar's technically a canvas would mean anything attacking it…"

"…would just get trapped inside that painting," Gideon realized. He stopped pacing abruptly, his eyes widening. "My god, it's brilliant!"

Bella broke out into a smile.

"It is?"

"It is!" Gideon exclaimed. He gave her a funny look then.

"What?" she asked.

"You know, that's the sort of thing your mother would've come up with. She was always thinking differently than everyone else."

"Strangely?" Bella inquired with a smile.

"Very," he agreed. He crossed his arms over his chest then, arching an eyebrow at her. "You know what would make a *perfect* surface for painting?"

Bella frowned, eyeing him suspiciously. She did *not* like Gideon's expression. He stepped right up to the painting, putting a finger on one of its wings.

Bella turned to the canvas set upon her easel. She imagined her dragon, its wings spread out wide. Imagined the black skin between the bony fingers of its wings as canvas instead, painted with all sorts of wonderful things. But not the inner surface, only the exterior. If she needed protection, it could fly to her, and wrap its wings around her. Wings with painted skin that could absorb nearly any attack.

She felt a rush of excitement, her heart starting to race. Gideon grinned at her.

"I know that look," he stated. "Should I leave you to it?"

"I don't know," she hesitated. "I don't think I'm ready to paint her."

"You need a Familiar, Bella," he pressed. She crossed her arms over her chest.

"I'm not good enough at painting yet," she retorted.

He grabbed a paintbrush, offering it to her.

"Then get good," he replied. "Enough sketching. I want five paintings a day."

Her eyes widened.

"Five?" she blurted out.

"That's right," Gideon confirmed. "I don't care what they're about – as long as they aren't of people – or if they're good. Just paint."

"But…"

"It's the only way you'll get good," he interrupted.

"Yeah, but…"

"Paint!" he commanded, shoving the paintbrush in her hand.

And then he left her to it.

* * *

So Bella painted.

She painted her mushroom-person, Gideon be damned. And she painted ravens picking the hay out of a scarecrow in the middle of a cornfield, eating at its hay-intestines as they spilled out of his torn shirt. She painted a floating skull surrounded by an aura of sickly green light, its eyes glowing with a terrible inner fire. She painted dead things and living things and things that were somewhere in-between.

And, forced to paint five paintings a day, she stopped caring so much about how her paintings were going to turn out. In fact, she stopped planning her paintings altogether, merely plucking each finished painting off her easel and starting a fresh one immediately afterward. Dip brush in paint, slide paint across canvas.

Over and over again.

Freed from the constraints of quality and deliberation, Bella found that the quality of her work actually improved. Sure, she started off rough, using broad strokes to place things where they should go. But with refinement, her paintings came to life. Her colors became bolder, her palette broadening. She began to use different tools, playing with her process. Some experiments failed miserably, but others were surprisingly successful.

After nearly a week, she was painting *seven* paintings a day...and with hardly any effort at all.

Of course, after a week of being holed-up in the depths of an underground mansion, Bella found herself going a bit stir-crazy. So she forced Grandpa to leave his writing desk and accompany her and Gideon on a day trip in Havenwood.

Which turned out to be rather lovely.

Gideon drew Myko out of his painting to join them, and after many slobbery kisses, the great silver wolf walked at Bella's side all the way up to the surface. The sun shone brightly in the late-morning sky, puffy white clouds floating lazily in that brilliant blue. After everyone squinted and stretched, they made their way to the spiraling cobblestone street winding down the mountain, following it all the way to the bottom. They continued on the path along the shore of Lake Fenestra, gazing at the glittering waterfall.

"It's just as I pictured it," Grandpa mused, taking it all in. "The Pentad was none too pleased with me after their artists started flocking here. They accused me of doing it on purpose...creating a haven for artists that wanted to get out from under the Queen's thumb. Like your mother," he added.

"Did you?" Bella pressed. Grandpa's eyes twinkled, and he gazed up at the top of the waterfall, reciting the following:

> "And beyond the belly of the beast,
> Deep within Dragon's Peak
> Sat a haven in Havenwood,
> Far from danger's reach.
>
> For its tail did reach

Across an impossible space,
To bring the traveler home
To her strange, dark place."

Bella's eyebrows furrowed.

"The traveler was Mom," she realized. "And the strange dark place was home." She glanced up at Grandpa. "You created Havenwood…"

"For her," Grandpa confirmed. "Such a small part of the book, really. The Pentad's editors didn't even catch it…not until it was too late."

"So Mom traveled to Havenwood so the Pentad wouldn't arrest her?" she pressed.

"Oh no," Grandpa replied. "Your mother stayed right in her home. It was already underground, you see. In a cave. My book created a connection to that cave, and your mother simply collapsed the existing tunnel that led to it. Her mansion isn't in Havenwood at all…only surrounded by it."

"So Havenwood was the only way to get to her home," Bella realized. "Wow…that's brilliant!"

"Yes," Grandpa agreed. "Can't imagine why they haven't published any of my work since."

"Which begs the question," Gideon piped in, "…how exactly are you going to distribute this sequel? Without enough people reading it, nothing within it will become reality."

"We'll need to distribute it on the black market," Grandpa answered. "I have a smuggler that would be more than happy to get exclusive rights to sell it."

"And how are you going to get it to this smuggler?" Gideon pressed.

"I'm not," Grandpa replied, pointing a finger at Gideon. "You are."

Gideon's eyebrows rose.

"I'm done with the first draft," Grandpa continued. "I'll have it edited in a few more days, and then you'll need to get it published and distributed. There is a publisher in the Twin Spires that owes me a favor."

"In the Twin Spires?" Gideon inquired.

"A black-market publisher," Grandpa clarified.

"Who owes you a favor," Gideon stated, clearly unconvinced.

"You may have heard of her," Grandpa continued. "A woman by the name of Petrusa."

Gideon's eyebrows rose even higher.

"Petrusa?" he blurted out. "*The* Petrusa? Are you serious?"

"She has the manpower," Grandpa insisted. "She's the only one who can publish and distribute my book quickly."

"At what cost?"

"Petrusa owes me," Grandpa repeated. "The cost has already been paid."

Gideon ran his hand through his hair, shaking his head. Bella frowned at both men.

"Who's Petrusa?" she asked. Both turned to her.

"Ah…" Grandpa began. He glanced at Gideon.

"A…an associate of your mother's," Gideon answered. "She sold paintings on the black market for Petrusa's…people after she ran away from home. Before she and I got together."

"She knows?" Grandpa inquired.

"A bit," Gideon admitted. Bella's frowned deepened, and it was her turn to cross her arms over her chest.

"Okay, enough secrets. Tell me everything," she demanded.

Both men glanced at each other again.

"Well?" Bella pressed.

"Your mother was a member of the Guild of the Golden Coin," Grandpa answered. "Ostensibly a guild of merchants. They have branches in nearly every country in the world. Very powerful, you see."

"Very," Gideon agreed.

"The leader of the guild is a woman named Petrusa," Grandpa continued. "She's even older than I am, if you can believe it. A truly gifted Sculptor. She was ancient when I was young."

"And?" Bella pressed.

"Petrusa is also the leader of a…group of people who dabble in forbidden magic," Grandpa explained. "And sell information and paintings and such on the black market."

"Like books," Gideon added.

"She has a vast distribution network, and can make an enormous quantity of my books and send them across the world in very little time," Grandpa said. "Faster than the Pentad."

"Makes sense," Bella stated. Grandpa turned to Gideon.

"Petrusa can be accessed through a tomb in downtown Twin Spires," Grandpa told him. "I'll write down detailed instructions on how to reach her."

"Wonderful," Gideon grumbled.

"You'll be fine," Grandpa reassured. "Especially considering your relationship with Lucia."

"Why not just send your book to the Pentad to have it published?" Bella inquired. "Wouldn't they jump at the chance to get the edge on the Collector?"

"Maybe not," Grandpa countered. "They probably don't see him as being a big threat, fools that they are. And they have every reason to distrust my work after what happened with the last book."

"Oh," Bella murmured. "Right."

"And you can't *imagine* how slow traditional publishing is," Grandpa continued. "Miles of administrative red tape, months to years of review processes to go through. We can't afford to wait that long." He made a face then. "Besides, they'll make me write a synopsis, and frankly I'd rather have my hair set on fire."

"Very well," Gideon replied with a sigh. "Petrusa it is."

"When will you be done?" Bella asked.

"The first draft is already complete," Grandpa declared.

"You're already finished with the first draft?" Bella blurted out incredulously. "It's only been a week!"

"I've been thinking about this book for ten years," Grandpa reminded her. "Ten years without feeling the Flow," he mused, shaking his head. "I missed it terribly…and apparently it missed me more."

"You couldn't feel the Flow in the apartment?" Bella asked.

"That's why you can't write a magical book within a book," he explained. "A Painter can feel the flow in a book, although less so, but a Writer cannot. And no one can feel the Flow in a painting, because there's no time within one."

"Oh."

"So what's the book do?" Gideon inquired.

"Nothing that the Pentad would be able to point to as being illegal," Grandpa answered. "But there's a very specific word-choice error…one that will give us the manpower we'll need to fight the Collector's army."

"Why not just get the Pentad to attack him?" Bella asked. "Don't they have huge armies?"

"They do," Grandpa confirmed. "But keep in mind the Collector hates your father. And if the Pentad ever found out that Gideon was the one who painted him…"

"Right," Bella muttered. Then she frowned. "Why hasn't he told them already?"

"I don't know," Gideon admitted. "Maybe he wants me to live in fear of the possibility."

They continued down the cobblestone path, reaching a fork in the road. One turned left, toward the mushroom forest and the entrance to Havenwood, while the other continued along the shore of the lake. A black-cloaked figure was strolling down the leftmost path toward them.

"Raising an army is all well and good," Gideon pointed out, "…but we still don't know where the Collector is. How are we going to find him?"

"It's all in my book," Grandpa replied. "You see, I…"

"Don't need a book to find the Collector," a gruff male voice interrupted. "Give me what I want and I'll tell you exactly where he is."

Chapter 33

The black-cloaked man stopped before Bella, Gideon, Grandpa, and Myko, barring their way forward. They all stopped, realizing that the man who'd been walking toward them had been the one to speak. Myko growled, stepping in front of Bella protectively.

The cloaked figure stood before them, his hands at his sides. He was imposingly tall, and even with his body nearly completed covered by his thick black cloak, he was obviously very well-built. His face was hidden within the depths of his hood, giving not a hint of what lay beneath.

And then something very strange happened.

His cloak thinned, seeming to melt into his body…and revealed a golden shirt and pants beneath. At the same time, he seemed to shrink a few inches, until he was as tall as Grandpa. His hood vanished, revealing a handsome face, like a movie star's. He had a finely trimmed black goatee, with dramatically arched eyebrows and attractive blue eyes.

Gideon glared at the man, pulling his cane from his chest-painting and slamming the butt of it against the cobblestones. Then he pointed it at the man in gold.

"I suggest you leave," he growled. "Now."

The man held up both hands.

"Whoa there," he replied, taking a step back. "I'm unarmed."

"Right," Gideon shot back. Myko growled again, baring his teeth at the stranger. "Come to spy on us for the Collector?" Gideon inquired. "I thought you were smarter than that, Piper."

"I am," the man called Piper replied. "I'm not here for him."

"Bullsh-"

Grandpa cleared his throat, glancing at Bella.

"It's not like I haven't heard the word before, Grandpa," Bella pointed out.

"Even so," Grandpa replied. He turned to Piper. "You have a lot of nerve showing up here after everything you did."

"Yeah, about that," Piper replied with an apologetic look. "It was just a job."

"You hunted us for ten years!" Grandpa shot back.

"Worked out well enough, didn't it?" Piper countered, gesturing at the three. And taking another step back when Myko took a step toward him, still baring his fangs. "Look, it wasn't like I was mean to her or anything. That was all Stanwitz."

"Wait, what?" Bella asked. "Who are you?"

Piper hesitated, then transformed, a police uniform forming around him. His skin darkened, and soon he was all-too recognizable. Bella gasped.

"Reynolds!" she blurted out.

"Guilty as charged," he admitted.

She stared at him, hardly believing her eyes. He looked completely different...even *sounded* different.

"How..." she began.

"He's an Actor," Gideon explained. "Reynolds is a character he plays."

Reynolds transformed again, back into the golden-uniformed man named Piper.

"Like I said, it was just a job," Piper insisted. "Stanwitz was a complete psychopath," he added. "He was never supposed to hurt you, kid. Or your grandfather. We were just supposed to find you and take you out of the book."

"Uh huh," Bella grumbled, crossing her arms over her chest.

"Look, Stanwitz got what was coming to him," Piper insisted. "And not for nothing, I saved your ass when Stanwitz tried to shoot you in the head, remember?"

Bella grimaced; it was undeniably true.

"I'm not here because of the Collector, or to try to kidnap you or anything like that," Piper insisted.

"Then why *are* you here?" Grandpa inquired. Piper sighed.

"Because the Collector took Kendra," he revealed. "And he tried to kill me."

"And you're surprised?" Gideon inquired.

"I never trusted the Collector, but my wife did," Piper told them. "She got promoted over a week ago, and I haven't seen her since. I started asking questions, and the Collector sent an assassin to murder me in my sleep."

"Pity it didn't work out," Gideon muttered.

"Point is, the Collector is either holding my wife hostage, or he's already killed her," Piper continued, ignoring the quip. He crossed his arms over his chest, his jawline rippling. "And I'm not about to let him get away with it."

"Then why come here?" Gideon inquired. "So the Collector can't kill you?"

"No," Piper retorted. "I came here for you.'"

Gideon's eyebrows rose, and he glanced at Grandpa, then back at Piper.

"For me?"

"That's right," Piper confirmed. "And Thaddeus."

"Kendra tried to kill us," Gideon reminded him. "And I spent ten years trying to stop you from getting to Thaddeus and Bella. If you think we're going to help you after everything you two did, you're insane."

"You're the only men I know that can take on the Collector and win," Piper insisted. "And if you agree to help me, I can offer you something that no one else can."

"What's that?" Grandpa inquired.

"My services as an Actor," Piper replied. "And the exact location of the Collector."

* * *

Bella, Gideon, and Grandpa sat across from Piper at a table in the Painted Feast, Bella's favorite restaurant in downtown Havenwood. Myko sat at Bella's feet, gnawing at a bone the chef had been kind enough to paint the wolf. Piper had convinced them to hear him out, although it was clear that no one was particularly pleased at the prospect.

"So you're saying there's a series of underground tunnels that connect different places in the world together?" Grandpa inquired, pushing his glasses up the bridge of his nose. "Fascinating!"

"The Collector uses them to transport valuables and high-ranking personnel," Piper explained. "I'm the first high-ranking artist to defect...without being killed first, that is."

"So where does the Collector live?" Gideon inquired.

"In a castle on top of Mount Inversus," Piper answered.

"Never heard of it," Gideon admitted.

"It's technically two mountains," Piper explained. "There's an upside-down castle on top of the first one, and an upside-down mountain on top of that."

"An upside-down mountain?" Gideon exclaimed, his eyebrows going up. He glanced at Grandpa, who frowned.

"I seem to recall having heard something about a place like that," he said. "A long, long time ago. But it must be very far away for me to have never been there."

Bella supposed this made sense. Grandpa would have had the opportunity to travel quite a bit in the last nine hundred years or so.

"I'm sure it is," Piper agreed. "The Underground is the only way I know to get there."

"And how do we access this Underground?" Gideon pressed. Piper leaned his elbows on the table, steepling his fingers.

"I can show you," he answered. "But you have to promise to help me get Kendra back."

"It's unlikely she's alive," Grandpa warned...and grunted as Gideon elbowed him in the side.

"I have to try," Piper insisted. "And either way, I'm going to get the Collector back for what he did to her...and what he tried to do to me. That's what you want, right? To stop the Collector?"

"We do," Gideon agreed.

"Then I'm the best chance you've got," Piper stated, folding his arms over his chest. "What'dya say?"

Bella glanced at Gideon, who glanced at Grandpa. Grandpa cleared his throat.

"I say we'll think about it," he decided. Piper nodded.

"Fair enough," he replied. The Actor stood then, pushing his chair in. "I'll be around until you make your decision," he informed them. "Don't wait too long," he warned. "The Collector is only going to get stronger the longer you wait."

"We'll make our decision as soon as we can," Grandpa promised, standing as well. This cued everyone else to stand, including Myko, who kept his bone firmly between his jaws. "Until next time, Piper."

They left then, and Bella, Gideon, and Grandpa walked back up Dragon's Peak to the waterfall, Myko trotting at Bella's side. They entered the mouth of the Water Dragon, returning to Mom's estate. Once inside, everyone went to the nearest living room, plopping themselves on the couch Grandpa had grown fond of taking naps on. Both Grandpa and Gideon looked troubled.

"What do you think?" Gideon inquired, eyeing Grandpa. Grandpa sighed, slumping into the couch cushions.

"I think he's telling the truth."

"It could be a trap," Gideon warned. "A way to lure us out of Havenwood so the Collector can get to us."

"True," Grandpa conceded. "That would be the worst-case scenario. So that's what we have to prepare for."

"How?"

"By getting my book to the Twin Spires," Grandpa answered. "If we can get enough people to read it, we'll have more than enough manpower to deal with Piper and any force the Collector would throw at us."

"What exactly is in that book?" Gideon pressed. Grandpa glared at him.

"And spoil the sequel? Never!"

Gideon sighed, rubbing his face with his hands.

"All right," he decided. "So you're saying we should let Piper help us, but expect him to double-cross us."

"Naturally," Grandpa agreed. "Unless you see another way."

"Not really," Gideon admitted. "Very well. So the plan is to finish your book, then have me bring it to the Twin Spires. Then take the Underground to the Collector's castle to take him out once and for all."

"Easy-peasy," Grandpa concluded. Gideon hardly looked convinced, but he nodded.

"Very well. When will you have the book finished?"

"Give me a few more days," Grandpa replied. "It'll be a bit rough, but it'll do the trick."

Chapter 34

Grandpa was as good as his word.

He worked furiously night and day until he was finally finished. That done, he handed the book to Gideon, who said his goodbyes to Grandpa and Bella before leaving. Myko did as well, giving Bella enough wolf-kisses to last a lifetime, and even giving Grandpa one or two. Then they waved goodbye, following the path down to the base of Dragon's Peak and vanishing into the mushroom forest beyond.

Then it was back to just Grandpa and Bella, as it'd always been.

And as it'd been for the few weeks before coming to this world, Bella found herself spending much of her day painting while Grandpa wrote. To her relief, he did venture out into the town daily, meeting with his fellow Writers and the other artists. Bella got to tag along when she wanted to, and she found meeting new people to be refreshing. There was no more fear of others, no rush to get home. No secret password just to get inside her own room.

For the first time in a long time, Bella felt…normal. As normal as a girl like her *could* feel, that was.

And Grandpa…well, he filled out quite rapidly, eating like a man starved half to death, which Bella supposed he had been. He too seemed at peace, as content as she'd ever seen him. Seeing him this content made her realize that he'd been terribly depressed, a fact that, in retrospect, should have been obvious. Every night, as was their ritual, he told her a bedtime story…after she made them a home-cooked dinner.

"I still don't get why you want me to cook," Bella said as she tossed some chicken onto a frying pan. Grandpa stood beside her, cutting up a few bell-peppers. She'd gotten the ingredients from her mother's pantry, which was a big room containing tons of paintings of various food items. The food came out fresh every time.

"What do you mean?" Grandpa inquired, handing her some peppers, which she tossed into the pan with a sizzle.

"The food at the restaurants is better," she explained.

"Hmm, maybe it *tastes* better," he conceded. "But that's not why we have meals, Bella."

Bella frowned, turning to him and putting a hand on her hip.

"Going to have to explain that," she stated.

"Well, people eat food to sate their hunger," Grandpa replied. "But they eat *meals* for the story."

Bella stared at him.

"The story?" she asked. "You're saying *meals* have a story?"

"Oh yes," Grandpa confirmed, smiling at her while he cut more peppers. "Tell me…when you sit down and eat this meal, what will it remind you of?"

"Of being in the apartment," Bella answered. "And you not eating enough of it."

"Ha!" Grandpa exclaimed. "It will remind you of *our* story, Bella. Of you and I, two people trying to survive with barely a dollar to our names." His smile broadened. "When I eat this, it reminds me that you cooked it for me because you know it's my favorite. That you love me and care about me. That you worry about me and want to nourish me. Right?"

Bella smiled back.

"Right," she agreed.

"That's the story it tells," Grandpa declared. "And it's one of the reasons why I love it so much. Not just because it tastes good, but because it tells a wonderful story. A kind of love story."

"I get it, Grandpa," Bella said. She leaned in, giving him a hug with one arm. "I love you too you know."

"And I you," Grandpa replied. "More than I can ever say."

"So meals tell stories, huh?" Bella mused, getting back to her cooking. "Seems like everything does."

"Correct!" Grandpa agreed, handing her some more chopped-up peppers. "People think in stories, Bella. Not facts or such. That's why most teachers are terrible...they aren't storytellers."

"Like Mrs. Pittersworth," Bella muttered.

"Definitely," Grandpa agreed, making a face. Bella laughed, and he winked at her. "She was written boring, you know. They all were in that dreadful book. 'The Chronicles of Collins Dansworth,' what a pile of rubbish!"

"Why'd you choose it then?" Bella inquired.

"Because it was very long and detailed," Grandpa explained. "With a huge world to get lost in. I knew that would make it harder for the Collector's men to find us, even if they *did* pick the right book to look in."

"Ah."

"Before we got lost in it, Animus had knocked over quite a few bookshelves in the library," he continued. "That's why they had a hell of a time figuring out which book we got lost in."

"Clever," Bella murmured.

"Onions?" Grandpa inquired, eyeing the frying pan. Bella nodded. "Coming right up!" he proclaimed, grabbing one and starting the painful process of mincing it. Soon their eyes were stinging, tears dripping down their cheeks. A pain that was more than worth the sweet, caramelized treat the onion would be transformed into.

At length they finished, and sat down to eat their meal. And it was, Bella realized, just as Grandpa had described. By the time she was done, she found herself smiling at him. At Thaddeus Birch, the world's greatest Writer, nearly a thousand years old...and her sole companion for most of her life.

"Love you Grandpa," she said, reaching over the table and grabbing his hand. She gave it a squeeze.

"And I love you, Bella," he replied, his eyes twinkling. "Now, let's clean up so I can tell you a story!"

* * *

Bella's bedroom in Mom's house was far larger than the one in her old apartment, and filled with paintings of various scenes from her childhood, according to Grandpa. They laid side-by-side, gazing at the ceiling while Grandpa spun a tale. A remarkable tale of adventure, as per his usual. When he was done, Bella turned to him.

"How do you come up with stories so easily?" she asked.

"I've lived a long life," he answered. "The more you've lived, the more stories you'll have to tell."

"I still can't believe you're over nine hundred years old," she admitted. Grandpa chuckled.

"I can hardly believe it either."

"Guess that explains why you're so wise," she mused.

"You can learn a lot in ten lifetimes," he agreed. Then he sighed. "I wish I'd learned this a lot earlier," he admitted.

"Learned what?"

"This," he repeated, gesturing at the two of them. "How it could change me. I waited so long to have children, you know. Nearly a thousand years old, and you're my only grandchild."

Bella gazed at him.

"You wish you had more?"

"I will," he replied. "When Gideon comes back, I'll step into his canvas and regain my youth. What should I go for...my thirties?"

"That's going to be weird," Bella realized. Grandpa was supposed to be, well, a grandpa.

"You'll get used to it," he reassured.

'So..." she began, clearing her throat. "When Gideon comes back, what then? How are we going to beat the Collector?"

"I have a copy of my book in my desk," he answered. "If you want to find out, you'll have to read it."

He leaned over then, giving her a kiss on the forehead.

"Goodnight sweetheart," he murmured.

"Night Grandpa. Love you."

"Love you too," he replied, standing up and putting a hand on his chest. "With all my heart."

Bella smiled, putting a hand on her own heart, feeling her mother's amulet there. Then she watched as Grandpa left the room, closing the door gently behind him.

The room trembled.

Bella stiffened, wondering if she'd imagined it. The sensation had been subtle, almost imperceptible. She waited nearly a minute, staring up at the ceiling, but felt nothing more.

Suddenly the room trembled again, far more powerfully this time. The paintings went askew on the walls, her legs of her nightstand clattering on the floor. Her bedroom door burst open, and Grandpa stepped through.

"Did you feel that?" he asked.

"Yes," she answered…and the room trembled again. Bella rolled out of bed, walking up to Grandpa. "What is it?"

"I don't know," he replied. "Let's go," he added, grabbing her arm and pulling her out of the room. They made their way down to the foyer, and the floor quaked under their feet, dust falling from the ceiling.

"It's an earthquake," Bella realized. "Does Havenwood get earthquakes?"

"I certainly didn't write it to."

They left the estate, making their way quickly across the mushroom-lit cavern to the Water Dragon's tail. But it was pitch-black beyond; Bella went back to pluck a large glowing mushroom, bringing it with them up the Water Dragon's innards. They reached the mouth of the cave, spotting starlight beyond, and a hint of the pale moon.

The earth quaked yet again, a thunderous *boom* echoing through the air.

They reached the end of the cave, walking beside the stream leading to the waterfall ahead. Grandpa stopped at the edge of the drop-off, gazing downward, and Bella joined him. Havenwood lay spread out before them, bordered by the mushroom forest, and the massive body of the White Dragon.

Which was *moving*.

Bella drew in a sharp breath, clutching onto Grandpa's arm. She watched as the dragon's head rose, its eyes focusing on something in the distance. Something in the forest beyond Havenwood.

Bella peered into the forest, but saw nothing.

The White Dragon pushed its huge body up off the ground, the earth trembling with the movement. Seconds later, she heard a low rumbling sound.

"What's happening?" she asked. Grandpa shook his head.

"I don't know," he answered. "But it can't be good."

The White Dragon extended its long neck, crouching low to the ground. She saw its enormous wings unfurl, spreading out so wide that its right wing completely covered the lake.

"My god," Bella breathed.

"Look!" Grandpa exclaimed, pointing beyond the dragon.

302

Bella peered into the darkness beyond, at the wide swathe of forest ahead. She caught a hint of movement there within the trees, near the tree line. Tiny shadows spilled out of the forest, thousands of them swarming over the grassy plain. An army charging toward the White Dragon.

Toward Havenwood.

"What are those?" she asked.

Grandpa didn't answer.

"Grandpa?"

"Come on," he urged, pulling her to the left. They made their way to the spiraling main street leading up to the top of Dragon's Peak. She spotted a crowd of people standing by the street a ways down the mountain, staring down at the scene unfolding far below. Grandpa hesitated, then went down to join them, Bella at his side.

"What's going on?" he asked as they reached the men and women gathered there.

"I don't know," one of the women answered, a short, rotund woman that looked to be in her fifties. A small owl was perched on her shoulder. "I'll send Videre," she said, patting the owl's back. The owl leapt off her shoulder, flying forward, then diving quickly downward. It soared over the land, flying past the White Dragon to the open fields beyond.

"What does she see, Ula?" a man asked.

"An army," the woman answered. Her eyes narrowed. "Black humanoids with eyes of flame, all identical to each other. Thousands of them."

"The Pentad's men?" another asked. Ula shook her head.

"They're not wearing armor," she answered. "I've never seen anything quite like them."

Bella glanced up at Grandpa, who was staring down at the approaching army. The White Dragon lifted its head high, arching its neck. A blast of air shot out of its nostrils, so loud that Bella could hear it...and so powerful that it swept through the grass below, flattening it.

Then it drew its head back, sucking air in through its nostrils. It opened its huge maw, its eyes rolling back and its eyelids closing.

The army of shadows stampeded toward the dragon, only a mile away...and closing fast.

Blue light burst from the White Dragon's mouth, a blinding ray that slammed into the plains below. Red-hot flames roared to life where the light touched the ground, thick smoke billowing upward from a huge swath of charred grass.

But the shadow army parted before the deadly beam, flowing around the flames and the rising column of black smoke like water around a rock. The light faded, and the White Dragon's eyes opened.

The two halves of the army came together as they passed the scorched field, and then...

...then they *merged*.

The soldiers threw themselves at each other, forming a writhing mass that grew as it continued forward. A mass that quickly took shape, transforming into a monstrosity as big as the White Dragon's head. An inky-black creature with a humanoid head, but with huge jaws lined with razor-sharp teeth. Possessed of a long, serpentine neck and a muscular body, it had three pairs of arms and one pair of legs...and no tail. Fire raged in its eye-sockets, and flickered between its jaws. It was hideous, bizarre. A nightmare unlike anything Bella had ever seen.

And it moved with terrible speed and purpose, charging at the White Dragon's head, then leaping up into the air!

Upward it soared, toward the dragon's closing maw. But the White Dragon simply drew its head upward and backward, and the dark creature missed, falling to the ground. It landed with a *thump* that Bella heard seconds later, then continued forward until it was near the dragon's chest. It leapt again, extending its six arms and slamming into the White Dragon.

Then it crawled up the dragon's chest to the front of its neck, circling around to its spine. It scaled upward easily with its claws, making its way toward the dragon's head.

"Oh!" Ula gasped, putting a hand to her mouth.

"What?" Grandpa asked.

"It's breaking apart," the woman explained. "Back into the soldiers!"

And it was true; the pale creature seemed to disintegrate even as it made its way up the White Dragon's neck, breaking up into thousands of soldiers once again. These sprinted to its head, swarming over its face, crawling over its eyes and leaping into its nostrils.

The White Dragon jerked its head backward, then thrashed from side-to-side, its jaws opening in an ear-blasting roar.

Some of the soldiers fell off, landing on the ground and shattering into pieces. But those pieces merely flew back up to join the other soldiers, re-forming there.

The White Dragon closed its eyes, flinging the side of its head into the grassland below. The impact sent an explosion of dust and rocks skyward, a thunderous *boom* echoing through the night air. Hundreds of the soldiers were crushed.

And yet, as the dragon lifted its head from the earth, the broken pieces of their bodies came back together, and in moments the soldiers were whole again.

Bella felt a hand grab hers, and she looked down at it, realizing it was Grandpa's. He turned to her, his expression as grave as she'd ever seen it.

"We should go," he prompted.

"Go?" Bella asked. "Where?"

"Um, guys," Ula warned. "There's more of them coming this way."

"What?" a man asked.

"More of the soldiers," she explained. "They've gotten past the White Dragon. They're coming up Main Street!"

All eyes turned to the mushroom forest…and the path leading from it to curve around the lake toward the mountain. Shadows were sprinting across it. Demonic soldiers with fiery eyes, following the spiraling path up the mountain.

Dozens of them.

"Let's go," Grandpa urged, pulling Bella up the street and toward the ledge leading back to the Water Dragon cave.

"Grandpa…"

"Now!" he snapped, yanking her bodily forward.

Bella did as he commanded, fear twisting her guts. He'd never spoken like that to her before. Not ever.

"Get indoors if you want to see tomorrow!" Grandpa cried, gesturing for the crowd to follow him. "To the castle, or with me. Go!"

The crowd hesitated, turning back to face the White Dragon. It was bashing its head against the earth again and again, trying in vain to obliterate the army assailing it.

Then there were screams from far below. From downtown Havenwood, near the base of the mountain.

Screams that made Bella's blood run cold.

305

"Run!" Grandpa cried, sprinting from the crowd. Bella followed at his side, struggling to keep up with him. She glanced back, seeing some of the people following them, while others made their way up the street toward the castle. Ula was among those jogging to catch up with them. But the portly woman tripped, falling face-first onto the rocky ground...and the men around her ran right by her.

"Grandpa," Bella urged, yanking on his arm. He skid to a stop, glancing back, then cursing.

"Keep going!" he ordered, rushing back to help Ula. "Get to the house!"

"I got her," a man declared. To Bella's surprise, it was Piper. The Actor transformed in front of her very eyes, growing into a tall, muscular man with a buzz-cut. He scooped Ula up into his arms, carrying her easily as he rushed after Bella and Grandpa.

More screams from below, closer now.

"We have to help them!" Bella cried, glancing back.

"Save who you can," Grandpa retorted, "...not who you can't."

They rushed up to the stream leading to the waterfall ahead, then turned right at its shore, seeing the gaping maw of the cave in the distance, nearly hidden in shadow. Bella glanced back the way they'd come...and saw *something* coming up the street. It looked human, but had pitch-black skin, with hunched shoulders and fingers that terminated in vicious-looking claws. Two flaming eyes bobbed in the darkness as it came closer.

Bella's blood ran cold.

The figure spotted them...and sprinted after them. Another followed...then another.

"They're coming!" Bella warned, following Grandpa. She lost sight of the figures, and focused on the mouth of the cave ahead. Piper beat them to it, despite carrying Ula, vanishing into the shadows beyond. Grandpa and Bella followed, plunging into darkness.

"We need light!" someone yelled. The only source of light was Bella's glowing mushroom, which barely illuminated the path ahead. Bella reached reflexively into her chest-painting...or at least she tried to. She was wearing her nightclothes, not her Painter uniform. But one of the others managed to draw out a torch, holding it high. It illuminated the skeletal cave in a flickering orange glow, casting long, ghastly shadows ahead of them.

They sprinted down the large cave, the dark waters of the Everstream flowing to their left.

The sound of footsteps echoed through the cave, coming from far behind. Bella looked back, seeing the group of artists following them...and far behind them, at the mouth of the cave, four shadowy figures silhouetted by the moonlight beyond, their terrible eyes glowing brightly in the darkness.

Sprinting after them.

"Behind us!" Ula warned.

"Silence!" Grandpa hissed.

The tunnel grew as they reached the end of the neck of the cave, entering into the Water Dragon's body. The Everstream was a torrent here, the roar at its source almost deafening. A blue light pulsed beneath its surface, casting the walls in its glow. They rushed toward it, but Bella noticed that Grandpa was slowing down, his face pale and slick with sweat, his breath coming in short gasps.

He stumbled, falling forward onto his hands and knees. A loud *pop* reverberated through the cavern like a gunshot.

Grandpa bit back a scream.

"Grandpa!" she hissed, rushing back to his side and helping him up. He clutched his right wrist to his chest, his face twisted with pain. The end of his forearm was bent like an "S."

Grandpa grunted, continuing forward, but what little color remained in his face drained away, and his eyes rolled up into the back of his head. He fell forward like a stone, and Bella caught him. But his weight pulled her down with him, pinning her to the ground.

"Help!" she cried.

"Take her!" Piper barked, shoving Ula into two men's arms. He ran back toward Bella and Grandpa...

...just as Bella felt a hot, hard arm wrap around her waist from behind. She looked down, seeing a black arm clutching her, its skin riddled with cracks...and terminating in a hand with long black claws.

"Grandp-!"

She was yanked backward, torn away from Grandpa. She struggled, kicking and screaming, and desperately trying to pry that awful arm from around her waist. But she may as well have been fighting a statue...and the thing's hot, stone-like skin burned her palms.

Another black soldier burst out of the shadows, grabbing Grandpa and dragging him backward the way they'd come.

"Help!" he cried at the artists further down the cavern, most of whom were still running away. "For god's sake, you're Painters. *Do something!*"

They glanced back, but kept running...including the man with the torch.

Suddenly a huge hand grabbed on to the arm clutching Bella, tearing it off of her...and off of the soldier it was attached to.

It was Piper!

The Actor grunted, swinging the disembodied arm at the soldier. It struck the thing in the face, shattering its left cheek. Piper executed a perfect spinning back-kick, sending the soldier flying into the Everstream in a burst of steam.

The stream's powerful current pulled it up and away, and it vanished into the darkness.

"Run!" Piper ordered, shoving Bella down the tunnel. He rushed after Grandpa, who was being pulled backward by the other black soldier. But two more of the awful things leapt from the shadows, intercepting Piper. One swung its hand at his head, raking its claws across his face. Piper stumbled to the side, blood spurting from deep gashes in his temple.

"Grandpa!" Bella cried, watching as the other soldier dragged Grandpa toward the edge of the blue light from the heart of the Everstream.

Piper tried to run after Grandpa, but the two soldiers leapt on him, raking at his body with their terrible claws. He fell to one knee, blood pouring from fresh wounds on his chest.

Then he transformed again.

His back swelled, his muscles growing even larger, his arms as big as tree trunks now. He roared, grabbing the soldiers and flinging them from him, sending them flying into the Everstream. Then he charged after Grandpa.

"Bella!" she heard Grandpa cry. He struggled against the soldier pulling him backward, digging his heels into the ground. But it was no use. The soldier dragged him away, and they vanished into the darkness beyond the light from Bella's mushroom.

"Grandpa!" she screamed.

Piper roared, throwing aside a soldier that dared to attack him. He sprinted after Grandpa, vanishing into the darkness.

Thump.

There was a *splash*, followed by another. Then the sound of footsteps barreling toward her.

Bella backpedaled, her heart leaping into her throat. The footsteps got louder, and she turned to run…just Piper burst out of the shadows, Grandpa in his arms!

"Run you idiot!" Piper cried, shrinking to become the tall military man again, all while sprinting down the cavern. Bella obeyed, struggling to keep up. The tunnel spiraled deeper into the earth, getting smaller as it did so. They were in the tail now, close to the end.

Close to home.

Bella heard footsteps from far behind, growing steadily louder.

"They're coming after us!" Bella warned.

"Got that," Piper snapped.

They reached the end of the Water Dragon's tail, the narrow tunnel beyond bringing them to the huge cavern housing Mom's estate. Bella squinted against the glow of the mushrooms all around them, spotting a group of men and women ahead. They were the cowards who'd abandoned Grandpa, stopped by the closed portcullis at the entrance to the estate.

Bella and Piper rushed up to join them, and the Piper shoved his way through the crowd to the portcullis.

"Open the door!" he growled. Even as he did so, she realized he was shrinking. His muscles all but disappeared, his clothes shifting to a familiar yellow uniform. "Open the damn door or we're all dead!" Piper snapped. She faced the portcullis, seeing Animus flowing toward them from beyond it.

"Let us in!" she pleaded.

The portcullis began to rise…and then a bright purple light flared to life from behind. Bella spun around, her eyes widening.

There, at the entrance to large cavern, were two more of the black soldiers. One of them was holding a purple crystalline key…up to a translucent, dark purple door made of pure energy standing in the middle of the cavern. The door opened, revealing a long hallway beyond…and something else.

Not something. Some*one*.

It was a man, tall and slender, dressed in an elegant black suit. A blood-red handkerchief peeked out of a pocket at his left breast, the only hint of color he wore. His hair was slicked back over his head, with a gray hair on the right, black on the left, and he had piercing green eyes that seemed to glow in the darkness.

And they focused right on Grandpa.

"Thaddeus," he greeted. His voice was smooth and calm, and sent a chill down Bella's spine. It was somehow terribly familiar, as if plucked from her very nightmares.

Grandpa grit his teeth, clutching at his broken wrist and glaring at the man in black.

"We meet again, Collector," he shot back. The man inclined his head. "You're awfully bold. The White Dragon is distracted now, but it will come after you once its done with your army."

"If," the Collector corrected. "And I'll be long gone by then anyhow." He crossed his arms over his chest. "You're awfully clever," he continued. "Or was it Gideon who came up with the idea to fake your death?"

"A joint effort," Grandpa answered, clinging to Bella. "What do you want?"

"Your daughter cursed me," the Collector answered. "I want you to undo her work."

"I'll never work for you," Grandpa vowed.

"You'll never work against me."

The Collector reached into his breast pocket, retrieving the blood-red handkerchief and unfolding it. One side was black; he reached *into* this with his left hand, pulling out a long, slender silver blade. It had no crossguard, its blade barely an inch wide…and it hummed almost imperceptibly.

"There's no need for a struggle, Thaddeus," he reasoned. "Come with me peacefully and my army will withdraw from Havenwood. No one else has to get hurt."

"Your promises mean nothing to me," Thaddeus retorted. The Collector stepped forward, and the other artists scrambled away from him. But several of the black soldiers came through the doorway behind the Collector, rushing at the artists.

"No!" Ula cried.

One of the soldiers grabbed her, dragging her kicking and screaming through the energy door. The other artists were similarly abducted, until only Grandpa, Piper, and Bella remained in the cavern.

"I'm not an unreasonable man, Thaddeus," the Collector insisted. "No matter what Gideon might have said about me."

"You murdered my daughter!" Grandpa retorted, stepping in front of Bella protectively. The Collector grimaced.

"I didn't know it was her, Thaddeus."

"Does it matter?" Grandpa shot back.

"It does to me," he insisted. "I've had to live with that regret for a long time now."

"To hell with your regrets," Grandpa spat. "I'll never forgive you for what you've done."

The Collector raised an eyebrow.

"Yet you forgave Gideon."

The Collector took another step forward, then another, and Grandpa backpedaled, pushing Bella back with him.

"I killed your daughter out of ignorance," the Collector continued. "But Gideon knew exactly what he was doing when he painted me. When he drew me out. He *knew* that every word he told me was a lie. And he did it anyway."

"He didn't make you become what you are," Thaddeus retorted. The Collector gave a grim smile.

"You of all people know that a painting can only be what its Painter makes it to be. We're not real, Thaddeus. Not like you."

"You're wrong," Grandpa argued. The Collector's eyes hardened.

"Bullshit."

"You are," Grandpa insisted. "You don't know the first thing about art, *Xander.*"

The Collector froze, his jawline rippling.

"Don't call me that."

"Great art tells a story much larger than we could ever intend," Grandpa lectured. "And you are great art, Xander. You're the greatest painting Gideon ever painted."

"I said don't *call* me that!" the Collector shouted. He lunged forward, closing the distance between them in a split second, raising his sword at Thaddeus. Piper ran between them, kicking the Collector square in the chest...and flew backward through the open portcullis into the mansion.

"Piper!" Bella cried, rushing to his side. She helped him up, and he clutched at his chest, gasping for air.

The Collector just stood there, having not budged an inch.

"You can thank Gideon for that," he declared. "My suit is also one of his greatest creations. It does unto others what they would

311

do unto me." He smiled grimly. "He made sure nothing would ever be able to harm me."

"Run!" Bella cried. She pulled Grandpa into the mansion, and Animus closed the portcullis behind them. The Collector walked right up to it, slashing the portcullis with his glowing sword. The blade cut through the crisscrossing metal slats like they weren't even there, and the portcullis fell to the ground with a clatter.

He stepped over it, and into the short hallway beyond.

"Run!" Grandpa cried, shoving Bella backward with his good hand. They retreated into the foyer, Animus swirling around them.

"What do you want with us, Xander?" Grandpa demanded.

The Collector went furious, lunging at Grandpa, and Bella cried out, rushing forward to stop him. The Collector shoved her backward with one hand, and she fell onto her butt. He stepped up to her, pointing the tip of his glowing sword at her chest.

"Don't!" Grandpa cried, rushing to her side. "She's just a child!"

The Collector's eyes never left hers.

"So was I," he retorted.

And then a white light appeared around his sword-arm, and his eyes grew wide, his mouth opening in a primal scream.

He raised his sword high into the air, thrusting his sword at Bella's heart.

Chapter 35

The maze-like streets of The Twin Spires were narrow, dull brownstone buildings looming on either side. Many of the windows looking out over the street were shattered or boarded up, while other establishments had bars before the windows. In prison, such bars served to keep criminals in. But in the poorer sections of the Twin Spires, they served to keep criminals out. For while the wealthier portions of the city were beautiful and well-maintained, much of the city consisted of slums.

During the day, the streets were typically congested with traffic, pedestrians and horse-drawn carriages clogging the throughways. But after the sun set, everyone went indoors. Everyone with any sense, that was. Only the very powerful – or very stupid – walked the streets at night.

So it was that Gideon found himself walking down a narrow, winding cobblestone street in the dead of night, his cane *clacking* with every other step.

He peered ahead, scanning the street as he walked. Many of the street-lanterns hanging from posts high above were unlit, having been vandalized so many times that the city had stopped bothering to fix them. The few that remained functioning only served to deepen the shadows in-between.

Shadows that hid god-knows-what.

While there was little Gideon feared from the scum and vagrants that lived in this part of the Twin Spires, being attacked – and having to defend himself – could reveal his true identity. And that, he knew, would be disastrous.

Gideon tipped his hat forward a little as he passed underneath one of the few functioning street lanterns, letting its brim cast a shadow over his face as he walked. His eyes darted from shadow to shadow, scanning them carefully. Normally he wouldn't have been able to see a thing, but the magical monocle he wore over his left eye gave him remarkable night-vision.

To his relief, the street was barren.

He followed the winding street, barely wide enough at times for him to squeeze his shoulders through. This avoided most of the city guards – who tended to be very inquisitive about those traveling the streets at night-time – but forced him to squeeze past the city's hidden population. Those unsavory types deemed unacceptable to polite society, effectively swept under the proverbial rug. Drug dealers, homeless people. And the psychotic; those whose inner stories did not match any sort of reality. In that way, it was as if their minds were lost in a book, while their bodies walked the real world.

They stared at him as he passed, these people. As he invaded their turf. He felt them studying him, sizing him up. Determining if he was a someone to be trifled with. Most decided quite correctly that he was not.

Most…but not all.

A young man, very tall and beefy, leaned against a wall ahead. He was muttering to himself, clearly suffering a constant stream of internal stimulation, the poor soul. As Gideon neared, the man glared at him, his mumbled utterances growing more agitated. Gideon did his best to ignore the man, avoiding eye contact.

"Hey," the man blurted out. And not in a friendly way.

Gideon glanced at him, tipping his hat forward and inclining his head…and kept walking, passing by the man. Or trying to; the man stepped to block his way, looming over him.

Damn.

If the man made too much of a ruckus, the city guard would be alerted…and they'd take Gideon into custody.

Gideon let go of his cane, whipping his left hand out at the man. His magic glove flew off, grabbing the man by the throat…and squeezing. The man stumbled backward, trying to cry out in surprise, but only a strangled gurgle came out. Gideon grabbed his cane before it tipped over, striking it hard against the wall, then whipping it at the man's temple.

He flew into the wall, his head ricocheting off of it, and tumbled to the ground.

Dead.

Gideon stepped over the man, tucking his cane in his armpit, then calling for his glove. It flew back onto his hand, and he sighed, continuing onward down the narrow street.

He picked the wrong guy at the wrong time, he muttered to himself. It hardly made him feel better. That poor man could never have been anything more than what he was. Not in this city. And in ordinary circumstances, Gideon would have let the man off with nothing more than a bruise or two.

But circumstances were far from ordinary.

The street eventually opened up into a large park within the city, big buildings giving way to grassy fields and tall, beautiful trees. All protected by a gated fence ten feet tall, of course. But Gideon merely walked up its surface, his magical boots carrying him to the top. He leapt down, his cloak slowing his fall to the grass beyond, and continued forward. After a few minutes, he spotted what he was looking for: a large graveyard.

Gravestones stood in even rows throughout the newer section of the graveyard, but beyond this, the rows were more irregular. The poor were clustered in tighter rows, with small, plain tombstones. The more wealthy had quite large plots, with ornate gravestones marking their resting spots. But the wealthiest of all had large tombs, stone buildings with locked doors leading into crypts that often held generations of family members.

As in life, so in death.

He passed between row after row of tombstones, eventually reaching the tomb he was looking for. One of the largest in the graveyard, and certainly the most ornate. The door at the entrance was made of solid metal, and a twist of the knob proved it to be locked.

Luckily, Thaddeus had given Gideon the key.

He unlocked the door, opening it. To his surprise, it swung inward without a sound. Beyond was utter darkness, for the tomb had no windows. He tucked his cane in his armpit, then unsnapped his cloak in the front, exposing his chest-painting. Pulling out his magical lantern, he held it before him. Powered by the sun in much the same way as Myko was powered by the moon, it was fully charged after days of travel.

"Luminos" he incanted.

The lantern flared to life.

Gideon found himself standing in a narrow hallway, with doors on either side and stairs leading forward and downward into darkness. He took these, and they led to a maze of underground tunnels. Having long-since memorized Thaddeus's written instructions, he went right, then left, then down another set of stairs, one that led to a crypt with six stone coffins. He ignored these, walking up to the far wall...and passing right through it. An illusion, just as Thaddeus had said it would be.

The chamber beyond was circular, about ten feet in diameter. In the center of the pool was a single coffin, covered entirely in black velvet, a symbol of a golden circle surrounding a triangle embossed on its lid.

Necromancers, Gideon thought with a grimace. The irony of his disgust did not escape him.

Gideon took a deep breath in, then strode up to the coffin, staring down at it. A golden circle surrounding a golden triangle had been embossed on its surface, a symbol whose significance did not escape him. This coffin was the property of the Dark Circle, the ultra-secret group of Necromancers Lucia had been a member of.

He stared at it for a while, dread coming over him. Despite every instinct telling him not to, he curled his fingers under the coffin's lid, lifting it up.

It was empty.

Gideon took a deep breath in, then laid down in the coffin, staring up at the ceiling above. Then he pulled the lid closed, and was plunged into darkness.

"YOUR NAME," a deep, disembodied voice asked.

"Gideon Myles," he answered.

There was a long pause.

"YOUR PURPOSE."

"To publish Thaddeus Birch's latest book," he answered.

There was a low rumbling sound, and then the coffin began to rotate.

Gideon braced himself, feeling the coffin spin, turning him slowly onto his side. It continued to spin, and he felt gravity pull him onto his back once again. Not onto his belly, as he would have expected.

The spinning stopped.

Gideon hesitated, the pushed up against the lid of the coffin. It swung open, revealing a black, domed ceiling far above.

He sat up, then got out of the coffin, standing beside it.

The small room within the tomb was gone. In its place, Gideon found himself in a large, rectangular room filled with row after row of coffins. Each of the coffins seemed to be fashioned of pure gold, including the coffin he'd laid in only moments before. Each with a black symbol – the circle enclosing a triangle – embossed on their lid. The floor and walls were made of black stone, with skulls embedded in it, their gaping jaws open in eternal screams.

Gideon straightened his suit, holding his lantern before him. There was only one way out of the room – a wide stairwell leading upward ahead. He steeled himself, then strode up to it, ascending the stairs. They led to a wide hallway, one with a stone archway. A huge ivory skull had been carved at the apex of the arch, its deep, empty eye-sockets staring down at him.

He stepped forward, and a faint glimmer of light appeared from deep within those sockets. The skull changed color, turning from ivory to black…and blood began to spill from the skull's eye-sockets.

"WELCOME, GIDEON MYLES," its voice boomed, the light within its eye-sockets growing brighter.

"Thank you," Gideon replied, trying his best to sound nonchalant. This, he knew, was a mouthpiece for the personification of Death, guardian of the Plane of Death. As powerful as Gideon was, if this thing wished, it could destroy him instantly. "I seek Petrusa."

"YOU EXIST OUTSIDE OF THE CIRCLE," the guardian boomed. "STAY ON THE PATH OR KNOW OBLIVION."

"Much appreciated," Gideon replied, inclining his head.

The huge skull shifted back to ivory, the light within its sockets fading. Gideon strode forward, holding his lantern before him. Beyond the arch was a simple wooden door. He opened it, stepping through.

And found himself in a graveyard quite different than the one he'd come from.

Dark, swirling clouds blanketed the sky far above, a blood-red moon looming over the horizon. Its crimson rays cast the black dirt and the gray tombstones all around him in a bloody hue. Tombstones set in haphazard rows, their stone cracked and crumbling. A tall black fence surrounded the large graveyard, its twisted metal topped with long, blood-stained spikes. Disembodied heads in various states of decay were impaled on some of the spikes.

Gideon spotted a narrow dirt path to his left, littered with half-buried skulls and various other human and not-so-human bones. The eye sockets of the skulls began to glow a faint blue, illuminating the path. He followed it, eventually reaching a small black metal gate, and opened it with a loud *creak*, leaving the graveyard.

The glowing skeletal path continued forward, winding up a small hill. Leafless trees littered the landscape, their twisted trunks covered in black, peeling bark. A dull red light shone from their flesh between the strips of bark, blood oozing from the cracks in a slow, steady stream. The path wound between these trees, leading Gideon to the top of the hill…and an extraordinary view.

For there, beyond the downward slope of the hill, was a massive city. One he'd only seen in Lucia's paintings.

Tall, narrow buildings made of black and gray stone rose to form the cityscape, many connected by bridges that crossed over the bustling streets below. Some were only a few stories tall, while others rose hundreds of feet up like eerie skyscrapers. The streets themselves were filled with horse-drawn carriages and legions of the undead congesting the wide streets. There were no lanterns in the city per se; instead, ghostly light came from the eye-sockets of countless skulls embedded in the streets and the walls of the buildings, and set upon tall spikes along the city streets. Most of that light was an eerie blue, some green, and occasionally a few other colors. But most of the city was shrouded in darkness.

And in the center of the city, a single, massive stone pillar stood easily a hundred feet in diameter. It had a broader base that tapered as it rose upward, then broadened again as it pierced the dark clouds far, far above. And halfway up the column – high above the rest of the city, and connected to this column – was a long, flat platform upon which a great black castle stood.

318

Arx Mortus, city of Petrusa, ruler of the Plane of Death.

Gideon got goosebumps looking at it. Lucia had described this place to him many times, but he'd never seen it with his own eyes. Only the dead and Necromancers were allowed to come here…and any who Petrusa deigned to make an exception for.

She must have owed Thaddeus quite the favor…or perhaps Petrusa wanted something from Gideon himself. Everything with her was transactional…and nothing was for free.

The glowing path ended at the top of the hill, and Gideon stood there, not quite sure where to go next. But he didn't have to wonder for long; the earth trembled under his feet, the dirt parting ahead of him to reveal the ivory dome of a huge skull. It lifted out of the hill before him, its mouth opening wide enough for him to walk through with ease…and revealing a shimmering blue portal within.

Gideon hesitated, then stepped into the portal…and emerged onto the stone ledge looking out over the city, the ledge upon which the great castle stood, the tops of the tallest buildings visible hundreds of feet below.

"Beautiful, isn't it?" a woman's voice stated from behind.

Gideon turned around.

There was a woman standing before him. A tall, slender woman with skin as pale as death, her long black hair cascading down over a multilayered suit of armor made entirely of intricately interconnected bones. She was quite beautiful, with arched eyebrows and high cheekbones, and glacier-blue eyes that never seemed to blink…and stared into his with an intensity that made him want to squirm. A skeleton stood guard behind and to one side of this woman, a golden ring etched into its forehead.

"What do you want, Gideon?" the woman inquired.

"Petrusa I presume," Gideon ventured. She didn't respond…nor did her expression change. It was utterly flat. Unreadable.

He cleared his throat, knowing that this *was* Petrusa. Her non-answer was answer enough.

"Thaddeus Birch wrote a sequel to 'The Magic of Havenwood,'" he continued. "I need it published and distributed as rapidly as possible."

"Why?"

"To build an army to defeat the Collector," he answered.

"Revenge?" she inquired, arching an eyebrow. He hesitated, then shook his head.

"Not revenge. To protect my daughter...and right a terrible wrong."

"Ah," Petrusa murmured, the faintest of smiles curling her pale lips. "You wish to complete the cycle."

"The what?"

"The cycle," she repeated. She stepped past him, standing inches from the edge of the stone ledge and gesturing with one long, slender arm. "Life. Death. And from death, a multitude of life." She turned to him. "Forever."

"In a way, yes," he conceded.

"*Exactly* yes," she corrected. "Or do you think Lucia didn't tell me your darkest secrets?"

Gideon grimaced, wiping sweaty palms on his pants. Though every inch of him wanted to lower his gaze, he didn't.

"Dark secrets are my currency," Petrusa mused. "I buy them, invest them. Sell them." She stared at him with those unblinking eyes. "Shame is such *effective* leverage."

"Can you do it?" he asked. She dismissed his question with a wave of her hand.

"Of course," she answered. "I could have hundreds of thousands of my people start copying it within the hour. And have it in the hands of thousands of readers within a day."

"Will you do it?"

"That," she replied, "...is a far better question." She eyed him silently for a moment. "Thaddeus did me a favor years ago. This will pay for...most of your request."

Gideon took a deep breath in, knowing full-well he was being toyed with. Petrusa held all the power, and could name any price she wanted. And she damn well knew it.

"The remainder?" he inquired.

"Hmm," she murmured, gazing down at the city. "Do you miss your wife, Gideon?"

Gideon froze, his heart skipping a beat. Petrusa glanced at him.

"Do you?" she pressed.

"More than anything in this world," was all he could say.

"Such a short life, yet she became one of my finest Necromancers," Petrusa mused. "She was the first to earn entry into the Dark Circle before she was thirty. I was hardly surprised, of course. She's a…kindred spirit."

Petrusa eyed him for a long, uncomfortable moment, and he resisted the urge to squirm.

"I admit I've been tempted to…persuade you to become one of us," she confessed. "But you're not meant for it, are you?"

"Not like Lucia was."

"And your daughter?" she pressed. Gideon grimaced, hating the fact that this woman knew about Bella. And hating the answer he was about to give.

"She takes after her mother," he admitted. Petrusa gave the slightest of smiles.

"Marvelous," she murmured.

"She needs to make her own choice," Gideon warned. Petrusa arched an eyebrow.

"And *you* need to let her make it."

Gideon grimaced, but nodded reluctantly.

"This is my proposal," she declared. "I will publish and distribute Thaddeus's book. It will be within the hands of thousands of readers by tomorrow. As to what happens then, that is up to Thaddeus's story." Her expression grew stony. "In return, you must bring Bella to the Guild of the Golden Coin…and let her make her choice."

Gideon sighed, then inclined his head.

"You have yourself a deal," he agreed.

"You of course understand the folly of not paying the full price."

"No," he admitted. "But I don't need to. I made a promise and I'm going to keep it."

She inclined her head.

"A good man," she replied. "Few powerful men are. Come to me again when this is done," she commanded. "Bring Bella to the Guild of the Golden Coin in the Twin Spires."

"As you wish," Gideon replied.

"It seldom isn't," Petrusa mused. She broke their gaze, gesturing at the city far below. Throngs of undead clogged the streets, going about their day. "See all of those souls Gideon? The vast majority were desperate to come here. To live in this wretched place. To become my servants for eternity."

Gideon said nothing, staring at the masses far below.

"Do you know why?" she inquired.

"They were afraid of death," he answered.

"Why?" she pressed. Gideon frowned, turning to give her a questioning look.

"Isn't everyone?"

"Lucia wasn't," she pointed out.

"Granted."

"You should know the answer," Petrusa scolded. "You're an artist, after all."

"Teach me."

"There is magic in stories, Gideon," Petrusa declared. "Magic brings our stories to life...and our life is a story in and of itself." She gazed down at the vast network of city streets. "And none of these people wanted their stories to end."

She turned to him again, arching an eyebrow.

"You of all people should understand that."

"My story..." he began.

"I wasn't talking about *your* story," she interrupted.

Gideon lowered his gaze, swallowing past a lump in his throat.

"Tell me Gideon," she continued. "Do you know why Heaven doesn't exist, but this place does?"

He shook his head mutely.

"Because Heaven is a terrible story," she answered. "The Plane of Death is about sacrifice. About souls being doomed to walk the land of the dead, never to return to the living world. About eternal longing for a chance at eternal life. It's a curse and a gift, Gideon. Heaven," she added with a dismissive wave of her hand, "...is what happens at the *end* of a story. The 'happily ever after' that inane fairy tales love so much."

Petrusa turned then, facing away from the city, toward the palace nearby. Gideon followed her cue; the great black castle stood before them, and in front of it hovered the huge skull that had brought him here only moments ago. It floated toward them, stopping before Gideon and opening its mouth wide to reveal its shimmering blue portal.

"Your time here is up," Petrusa announced. "Good luck defeating the Collector, Gideon."

"Thank you."

"And Gideon," she added as he lifted one foot into the skull's mouth. He stopped to glance back at her. "Don't die." She smirked. "Yet."

Chapter 36

ella didn't even have time to raise her hands to defend herself as the Collector thrust his deadly blade at her chest. Didn't even have time to scream. Bright white light flared around his right arm as the deadly point shot toward her, glowing with unholy power.

But his sword stopped an inch from Bella's chest...and then was flung backward by an invisible force, flying from his hand. The strange white light crawled up his arm to his shoulder, then to the right side of his face. Then it shot forward, plunging into Bella's chest.

"Run!" Grandpa cried.

The Collector stumbled backward, staring at his glowing right hand in horror.

"No!" he blurted out, stumbling backward. White light flowed from his body in a continuous stream to Bella's chest. Bella looked down at herself, seeing a red glow from under her shirt. She glanced back up.

The fine lines on the right side of the Collector's face were deepening, his hair on that side turning stark white...before her very eyes.

"Go Bella, go!" Grandpa pressed, turning and running from the Collector and pulling her with him.

"Get Thaddeus!" the Collector barked. "Detain the girl!"

Black soldiers spilled into the foyer through the broken portcullis, rushing toward Grandpa. The soldiers reached him quickly, grabbing his arms and legs, then dragging him toward the exit...and the glowing energy door beyond.

"Grandpa!" Bella screamed, running back toward him. But Piper hauled her backward, pulling her out of the foyer into the narrow hallway.

Animus burst into action then, flowing upward into the golden statue in the center of the foyer and bringing it to life. The statue leapt down from its pedestal, attacking the Collector and his soldiers. It swung its golden sword at the leftmost soldier, slicing through its neck in a single blow.

The soldier's head toppled from its shoulders in a burst of flame...and promptly flew back up, reconnecting with its neck.

"Come on!" Piper shouted, turning around and sprinting down the hallway...and then cursing as a huge undead boar charged right at them!

Piper dodged out of the way, pulling Bella with him.

The boar barreled right past them, entering the foyer and lowering its head to gore the soldiers. The impact sent them all flying...and the golden statue slashed at one of the fallen soldiers over and over, cutting it to pieces.

"Down the hall," Bella instructed, following her own advice. "Up the stairs!"

But more of the black soldiers rushed into the foyer, avoiding the boar and the statue and chasing after Bella and Piper. They moved incredibly fast, closing the distance rapidly.

"We're not gonna make it!" Piper warned. Bella focused on the stairs ahead, reaching them and bounding up three at a time. She heard the footsteps of the soldiers behind her, growing nearer with every second.

Bella and Piper made it to the top of the stairs, and that's when the enemy caught up with them.

One of them slashed at Piper's right shoulder, its claws raking his flesh. Piper grunted, then kicked the soldier down the stairs, toppling two of the other soldiers behind it. Then he followed Bella, reaching the top of the stairs...and the small room beyond. The one with the lone coffin in the center. Bella skid to a stop before the coffin, throwing the lid open.

"Come on!" she urged, glancing back. The black soldiers dashed after her, reaching the top of the stairs. They lunged at her and

Piper…just as Death's black skull rose from the depths of the coffin, its huge mouth gaping open.

It wailed, the sound filling the small room, sending chills down Bella's spine.

The soldiers switched targets, leaping at the head and attacking Death with their vicious claws.

Which went precisely as one might expect.

Death's black tongue shot out, wrapping around both of the soldiers and pulling them into its gaping maw, swallowing them whole.

The Collector appeared at the top of the stairs, jerking backward when he saw Bella…and the personification of Death itself.

"LEAVE," its bone-chilling voice boomed.

The Collector glanced at Bella, then the creature…and the coffin it came from.

"Right," he muttered.

And then he turned and ran.

* * *

Bella sat on the edge of the stone bowl of her mother's foyer, the golden statue once again standing on its pedestal. Animus hovered above the floor at her feet, and Piper paced nearby, chewing on a fingernail as he did so. The horrible black soldiers were gone, as was the Collector.

Grandpa was gone.

She stared at the damaged portcullis ahead, and at the empty cavern beyond. Part of her hoped beyond hope that the purple energy door would reappear, that Grandpa would step out of it. That everything would be back to the way it'd been.

But no matter how long she sat there for, nothing happened.

Bella lowered her gaze to Animus, feeling numb.

"You sure you don't know when Gideon will be back?" Piper asked for the umpteenth time. Bella didn't even bother to answer. He sighed, continuing his pacing. "If that…thing that attacked the White Dragon is still around, Gideon'll be in deep trouble," he warned.

"I think he'll notice," Bella muttered.

"Yeah, but what if it wins?" Piper pressed. "What if it comes down here and decides to take *us* out?"

"Then we hide in Mom's conclave," she answered.

"And stay in there forever?"

"Just until it leaves," Bella replied. Piper gave her a look.

"And how are we gonna know when it does?"

Bella sighed, lowering her face to her hands and rubbing her eyes wearily. It had to be early morning, and neither one of them had gotten any sleep for nearly twenty-four hours. She was beyond exhausted...but Piper was right. If the huge creature was still out there, they were in big trouble.

"Let's go," she prompted, sliding off the stone bowl and walking toward the stairs leading to her bedroom on the second floor.

"Wait, where?" Piper asked.

"Out there," Bella answered, gesturing at the cavern ahead. "Let me get my Painter's uniform first." She went upstairs, changing into her uniform and stuffing her thigh-holsters with paintings. Then she went back downstairs, finding Piper still standing there in the foyer, staring at her with an incredulous expression. She ignored him, passing through the broken portcullis and continuing to the gate ahead. Piper followed behind her.

"You're going outside?" he pressed. "Are you crazy?"

"We have to know what happened," Bella explained. She pulled out one of her paintings from her thigh-holster. "Apertus," she commanded, and the painting unrolled itself. It was the painting she'd stuck Goo in. She drew him out, and he landed with a wet *plop* beside her. "Clausus," she muttered, and the painting rolled back up. She stuffed it in her thigh-holster, continuing forward.

"What the hell is that?" Piper asked.

"Goo, this is Piper," Bella introduced. "Piper, this is Goo."

"Goo?" Piper repeated.

"Goo."

"Creative name," he muttered. Goo pointedly ignored him, oozing behind Bella as she strode across the cavern toward the tunnel leading back to the Water Dragon's tail.

"The Collector got Grandpa," Bella notified Goo. "He attacked Havenwood."

Goo's body rippled, indicating his understanding.

"You got a light?" Piper inquired as they neared the tunnel. Bella paused, then made her way to a cluster of the glowing mushrooms nearby. She took a whole bunch of them, dropping them onto Goo.

"Can you carry these?" she asked.

Goo sucked the mushrooms into himself, and they made him glow bright green, providing plenty of light. They made the long journey up the Water Dragon's tail and body, and thankfully there were no more of the Collector's soldiers waiting to attack them. The Everstream flowed upstream as they made their way to the mouth of the cavern. Bella slowed as they neared the opening, staring at the starry night sky beyond. The pale moon shone its silver light on the rocky outcrop leading to the waterfall, the gurgling water the only noise.

No sound of fighting. No earthquake-like shuddering of the earth at her feet.

She hesitated, then exited the cave, Goo at her side. Piper, she noted, stayed behind in the relative safety of the cave. A twinge of fear gripped her as she walked up to the edge of the waterfall, and she steeled herself for what she was about to see.

Bella gazed down at the landscape spread out before her below, Goo stopping at her side.

The waterfall fell to Lake Fenestra below, but the lake was no longer blue. Its waters were black with soot. For the mushroom forest surrounding Havenwood was on fire, thick black smoke rising into the air all around. Downtown Havenwood was in ruins, many of the buildings charred or collapsed.

She closed her eyes, taking a deep, steadying breath in. Then she opened them, looking beyond the mushroom forest.

The White Dragon was there, as it had been before the siege on Havenwood, its massive body encircling the mountain. But its body was covered with gigantic streaks of blood, many of its scales charred or missing. The flesh of its wings was riddled with tears, its face bloodied.

It looked...dead.

Oh god, she thought, putting a hand to her mouth.

"Well?" she heard Piper call out from behind. She ignored him, staring at the White Dragon. Waiting for it to breathe.

But it didn't.

Bella lowered herself to sit down, feeling suddenly exhausted. She lowered her face into her hands, taking a deep breath in, then letting it out. A vision of Grandpa being dragged away by the

Collector's soldiers came to her. Tears welled up in her eyes, and she took another, shuddering breath in. She heard footsteps from behind, and felt Piper's presence behind her. He swore, shaking his head grimly.

"We're screwed," he muttered.

Bella said nothing.

"We can't beat the Collector," he stated. "No one can. He killed the damn White Dragon!"

Still she said nothing.

"We're going back inside," he muttered, turning back toward the cave. But Bella didn't stand up to follow him. She just sat there, staring at the White Dragon. Staring at its gigantic chest.

As she watched, it rose up ever-so-slowly…then fell. Her heart skipped a beat, relief coursing through her.

"It's alive!" she exclaimed, pointing to the dragon. "Look!"

Piper did so, and nearly a minute later, the dragon's chest rose and fell again.

"Yeah, but barely," he conceded. "If that *thing* attacks again…" He turned to face Bella. "Come on, let's go home," he insisted.

"No."

Piper blinked.

"What do you mean, 'no?'" he demanded.

"I'm not going back inside," she answered.

"Excuse me?"

"I'm not going back inside," she repeated, standing up. She turned away from the White Dragon, facing him. "I'm not hiding anymore, Piper. I won't be a victim again. I *refuse* to be a victim again."

"Bella, we're not safe here."

"We're not safe *anywhere*," she retorted. "And what are we going to do, hide for the rest of our lives?"

"If we want to *have* lives, yes."

"That's not a life," Bella pressed. "I spent most of my life lost in a book, hiding from the Collector. How is hiding here any different?"

"Well it's the only reason you're still alive," Piper pointed out.

"Maybe so," she conceded. "But I don't want to just be alive. I want to *live*."

"Bella…"

"When I came here, for the first time in my life, I felt free," Bella stated. "I felt like I belonged somewhere. Like I wasn't some freak trying to fit in where I didn't belong." She crossed her arms over her chest. "And for the first time in my life, I saw Grandpa happy. *Truly* happy."

Piper grimaced, but held his tongue.

"The Collector hunted us for ten years, and for ten years Grandpa kept me safe," Bella declared. "And now the Collector has him."

"He's probably…"

"And your wife," Bella interrupted, glaring at him.

Piper drew back as if he'd been slapped.

"Do you love her?" she asked. Piper swallowed, then nodded.

"More than anything in this world."

"Well I love my Grandpa," she replied. "And I won't stop until I get him back."

Piper sighed.

"What're we gonna do?" he inquired, raising his arms up to the sides. "Storm the Collector's castle and demand he give them back?"

"We have to do *something*," Bella insisted.

"That's not a plan."

"Fine, we'll come up with a plan then," she replied. Piper's eyebrows went up.

"Oh yeah?" he said. "Just like that?"

"Just like that."

"You're gonna need an army to take on the Collector," he warned. "Either that or some pretty damn powerful magic."

"I think we already have some," Bella replied. She looked down at her amulet, holding it in one hand. Remembering the white light that had surrounded the Collector, streaming into her amulet.

"What'd'you mean we already have some?" Piper demanded.

"Did you see the Collector's face?" she asked. Piper nodded. "It was older on one side," she explained. "And it got even older when he tried to attack me. The light…it when into here," she added, pointing at the heart-shaped ruby. She studied it…and frowned. The large crack in the ruby looked…different. It extended two-thirds of the way through the heart now, instead of going all the way through.

"So…"

"Huh?" she asked, glancing up at Piper.

"So what?" he pressed.

"So...he can't attack me," Bella concluded. "That must've been how Mom's amulet saved me the first time."

Piper's eyebrows furrowed.

"The first time?"

"I think it happened before," she reasoned. "Grandpa said the Collector attacked Mom, and...killed her. Then he tried to kill me."

"And the same thing happened."

"His face was already old on one side," she pointed out. "So yes, it must have."

"So you're saying if he comes near you, he'll be...drained again?"

"I think so," Bella confirmed.

"Alright, maybe so," Piper conceded. "But how exactly do you plan on getting close to him again? His defenses are incredibly powerful. And *he* might not be able to kill you, but his army will."

"Then it's time for me to get real creative," she decided.

"Why's that?"

"Because the more creative I am, the more powerful my magic will be," she answered. "Let's go," she added, turning left and following parallel to the edge of the cliff.

"Go where?" he asked, following behind her.

"We need to look for survivors."

"It's still too dark," he countered. "We should wait for the morning."

"I'm not afraid of the dark," Bella replied with a grim smile, stuffing her amulet under her shirt. "But it's about time I made the darkness afraid of me."

Chapter 37

The Collector eased himself into his chair before his desk in the inverted Castle Over, wincing at the pain in his right hand as he did so. It throbbed something fierce, a constant, reminder of his terrible mistake.

He squeezed his eyes shut, cursing under his breath.

Idiot!

The Collector slammed his left fist onto the desk, his jawline rippling.

It was the damn girl!

He should have known better. That terrible white light had drained him after he'd attacked the girl the first time, ten years ago at Blackthorne. After he'd thrust his sword into Lucia's heart. It made perfect sense now. Lucia had cursed him...so that any time he got close to her daughter, he'd be drained.

You never should have gotten close to the girl, he told himself. *You should have known better.*

He opened his eyes, staring down at his gloved right hand. Feeling the pain there. Dread twisted his guts, fear at the thought of what horrors might be waiting for him under that black cloth.

Despite every inch of him screaming not to, he pulled the glove off.

A flap of skin on the back of his hand came with it.

He drew in a sharp breath at the sudden pain, watching as blood welled up from the large skin tear. His hand was practically skeletal, the skin so thin it clung to his bones like tissue paper. His fingers were bent at odd angles, his fingernails chipped and yellowed.

Blood dripped off the sides of his hand, pooling on the desktop.

The Collector stared at his ancient hand, watching as the blood continued to ooze from it. For the first time in a very long time, he reconsidered his vow to never return to the canvas.

You could have one of your Painters heal you, he told himself. *Just this once.*

He reached down to pull open one of the desk drawers, retrieving a small mirror within. He closed the drawer, then held up the mirror with his good hand, staring at his reflection.

The left side of his face was much as it had been, but with some new, fine wrinkles here and there. But the right side…

He almost dropped the mirror.

The hair at his right temple was pure white, and much sparser than it had been. And his skin was deeply wrinkled, like an old man's, the skin there loose and thin, with liver-spots on his cheek. The skin on the right side of his neck was loose as well, in stark contrast to that on his left.

He lowered the mirror to the desk, setting it down gently.

And then he lifted his left fist up, sending it crashing down on the mirror with a loud *bang!*

The mirror shattered, pieces flying across the desktop and falling to the floor with a clatter.

That damn witch!

Even in death, Lucia was getting her revenge.

You should never have killed her.

The Collector closed his eyes, remembering how she'd stood defiantly before him, guarding her daughter and Thaddeus. Short and slender, with chocolate-colored skin and curly hair that sprung from her head, wild and free.

Just stood there, smirking at him as he'd thrust his sword into her heart.

And how, as she'd slumped to the floor, as he'd strode up to finish off that screaming little brat, a white light had appeared on his right hand. His sword hand.

And how that light had crawled up his arm, then shot outward at the girl, flowing into her chest.

He opened his eyes, staring at his right hand.

If only he'd known then what he knew now. He'd been young. Brash. Stupid enough to attack a Necromancer. Callous enough to try to kill an innocent little girl.

The Collector stood abruptly, his chair tipping back and falling onto the floor with a *thump*. He strode out of his office, to the tall inverted tower with the spiraling staircase that would bring him back to Castle Under. He'd vowed never to step into another canvas, but he'd never anticipated *this*. There was too much work yet to be done. His sacred mission was not even close to being complete.

He needed more time.

Just this once, he told himself as he entered the tower. With a thought, he activated his boots, and shot upward into the air at breakneck speed, the spiraling staircase of the tower a blur around him.

Then never again.

Chapter 38

Without Grandpa, the magic of Havenwood was gone. Ash coated the ruins of downtown Havenwood, the tightly-clustered buildings near the base of Dragon's Peak bereft of life. After hours of searching – well through the night and into the next morning – neither Bella nor Piper found a single soul. No survivors, no corpses.

The town was deserted.

Eventually they made their way up to the top of Dragon's Peak, to Castle Havenwood. The Studio, once filled with people and paintings, was also deserted. The paintings were gone, only sculptures remaining. And one entire wing of the castle – one supported by a giant mushroom stalk – had collapsed completely after the stalk had been severed by the horrible beast that had attacked the White Dragon.

After another hour of searching the castle, they found a couple dozen survivors huddled in a locked vault in one of the upper floors. It took quite a bit of convincing to get them to unlock the door, after which everyone was relieved that the attack was over…and that the White Dragon was still alive.

But as the artists followed Bella back down to the ground floor of the castle, walking out of it and traveling down the spiraling cobblestone road to downtown, relief turned to horror.

For their families were gone. Their friends. And their homes had been all but destroyed.

And, curiously, their paintings – every last one in Havenwood – had vanished.

The sun was already well above the horizon by the time Piper pulled Bella away from the others, facing her with dark circles under his eyes.

"Let's go back to your place and get some sleep," he prompted, walking toward the spiraling cobblestone street.

And so they made their way, one foot in front of the other, until they were home.

* * *

The next afternoon, Bella woke, and the survivors of Havenwood had a meeting in The Studio.

"The White Dragon will heal," one man stated. He was Griggins, an older Sculptor who was short, squat, rotund, and had a long, curly white beard. He appeared to be the de-facto leader of the group. "But it's going to take a long time. We need to paint a potion or something that will help it heal faster."

"I can do that," a woman offered.

"We need to do more," Piper piped in.

"The dragon is still our best option for defending Havenwood," Griggins insisted.

"Tell that to everyone who *isn't* here," Piper retorted. Griggins grimaced.

"If you have a better idea, please enlighten us," he replied.

"You're artists," Piper stated. "You can make whatever you want. Build an army. Make weapons. Defend yourselves."

"We're not combat Painters," someone else protested. "That's who the Collector hires. We can't compete against that!"

"He's got paintings from Blackthorne, for gods' sake," another argued.

"So that's it?" Piper exclaimed incredulously. "You're just gonna give up?"

"Why don't we ask the Pentad for help?" someone else inquired.

"And have them arrest all of us for illegally painting?" Griggins countered. "We're all technically criminals, in case you forgot." He shook his head. "Our best bet is to help heal the White Dragon," he insisted. "Then have an emergency plan. We'll all go into the vault like we did before if there's another attack. It worked yesterday."

"And if they force their way in next time?" Piper pressed.

"Well, Gideon is coming back, isn't he?" a woman pointed out.

"That's right," Griggins realized. "Gideon's a combat-Painter. The best!"

"What if he doesn't come back in time?" Piper asked.

"Then we hide in the vault."

Piper threw up his arms, storming out of The Studio and into the grand foyer of the castle. Bella hesitated, then followed him. Piper stopped before one of the statues of the Dragonkind, leaning against it. He seemed to be swearing under his breath.

"What's wrong?" she asked.

"These damn artists," he complained. "Everyone in Havenwood has their head in the clouds, making fanciful crap and expecting the White Dragon to protect them. Even when there's proof that it won't." He shook his head, turning to face her. "This is what happens when you convince people they aren't responsible for their own fates. They all turn into useless victims waiting for a damn hero to come and save 'em."

"Well, we can't wait for Gideon to get back," Bella argued. "We have to get Grandpa, and your wife."

"Great idea," Piper sneered. "Let's just go strolling into the Collector's castle and ask him to give 'em back."

Bella gave him a look.

"We're not going to ask him," she retorted. "We're going to *make* him."

Piper's eyebrows went up.

"And how exactly do you plan on doing that?" he inquired.

"Grandpa told me the secret to defeating the Collector was in his new book," she answered. "We just have to read it to find out what it is."

"Okay…"

"And in case you forgot, I'm a Painter too," she reminded him. "I can paint things that will help us."

Piper gave her a doubting look.

"You any good?" he inquired. Bella squared her shoulders.

"If I want to get Grandpa back, I'll have to be," she replied.

* * *

And so Bella returned to her studio in Mom's estate, deep in the bowels of Dragon's Peak. But she didn't paint, not at first. First, she studied.

Every room of Mom's house had paintings in it. Bella looked at each one, studying the brushstrokes, the colors. Not only did she study the story each painting told, but she deconstructed *how* Mom had told them. All the tiny details that were the difference between a novice painter and a master.

After all, according to Gideon, Mom was the second-best painter he'd ever met.

In-between these sessions, Bella sat on the couch in the living room Grandpa had become fond of taking naps in, reading Grandpa's first book on Havenwood, titled "The Magic of Havenwood." Of course, since she was already *in* Havenwood, reading the book didn't transport her to another world. Still, she found herself lost in Grandpa's prose, a story every bit as good as the bedtime stories he'd told her.

And when she was done with that, she read the sequel...and was about two-thirds of the way through when she saw it.

"I found it!" she cried, leaping up from the couch she'd been reading in. Piper – seated in a comfortable chair nearby taking a nap – jolted awake.

"What the...!" he blurted out. "Damn kid, don't scare me like that!"

"I found it," she repeated, holding the book before her. "I found Grandpa's secret to fight the Collector!"

Piper stood up, reaching for the book, and Bella handed it to him.

"What is it?" he asked.

"There's a Plane of Reflection," she explained.

"Duh."

"Grandpa wrote about it in the first book, that the Dragonkind lived in Havenwood – they *built* Havenwood in the Plane of Reflection, and so its mirror-image appeared in the real world. And the White Dragon was born in the Plane of Reflection, but somehow managed to come into this world."

338

"I read the first book," Piper stated wryly. "Everyone in the damn world has."

"Well, the first book says that after the White Dragon went through, the Dragonkind lost the ability to travel into the real world," Bella continued. "But in *this* book, I think he created a way."

Piper frowned, reading the passage Bella had pointed out:

"The Everstream flowed into Lake Fenestra at the foot of Havenwood, a reflection plane to see. And through its waters the land of the Dragonkind, where a multitude will bend its knee."

Piper looked up at her.

"I don't get it," he admitted.

"It's the typo," she explained, pointing at the page. "A reflection *plane* to see."

"And?"

"He put it there on purpose," she replied. "A Reflection Plane to see, and through its waters…"

"A multitude will bend its knee," Piper finished, his eyes widening. "So he made the lake…"

"A way to get into the land of the Dragonkind," Bella concluded excitedly. "Where an army of Dragonkind will bend its knee!"

Piper re-read the passage silently, then lifted his gaze to Bella, giving her a rare smile.

"I think you're right," he breathed.

"Let's go," she prompted, leaving the living room.

"Where are…"

"To the Dragonkind," she interjected. "It's time we got ourselves an army!"

She led him out of the mansion and up the Water Dragon tunnel, emerging at the mouth of the cave. They both squinted at the bright light from the sun high above, waiting until their eyes adjusted, then continuing down the spiraling path to the base of Dragon's Peak. The lake, filled with ash and debris after the attack, had already cleared completely, its waters recycled continuously by the twin heads of the long-dead Water Dragon.

"I'm going in," Bella stated, walking to the very edge of the lake. She peered into the water, seeing the rippling reflection of the sky and part of Dragon's Peak. And a few Dragonkind standing at the edge of the water in that reflection, one of the pointing at her and saying something to a colleague.

She took a deep breath in, then jumped into the water!

And stood there, ankle-deep in the lake.

She spun around, looking up at Piper.

"Well that didn't work," he quipped. "Try jumping up and down."

She did so, hopping over and over, but nothing happened. Piper watched her, a smirk on his lips. She frowned at him.

"You knew that wouldn't work," she accused. "Why'd you have me do that?"

"Umm…"

"I don't get it," she grumbled out, walking back onto the shore. "I'm *sure* that's how we're supposed to do it!"

"Just because he wrote it doesn't mean it's real," Piper reminded her. "Maybe Gideon hasn't gotten the book published yet…or not enough people have read it.

Bella realized he was right, and her shoulders slumped.

"Oh."

"It's okay," he reassured. "We'll just keep trying. It might take a while."

"Alright," she agreed.

They trudged back up the mountain, returning home. And after she'd finished the second book – and found no other clue as to how to reach the Dragonkind – there was nothing else to do but wait…and paint.

* * *

With no way to tell what time it was, Bella fell into a pattern of napping when she got tired, then waking up and getting to work. Perhaps inspired by her work ethic, Piper got to practicing his Acting, a process that was fascinating to behold. Transforming from one character to the next with ease, Piper went from being a humpbacked old man to a mysterious cloaked stranger in a matter of seconds.

"How do you do that?" Bella inquired. "Do you just pretend and it happens?"

340

"It's not pretending," he countered. "It's *being*. When I act, I *am* my characters. I feel what they feel. I become them."

"Oh."

"I create them the same way you paint things," he explained. "By creating a story about them."

Bella supposed that made sense. Magic, as Gideon had told her, loved stories. In fact, stories *were* magic, as far as she was concerned.

Which meant that if she wanted to stand a chance against the Collector – and his Painters – she needed to tell a better story than they could.

But what exactly?

"Oh, by the way," Piper said, breaking her from her train of thought. "A few of my characters are beat up…and one is dying. I need you to heal them for me."

"By painting them?"

"Right," Piper confirmed. "I'll change into each character and go into a canvas, and you heal them." He gave her a doubting look. "You ever do that before?"

"Yup. To Gideon."

"Alright, well if he trusted you to do it, I will," Piper decided. "Want to do it now?"

"Whenever," Piper replied. "Time stands still for my characters when I don't use them, so there's no rush. Go paint some more first."

Bella did so, making her way back to her studio. She grabbed a fresh canvas, placing it on her easel. Then she sat down on the floor, her chin in her hand, staring up at that blank space. She needed to tell a story…a better story than the Collector's Painters. But what?

What would Grandpa say?

She closed her eyes, remembering how she'd laid in bed beside Grandpa, asking him what she should paint. Remembering what he'd said.

Something that makes you feel something.

She sighed, opening her eyes and gazing up at the canvas.

Throwaway art pleases the eye, good art changes people's minds, and great art…great art opens their hearts.

Her hand went to her heart, and she felt the hardness of her mother's amulet there. She withdrew it from her Painter's uniform, staring at the cracked, heart-shaped ruby. Her mother's heart.

She reached into her pants pocket then, finding a folded-up piece of paper there. It was Grandpa's letter; she retrieved it, unfolding it and reading the final sentence:

> *Remember that love is something you give, as I gave mine to you. Give it to your art and heal your heart.*
>
> *A friend awaits.*
> *Grandpa*

Her own heart skipped a beat, and she leapt to her feet, clutching the amulet. She turned, spotting one of the many sketches she'd made of her dragon…and her eyes went to the heart-shaped ruby embedded in its sternum.

"My dragon," she blurted out. She reached down excitedly to grab a pencil, then froze.

I'm not ready.

Bella hesitated, then grit her teeth, grabbing the pencil and turning to the canvas. If she was going to have any chance at saving Grandpa, she couldn't wait any longer. Her dragon was the memory of her mother, a fierce, dark protector who would never leave her side. She had to paint its story – *her* story – with all of her heart. She *had* to be ready.

Grandpa's life depended on it.

Chapter 39

imon stepped into the Collector's office, walking up to the Collector's large desk. He'd been called in only moments before, having waited in the waiting room with Miss Savage for over a half-hour. The Doppelganger had been forced to wait all the way back in his studio, and Simon could feel the Familiar pacing. But he hardly noticed, his eyes on the Collector.

It took every ounce of self-discipline for him to keep his expression neutral.

The right side of the man's face had aged terribly, his hair white and thin, his skin thin and wrinkled. It was as if half of him were a hundred years old. Even the man's right eye was glazed over, so much so that Simon suspected he couldn't even see out of it.

"Hello Simon," the Collector greeted.

"Hello sir," Simon replied automatically, bowing his head.

"I have some news for you," the Collector announced, leaning forward and resting his elbows on the desk. He steepled his fingers. "Good and bad, I'm afraid."

Simon waited.

"Your creation was a success," the Collector declared. "It attacked Havenwood and badly wounded the White Dragon. Your dark army took down nearly every artist in Havenwood…and their paintings are now mine."

"The bad news?" Simon asked.

"The White Dragon destroyed most of your creation," the Collector answered. "A few dozen of the dark soldiers remain, but the rest are gone."

Simon lowered his gaze, swallowing past a lump in his throat.

There was a long silence, and Simon lifted his gaze, staring at the Collector. The man was watching him silently, his hands still steepled.

"How does that make you feel, Simon?" he inquired.

Simon hesitated.

"I loved them," was all he said. All he *could* say.

The Collector sighed, lowering his hands to his desk. He stood then, stepping around his desk and standing before Simon.

"Simon, do you trust me?"

Simon just stared at him.

"You can tell me the truth," the Collector reassured.

Don't tell him the truth, the Doppelganger warned.

"I want to," Simon answered. Which was true enough.

"And I want to trust you," the Collector replied. "I'm *going* to trust you. With something very important. Something I've never let anyone do before."

"What's that?"

"I want you to paint me," the Collector answered. He gestured at the right side of his face. "I want you to fix this."

"Yes sir," Simon replied. "What…happened?"

"A woman cursed me," the Collector answered. "A Necromancer. Do you know what that is?"

Simon nodded. Necromancers were artists that walked two worlds, that of the living and that of the dead. They were the stuff of fairy tales, a threat used to scare kids into behaving. The Collector must have noticed his doubting look.

"They're real, Necromancers," he informed Simon. "And the one who cursed me was very powerful. I need you to undo her curse."

"Okay," Simon agreed. The Collector smiled.

"Good," he replied. He stood then. "Let's go to your studio."

* * *

The Collector set a small mirror on the floor, then stood before the huge canvas Simon had used to create Legion, the beast that had attacked Havenwood, gazing at it. With the countless Doppelgangers drawn out of it, only a drab landscape remained. For the first time in a very long time, he felt a nervous energy within him.

He felt Simon staring at him, and glanced down to eye the boy. Simon had barely said anything during their trip across the castle. The boy's shoulders were less rounded than before, his posture better than when they'd first met. But he was still so quiet. When he walked, his footsteps were barely audible.

As if he were terrified of being heard.

"It's time," the Collector stated, turning to Simon. He forced himself to keep his tone calm. Authoritative. Simon glanced up at him.

"Are you nervous?" the boy asked.

The Collector tried not to grimace. Simon was an incredibly sensitive boy, highly attuned to the emotional state of others.

A skill learned by necessity, he suspected.

"Yes," the Collector confessed. There was no point in lying. Simon already knew the answer, and only the weak felt the need to lie.

"I'll do a good job," Simon promised. The Collector smiled.

"I trust you."

And to his surprise, it was true. He trusted the boy implicitly, in a way he trusted only one other: Miss Savage. Simon was…pure. There was no duplicity about him. And despite his outer frailty, the boy had an inner strength that continually surprised the Collector. So much like the Collector when he'd been Simon's age.

He trusts you, the Collector thought. And in that moment, he felt a sudden twinge of guilt, knowing that he was unworthy of that trust.

The Collector grimaced, looking down at the glove on his right hand.

Focus.

Slowly – carefully – he pulled it off, wincing at the pain there. This time he didn't bother to hide the expression. Let Simon see that he was…human.

The Collector noticed Simon staring at his ancient hand, and resisted the urge to hide it at his side. Unbuttoning his black suit jacket, he folded it neatly, placing it on the floor beside him. He wore a simple black shirt underneath; this too he removed, revealing his bare chest and belly. The body of an ordinary man. Mere flesh and blood.

Exposed for what he *really* was.

He felt Simon's eyes on him, and knew the boy was admiring his body. He allowed this, keeping his gaze on the canvas so as not to interrupt. Though he didn't share Simon's preferences, he understood the inevitability of the boy's attraction. It was the boy's truth, something he could not change. And therefore it deserved the Collector's acceptance.

"Take your time, Simon," he advised.

And then, before he could give himself enough time to change his mind, The Collector stepped forward, becoming one with the canvas.

And felt a hand grab his wrist, pulling him out immediately thereafter.

The Collector blinked, seeing Simon before him. The boy looked utterly exhausted, his eyes glassy and dark circles under his eyes.

"It's done," Simon notified him.

The Collector looked down at himself. At his right hand. It was a mirror-image of his left, the skin smooth and supple, the wrinkles and age spots gone. He flexed and extended his fingers, turning his hand over to gaze at his palm. No pain, no stiffness.

It was perfect.

He brought a hand up to his face, feeling the skin there. It too was smooth. Retrieving the mirror he'd set on the floor, he gazed into it. His face was as it'd been before being drained by that girl, his hair jet-black. Again, it was perfect.

He felt a wave of emotion, and grit his teeth, composing himself. Lowering the mirror, he turned to Simon.

"Well done, Simon," he congratulated. "You're the only one I trusted to do this for me."

Simon broke out into a relieved smile, which he quickly suppressed, almost by reflex. The boy lowered his gaze to the floor.

"What's wrong?" the Collector inquired. Simon hesitated, then shrugged his frail shoulders.

"No one ever…said something like that to me before."

The Collector resisted the urge to talk, sensing that this was a critical moment for Simon. Now was the time to listen.

He waited, and Simon lifted his gaze to meet his.

"My mom died when I was born," Simon confessed. "*Because* I was born. My dad…" He lowered his gaze again, his eyes moist. "He didn't love who I was inside, so he tried to beat it out of me.

"My…mother left my father," the Collector confessed. "My father raised me too. Like yours did."

Simon looked up at him, his gaze intense.

"Did your father…care?" he asked. The Collector sighed.

"He thought he did. But the only person he really cared about was himself."

Simon frowned, considering this.

"My father never lied about how he felt about me," he muttered.

The Collector said nothing, finding his gaze drawn to the scars on Simon's arms. He glanced at the Doppelganger, the boy's Familiar, always at Simon's side. It stood there, its shoulders slumped, that brown bottle forever clutched in its hand. A beer bottle. He gazed at the fine cracks in the Doppelganger's porcelain skin. Broken over and over, it somehow pulled itself back together each time. And each time it had to, it grew a little stronger.

A vision of the Glarg it'd killed came to him, its head beaten to a bloody pulp.

He felt a warm hand touch his, holding it gently.

The Collector resisted the urge to yank his hand out of the boy's, surprised by the unexpected touch. Simon gazed up at him with a warm smile, his expression still guarded…but hopeful.

The Collector felt a sudden, powerful affection for the boy, and found himself smiling back.

A bolt of fear struck him then, and he recoiled from the sudden emotion, gently slipping his hand away from Simon's after a long moment, so as not to offend the boy. He struggled to remember the last thing Simon had said.

"Your father was a fool," he forced himself to say.

Simon's smile broadened, and the Collector turned away, gazing up at the huge canvas before them. Mostly as a way to stop the boy from studying his expression…and to collect himself. The affection he'd felt had been unexpected, but not unreasonable. They had a lot in common, after all. But he couldn't afford to feel that way toward Simon. *Especially* toward Simon.

Their relationship was built on a lie, after all.

You're just like the man who made you, the Collector realized, a chill running through him. *Lie after lie after lie.*

The thought horrified him.

He glanced down at Simon, who was still smiling at him…and was struck with another burst of fear.

But what if his feelings for Simon *weren't* a lie? What if they were real?

Remember the plan, he told himself.

He took a deep breath in, steeling himself. Then he turned to face Simon.

"You're too good to be wasted here, Simon," he declared.

Simon gave him a questioning look.

"You'll be joining me tomorrow," the Collector continued. "I have something very special I want to show you."

"What's that?"

"Castle Over," the Collector answered.

Simon's eyes widened, and he broke out into a grin.

"Castle Over?" he breathed. The Collector nodded.

"It's time for your promotion," he announced. "Congratulations Simon," he added. "You earned it."

Chapter 40

Bella stood before a large canvas propped on its easel in her studio, making the finishing touches to her latest sketch with a fine-tipped pencil. Then she set the pencil down, taking a few steps back and staring at her work.

It was a sketch of her dragon – the best version yet. But what really mattered, she knew, was the story *around* the dragon. And for that, she'd started with the few fragments of her past she'd remembered painting way back when she'd been lost in the book with Grandpa. The double-doors of the library at Blackthorne, fingers of mist crawling up their surface. And that mist obscuring a transition to the inside of the library, where the two cloaked, bone-scythe-wielding creatures levitated above the polished floor. Both flanking the Collector, who raised his silver sword, face twisted in rage. And the ghostly light pulling from his face and arm, converging on her mother's amulet…embedded in the bony sternum of her dragon.

And protected within the embrace of those translucent wings, a shadowy silhouette of a small girl holding a paintbrush.

There were countless other details, of course. They'd come to her as if by magic as she'd sketched, a trickle of the Flow affecting her. It would grow much stronger once she painted, for the act of painting was when the *real* magic happened.

She glanced down at Goo, plopped on the floor to her left.

"What do you think, Goo?" she asked. Goo quivered quite violently. "Really?" she pressed. He quivered again in confirmation.

Bella frowned, grabbing the pencil from her easel and tapping her chin with its eraser.

"I still need to make it my Familiar," she realized. "Which means I have to make her connected to me somehow."

But how?

Sure, having her dragon protect her – and having her mother's heart-shaped amulet – might be connection enough. But then again, maybe not. How to show a mental connection? A mental *and* emotional one?

She stopped tapping her chin with her pencil, looking down at the eraser.

Suddenly, she had an idea.

Stepping up to the drawing, she used her eraser to create a faint light around the silhouette of her head behind the dragon's translucent wings. She extended the light, making it travel all the way up to encircle the dragon's head.

"There," she declared, setting the pencil down and crossing her arms. She glanced at Goo. "Think it's ready?"

A lump protruded from Goo's surface, nodding once.

"All right then," she decided, grabbing a bunch of paint canisters and sliding them across the floor next to the easel. She began to mix paints onto her palette, glancing up at her sketch as did so. The canvas was huge, with far more detail than she'd ever attempted before. Doubt trickled in again, but she pushed it aside.

She had to forge ahead if she ever wanted to see Grandpa again.

"Just paint, huh?" she mumbled to herself. She took a deep breath in, squaring her shoulders and focusing on the canvas. "All right Bella, you can do this."

And she refused to stop until she proved herself right.

* * *

"Wow," Piper breathed, staring at the canvas.

Three days had passed since Bella started painting her dragon, spending day and night slaving over it. Her clothes were spattered with layer upon layer of paint, as were her hands. The few times she'd taken a break, she'd worked on other things. Healing Piper's many characters came first, then creating some magical items she'd need on her journey to the Collector's castle.

But none compared to the one they were standing before now.

She'd obsessed over this painting. Spent almost every waking minute thinking about it. Loved it. Hated it. Raged against it. She'd painted the Collector with dark, angry lines, and the white light drawn out of him with a sense of grim satisfaction. Painted Animus with softness and warmth mixed with somber grays.

And the dragon – *her* dragon – she'd painted with love. It'd given her goosebumps, seeing her creation slowly come to life. What had once been mere strokes of a pencil in her notebook, but so vibrant and *alive* in her mind, in her daydreams, was now before her in full, majestic color.

Its wings curled inward before it, and within them was a deep red glow. A glow of its heartstone, her mother's broken heart. And silhouetted within was a hint of a girl. A girl with wild, curly hair. A ghostly light rose from the girl's head, arcing to the dragon's…while the girl crouched within the radiant warmth of its heart.

Bella stared at that silhouette, picturing her mother's arms wrapped around her. The warmth and softness of her embrace. Not for the first time, she blinked away tears.

Ten years she'd been lost, adrift in a cruel, uncaring world with her Grandpa. With only her mother's amulet to remind her of what she'd had before. Of what had been taken from her. Now she would carry a piece of her mother with her. A dragon with her mother's heart.

Bella would never be alone again.

"Damn," Piper murmured. He leaned in, his brown furrowing as he took in all of the details of the painting. While similar to her sketch in composition, in execution it had transformed greatly. Rich colors in the foreground contrasted sharply with deep shadows in the background. Indeed, her dragon was so vibrant that Bella half-expected it to leap out of the canvas all by itself.

"Right?" she replied, watching his expression. He must've realized his mouth was hanging open, because he snapped it shut, blinking and turning to her.

"This…" he stated, gesturing at the painting. "I didn't know you could paint like *this*."

"You like it?"

"Bella, this is…it's not normal," he informed her. She frowned at him. "Do you know what this is?"

"My Familiar."

"No, it's more than that," he insisted. "I've seen a painting like this before, but only once. Kendra showed me it. A painting from one of the old masters. It was like this."

"Like what?"

"Like this," he repeated. "Like…it could almost come out of the painting without you."

"Could it?"

"No," Piper answered. "But it means the Flow was extremely strong while you were painting. There's powerful magic here, Bella."

Bella turned to the painting.

"I painted the story inside of me. One that mattered."

Piper, for once, didn't comment. She turned to face him.

"What's it like for you?" she asked. "The Flow, I mean."

"The same," he admitted. "People think that acting is just pretending. Like you just pretend to be happy or sad, memorize some lines, and that's it. But I don't pretend when I act," Piper continued. "When I act, I *am* my character. I feel what they feel. I live what they've lived. They're as real to me as…" He gestured at her painting. "As that dragon is to you. And as Havenwood is to all of these people."

"Huh."

Art is art," he declared. "We're all storytellers. We just do it in different ways." He smiled. "And it's all magic."

It made sense, of course. Magic, as Gideon had told her, loved stories. She smiled back at Piper, then eyed him silently for a while, until he squirmed.

"What?" he asked.

"You're not such a bad guy after all," she observed. "Now that you're not with that jerk Stanwitz."

"He was a psycho," Piper agreed.

"How'd you end up working for a guy like the Collector?" Bella inquired. Piper shrugged.

"I was just following Kendra," he answered. "She's a lot like your mother was, you know." Bella's expression soured.

"Your wife tried to kill me, remember?"

"Nah, she wouldn't have killed you," Piper countered. "She wanted you alive, trust me. That's why she sicced Nightmare on you, to take you away safely. Gideon fought back, so she had to do what she had to do."

"Nightmare?" Bella asked.

"Her Familiar," he clarified. "The cube with the tentacles."

"Oh, right." She paused. "Why is she like my mom?"

"They were both free spirits," he answered. "They hated that the Pentad tried to control us artists. Telling us what we could and couldn't create, then taking most of our creations away from us to increase their own wealth and power." He gave a wry smirk. "That's what people who can't create always do. We create all the value, then they steal most of the profit from us artists, and hand us a pittance for our efforts."

"Is that why Mom ran away?" Bella pressed. "Gideon said she sold most of her paintings on the black market."

"According to Kendra, yeah," Piper replied. "Anyway, the Collector offered Kendra a job…freedom to work on whatever she wanted, and to keep most of the profits if she sold it. All he asked was to collect a small percentage. If he wanted to keep something she made, he'd pay full price for it."

"Huh."

"With that kind of deal, you can imagine why so many artists – including the ones from the Pentad – flocked to him. The Pentad couldn't have that, of course. For one, it violated their laws, and two, if they let *him* get away with it, lots of others would try to get away with it too. So they tried to have the Collector arrested."

"I'm guessing that didn't work out so well," Bella ventured.

"Right," Piper agreed. "The Collector fought back. Hard. So the Pentad declared war. That's when the Collector did a pre-emptive strike, taking Blackthorne…one of their most valuable assets."

Bella frowned, taking this in.

"So…you're saying the Pentad started all this?"

Piper shrugged.

"Depends on whose side you're on, kid," he answered. "The Pentad will say the Collector violated the law…so he started it. If you ask the Collector, he'll say he's helping to free artists from a tyrannical government."

"Yeah, well the Collector murdered my mother," Bella reminded him. "And he kidnapped Grandpa. And he tried to kill *me*."

"I know," Piper murmured. He hesitated, then put a hand on her shoulder. "Sorry kid."

She lowered her gaze, feeling suddenly glum. She'd spent the last few days trying not to think of what'd happened to Grandpa. Every time she did, she felt like lying in bed and doing nothing…and she couldn't afford to do that.

"The Collector isn't a nice guy," Piper admitted. "Kendra knew that. I knew that. But to Kendra, he was better than the Pentad…and where she goes, I go."

Bella glanced up at him.

"So what do *you* believe, Piper?" she asked. He sighed, taking his hand off her shoulder.

"I'm an Actor, kid. Sometimes I have to play the hero, sometimes the villain." He paused. "And you know what?"

"What?"

"When I'm playing the hero, I feel like the hero," he answered.

"Duh," she replied. "And when you're playing the villain?"

"I feel like the hero."

Bella stared at him, processing this.

"So, from where I'm standing, a lot of the time, heroes and villains are just different teams playing the same game," Piper concluded.

"So…how do you know what's right?" she asked. He smiled, wrapping an arm around her shoulders.

"Honestly, I just try not to be an asshole," he answered.

Bella smirked.

"I take care of the people I care about," he added. "Because that's *my* team."

Bella arched an eyebrow.

"Am I on your team?" she asked.

"You are now, kid," he answered, giving her a squeeze. "You are now."

There was a moment of silence, and Bella slipped her arm around *his* shoulders. They held each other for a while, until Bella cleared her throat.

"You really love her, don't you?" she asked.

Piper gave her a sad smile, his arm slipping away.

"I've lived a few lifetimes kid," he replied. "And trust me when I say it's hard to find someone you'll get along with after a few years, much less someone that'll make you feel the way Kendra makes me feel."

"What *does* it feel like?" Bella pressed. He slipped away from her touch, turning to the painting.

"Like having a Familiar, but it's another person," he answered. "You'll know when you feel it," he added. "If you're ever lucky enough to."

Bella nodded silently. She'd never really dated. Grandpa wouldn't have allowed it, and besides, she'd found the boys at school to be a bit...one-dimensional. No surprise, she supposed. They couldn't be anything more than what they'd been written to be, and Belthazar Squib's name was easily the most impressive thing about the author.

Piper cleared his throat.

"So, you gonna draw that thing out?" he inquired, gesturing at the dragon. Bella glanced at it, feeling sudden trepidation. How many times had she imagined her dragon becoming real, back when she'd been in school? Of it leaping off the page and becoming her constant companion?

"I don't know," she mumbled.

"Nervous?"

"Yeah," she confessed. "I'll do it when I'm ready."

Piper smirked, putting a hand on her shoulder.

"Gonna let you in on a little secret, kid," he replied. "People who wait until they're ready to do things never end up doing them. If you want to get ahead in life, you gotta take a leap into the unknown...and trust yourself enough to deal with whatever comes next."

Chapter 41

few days had passed since Bella had completed her painting of her Familiar…or at least, *thought* she'd completed it. She kept finding more and more things to add and change every time she looked at it. Small details, but important; it was as if gazing at the painting summoned the Flow, demanding that the alterations be made.

So she did.

In the meantime, she made a few more paintings, of things she'd need for the upcoming battle…like a weapon. She chose to paint a long whip made of human vertebrae, with a femur for a handle. It was Sleep Terror, a whip that, in her story, was owned by a great demon that planted nightmares into people's brains. A single lash from the whip instantly put any opponent to sleep, making them suffer horrifying nightmares. So horrifying that even when they awoke, most would be so fearful that they could only run from battle. She practiced using this for hours, then continued building her arsenal of magical items.

Bella also needed a light source like Gideon's lantern. For this she painted a will-o-wisp, a forest spirit that drew power from being around living beings. It was intelligent, a product of magic from forest sprites, and understood a few commands. And it was drawn to Bella's heart-shaped necklace…a way to ensure that it wouldn't just go wandering off when it felt like it, and never come back.

For a heat source, Bella painted a Lava shroom, a glowing red mushroom that was not hot to touch, but radiated a comfortable heat and as much light as a small campfire. Like a real mushroom, it derived its nutrition from dirt and decomposing things, making it radiate more heat when placed on top of such things.

Each time she painted, she found the stories behind her paintings easier to create and tell. So much so that it was hard to believe that, only months ago, she'd struggled just to paint a flower. The more she told stories, the better she got.

If you want to be it, do it, she found herself reciting.

Lastly, she rolled up some of the paintings of various food items from her mother's pantry, as well as plates, bowls, and utensils. A girl had to eat, after all.

Piper kept himself busy by practicing Acting, which Bella often paused her own work to watch. While at first blush it seemed like Acting would be a relatively weak magical art, she soon found otherwise. For Piper could change from one person to the next at a whim, impersonating anyone he studied for long enough. And he could turn into beastly characters that didn't exist in real life…characters he'd created. All of them seemed to represent a different aspect of his personality…good, bad, weak, strong, and everything in-between.

Eventually Bella found herself returning to her dragon painting…and just staring at it. No new ideas came. No alterations. But she couldn't help worrying that there might be something missing. That it wasn't quite perfect yet.

But what that something was, she couldn't say.

She stood there in her studio, chin in hand, studying it.

"Hey," Piper greeted from behind. He stopped by her side. "How's it going?"

"It isn't," Bella replied. "I have no idea what else to do."

"Must be done."

"Done?" Bella blurted out, glaring at him. "It's not done."

"It's done enough," he countered.

"Mmm…no."

"Look, I'm no Painter," he told her, "…but I've seen a lot of paintings. Kendra's, Gideon's, and quite a few of the Collector's Painters' paintings too. This painting is one of the best I've seen."

"Really?"

"Yeah, really," Piper confirmed. "You got talent kid. Loads of it. And this story…it's *good*. It's…you."

She smiled.

"Yeah?"

"I don't make a habit of lying," Piper told her. "Too much work."

"I still think it's missing something," she insisted, turning back to the painting. Piper put a hand on her upper back.

"It is," he agreed.

"What's that?"

"Your signature," he answered with a smile. She smiled back, nudging his side with her elbow.

"Alright, I'll give it to you, that was smooth."

"I'm an Actor," he replied with a wink. "Smooth is what I do. Now go sign that thing and meet your Familiar."

Bella took a deep breath in, then let it out, squaring her shoulders. She reached down for a fine paintbrush, dipping it in pale blue paint. Then she walked up to the lower right corner of the canvas.

And hesitated.

"What's wrong kid?"

"I…kinda wanted Gideon to see this," she admitted. "I think he would've wanted to be here."

"I'm sure he would've," Piper conceded. "But we don't know when he's coming back, and the longer we wait…"

He trailed off, giving her an apologetic look.

"You're right," she decided. "I'll draw her out…soon."

"Her?"

"Yeah," she confirmed. "But first I'm going to try the lake again. We aren't going anywhere until we have the Dragonkin on our side."

"Good point."

"Let's go," she prompted…and promptly left the studio, starting the long journey to the base of Dragon's Peak. They reached the mouth of the cave, spiraling down the mountain to Lake Fenestra far below. It looked much as it had before, its waters placid. Bella stood at the edge, staring at the surface of the water. Again, she saw the reflection of the sky and Dragon's Peak…but this time, she couldn't see her own reflection.

"Alright," she declared. "I'm going in."

She jumped forward, landing feet-first in the lake…and felt her legs immediately burst through to air below, then her body…and her head. The world *shifted*, and then she fell head-first into the water again…and her head burst through the surface again. She bobbed up and down, then reached an equilibrium, floating waist-deep in the water.

Piper stared at her from the shore, his mouth open.

"Get me out!" she ordered. Piper extended an arm, and she grabbed it, letting herself be hauled out of the water. She turned back to face the lake, soaking wet.

"What the hell happened?" Piper asked.

"I think I went through," she answered. "Everything shifted…it was upside-down. I think I need to go head-first, so I'll emerge on the other side and be able to grab onto the shore."

"Okay, try it."

Bella took a deep breath in, then dove into the water, head-first.

She plunged through…and found herself bursting head-first *out* of the water near the shore. She extended her arms, grabbing onto the shore, then hauled herself up.

And found herself surrounded by Dragonkin.

* * *

Bella froze.

Over a dozen dragon-like creatures were standing around the lake nearby, some with children on their backs, others in mid-stroll down the path toward Dragon's Peak. All with long necks, dragon-like faces, and wings folded on their backs. More of them flew in the sky high above, their wings and long bodies silhouetted by the sun.

And Piper was nowhere to be found.

Bella stared at the Dragonkin, and they stared back at her. She swallowed in a dry throat, waving rather lamely.

"Hey," she greeted.

They continued to stare.

"I'm um, Bella," she introduced. "I'm Thaddeus Birch's daughter."

Still no response.

359

Bella lowered her hand, trying her best to smile. No one said anything. She began to wonder if any of them understood her. There was no guarantee that they spoke English, after all.

"I've come to speak with the king," she announced. "Thaddeus was kidnapped. I need your help to save him."

One of the Dragonkind, obviously a woman, strode up to her, inclining her head.

"We have witnessed the attack on your realm through reflection," she declared. "If perchance you are indeed our Creator's daughter, then we shall do any deed you require. Come, I shall take you to our castle with great haste, so that you may have audience with our king."

Bella blinked, taken aback by the woman's odd way of speaking. She found the dialogue rather stilted, but it'd been that way in Grandpa's book as well…a fact that had made parts of it painful to read. But apparently some people liked that sort of thing.

"Thank you," she replied.

The Dragonkin woman led her leftward around the lake – rather than rightward, as it would have been in the real word – bringing her to the base of Dragon's Peak. Everything was a mirror-image of the real world, or rather, the *original* world. For this world was as real as any other, the sun, ground, and air indistinguishable from that of the world Bella had just come from. And, given that this world had been created by a book, but was now part of the real world, she should be able to feel the Flow here. Indeed, the Plane of Reflection had existed even before Grandpa's first book; 'The Magic of Havenwood' had merely created a new land within that realm. The idea that a book could create a whole alternate world, wherein other books could add to it…

It was a lot to process.

Bella followed the Dragonkin woman to the top of Dragon's Peak, seeing the Castle Havenwood ahead, a familiar bridge arcing over the moat. She glanced down the side of the mountain, seeing the mushroom forest…but no White Dragon. Which made sense; the White Dragon had crossed over in the original world long ago…at least in the book. The idea that history could be created in a book, and then retroactively become true for a place, was mind-boggling.

They made it to the entrance to the castle, passing through to the foyer beyond. It was identical to the one in the original world, except of course for all the Dragonkin milling around. There were far more Dragonkin here than there were artists in the original Havenwood. This Havenwood was densely populated, with crowds of Dragonkin all around.

And all of them where staring at her.

Bella kept her shoulders back and her chin up, forcing herself to appear confident and relaxed. She had a mission to focus on.

Grandpa's life – and Kendra's – hung in the balance.

She followed the woman through the lobby to the room that was The Studio back home, but appeared to be a large meeting hall here. They made their way past it, up some stairs, through a maze of corridors, up more stairs, and finally to what was obviously the throne room…a long room with a single, massive throne at the end, the seat back a huge marble carving of a dragon rising up a good twenty feet in the air, its head nearly touching the vaulted ceiling. A very large Dragonkin man was seated upon it, dressed in golden armor and wearing a golden crown resplendent with shimmering jewels. He was easily four times the size of the other Dragonkin, filling his huge throne easily, a golden staff in one hand.

"Your majesty, King Draco, I bring forth to you the esteemed Bella Birch, sole granddaughter of the Creator," Bella's guide announced, bowing before the man. Bella bowed as well, following her lead.

"Are you truly kin of our great Creator?" Draco inquired. Bella nodded.

"I am, your majesty," she confirmed. "I've come to make a request."

"Make it and it shall come to pass," King Draco declared.

"Thaddeus Birch has been taken by the Collector," she informed. "Kidnapped…or worse."

There were a few gasps from the guards and Bella's guide.

"Who is this 'Collector?'" the king demanded.

"A dangerous man," Bella answered. "He lives in a castle far away. A castle with an upside-down castle on top of it, on top of a mountain."

"This castle is known to us," King Draco revealed. "There is a great mirror in the sky between the two castles…a magical one that serves as a doorway between our worlds. It is called Chiral, and was created long before the castle it reflects."

"I need to save my grandfather," Bella told him. "But I can't fight the Collector alone." She paused. "I need your help. The help of the Dragonkind."

King Draco stood, slamming the butt of his staff against the floor. The sound reverberated through the royal chamber.

"We are ever loyal servants of our Creator, our very existence owed to his great kindness," he declared. "I shall command my armies forthwith to lay siege to this villain and reclaim Thaddeus Birch from his evil clutches." His tone turned grave. "Any enemy of the Creator is a sworn enemy of the Dragonkind."

Bella bowed.

"Thank you, your majesty," she replied. She hesitated then. "I have a…friend who says the Collector uses a series of tunnels called the Underground. They have doorways that lead to places all over the world. Lake Fenestra is a portal to my world now. If your army crosses over, they can take the Underground to reach the Collector quickly."

The king considered this.

"If the Underground exists in your realm, then its sister exists in ours," he reasoned. "We shall navigate this Underground in our world, and cross through the giant mirror Chiral to lay siege to the Collector's defenses."

"Thank you your Highness."

"I shall require intimate details of the Collector's defenses, and the layout of his castle," King Draco stated.

"I have a friend that might be able to help."

"Then summon him to me at once," Draco ordered. "We shall spend this day planning our assault, and readying my army. Tomorrow, we shall mobilize…and if the Creator wills it, we shall rescue Him from the clutches of this 'Collector.'"

Bella bowed again, more deeply this time.

"Do not bow to me, granddaughter of the Creator," the king requested. "We owe our existence to the Creator. It is my pleasure to serve Him…and you."

And with that, King Draco stood from his throne, lowering himself to one knee and bowing before her. Bella accepted this, feeling rather awkward. He stood then.

"Go," he stated. "Bring your friend to me. Return tomorrow morning, and we shall commence with our mission to save the Creator."

Bella did as the king requested, returning to the original world and bringing Piper this time. Piper told Draco everything he knew about the Underground and the Collector's defenses, then returned to the original world with Bella. By that time, it was well after sundown, the night sky alight with countless shimmering stars. They made their way back to Mom's estate, passing through the broken portcullis into the foyer. Animus greeted them by swirling around Bella's feet, and she smiled at the Familiar.

"Hi girl," she greeted.

"Better head off to bed," Piper recommended. "Gonna need all the sleep we can get for tomorrow."

"I will," she promised. "Just going to stop by the studio for a sec."

They split up, Piper following his own recommendation. Bella went to her studio, closing the door behind her and standing before the painting of her dragon.

It was then that she realized she hadn't named it yet.

"Well duh," she scolded herself. Assigning a name was a simple matter; all she had to do was print it on something the dragon owned. Or perhaps put it in the title of the painting.

But what to name it?

She thought back to her mother's story. Of the Collector killing her mother in Blackthorne, and of the Collector being attacked by Lucia's curse afterward.

She was like a dragon, Grandpa had said. *Powerful and fierce. And always there to protect you, even in...*

Even in death.

In killing her mother, the Collector had activated Bella's ruby necklace...protecting her from him, and sealing his doom if he drew too close.

Vengeance, she thought.

"No, already taken," she muttered. She couldn't steal Piper's character's name. "Revenge...Curse. Cursa?" She made a face. "Enemy...Nemy...Nemesis..."

She stopped.

"Nemesis," she murmured, breaking out into a smile. "Now *that's* a name!"

363

She walked up to a little stand beside the painting, getting some ivory paint and dabbing it on her palette. Then she grabbed a fine paintbrush, dipping it in the paint and walking up to the canvas.

"Nemesis," she wrote in neat, cursive letters on one of the dragon's ribs.

She stood back then, feeling rather pleased with herself.

Bang!

Bella whirled around to face the closed door of her studio. The sound had come from the hallway beyond it. She reached into her chest-painting for Sleep Terror, drawing the magical bone-whip out. Rapid footsteps approached from the hallway beyond, getting closer and closer.

Then the door burst open in a flash of silver light!

Bella took a step back, raising her whip to strike…and saw a big, glowing silver wolf burst into the room.

"Myko!" Bella cried, rushing up to the wolf and giving him a big bear hug. Myko *wuffed*, then showered Bella with wet kisses. She laughed, kissing his nose, then hugging him again. "Oh Myko, I missed you so much!"

Another set of footsteps approached, and Bella looked past Myko. There, standing in the doorway, was none other than Gideon Myles.

"Bella!" he cried, rushing up to Bella and embracing her. He lifted her clear off the floor, twirling her around, then setting her down. He held her at arms' length then, looking terribly relieved. "Oh thank the gods you're okay!" His expression darkened. "When I saw the White Dragon, I knew something was terribly wrong. I came up here as quickly as I could. What happened?"

"The Collector," Bella answered. "He attacked the White Dragon with this…*thing*. An army of soldiers that combined to form this huge monster. It destroyed downtown, and hurt the White Dragon. Bad."

"So I saw," Gideon replied. "I take it the White Dragon prevailed."

"It did," she confirmed. "But…the Collector, he…"

She stopped then, feeling a lump form in her throat. Tears welled up in her eyes, and she lowered her gaze, shaking her head.

"He got Grandpa," she forced herself to say.

Gideon stood there, the color draining from his face. Then he dropped to one knee before her, putting his hand on her shoulder.

"We'll get him back," he promised. "I'm going to make things right, Bella." His jawline rippled. "I should have done it a long time ago."

"I'll help," she promised, meeting his gaze. "Grandpa's plan worked. His second book made the lake a portal into the Plane of Reflection. I went there today and got the king to help us."

Gideon's eyebrows went up.

"Really?"

"King Draco wants us to join him tomorrow in the Plane of Reflection," she informed him. "We're taking the Underground – in the Plane of Reflection – to the Collector's inverted castle. The Dragonkin army will attack, and we'll grab Grandpa and Kendra."

"I see," Gideon replied. He stood then, regarding her with newfound appreciation. "You've been busy."

"I've had a reason to be."

He nodded, then turned to regard Bella's painting. The painting of her Familiar...of Nemesis. His eyebrows and his jaw went in opposite directions...so much so that Bella had to smile.

"You like it?" she asked.

He stood there for a moment longer, then strode right up to the painting, his chin in his hand. He studied it intently, drinking in every detail. After several long, silent minutes, he turned to Bella.

"Bella, this..." he began, then stopped. He shook his head. "This is just..."

"What?"

"Do you see this?" he asked, gesturing at the undead dragon. "See how it looks like it's ready to leap from the canvas?"

"Piper said that means it has powerful magic."

"He's right," Gideon confirmed. He gestured at Myko with his stump. "It was the same with him."

"It was?" Bella asked.

"Yes," Gideon confirmed. "You've outdone yourself, Bella. You told your story...*your* story. The one in your heart. The one you were most afraid of." He smiled. "That took a lot of courage. I'm proud of you."

"Thanks," she said with a smile of her own. "Um, Dad."

"Still awkward, eh?"

"Yup."

"We'll get used to it," he promised. "In any case, this means that your Familiar is going to be incredibly powerful."

"In what way?" she asked.

"We won't know until you draw it out," he answered. "But there's something missing."

"My signature?" she guessed.

"Right."

Gideon grabbed the paintbrush she'd used to entitle the painting then, handing it to Bella. She paused, then took it, dipping it in the ivory paint on her palette, then gazing one last time at her painting.

"How do I know if it's finished?" she asked.

"When your changes stop mattering," Gideon answered. He raised an eyebrow. "Have they?"

"Pretty much."

"Art is never really finished," he admitted. "But eventually we have to abandon our works. There are other stories to tell, and sometimes good enough is good enough." He put a hand on her shoulder. "And believe me, this painting is more than good enough."

"You're my dad," Bella countered. "You have to say that."

"The good fathers do," Gideon conceded with a wry smirk. "I don't think I qualify."

Bella gave him a look.

"Go on," he insisted, gesturing at the painting.

She turned back to the painting, then took a deep breath in, squaring her shoulders. Then she leaned in, signing her name below the title: *Bella M. Birch.*

A gentle breeze caressed her from behind, and a chill ran down her spine.

"Good," Gideon declared. "Now...ready to meet your dragon?"

Bella took a deep breath in, then squared her shoulders, nodding at Gideon.

"Ready."

She reached into the painting, feeling the warm pulsing of the magic there as her fingers dipped into the canvas. She felt her hand brush up against the hard shaft of the bone of her dragon's upper arm, and she pulled, bringing her Familiar to life.

Chapter 42

Simon sat patiently on the bench in the Collector's waiting room, staring down at the simple black cloak he was wearing, a very special uniform he'd been given to wear today. Mrs. Savage had seen to it that the cloak had been placed on top of his bureau that morning. A garment he'd spotted other Painters wearing when they'd earned their promotions.

He smiled, hardly believing that *he* was wearing it now. That, after such a short period of time, he'd earned the right to ascend to Castle Over. For the first time since he could remember, he felt completely at peace. He hadn't needed to cut himself for weeks now.

It was liberating.

"The Collector will see you now," Miss Savage declared, standing up from her desk and walking toward the Collector's door. Simon bolted up from the bench, following her to the door. She opened it, giving him a little smile and gesturing for him to walk through.

"Congratulations," she murmured. Simon smiled back, then stepped into the Collector's office. The Collector looked up from the papers on his desk, gazing at Simon with those exquisite green eyes.

"Ah, there you are Simon," he stated. "Did you sleep well?"

"No sir."

"Why not?" the Collector inquired.

"I was too excited sir," he confessed. "About today."

"Understandable," the Collector replied. He hesitated, but only for a split-second. "I didn't sleep well either, to be honest."

Simon gave him a questioning look.

"I too have a lot on my mind," the Collector admitted. Simon nodded at that. The Collector was a powerful man, with a great deal of responsibility. He could only imagine how difficult being in the man's shoes would be.

There was an uncharacteristically awkward pause, and the Collector cleared his throat.

"Come, let's not delay your promotion any further," he stated.

And with that, the man stood, gesturing for Simon to follow him to a door on the opposite end of the office. The Collector retrieved a key from his pocket, inserting it into the lock and turning it 90 degrees clockwise. It was clearly a magical key, created for this very door. Simon suspected the two had been painted on the same canvas.

There was a *click*, and the Collector pulled the door open, gesturing for Simon to take the lead.

Simon stepped through the doorway, emerging into a circular room. A tower, in fact; he knew that it was the tallest spire of the castle. The one that rose to meet the inverted castle far above. He gazed upward, seeing a seemingly endless spiraling staircase leading to the top…and beyond, to the bottom of the inverted tower.

It was enough to give him goosebumps.

He glanced at the Collector, who gestured for him to ascend the stairs. Simon did so, starting the long journey upward, the Collector following behind him. The man seemed uncharacteristically distracted, almost melancholy…and was trying to hide it from him. A noble effort, to not want to spoil Simon's promotion. Simon decided not to ask what the Collector was thinking about, not wanting the man to realize his efforts had been in vain.

We shouldn't be apart, he felt his Familiar insist.

Doppelganger – still in Simon's studio, pacing before the huge canvas he'd painted Legion on – was clearly vexed, transmitting an irritated, nervous energy. Simon agreed silently. But the Collector had demanded it…at least until the ceremony was complete.

He's separating us for a reason.

Simon ignored the sudden trickle of paranoia coming from his Familiar, focusing on his ascent. Doppelganger was *always* paranoid...about everyone.

Trust no one, Doppelganger argued. *You know what would happen if he knew what you really were.*

Simon swallowed, feeling the Collector behind him. The warmth radiating from the man's body.

It made his skin tingle.

Simon realized he'd slowed down, and focused on the stairs ahead, maintaining an even pace. It was many minutes later that he reached the end of the spiraling staircase. It stopped halfway up the tower, with a landing that dropped off suddenly. There was another landing – and staircase – above, a perfect mirror-image. Which meant that this was the transition point...the entrance to Castle Over.

A horizontal bar was set between the two landings, roughly six feet above the landing he was standing on.

Simon felt the Collector standing behind him, and glanced back at the man questioningly.

"I'll pick you up," the man stated. "Grab onto the bar and swing as high as you can. You'll have to clear the midway point between the two castles...gravity will do the rest."

"Yes sir," Simon murmured.

The Collector stepped up behind Simon, putting his hands under Simon's armpits. Simon felt the man's chest and abdomen press against his back, and grit his teeth, willing himself to not react to the sudden and unexpected closeness. The Collector lifted him up, and Simon grabbed onto the horizontal bar, feeling the Collector's hands slip away.

Simon focused, swinging back and forth, going a little higher each time. Then he reached the invisible border between the two castles...and felt a force *pull* on his outstretched legs, forcing him to continue his forward swing. The tower rotated alarmingly around him...and he found himself hanging above the landing...opposite the Collector.

He let go, landing with a *thump*, then glancing upward. The Collector was standing upside-down on the landing above. Simon went a few steps down, giving the man ample room to swing and land.

Moments later, the Collector did just that, dropping gracefully to the landing.

"Continue," the man prompted, gesturing for Simon to start the journey downstairs. He did so, spiraling downward to the bottom of the inverted tower. There was a door here, identical to the one far above, but the doorknob was on the opposite side. The Collector unlocked it, and they stepped through into the room beyond. The Collector's office...but with different furniture.

"My study," the Collector explained.

"What do you study?" Simon inquired, gazing at the books on the large desk in the center of the room, and the countless other books on the shelves built into the walls.

"History," the Collector answered. "Art History, specifically."

"To know what paintings to...take?"

The Collector gave a slight smile.

"Among other things," he answered. Simon spotted a whole shelf devoted to the history of literature.

"What about those?" he asked.

"Books created much of this world, Simon," the Collector replied. "To know the history of books is to understand the history of the world...and to discover lands long forgotten."

He led Simon through the office into the room beyond, a mirror-image of the waiting room. Simon half-expected Miss Savage to be there, but neither she – nor her desk – were. In fact, the room was utterly empty, with no furniture or adornments of any kind.

And, as the Collector led Simon through the hallways and stairwells of Castle Over, Simon realized that this was the norm. The entire castle seemed abandoned. Unadorned. Uncared for. As if Under had been a show of power and prestige, while Over was merely...functional.

"What is this castle for?" he asked as they walked. The Collector slowed, looking down at Simon.

"No one's ever asked me that before," he admitted. He paused. "It used to be a storehouse for an ancient Writer named Persnickity Gibbons," he answered. "The man who created Castle Under, in fact."

"And Over?"

"No, Castle Over exists in the Plane of Reflection," the Collector explained. "Where we are now. When Castle Under was created, its mirror-image automatically appeared in the Plane of Reflection."

Simon nodded. Made sense.

"The Writer merely arranged for a giant, magical mirror to exist in the sky above the original castle," the Collector continued. "One that would serve as a portal between the two planes."

Simon frowned.

"Isn't that illegal?"

"It's carefully regulated now," the Collector corrected. "But not so much back then."

"What do you use it for now?"

"For my collection," the Collector answered.

And then he fell silent, and it was clear to Simon that the conversation was over.

They continued walking through the empty rooms and corridors of the inverted castle, until at last they stopped before a narrow wooden door. There was no doorknob, nor other obvious way to open it; only a human skull embedded in its center.

"This is it," the Collector declared. His tone was curiously flat. He glanced at Simon for a moment, then pressed his forehead against the skull's. A faint red light flashed in its eye-sockets, and the door swung open of its own accord.

The Collector turned to Simon, gesturing for him to step through. Simon obeyed, stepping through the doorway, and found himself standing on a white marble balcony, pale, weak light from a lantern the only illumination amidst utter darkness. A few feet ahead, the balcony ended.

Simon felt a cool draft, and cleared his throat, hearing the sound echo as if across a vast space. The hairs on the back on his neck stood on-end.

Something's wrong, he felt Doppelganger warn.

You always say that, he shot back.

The Collector stepped onto the balcony, stopping at Simon's right side. He looked at Simon for a long, silent moment, his expression unreadable.

"Are you ready Simon?" the man inquired.

Simon nodded.

The Collector snapped his fingers, and the room was suddenly filled with bright, golden light.

Simon's breath caught in his throat.

They were standing on a balcony near the top of a huge tower, the floor hundreds of feet below…and the walls were covered in paintings. Thousands of paintings.

He felt the Collector's eyes on him.

"Behold, my collection," the Collector declared.

Simon said nothing, his eyes darting from painting to painting, taking it all in. Some of the paintings were rather barren, merely landscapes or backgrounds with nothing in the foreground. Live canvases whose original foreground contents had been drawn out. Which meant they were ready to have other things put *in* them.

It didn't take long for him to find out what those things might be.

For many of the other paintings had *people* in the foreground. Men and women of various ages, some facing away from him, some facing forward. All of them appearing terrified or surprised.

And all of them wearing the same black cloak *he* was wearing.

He felt Doppelganger's voice screaming in his head.

"What do you think, Simon?" the Collector inquired. Simon swallowed in a dry throat.

"Why are you collecting Painters?" he asked bluntly. The Collector sighed.

"That's a long story, Simon."

Simon looked up at him.

"They hurt you, didn't they," he guessed. The Collector stared back at him for a quiet moment.

"One did," he confessed.

"Your father," Simon guessed again. The Collector's green eyes bored into him.

"Yes."

"My father hurt me," Simon confessed, lowering his gaze to his forearms. Scars crisscrossed the pale skin there, and beneath the skin of his right forearm was a small lump. A piece of glass he hadn't been able to get out.

"What did you do about it, Simon?"

"I learned not to love someone that can't love me back," Simon answered.

The Collector took a deep breath in, letting it out slowly.

"My…father told me he loved me," he confessed. "He said he loved me more than anything in the world. He spent time with me. He…was everything a father should be."

He lowered his gaze, his jawline rippling.

"Growing up, I had problems remembering things," he continued. "I couldn't remember much of anything that had happened before I turned eight. My father said it was because I'd gotten into a horrible accident then, and lost most of my memories. But that it didn't matter. That I was perfect the way I was."

He paused.

"He was a Painter, my father," the Collector admitted. "So was my mother. I wanted desperately to paint...I had these memories – very vague, but there – of what it felt like to feel the Flow. The magic of it. But my father would never let me. He'd always say he'd teach me later. Kept putting it off. Until one day, when he was sleeping, I stole one of his canvases and starting painting."

Simon gave a little smile. He'd done the same thing, in his attic. Painting without a license, feeling the Flow in secret. Until his father had caught him, and...

"I painted, but nothing happened," the Collector continued. "I couldn't feel the Flow, no matter how hard I tried. I felt...nothing."

"Why?" Simon asked.

"I asked my father the same thing the next morning," the Collector answered. "He told me some nonsense about my injury having stopped me from being able to feel the Flow. I didn't believe him. I called him a liar, and demanded to know the truth. I told him..." He paused, swallowing visibly. "I told him if he really loved me, he'd tell me the truth."

He gave a wry smirk.

"So even though he didn't, he did."

The Collector's fingers curled into fists, and he went silent for so long that Simon almost thought he was done. But then the Collector turned to face Simon, with a gaze so intense it made Simon take a step back.

"I did have an accident," he revealed. "It was my eighth birthday. I was playing with my friends...we were taking turns jumping off a raft in the middle of a lake. Apparently I slipped when jumping off, and hit my head on the edge of the raft. I was knocked unconscious, and slipped below the surface. My friends tried to save me. Then my mother tried. But they were too late."

The Collector swallowed.

"So I died," he concluded.

Simon frowned, shaking his head.

"I don't…"

"My mother left my father, and my father – struck with guilt and grief – did the unthinkable. He painted his son. Painted him to be as close to the original as possible. And then, one night, he drew that painting out."

Simon's eyes widened, a chill running down his spine. The Collector turned away from him, gazing at the paintings hanging on the wall of the tower.

"You see Simon, my father wasn't my father at all. He never loved me. He loved his son. His *real* son. He pretended that I was his son, deluded himself into believing it. But deep down inside, he knew I wasn't. And so did I."

He gave a bitter laugh.

"My entire childhood was a lie, Simon. Everything he told me was a lie. *I* was a lie. I wasn't real…I was a copy of something real. A forgery. What little memories I had of before I'd been painted, those were *given* to me. They weren't mine." He shook his head. "His love was for his son, not for me."

Simon didn't say anything. Didn't dare say a word.

"So I left," the Collector revealed. "At first I wanted to kill myself. I didn't think I was worthy of existing. I was just a copy, after all. A creation of a delusional mind. But I didn't kill myself, Simon. I vowed to make something of myself instead. Something more than what my Painter had painted. Something *far* more."

"You did," Simon murmured.

"I did," the Collector agreed. "And now I've created this," he declared, gesturing at the thousands of paintings before them."

"You've turned Painters into paintings," Simon realized.

"And Painters turned paintings into people," the Collector pointed out. "That's all we are, Simon."

"I don't understand."

"Why is it that most people can't paint, Simon? Or Write, or Act? Why do some people feel the Flow, but the majority can't?"

Simon shrugged.

"It's hereditary, Simon. If either of your parents can sense the Flow, you'll be able to. If both can, you'll be able to sense it more powerfully. But if neither parent can feel the Flow, their children won't be able to either…and most people can't feel the Flow." He paused. "Why?"

Simon just stood there.

"Because they're paintings," the Collector revealed. "Like me."

"But…"

"Humanity was created, Simon. By artists. Writers and Painters. They created a people in their image, identical in every way…except for the ability to feel the Flow. From those ancestors, all non-artists were born…except for me."

Simon lowered his gaze, hardly believing what he was hearing. It was impossible…but it had to be true. There was no other explanation.

"They know this," the Collector continued. "The aristocracy. The Pentad. Other governments. They know the truth, and have been hiding it from humanity. Most of them are humans themselves. Descendants of paintings. And they've taken power from the artists, forcing them to be licensed, to paint only what they're allowed to paint. And reaping most of the profit." He smiled grimly. "The humans have taken over, Simon. They've all but conquered their creators."

Simon stared at the Painters trapped in their paintings. Hundreds of them, frozen in the canvas. Not quite alive, not quite dead.

"You're turning Painters into paintings because…Painters turned paintings into people."

"They're pretending to be gods, Simon," the Collector explained. "People creating living things, making them exactly the way they want them, like my father did. Painting things and giving them false memories. False emotions. Forcing the paintings to love them and do things for them. Lying to them and telling them they're real."

He paused for a moment, collecting himself.

"My creator never loved me, Simon. He loved a real person…not some paint on a canvas. If he could have brought his son back from the dead, he would have discarded me in a heartbeat, ashamed that I ever existed."

Simon lowered his gaze, swallowing past a lump in his throat.

"My father loved the person he thought I was. But it wasn't me." He swallowed past a lump in his throat. "When he found out, he…tried to change me."

The Collector said nothing, and Simon grit his teeth.

"Then he found out he couldn't change me," he added. "And that who I was…was something he couldn't love."

He lifted his gaze to the Collector's, almost defiantly.

"Paintings are the only things that've ever cared about me. Because I made them that way. But I didn't make you." He swallowed. "Was everything you told me a lie?"

The Collector stared back at him silently, not answering. Simon turned away from him, gazing at the vast collection of paintings before him. His vision blurred with tears, and he let them build up, rolling down his cheeks. He refused to hide them. Refused to ever hide again.

I told you, he felt the Doppelganger say. Simon grimaced, shoving the Familiar from his mind.

Eventually, the Collector stirred.

"I remember what it was like to feel the Flow," he murmured. "Even though it's not a real memory, it feels real to me. But I'll never be a Painter, because I'm not real."

"You're real to me," Simon retorted.

They stood there, side-by-side, staring at the paintings lining the curved walls of the tower for a long moment. Then Simon cleared his throat.

"You're not a Painter," he declared. "But this..." he added, gesturing at the collection, "...is your story. This is your art. These paintings. The castle. Your armies. All of it. Your story is your power, and it wasn't given to you. You took it."

He looked up at the Collector then.

"It's a masterpiece."

The Collector didn't respond, and Simon returned to gazing at the man's collection. They stood there for a long while, at the edge of the marble balcony.

"I love it," he stated.

Still the Collector said nothing.

I'm coming, he felt the Doppelganger declare. But as quickly as his Familiar was moving, there was no way it would reach him in time. And there was nothing it could do against a man like the Collector.

Simon gazed at the countless Painters trapped within their framed prisons, all dressed in identical black robes. The same robe he was wearing. He clenched his fists, his heart hammering in his chest. His whole body seemed to tremble, desperately trying to keep in the secret that had destroyed his previous life. That had proven his father's love a lie...just as it would the Collector's.

376

"I love you," he confessed.

A bolt of terror shot through him as soon as the words left his lips, his breath seizing in his throat. He had the sudden mad urge to fling himself off the edge of the balcony, to escape the consequences of what he'd just done.

But though Simon felt the Collector's eyes on him, the man said nothing in reply.

An eternity seemed to pass, the silence between them growing so vast that it seemed that nothing could end it. Simon's vision blurred, and he closed his eyes, feeling wetness trickle down his cheeks. For the first time in weeks, he was struck with the terrible need to cut himself. To feel the pain that would make everything better, if only for a moment.

And then he felt the Collector's warm hand come to rest on his upper back, between his shoulder blades.

Chapter 43

Bella *pulled.*

She saw her hand withdraw from the surface of her canvas, grasping onto a skeletal, black-clawed hand a little larger than hers.

A chill ran down her spine, the realization of what she was doing striking her. Finally, after so many years of dreaming, she was bringing her dream to life. It was being born, as if pulled from a womb.

Still she pulled, seeing a bony forearm, then an upper arm bone, and a shoulder.

Then a skeletal dragon head appeared through the canvas, twin points of blood-red light in its eye-sockets turning to focus on her.

A burst of surprise struck her, followed by a sudden realization. *Bella,* she thought.

A warmth spread through Bella, and she nearly dropped her dragon's hand. She felt a profound happiness, one that made her want to weep.

"Pull her out, Bella," she heard Gideon prompt from behind.

She focused, pulling her dragon out all the way. A long body emerged from the canvas, wings folded on its back. And a long, skeletal tail.

It was done.

Bella stared, hardly believing what she was seeing. An undead dragon, plucked from her wildest dreams, standing before her. Looking at her. Its body was roughly the same size as Bella's, but its long neck and wings made it seem much bigger. It spread those wings out wide, seeming to fill the room with them…and bowed its head to Bella.

Bella let go of its hand, reaching up to touch the side of its face. "Hey you," she greeted.

The dragon lifted its gaze to meet hers.

Hey girl, a voice replied. It took a second for Bella to realize the voice wasn't sound, but thought; she'd heard it inside of her mind.

"I'm Bella," she introduced.

I know who you are.

"Oh, right," Bella stammered, feeling herself flush a bit. She glanced back at Gideon. "She knows who I am."

"Naturally," Gideon replied. "You can hear her thoughts?" Bella nodded. "Then she is truly your Familiar," he declared. He stepped up to Bella's side, inclining his head at the dragon. "I am Gideon Myles, Bella's father," he introduced. "A pleasure to meet you, Nemesis."

Nemesis eyed Gideon.

He's so old.

"Um, yes," Bella admitted, flushing again. "But he's good, I promise."

Gideon raised an eyebrow, and Bella grimaced.

"She says you're old," she admitted apologetically.

"Oh *really*," Gideon replied, eyeing Nemesis. "Well you're looking a bit undernourished."

Tell him I could always eat him, Nemesis requested.

"She says she could always eat you," Bella complied. Gideon chuckled.

"I think I like her already," he quipped. Then he turned to Bella. "We don't have much time…you should paint her wings."

"Oh, right," Bella remembered. Her wings were made of canvas, after all. If she painted them, and activated them, they could be used to shield her from any attacks, and serve as a storehouse for other paintings. She glanced at Nemesis. "If it's okay with you," she added.

Go on, Nemesis replied. *Make me look pretty.*

* * *

A few hours later, Bella finished painting – and activating – all of the canvas-like webbing between Nemesis's wing bones. Then she led Gideon and Nemesis out of the studio and into the living room, where Piper was practicing his craft. The Actor looked like he had when they'd first seen him in Havenwood, hidden behind a black cloak. He morphed back to himself when they entered the room, his eyes widening as he saw Nemesis.

"Wow," he breathed.

Who's this? Nemesis asked.

"Nemesis, this is Piper," Bella introduced. "Piper, this is Nemesis."

"Nice meeting you," Piper replied. "Sorry for 'dragon' you into this mess."

You like this guy? Nemesis asked, eyeing Piper dubiously.

"Yeah," Bella answered. "He's alright."

Piper arched an eyebrow, and she felt a flash of irritation. But it wasn't hers, it was her dragon's.

You don't have to talk to answer me, Nemesis pointed out. *I can hear your thoughts.*

"Oh, right," Bella replied. Then she grimaced. *Oh, right,* she thought. She paused. *Can you hear me now?*

Yes.

"I'm just alright, huh?" Piper grumbled.

Puns, Nemesis warned, *are a sign of a demented mind.*

"Back to the siege tomorrow," Gideon interjected, thankfully changing the subject. "Did the Dragonkin mention what time we'd meet?"

"Morning," Bella answered.

"I assume early morning," Gideon stated. "Very well then. It's getting late. I'm going to go to sleep, and so should you," he added, nodding at Piper. "We've got a big day tomorrow."

Bella narrowed her eyes, folding her arms across her chest.

"I'm sorry, that sounded like you thought I wasn't coming," she accused.

Oh, we're definitely coming, Nemesis promised. *Whether he wants us to or not.*

"You should stay here Bella," Gideon reasoned. "You'll be safe if you use the coffin upstairs to bring you to…that room you saw earlier. No one will be able to hurt you there."

"That's what you said about being in Havenwood," Bella reminded him. Gideon grimaced.

"Yes, well trust me, *no* one is stupid enough to attack you in…"

"In what?" Bella asked.

Gideon hesitated, then sighed.

"In the Plane of Death," he answered.

Bella blinked.

"The *what* now?"

"The Plane of Death," Gideon repeated. "That's where you went after Death brought you into the coffin."

"Wait," Piper interjected incredulously. "Are you saying…?"

Gideon shot him a deadly glare, and Piper backed down.

"Okay, what are you hiding?" Bella demanded, her hands on her hips.

"As I told you before, there are many planes of existence," Gideon explained. "Your mother traveled to the Plane of Death from time to time, and her coffin is a…doorway to get to her apartment there."

"Okay…"

"In any case, not even the Collector would dare try to get into the Plane of Death without permission," Gideon continued. Bella nodded, remembering how the Collector had stopped short when he'd seen Death…and the coffin. How he'd turned and ran.

"I'm still going," she insisted. "I spent my entire life hiding from the Collector. I'm *done* hiding." She drew herself up as tall as she could, squaring her shoulders. "I'm going to be the hero of my story, not the victim."

"No Bella."

"What if the Collector gets to me before I can get to the Plane of Death?" she inquired, raising an eyebrow at him. "Then you'll be leaving me. And you won't be able to protect me." She shrugged. "Anything could happen."

Gideon frowned at her, crossing his own arms.

"You're preying on my insecurities," he realized. "How deviously clever of you."

She gave him a wicked smile.

"I'm a teenage girl," she replied. "It's what we do."

381

Nemesis lifted a clawed hand, putting it on Bella's shoulder.

We're going to get along just fine, the dragon told her.

Gideon sighed.

"I still think..." he began, but she cut him off, holding up her ruby amulet.

"The Collector tried to attack me, and this stole his life force," she explained. "It aged him once, when I was a kid, and it did it again when he tried to kill me. If he tries to hurt me again, he'll just be drained again."

"And that makes her the best weapon we have against him," Piper concluded. The Actor put a hand on Gideon's shoulder. "She's got a point, Gid."

Gideon glanced at Piper, then at Bella. Even Nemesis crossed her bony arms, glaring at Gideon. He sighed, visibly deflating.

"Fine," he muttered. "You can tag along. But you need to stay with me."

"Deal," Bella agreed.

"All right, I'm going to bed," Gideon declared. "Who knew having a daughter would be so exhausting?"

"I second that," Piper said. "The going to bed part," he added hastily when Bella shot him a look.

"You two should stay up a bit and get to know each other better," Gideon recommended, nodding at Bella and Nemesis. "Then you can sleep."

"Alright," Bella agreed.

The two men said their goodnights, and Bella and Nemesis went to her bedroom. The dragon curled up on the floor, and Bella sat cross-legged on her bed.

"So," she began.

Awkward?

"Yeah, little bit," Bella admitted. "Can you...read my memories?"

No.

"But you *can* read my thoughts," Bella pressed. Nemesis nodded. "Even the ones I don't, um, say in my head?"

They're less clear, Nemesis answered. *But I can always feel your emotions.*

"I can feel yours too," Bella admitted. They were hard to distinguish from her own emotions. "So you know what we're doing tomorrow?"

No.

Bella told Nemesis all about the Collector, and Grandpa, and their plan to get him back. And of Piper and Kendra. Nemesis listened without interruption, other than the occasional emotion.

"And that's that," Bella finished at last.

We'll get him back, Nemesis promised.

"Yeah, I hope so."

If he isn't already dead.

Bella jerked back, her eyes widening in horror.

"You can't say that!" she protested.

The Collector might've already killed him.

"Yeah, but you can't *say* that," Bella repeated.

Why not?

"Because it's a terrible thing to say," Bella answered. She felt Nemesis do a mental shrug.

It's the truth.

"Yeah, but…it's mean," she insisted. She felt the dragon scoff.

I'm a dragon, she retorted. *If you wanted warm and cuddly, you should've painted a dog.*

Bella opened her mouth to argue, but realized her Familiar had a point.

You made an undead dragon. Called Nemesis.

"Ok," Bella grumbled. "I get it." She took a deep breath in to calm herself. "Let's just agree that if we have a chance at saving Grandpa, we'll save him."

Deal.

Bella grimaced, realizing that this was going to be a little more complicated than she'd imagined. Nemesis was truly alive – real, not something that just existed in her mind, or in a notebook. And it was going to take a while for them to get to know each other…and get used to each other.

"Maybe I should get some sleep," she said, flopping onto her back in her bed. "We have a big day ahead of us tomorrow."

Nemesis didn't answer, but walk-slithered on all fours toward the bedroom door, opening it up.

"Where're you going?" Bella asked. Nemesis looked back at her, and Bella could swear the dragon smirked at her.

Out.

And that's exactly where Nemesis went.

* * *

The next morning, Bella awoke to knocking on her bedroom door. She could tell that it wasn't the first round of knocking, either.

"I'm up," she called out, sitting upright. She stretched her arms up, then to the sides, yawning widely. It took her a moment to remember what day it was…and to realize that Nemesis had never come back to her room during the night.

Relax, a voice in her head said. *Coming to you now.*

Where are you? Bella asked.

Flying back to Havenwood.

"Are you decent?" a voice behind the door asked. It was Gideon's.

"Getting there," she grumbled, finding her Painter uniform on the floor and pulling it on. She opened the door then, seeing Gideon – already fully dressed, his black cloak covering his uniform, black cane in hand – standing there.

"Where's Nemesis?" he asked. For Myko was at his side.

"Out," Bella answered. Gideon raised an eyebrow. "Don't ask," she muttered.

"Is everything okay?"

"She's a bit of a b…"

I can hear you.

"…bother sometimes," Bella stammered. "But we're getting to know each other."

"Good," Gideon replied. "It can take a while to build a relationship with your Familiar," he added. "Be patient with it."

"Did it take long with Myko?"

"Um…no."

Myko *wuffed* his agreement, licking Gideon's cheek. Bella felt a few rather evil thoughts toward the wolf, and realized they were Nemesis's, not hers.

Be nice, Bella scolded.

"We'd better be off," Gideon advised. "Piper is already near the lake waiting for us. Get your paintings and we'll go."

Bella did just that, grabbing her paintings and rolling them up, stuffing them in her thigh-holsters. She put Sleep Terror in her chest-painting, and let Goo out. At Gideon's insistence, she placed a few fireballs and lightning bolts and such in her uniform. Not that she had any intention of using them.

384

Why not? Nemesis inquired.

I'm not a murderer, Bella answered.

Not yet.

Not ever, Bella insisted.

You might not have a choice.

Bella shook her head, remembering the guards who Gideon had killed back at Devil's pass. The heartbreaking screams as they burned alive.

There's always a choice, she argued.

She followed Gideon out of the mansion then, and they made their way up the Water Dragon tunnel to the surface. Somehow, she knew that Nemesis was near...at the mouth of the cave ahead, actually. A few minutes later, that feeling was proven right. For there, silhouetted by the sunlight behind her, was her skeletal dragon Familiar, wings folded on her back.

"Hey you," Bella greeted as she and Gideon approached.

"Morning Nemesis," Gideon greeted. He led them out of the cave and leftward toward Main Street, but Nemesis stopped near the edge of the waterfall.

Come with me.

"What?" Bella asked. Gideon frowned.

"Hmm?"

"Not you," Bella apologized. "I was talking to Nemesis."

"Best if you do it using your thoughts," Gideon advised. "Otherwise you'll confuse people...or they'll think you're..."

He made circles with one finger around his ear.

"Hold on," Bella requested. She walked back to Nemesis. "What's up?"

They walk, Nemesis replied. *We fly.*

And then Nemesis leapt up, grabbing Bella's shoulders in her feet-claws, and leapt off the edge of the cliff!

Bella screamed as they plummeted down the side of the waterfall toward the lake thousands of feet below.

Then Nemesis spread her wings out wide, and Bella felt a jolt as their descent slowed abruptly. She cried out again, half-expecting the dragon's bony grip on her shoulders to slip away. But they held fast...and suddenly they were gliding instead of falling.

They soared over the lake, and Nemesis turned in a wide circle, spiraling gradually toward the bottom of Dragon's Peak. A full minute later, Nemesis steered them toward the rapidly-approaching shoreline…and slowed their descent with a few flaps of her wings, depositing Bella gently on the ground.

Bella's legs wobbled, and she lowered herself to her hands and knees, feeling queasy. The sensation passed quickly, and she stood, turning to glare at Nemesis.

"Are you crazy? You could've killed me!" she accused.

Keep that in mind.

Bella blinked.

"Excuse me?"

Flying is faster, Nemesis reasoned. *You'll get used to it.*

And Bella had to admit, it *was* a lot faster to fly. It was a long while later before Gideon and Myko made it to the bottom of Dragon's Peak and joined up with them. Apparently Piper had been waiting on the road further up, because he was with Gideon and Myko when they arrived.

"Everyone ready?" the Actor inquired.

"Ready when you are," Gideon replied. Bella nodded, and Myko *wuffed.*

And then they all turned to the lake, and jumped in.

* * *

The Dragonkind army was *huge.*

It had assembled just outside of the mushroom forest, on the plains beyond where the White Dragon would have been in the original world. Row upon row of Dragonkin in blue and white armor polished to a mirror shine, thousands upon thousands of them.

An army many times larger even than General Craven's had been.

King Draco was in a tent at the head of the army, standing four times as tall as any of the other Dragonkin. They met in this tent, which housed a large table upon which a map had been placed. It was covered with markings that seemed to show troop movements. Draco inclined his head at Bella when she approached, and after introducing Gideon, Myko, and Nemesis, they got down to business.

"The Collector's castle in your world is named Castle Under," Draco informed them. "It is heavily guarded, far more so than

386

Castle Over, the castle in our world. My armies will attack Castle Under."

"Thereby capturing the attention of the bulk of its defenses," Gideon noted.

"While we slip in Castle Over and grab Kendra and Thaddeus," Piper concluded.

"Precisely," King Draco agreed. "We shall send a small contingent with you to aid in your defense, and you shall extract the Creator."

"While I go and deal with the Collector," Gideon finished.

"Not without me you're not," Bella reminded him. She put a hand on his shoulder. "We're a family. We stick together."

He nodded, giving her a smile.

"Your mother would've been proud of who you've become," he told her. "*I'm* proud of you, Bella."

"Yeah, well the Collector's got some really nasty beasts guarding his castle," Piper warned. "The most dangerous are the Reapers, but he's got other defenses. Hell, if he decides to hide behind that magic door protecting his office, we'll never be able to get to him."

"The more creative we are, the more powerful our magic will be," Bella recited. "And my dad's the most creative person I know."

"I'll give you that one," Piper conceded. "All right, so we're taking the Underground then. Nearest entrance is here," he noted, pointing to the map on the table. "That's a good twenty miles away, over some pretty rough terrain."

"Terrain?" Draco inquired with what appeared to be an attempt at a smirk.

"Well yeah," Piper replied. "There's hills and lakes and a marsh along the way. Gonna take an army this size a hell of a long time to get there. Unless you plan on flying," he added sarcastically.

Draco spread his wings out wide…so wide that their tips touched either side of the big tent. Piper grimaced.

"Right," he muttered.

"We shall fly ourselves and you to the Underground," Draco decided. "You shall stay at the shore of the lake in our world while we fly up to the great mirror in the sky and pass through to your world. We will begin our assault, and when the battle becomes heated, you will be flown to Castle Over to complete your mission. Any questions?"

"Um, lots," Piper replied. "These are real broad strokes here. We need more specifics."

"Leave the specifics to me," Draco reassured. "Concentrate on your mission."

"That's what I m-" Piper began, but Gideon elbowed him in the ribs, giving him a look.

"We appreciate everything you've done for us, King Draco," Gideon stated. "And what you're doing for Thaddeus Birch."

"T'was the Creator that gave us life," Draco replied. "It will be an honor to save His."

Chapter 44

The dungeon of the Castle Over was dank and musty, its underground cells small and cramped. The only amenity offered any prisoner unlucky enough to be find themselves trapped within it was a pot to piss in. No bed, no window. No light save for the dull glow of the magical lanterns illuminating the narrow hallways. Despite its dozens of cells, only one was occupied.

The Collector crossed his arms over his chest, glaring through the prison bars of that cell, at an old man standing within it. A man with deep brown skin contrasting sharply with white curly hair, a pair of golden glasses propped on the bridge of his nose.

"This doesn't need to be unpleasant, Thaddeus," he insisted.

"On the contrary," Thaddeus replied. "That is the only way this can be."

"Agree to work for me and I'll provide far more comfortable living conditions," the Collector offered.

"Working for you would be far more uncomfortable for my soul than these conditions are for my body."

The Collector sighed.

"Clever turns of phrase won't help you, Thaddeus."

"My words are the truth," Thaddeus countered. "Clever or not, I find they are the *only* things that can help me at this point."

"Then use your words for my cause."

"No," Thaddeus replied. Simply, without anger or defiance.

"I can make things much more unpleasant for you," the Collector warned. "I won't enjoy doing so, but if you push me, I'll be forced to do it."

Thaddeus raised an eyebrow.

"An old, unarmed man trapped in a cell forcing you to do something?" he inquired. "And here I thought you were powerful."

The Collector grimaced, resisting the urge to argue. There would be no winning a war of words with Thaddeus Birch.

"You will be tortured," he promised.

"Naturally," Thaddeus agreed.

"You won't be so calm about it when my men get started," the Collector warned, suddenly irritated with the old man. "Trust me when I say they're very good at their jobs."

"Unfortunately I'm in a position to test that assumption," Thaddeus replied. "I daresay I've been tortured by the best."

The Collector sighed.

"Then you leave me no choice," he muttered, turning away from the Writer.

"Wrong," Thaddeus retorted. "Nobody makes our choices for us but us. Still playing the victim I see."

The Collector paused, then turned back to Thaddeus.

"I'm not a victim," he retorted. Thaddeus raised an eyebrow.

"Oh really?" he replied. "You're seeking revenge, aren't you?"

"Against the Painters that…"

"Oh it hardly matters *why*," Thaddeus interrupted. "Only victims get revenge, Collector. By definition, they must have been victims of something or someone to *want* revenge."

The Collector said nothing.

"Heroes want justice," Thaddeus continued.

"And that's what I want," the Collector replied.

"Have you ever heard of a hero torturing a poor old man after murdering his daughter and hunting down his granddaughter?" Thaddeus inquired.

Again, the Collector found himself speechless.

"People think in stories, Collector," Thaddeus declared authoritatively. "Not facts, not emotions. Stories. And you don't even know the story you've chosen to live."

"And that is?"

"That of the Victim," Grandpa answered. "A victim of your own creation. Of your creator. Of your very nature, and your fate. No matter how much money you have or power you take, that story defines you…and everything that you do."

The Collector swallowed past a sudden lump in his throat, staring at Thaddeus. No words came to him. No rebuttal.

"You have a choice," Thaddeus continued, reaching out to grab the bars between them and leaning in. "Be the Victim…or do something heroic." He smiled grimly. "But we both know what you'll do, don't we? After all, only victims don't 'have a choice.'"

The Collector stared at Thaddeus for a long moment, neither man blinking. Then he turned away abruptly, striding down the hallway toward the prison exit. One of the Reapers was levitating there by the stairwell leading up to the ground floor. The Collector paused at the foot of the stairs, his jawline rippling.

Focus.

He pushed past Thaddeus's words, focusing instead on what he should do. Thaddeus wouldn't work for him…and even if he did, it was dangerous to trust his work. For Thaddeus had fooled the Pentad into allowing Havenwood…and he could only guess at what the wily Writer would try to pull next, if given a chance.

"Put him in with the rest of my collection," he told the Reaper.

Then he ascended the stairs, returning to the ground floor of the Castle Over.

* * *

The journey back to the Collector's office in Castle Under was long and tedious, offering the Collector ample time to think. But try as he might, he found himself ruminating on the past instead of the present. On the choices that had led him to this point.

Nobody makes our choices for us but us.

Thaddeus's words played themselves over and over in his head. They were wrong, of course. Someone else *had* made the Collector's choices for him. The choice to create him. To make him have Xander's personality. His looks. Even a hint of his memories.

He hadn't chosen to be a copy. A counterfeit of a dead boy.

You're still a victim.

It was obvious to him now, though his mind rebelled against the idea. It was clear that Thaddeus was trying to get in his head.

391

That the wily old man was trying to make him doubt himself. But at the same time, Thaddeus's logic was undeniable.

It defines you and everything that you do.

A vision of his collection came to him, of all the Painters he'd trapped. Each act of betrayal a facet of his revenge. His revenge against the Painters who'd dared to create life. To control it.

By the time he made it back to his office, he found himself so disturbed and anxious that he had Miss Savage come in to play him a tune.

She sat in her chair in the far corner of his office, her violin propped on her left shoulder. She drew her bow across its strings, a haunting, melancholy sound filling the room. It was her genius to sense his mood so expertly, and to evoke it with her song.

He resisted the urge to insist that she start with a happier tune, knowing that she would make the transition soon enough. She would start with what *was*, and transform it into what *would* be.

Miss Savage closed her eyes, feeling the music. Feeling the Flow. The Collector eased back into his chair before his desk, watching her.

He felt glum as the song continued, each note tugging at what remained of his heart. An organ he'd locked away long ago. But her music – and her music alone – drew it out from its prison. And with it came the memories.

The urge to resist her power came, as it always did. He let down his guard, allowing himself to be vulnerable. Closed his eyes and felt the music with her, letting it take him on its journey.

Visions of his father came to him then. His father's face the first time he'd seen it, being pulled from his painting. A face wet with tears, eyes red and puffy. The stink of booze. How his father had embraced him, weeping uncontrollably.

What's wrong, Dad?

Nothing, son. Not anymore.

The music gradually quickened, the notes rising, becoming sharper, more insistent. No longer melancholy but angry. Wrathful. His heart and mind followed, the memory of that fateful night coming to him, so many years after he'd been drawn out. Of himself standing before his father, paintbrush in hand. Demanding to know why he couldn't feel the Flow. Why it was gone.

Remembered his father's lies. Lie after lie after lie.

392

For the first time in his life, he'd refused to believe those lies. He'd found his painting, and then he'd called his father out. Demanded the truth.

And only then – faced with the realization that he could lie no more – his creator had told the truth.

The Collector opened his eyes, staring at the painting above the door. He looked down at his hands then, realizing they were balled into fists. There was a sudden, awful pain in his right hand, a throbbing that made him wince.

"Stop," he ordered.

Her eyes snapped open, and she froze, staring back at him. He felt the power of her music fade away, his heart returning to its self-imposed prison.

"It's not you," he reassured. "I'm…I need to be alone for a moment."

She hesitated, then stood, inclining her head.

"As you wish."

Then she left, closing the door behind her.

The Collector grimaced, staring at his right hand. It was throbbing fiercely now, the pain worse when he tried to move his fingers. He reached over to pull off his glove…and hesitated, dread coming over him.

He swallowed, steeling his nerves, then slowly pulled the glove off.

His breath caught in his throat.

Thin, translucent skin covered skeletal fingers, purple veins crawling over his bones. The ancient skin went up his wrist to his forearm…and almost certainly beyond.

The Collector reached up, touching the right side of his face. The skin there still felt smooth, but he knew now that it was only a matter of time before it wouldn't be. His heart sank.

It didn't work.

That witch's curse was still within him, and no amount of paint could hide it. Soon he would be as he had been, half of him ancient. Near death.

He took a deep breath in, letting it out. Centering himself.

This is reality, he reminded himself. *This is truth.*

To deny the truth was to be like the man who had pretended to be his father. And he'd vowed long ago to never be like that man.

"So be it," he muttered. He put his glove back on, being exceedingly careful not to tear his paper-thin skin.

Do something heroic.

He took a deep breath in, steadying himself. Then he lifted his gaze to the door of his office.

"Miss Savage!" he called out.

The door opened, and Miss Savage peered in.

"Bring him to me."

She closed the door, no other words needed. The Collector sighed, leaning back in his chair and staring idly at the paperwork on his desk. Endless paperwork, each stroke of his pen generating a mountain of work for those under his employ. Armies mobilized with ink, priceless treasures purchased with a single signature.

He resisted the sudden, powerful urge to shove the stacks of paper off his desk. To watch them fly everywhere, their pristine order reduced to chaos.

Not yet.

The Collector sat there, waiting for his anger to dissipate. As it always did. He'd vowed long ago to never make a decision in anger again. To never let his enemies – or his allies – have that power over him.

My story is coming to an end.

He accepted this, secure in the knowledge that it didn't really matter. He was a copy, after all. Identical in every way to the boy he'd been created to replace…except that that boy had been real. The only thing special about him was what he'd done. The only thing that differentiated him from his copy were his actions.

And those, unlike him, were very real.

There was a knock at the door, and his gaze jerked up to stare at it. He took a deep breath in, sitting up straight and squaring his shoulders.

"Come in," he called out.

The door opened, and a familiar figure stepped into the office.

"Hello Simon," the Collector greeted. "I have something I'd like to give you."

* * *

Simon stood before a full-length mirror in his small bedroom in the eastern wing of the Castle Under, staring at his reflection.

His blond hair, once too short to be grabbed or pulled – by design – was now long enough to be slicked back. A narrow face, but not as narrow as it'd been when Miss Savage had rescued him from his prison cell in the Twin Spires. Scars on his face, one going through his left eyebrow, the other his left cheek.

Dad had been right-handed, after all.

His gaze dropped, to his thin neck. His throat made even paler when contrasted with the midnight-black suit and magic boots he'd just put on. The jacket had five buttons, and came halfway up his neck, with a narrow rectangular notch cut out over his Adam's apple. The material shimmered slightly in the sunlight streaming through the lone window in his room. It was the Collector's suit, and it was far too big for him. But the fabric shrank magically to fit him, embracing him gently but firmly. Almost intimately, in a way he now knew the Collector never would.

"It suits you," the Collector murmured.

Simon turned sideways, glancing up at the Collector, who stood to his left, having donned a white suit jacket and pants. It was clear that the right side of the man's face was starting to age again, the fine wrinkles Simon had noticed a few hours ago already deeper. He lowered his gaze, feeling unworthy of this suit. Of the Collector's praise.

"What's wrong?" the Collector inquired.

"I failed you," Simon muttered. He felt the man's warm hand rest on his shoulder.

"Simon," the Collector began. He paused, then knelt down, turning Simon to face him. "Listen to me very carefully."

Simon met the Collector's gaze.

"The only way you can fail me now is to fail yourself," the Collector insisted. "You have to believe in yourself, even when you fail." He squeezed Simon's shoulder. "*Especially* when you fail."

"Yes sir," Simon whispered.

"You're a survivor, Simon. You always pull yourself back together, no matter what. Learn from your scars."

Simon nodded, and the Collector gripped his shoulder harder, staring at him intently.

"I want you to be more than just a survivor, Simon. I want you to be powerful. Successful. I want you to do what I did. Do you know what that means?"

"I need to take it," Simon answered.

The Collector smiled.

"That's right," he confirmed. "Most people are weak, Simon. They'll give you their power. They'll give you power over them, just for being stronger than they are. Or *seeming* stronger. And the ones who won't give it to you, you *take* it from them."

"Yes sir."

"Never apologize for who you are, Simon," he insisted, grabbing Simon's hand. He pulled Simon's sleeve up, exposing the scars on his forearm. "That's your truth. With this suit, you won't need to hide that anymore. And the only one who'll be able to hurt you is *you.*"

Simon nodded.

"Never be a victim again, Simon," the Collector insisted. "Don't cut yourself. Cut them."

Simon's eyes grew moist, and he swallowed visibly. His lower lip trembled, but he stood tall, nodding once.

"Yes sir," he whispered.

The Collector stood, letting go of Simon's shoulder and eyeing him approvingly.

"Does it fit?" he asked.

"Perfectly, sir."

"It certainly does," he agreed. Then he sighed. "I don't know how much time I have left, Simon. But when I'm gone, I want you and Miss Savage to have all of this," he stated, gesturing around the room. "My castle. My paintings. Everything."

"Yes sir."

"I can never love you the way you want me to," the Collector continued gently, "…but I can love you the way my creator never did. As a father."

Simon nodded, his eyes growing moist.

"Do you accept me as your father, Simon?"

Simon's lower lip trembled, tears streaming down his cheeks. He took a deep, shuddering breath in, doing everything he could to compose himself.

"Yes sir."

The Collector reached around, placing a hand on the back of Simon's neck, and drew him in for an embrace. Simon closed his eyes, burying his head in the Collector's chest.

"I've got a lot to teach you, Simon. And not a lot of time to do it."

"I'll remember everything you say, father," Simon vowed. The Collector pulled back from Simon, smiling down at him.

"I know you will, son," he replied. "Now…"

The door burst open, and Miss Savage stepped into the room. The Collector spun around, glaring at the woman. Her feet were bare, her heels carried in one hand. Her chest was rising and falling rapidly, her skin covered in a sheen of sweat.

"You need to come with me," she stated breathlessly. "Now."

"What's wrong?" the Collector demanded.

"The castle," she replied. "It's under attack!"

Chapter 45

Bella stood at the shore of the huge lake surrounding Mount Inversus in the Plane of Reflection, her gaze traveling up to the large castle at its peak. And beyond that, a second, upside-down castle balanced perfectly on the tallest tower of the first. Gideon stood at her right, Piper at her left. Myko and Nemesis were right behind them, along with a hundred or so Dragonkin soldiers. They'd all taken the Underground to get here, a vast, winding network of dark tunnels containing magical doorways to just about every land in the world. A trip that had still taken most of the day, given the sheer number of Dragonkin involved.

And high above all of them, the bulk of the Dragonkin army had taken to the sky, forming a flock so enormous and dense it looked for all the world like huge, angry thundercloud that blotted out the sunset.

One whose thunderous power would soon strike the Collector's castle high above.

Piper gave a low whistle.

"Now that's a sight you'll never see again," he declared.

"Indeed," Gideon concurred.

"What now?" Bella asked.

"Now we wait," Gideon answered.

"This is a magic trick Bella," Piper explained. "We get our audience to look one way, then we do the trick out of sight. Gotta make sure we've captured their attention first."

Bella felt restless, shifting her weight from one foot to the other. She suddenly wanted nothing more than to fly up there and fight. To find the Collector and…

She turned to Nemesis.

"That's what *you* want, isn't it," she told the dragon. Gideon gave her a look.

"Inside voice please."

Bella grimaced.

You want to fight, don't you, she thought.

Damn right, Nemesis replied.

Be patient.

She felt Nemesis's irritation, and ignored it. In fact, she tried to send calm, soothing thoughts her Familiar's way. After all, if Bella could feel Nemesis's emotions, the converse had to be true.

Quit playing with my emotions, Nemesis groused. Still, it seemed to work; Bella felt less antsy now, which meant Nemesis did too.

"Alright, let's go over the plan," Gideon began. "The Dragonkin will fly us up to the peak of the mountain on this side. Part of our Dragonkin escort will charge the front doors while we head to the windows on one of the higher floors near the tallest tower. Myko will break us in."

"Why Myko?" Bella asked.

"If the window is magically guarded, Myko can moon-dash through it. Even if it hurts him, the moon-dash will heal him while he's doing it."

"It does that?" she pressed, her eyebrows going up. If that was the case, Myko could moon-dash into pretty much anything…and as long as he struck it in the middle of phasing, he'd heal at the end. And be practically invincible.

"Now you know why those guards were afraid of him back in Craven's camp," Gideon replied with a wink.

"That's a brilliant ability," Bella admitted.

"The more creative you are…" Gideon began.

"The more powerful your magic will be," Bella finished. "Right."

"Once we're through, we'll fight our way to wherever Kendra is. We assume she's still in Castle Over, if…" He trailed off, glancing at Piper, who grimaced.

"If she's still alive, you can say it," the Actor grumbled.

399

"Grandpa may be with her, but it isn't guaranteed," Gideon continued. "We'll have to interrogate anyone we find inside. It may not be pleasant, Bella," he warned.

"If it means getting Grandpa back," she replied, "...I'll do it."

"Once we've rescued Thaddeus and Kendra, the Dragonkin will take them to safety. Then we go after the Collector...and take him down," Gideon finished. "Got it?"

"So just the broad strokes then, eh? We just wing the details," Piper stated. Gideon smirked at him.

"All the more room for creativity, Piper. Has it ever failed me before?" he inquired. Piper gave a rueful grin.

"Nope."

"Bella, if you find yourself in trouble, Nemesis can fly you out of the castle to safety," Gideon added. Nemesis inclined her skeletal head. "Everyone ready?"

"If I wait until I'm ready to do something, I'll never do it," Bella replied." Gideon smiled.

"Well said," he replied.

"I had a good teacher."

They all watched as the bulk of the Dragonkin army passed through the giant magical mirror in the sky, to the original world beyond.

"All right," Gideon declared. "Let's do this."

* * *

Bella felt her feet lift off the ground as Nemesis beat her powerful wings, her clawed feet gripping Bella's shoulders in a vise-like grip. Gideon and Piper followed, flown upward by their Dragonkin escort. Two had grabbed Myko, the giant wolf too heavy for just one to fly with. Upward they went with their Dragonkin escort, the shore of the lake pulling away quickly below. Bella felt queasy suddenly, and she focused ahead, at the castle at the top of the mountain. It wasn't long before they reached the mountaintop, and most of the hundred or so Dragonkin soldiers broke away from them, zooming toward the courtyard near the entrance to the castle.

Statues of giant warriors stood in neat rows in that courtyard, and as the Dragonkin approached, they came to life. Big, brutish creatures poured out of the castle double-doors, familiar puke-green, bald-headed warriors carrying large axes.

"Circle around," Gideon yelled. The Dragonkin did so, circling leftward around the base of the castle. "There," Gideon added, pointing ahead. "There's a large window on the fourth floor."

They flew up to it, a stained-glass window easily as tall as Gideon was, and then hovered before it.

"Myko, you're up," Gideon ordered. "Dragonkin, drop him on my count. Three, two, one!"

The two Dragonkin holding Myko let go of the wolf…and Myko shot forward in a streak of silver light, smashing through the window.

An explosion of sparks flew from the impact, and Nemesis curled her wings around Bella, shielding her from the onslaught. They began to fall, and Nemesis spread her wings out a moment later, regaining the altitude they'd lost.

The window was broken…but Myko was nowhere to be seen.

"Myko?" she called out.

A moment later, Myko peeked out of the windowsill, *wuffing* at them.

"He says it's all clear," Gideon translated. "Let's go inside."

His Dragonkin escort flew him up to the window, depositing him within. Piper was next, and finally Bella was dropped in. She found herself in a large room; it appeared to be a bedroom.

"These are the dorms for the higher-ranked artists," Piper explained. He paused, looking around. "Hell of a lot nicer than mine was."

"Myko will scout ahead," Gideon declared. "We'll go up to the tallest tower, then make our way down again methodically, to find Kendra and Thaddeus."

"This is a big castle," Piper warned. "Gonna take a real long time to find them if we're not lucky."

"We have to start somewhere," Gideon countered. "If we encounter the Collector's defenses, Myko can warn me telepathically and moon-dash back to us so we can fight together."

"Hold on," Piper interjected. "The best fight is the one we don't get into."

"What are you thinking?" Gideon inquired. Piper smirked.

"I'm thinking the more creative we are…"

And then he *shifted.*

A thick black cloak appeared around him as he grew taller, his face hidden deep within its cowl. Silver gauntlets appeared on his hands…and twin pinpricks of blood-red light glowed from the shadowy recesses of his hood.

"A Reaper," Gideon murmured. "Clever."

"You are my captives," Piper explained in a deep, whispery voice that sent chills down Bella's spine. "Put your hands behind you."

Gideon nodded, taking a painting from his thigh-holster and opening it. Myko jumped in, and he rolled it up, putting it back in its place. Then he crossed his wrists behind his back…and Bella did the same.

"What about them?" Bella asked, glancing at the Dragonkin who'd escorted them.

"Stay behind," Gideon ordered. "Make sure no one follows behind us."

The Dragonkin nodded.

"Follow," Piper murmured in that horrible voice. "Eyes on the floor. No talking."

He opened the bedroom door, leading them out into a long hallway beyond, one with white marble floors and expensive-looking wood paneling. It was, to Bella's relief, deserted. She kept her eyes downcast, following behind Gideon, with Nemesis taking the rear.

Eventually they reached the end of the hallway, which turned right down a second one…and right into three of the tall, bald creatures with axes guarding a door at the end of it.

Bella tensed, and Gideon slowed slightly, so that she bumped into him.

"Glargs," he whispered.

"Silence!" Piper hissed, his creepy voice echoing through the hallway. The Glargs stared at him, then at Bella and Gideon and Nemesis, shifting their weight from foot-to-foot and exchanging nervous glances. Piper went right up to them, seeming to glide over the floor. Then he stopped, staring them down with his glowing red eyes.

The Glargs scrambled to open the door and get out of his way.

Piper ignored them, continuing through the doorway, with Gideon and Bella and Nemesis following behind. The door closed behind them, and Bella let out a breath she hadn't realized she'd been holding.

That was no fun, she felt Nemesis grumble.

You'll get your chance to fight, Bella reassured her.

They entered into yet another series of hallways, which Piper led them expertly through, having been an employee of the Collector's for over a decade. They made it past another contingent of Glargs, eventually reaching a door guarded by two men in full black plate-mail armor. They each carried a long spear, and peered through their helmet visors at Piper and the rest.

Piper stopped before them, gesturing with one gauntleted hand for them to open the door.

"Who are these people?" one of the guards demanded.

"Prisoners," Piper hissed. The guard's eyes narrowed.

"Where is your scythe?" he demanded, raising his spear to point it at Piper's head. "And why aren't you levitating?"

"It's an Actor!" the other guard blurted out...and thrust his spear at Piper's face!

Gideon's cane was already in mid-swing, batting the spear to the side with a loud *clang*. He followed up with an attack, smashing his cane into the side of the guard's helmet.

The guard's neck snapped to the side...but his helmet remained intact.

The man thrust his spear at Gideon this time, but Gideon leapt *into* the attack, batting the spear away with his cane, then jamming the butt of his cane through the guard's visor, striking him right between the eyes.

The guard stumbled backward, dazed...but only for a split-second. The guard thrust his spear again, striking Gideon right in the chest.

"Gideon!" Bella cried.

But the tip of the spear passed harmlessly into Gideon's chest-painting...and Gideon smashed his cane repeatedly into the guard's helmet, finally managing to dent it.

The helmet turned gray for a moment, the dent vanishing.

"Um, Gideon," Piper warned, staying back from the fight. "I think these guys are..."

"Statues," Gideon finished with a grunt, pulling himself away from the soldier's spear. The second soldier thrust at him, and he blocked the attack, backpedaling quickly away from the two.

403

"Could use a little help here," he grumbled, retrieving Myko's painting and tossing it to Bella.

My pleasure, Bella felt Nemesis reply.

The dragon leapt upward, spreading her wings and zooming through the air toward one of the guards while Bella drew Myko out from his painting. Nemesis grabbed his spear with both foot-claws, beating her wings and trying to tear the weapon from his hands. But he held on, and was far too heavy for Nemesis to lift into the air. She managed to pull the guard's hands above his head, leaving his body vulnerable...and Myko moon-dashed right into his chest. The guard shot backward, smashing into the wall beside the door. He ricocheted off...right as Gideon swung his cane.

The magical cane struck the guard in the belly, stopping his momentum instantly...and absorbing the kinetic energy. Gideon swung again, smashing the guard in the front of his helmet.

The guard's helmet – and face – crumpled with a sickening *crunch*.

But even as the guard flew backward into the wall again, his head turned to stone so that it could heal.

The second guard lunged at Piper, who dodged out of the way in the nick of time. Myko moon-dashed into the guard's side, sending him flying...right out of one of the windows.

A moment later, Myko moon-dashed back through the window, smashing into the other guard as he finished healing from Gideon's devastating blow. The guard slammed into the wall, but threw Myko off, jabbing his spear into the wolf's belly. Myko yelped, stumbling backward, blood gushing from the wound.

Bella drew Sleep Terror from her chest-painting, whipping it at the remaining guard. The bony tip struck his left shoulder, bouncing off with a *clang*...but nothing happened. The guard didn't fall asleep.

It's a statue, Nemesis reasoned. *Statues don't sleep.*

Nemesis flew at the guard as he drew his spear back to stab Myko again, grabbing the spear and tearing it out of his hands. Gideon charged, slamming the butt of his cane into the floor, then swinging it at the guard's head.

The guard dodged, kicking at Gideon's chest.

But his foot went *through* Gideon's chest-painting, and Gideon twisted, throwing the man off-balance. At the same time, Piper metamorphosed into Vengeance, an eight-foot-tall monster of a man. He roared, charging at the guard and ramming him with one boulder-sized shoulder.

Bella glanced down at her thigh-holsters, yanking out a painting. "Apertus," she incanted.

The painting unrolled, and she reached into it…and pulled out Goo.

"Get him!" she cried.

Goo rushed across the marble floor toward the guard, who shoved Vengeance off of him, then withdrew a sword from its sheath at his hip. He swung at Vengeance, who leapt backward…and Goo lunged at the guard, wrapping his gooey green ooze around the man's ankles.

The guard stumbled, looking down with surprise as Goo engulfed him, rising up his legs to his knees.

"Get back!" Bella ordered.

Gideon, Vengeance, and Nemesis backpedaled away from the guard, watching as the living statue struggled to free his legs from Goo's grasp. But it was as if the man were stuck in a giant wad of gum; no matter how hard he tried, he couldn't escape. Black mist seeped from his body, the dark emotions within him being drawn out by Goo's power.

And within moments, he seemed to lose the will to fight, standing perfectly still…and Goo seemed to grow a little as the guard relaxed, feeding off the man's rage.

Everyone stared at the guard, then turned to Bella.

"Well then," Gideon stated. "That worked."

"The best fight is the one we don't get into," Bella recited, winking at Piper, who'd transformed back into himself. He flashed her a wry grin.

"Well played kid."

Nemesis flew to Bella's side, eyeing the serene-appearing guard with irritation.

Spoilsport, she muttered.

"Quit complaining," Bella told her. "Or I'll put *you* in the goo."

"Think, don't speak," Gideon reminded her. Bella shot him a look.

"Why, because I'm a woman?"

"Let's go," he prompted, pointedly ignoring her.

Gideon led them through the doorway, which revealed a stairwell spiraling upward. Climbing the stairs, they reached a door at the top...which opened into a large chamber.

One with more than a dozen Glargs.

Myko moon-dashed into the nearest Glarg, throwing him backward into a few of his compatriots. They went down like so many bowling pins, and Bella cracked her bone whip, striking one after the other while they were still down. They went instantly to sleep, moaning and twitching in the throes of horrible nightmares.

At the same time, Gideon and Piper – morphing into Vengeance again – attacked the remaining Glargs, battering them with rapid-fire attacks. Nemesis flew at one of the Glargs, lifting him off his feet and dropping him right over Goo. The Glarg landed in Goo's green flesh, sinking partway in.

He struggled like a fly stuck in water, then gradually calmed, laying perfectly still.

Vengeance caught on, grabbing a Glarg and throwing him into Goo. Gideon smashed another with his cane, sending it face-first into Goo.

Within less than a minute, all of the Glargs were either dead, sleeping, or drained of their will to fight by Goo's magic. And Goo was even larger than before...nearly twice as big as he'd been when Bella had first drawn him out.

"Alright, let's keep moving," Gideon prompted. "Piper, where to next?"

"Everything's backwards," Piper said as he transformed back into himself, "...but the second-tallest tower should be ahead. There's a sky-bridge near the top of it that should lead to the upper floors, and the tallest tower."

"Lead the way," Gideon prompted.

Piper did so, bringing them through a maze of rooms and hallways. Some were guarded, others weren't. None of the guards were human, and all fell to the combined onslaught of Gideon's cane, Bella's whip, Piper's fists, Nemesis's claws, and Myko's moon-dash.

At length, Piper brought them to a door at the end of a short hallway. But this was no ordinary door; it was huge, easily twenty feet high and ten feet wide, and wrought of black stone. A face had been carved into it, a demon's face with horns and a mouth open in a snarling, toothy roar.

Its eyes were closed, but as they approached, they opened, revealing twin orbs that burned with an inner fire.

"WHO APPROACHES?" it demanded.

Bella froze, her eyes widening…and Piper and Gideon stopped in their tracks beside her. The voice hadn't been one of sound…it'd been in her head.

"Did you hear that?" she asked. Gideon nodded.

"There's *two* of them?" Piper blurted out. "That's it. We're screwed."

"I remember lecturing about these," Gideon recalled. "In an Art History class I taught a few decades ago."

"WHO APPROACHES," the door boomed, more insistently this time.

"So you know about this thing?" Piper asked. Gideon nodded.

"They're the Twin Demon Gates," he explained. "Quite ancient. The Pentad's archaeologists have been searching for them for some time now. Apparently there's a way to claim ownership of them. After you do, anyone who tries to pass through, the Demon Gates sense their intentions toward that owner…and if they're anything but benign…"

"Then what?" Piper pressed.

"Then they won't bring you to the other side," Gideon answered. "They'll bring you to Hell."

"Hell is a place?" Bella asked. Gideon gave her a rueful smile.

"Created by a book, of course," he confirmed. "No one's met anyone that's gone there, because no one that goes there ever comes back."

"Oh *great*," Piper muttered. "Well, we're done for."

"Don't give up just yet," Gideon counseled. Piper glared at him.

"Why, you think you can get past this thing?"

"You're speaking to the world's greatest living Painter," Gideon replied with a smirk. "No door is closed to me."

"Why don't we just get in Goo?" Bella interjected.

Everyone turned to her.

"If we're so worried about the door sensing our bad intentions, Goo can take them away," Bella reasoned. "He absorbs negative emotions."

Piper raised an eyebrow, glancing at Gideon. Gideon frowned, rubbing his chin.

"You know, that might just work," he admitted.

"What was *your* idea?" Piper asked him.

"Never mind my idea," Gideon grumbled. "Bella, I think you're right. But just in case, we should try it with one volunteer first."

"Like who?" Piper pressed.

Myko raised a paw.

"He says he'll do it," Gideon stated. Suddenly, Bella didn't feel quite as sure.

"What if it doesn't work?" she asked.

"It'll work," Gideon reassured. "Just a precaution, that's all."

With that, Myko stepped onto Goo, along with the various soldiers trapped in the translucent green ooze. His paws sank in, and he stood there, looking quite content.

"Go on Goo," Bella urged.

Goo quivered, then crawled forward. The Demon Gate's mouth opened even wider, and Goo went through, vanishing into the darkness beyond.

Bella held her breath.

A moment later, Goo returned, passing through the door as if it didn't exist. The guards were still stuck within him...but Myko was gone.

"Oh no!" Bella blurted out.

"Relax," Gideon soothed. "It worked. Myko's on the other side." He turned to Piper. "You're next."

Piper grimaced, but stepped into Goo, and his expression quickly turned serene. Goo went through again, and returned without Piper. Gideon went in next, and then Nemesis. Finally it was Bella's turn.

She stepped into Goo, feeling his warm...well, goo engulf her feet, then her ankles and lower legs. A sudden calm came over her like a warm, comfy blanket. She felt no anxiety whatsoever, and couldn't imagine why she would have felt nervous in the first place. Everything was just fine, after all.

They were going to be okay.

Goo ejected the Collector's guards onto the floor, then oozed forward, passing through the great open mouth of the Demon Gate. Bella passed into its shadowy maw, entirely unconcerned. It was just a door, after all...and everyone else had gone through without a problem.

A moment later, she found herself on the other side. A short hallway greeted her, with another – normal – door ahead. Everyone else was there, waiting for her.

Goo released her, and the moment he did, Bella felt that wonderful calmness fade. Anxiety slithered back into her consciousness, and she immediately missed being inside Goo. She had half a mind to ask him to carry her through the castle from now on, and was about to step back in when Nemesis flicked Bella's hip with her bony tail.

Don't even think about it.

"Ow," Bella said, rubbing her hip. "Okay, okay."

"Well, that worked," Piper noted. Bella smiled sweetly.

"You're speaking to the world's greatest Painter's daughter," she pointed out. "No door is closed to me."

Gideon rolled his eyes.

"Let's go," he prompted. Piper walked up to the door ahead, twisting the knob and pushing it open.

Beyond, there was utter darkness.

Gideon reached into his chest-painting, pulling out his magical lantern and holding it before him. He followed Piper into the darkness, gesturing for Bella and the others to follow. They all went inside, the meager light from the hallway behind them illuminating a small wedge of the floor they were standing on. Gideon lifted his lamp above his head.

"Luminos," he incanted.

The lantern flared to life, bright rays of light banishing the darkness around them.

Bella heard a sharp intake of breath, and she turned to see Gideon staring wide-eyed at the room around them.

"My god!" he blurted out in horror.

Chapter 46

The Collector limped as quickly as he could down the hallway, Simon and Miss Savage right behind him. He'd left Simon's room immediately after Miss Savage's proclamation, making his way toward his office on the other end of the Castle Under. His right hip ached terribly, each step sending a fresh burst of pain down the side of his thigh.

"Who's attacking us?" he demanded.

"An army of creatures, Collector," Miss Savage answered.

"Not the Pentad?"

"No," she confirmed. "They appear to be some sort of dragon-like race." She hesitated. "General Bowen estimates their numbers in the tens of thousands." General Bowen was the leader of the Collector's forces…a disciplined, but not particularly creative, man.

The Collector slowed.

"Tens of *thousands?*"

"Yes Collector."

He felt the blood drain from his face, and continued forward, not wanting Miss Savage or Simon to notice. Though, knowing them, it was too late.

"We've never seen creatures like this," she continued. "They came from the Plane of Reflection. We…"

"They're Dragonkin," the Collector snapped. His jawline rippled.

Well done, Thaddeus.

The corridor turned right, and the Collector followed it, spotting a row of windows to their right ahead. He stopped by one of them, peering out of it.

A cloud of dragon-like creatures swarmed in mid-air below, just above the mountaintop…and thousands more were on the mountain itself, facing his army of Glargs, various other creatures, and the eight forty-foot tall sword-wielding statues he called his Collosi. The bodies of countless Glargs littered the perimeter of the castle…and a much larger number of dead Dragonkin. But the enemy outnumbered them ten to one. And while the Reapers might be able to take down hundreds of enemies, and would likely be nigh invincible to mere soldiers, they couldn't stop the rest of the army from storming the castle.

And, having forced the vast majority of his Painters into becoming paintings, what few remained would inevitably fall.

At length, the Collector reached the Demon Gate, striding through its wide-open mouth without hesitation. Simon and Miss Savage followed behind him, and they all went into the waiting room of his office. General Bowen was already there. A tall, well-built man with short gray hair and a smooth-shaven face, his expression was grim.

"I know the nature of our enemy, general. Our status?" the Collector snapped.

"We've killed three for every one they have," Bowen answered. "But they're still annihilating us. They're using air superiority to their advantage. Our Painters and the Collosi are causing the most casualties, but it won't be enough." He paused. "They've breached the castle, sir."

"And the Reapers?" the Collector pressed.

Just then, long shadows spread across the floor of the waiting room…and the twin Reapers emerged from the floor, rising up from the shadows until they were levitating inches above the floor.

"Protect Simon and Miss Savage," the Collector told them. "Nothing is to harm them."

The Reapers inclined their heads in unison.

"There's…one more thing," General Bowen stated. The Collector turned to him.

"What?"

"Apparently a small contingent of the enemy was spotted at the base of Castle Over," Bowen revealed. "We believe that Gideon Myles is among them."

The Collector's blood went cold.

He lowered his gaze to his feet, forcing himself to keep his expression neutral. To keep his hands from balling into fists. He glanced to his right, spotting Simon staring at him.

My creator is coming for me.

He took a deep breath in, then let it out, squaring his shoulders. "Where is he now?" he demanded.

"According to our surveillance, he's making his way to the Demon Gate in Castle Over," General Bowen answered. "I doubt he'll be able to-"

"Do *not* doubt that man," the Collector snapped, glaring at Bowen. "If Gideon Myles wants to get through the Demon Gate, he'll do it."

General Bowen lowered his gaze, the color draining from his cheeks.

"Yes sir," he mumbled.

"Evacuate the castle," the Collector commanded. He turned to Simon then. "We can't let Gideon get to my collection before we do," he added, striding up to his office door and yanking it open. He let the obvious go unspoken; if Gideon reached his collection, the man would free as many of the Painters as he could. And their Familiars, which he'd also stowed in the collection. Hundreds of Painters.

They'd have no paintings, and wouldn't pose much of a threat to him. But if they were freed, all of his work would be for nothing.

"General Bowen, see to it that my orders are carried out. Then evacuate with the rest. Take the Underground."

"To where, sir?"

"Anywhere," he answered. "Wait by the Doorway there. If I die, Simon and Miss Savage will succeed me."

General Bowen glanced at Simon, but didn't question it. He saluted.

"Yes Collector."

"That is all," the Collector stated. But General Bowen hesitated. "Yes?"

"It has been a pleasure serving you, sir," the man declared, swallowing visibly. To the Collector's surprise, the man's eyes were moist.

The Collector strode up to Bowen, putting a hand on his shoulder. The man stiffened in surprise; the Collector touched no one.

Then the Collector turned about, gesturing for Simon and Miss Savage to follow him into his office. He closed the door behind them then, rushing to his desk and pulling open one of the larger bottom drawers. He retrieved a black sphere from it; its surface was smooth and highly polished, and cold to the touch.

The Collector paused to stare at it.

An invention of one of his…promoted Painters, the sphere could be activated with a single word. And once activated, it would glow red, and precisely three minutes later, would unleash an expanding inferno. One that would travel hundreds of yards in any direction it was free to do so, burning with enough heat to melt stone.

And even live canvases.

For once a canvas was activated, it was highly resistant to destruction from any element. Ordinary fire could not destroy it, but a flame specifically designed to do so…

He gripped it tightly, ignoring the pain in his withered hand as he did so. The sphere had always been a contingency plan, nothing more. He'd spent his life amassing his collection. Creating the ultimate gallery. A gallery of gods.

Gods reduced to being the very things they'd created. They'd turned fiction into reality, and he had made their reality a fiction.

He couldn't destroy it. Not now, when he was so close.

Lifting his gaze, he realized that Miss Savage and Simon were staring at him.

"Come," he prompted, leaving the sphere in the drawer. He closed it, striding toward the door leading to the castle's highest tower.

There was no point in running from his destiny. He would run *toward* it. He would face it head-on. Gideon was supposed to be his final painting. *Would* be his final painting.

But if he failed, Simon and Miss Savage would see to it that his life's work was not in vain.

413

Chapter 47

Bella squinted at the sudden bright light that shot outward from Gideon's lantern, banishing the darkness all around her. Then she blinked, taking a moment to get her bearings.

They were standing at the very bottom of a large, circular room. The floor and walls were made of gray stone, and fine paintings hung in neat rows in a circle all the way around. She took a step forward...and nearly tripped over something. More paintings had been laid on the floor in neat rows, nearly covering its surface. Unlike the paintings on the walls, the ones on the floor weren't framed. She glanced at Gideon, who was looking upward, his mouth hanging open.

She looked up......and gasped.

For the walls went up...and up, and up. And upon them hung row after row of paintings, as far as the eye could see. Indeed, though the light from Gideon's lantern went up a good hundred feet, the ceiling was still obscured by darkness beyond its reach.

"They're people," Gideon murmured, turning in a slow circle. He was right; most of the paintings were people, set against various backgrounds. All wore identical black robes...and all of them appeared to be either shocked or terrified, or some combination of the two.

"They're Painters," Piper corrected, his eyes widening. He turned to Gideon excitedly. "Look at those robes…they're for the ceremony!"

"What?" Gideon asked.

"The promotion ceremony," Piper clarified. "The Collector brought each Painter up to this castle when they were promoted!"

"And put them in these paintings," Gideon realized. "He stripped them of their defenses and forced each of them into a canvas."

"Along with their Familiars," Bella guessed. For, beside each Painter, there was a unique creature or object. Gideon nodded.

"Which means…"

"Which means Kendra is still alive!" Piper exclaimed. "Come on, we have to find her!"

"Hold on," Gideon cautioned, looking down. "I bet these paintings on the floor are live canvases. It's too dangerous to leave them here like this. We're wearing paintings, so we won't fall in, but Piper and our Familiars might." He squatted down, slipping his fingers under one of the canvases and lifting it up by its unpainted side. "Let's stack these face-down."

They got to work, carefully lifting each painting, then rotating them so they were face-down and stacking them in one corner of the room. After a few minutes, the job was done.

"Ok, first we search for Kendra and Grandpa," Gideon proposed. "Then we free the rest of them."

"Might get real ugly trying to get that many people outta here," Piper pointed out.

"How about we store their paintings in your Conclave and draw them out later?" Bella proposed. Gideon nodded.

"Good idea, Bella."

Bella turned to Nemesis.

"Can you fly Piper up there to find Kendra?" she asked.

Without dropping him? I'm not sure.

Bella rolled her eyes.

"Just do it," she grumbled.

Nemesis grabbed Piper by the shoulders, beating her wings and lifting him upward.

"Remember how to walk up walls?" Gideon asked. Bella blinked, then remembered their harrowing journey through Devil's Pass. She nodded, and Gideon walked up the wall, stepping between the narrow spaces between the paintings. Bella followed behind him, putting one foot on the wall, then lifting her other foot. Gravity *shifted*, and suddenly the wall was the floor. She paused, acclimated to the sudden change in perspective, then followed Gideon as he made his way carefully forward. Or rather, upward.

They walked between the paintings, scanning each of them, then continuing upward a row to repeat the process.

"I recognize some of these Painters," Gideon stated as they went. But none of them were of Grandpa...or Kendra. They were about two-thirds of the way up when they heard Piper call out. He and Nemesis were a good thirty feet above...and had stopped before one of the paintings. In fact, it was the second-to-last painting that had a person in the foreground.

"I found Kendra!" he cried.

Gideon and Bella made their way to Piper. There was indeed a painting of Kendra there...and beside it, another painting.

"Grandpa!" Bella exclaimed.

Her heart leapt with joy, and she knelt before his painting, reaching down to draw him out.

"Wait," Gideon said. "If you draw him out now, he'll fall...and since he's heavier than you, you'll fall with him."

"Oh," Bella replied. "Right."

"I'll draw him out, then we both grab him, and we'll have Nemesis fly him to that balcony," Gideon said, pointing up and to the left. Bella turned, seeing a marble balcony above and behind them.

"Okay," she agreed. Nemesis deposited Piper on the balcony, and Bella and Gideon positioned themselves on either side of Grandpa's painting. Gideon switched his lamp to his stump to free his hand; they reached in at the same time, and Bella felt the familiar warm pulsing sensation as her hand plunged through the canvas. She gripped Grandpa by the right elbow, remembering his broken wrist.

"On my count," Gideon prompted. "Three, two, one!"

They both pulled...and drew Grandpa out of the painting.

Bella felt Grandpa's weight yank her backward, and she braced herself, holding onto his arm as hard as she could. Nemesis grabbed Grandpa by the shoulders, flapping her wings powerfully to maintain altitude.

Got him.

"We can let go," Bella prompted. They did so, and Nemesis flew a very surprised Grandpa up to the balcony, lowering him next to Piper.

"What…!" Grandpa exclaimed. It took him a moment to realize where he was…but once he spotted Gideon and Bella, he broke into a relieved smile. Gideon and Bella circled around the tower walls, reaching the balcony and leaping down to land upon it.

"Grandpa!" Bella exclaimed, rushing forward and giving him a big bear hug. "You're okay!"

"It seems so," Grandpa agreed, giving her a big squeeze with his good arm. He separated from her then, clutching his broken wrist. "I had a feeling you'd come for me," he added with a smile.

"I thought you were…" Bella began, and then stopped, swallowing past a sudden lump in her throat. Grandpa chuckled.

"A goner?" he asked. "So did I." He glanced over her shoulder, at the paintings hung on the walls. "Luckily the Collector had a different plan for me. An apt name, don't you think?"

"Let's get Kendra out," Piper prompted. Bella and Gideon wall-walked back to her painting, reaching in and drawing her out as before. As soon as she came out of the painting, she screamed, flailing her arms. Then she froze, staring at Bella, then Gideon.

"Gideon…?" she blurted out.

"You were in a painting," Gideon informed her. "You're safe now."

She stared at him incredulously, then flinched as Nemesis grabbed her by the shoulders.

"It's okay babe," Piper called out from the balcony. "They're with me."

Kendra looked up, spotting Piper on the balcony…and immediately relaxed.

"Hey baby," she greeted. "Miss me?"

"Terribly," Piper replied, breaking out into a big grin. Nemesis flew Kendra up to the balcony, depositing her next to her husband. Piper drew her into his arms, embracing her tightly.

"Love you baby," he murmured.

She clung to him, burying her head in his chest. Then, after a long moment – long after Bella and Gideon had returned to the balcony – she drew back from him, shaking her head and smiling at him.

"My hero," she said, leaning in and kissing him passionately. Bella looked away, feeling rather awkward. It was hardly a kiss one should have in public, after all. "Told you you'd come and rescue me."

"Guess you're always right," he replied.

"How long have I been gone?" she asked.

"Way too long," Piper answered. "What happened?"

"The Collector betrayed me," she replied, her expression darkening. "He shoved me off this balcony. I don't get it...why would he do that?"

"Because he hates Painters," Gideon answered. Piper and Kendra turned to face him, and Gideon sighed. "I tried to warn you."

Kendra lowered her gaze.

"You were right," she admitted. "I'm sorry, Gideon. For everything." She shook her head, her jawline rippling. "The things I did for that man..."

"We'll talk about it later," Gideon interjected. "Right now we need to get you and Thaddeus out of here."

"And we still need to save all of these people," Grandpa pointed out, gesturing at the paintings all around them. Gideon nodded.

"Where's Nightmare?" Kendra blurted out, her eyes widening in fear. "I can't feel him!"

"He's in your painting," Piper reassured. Nemesis acted without having to be told, flying Kendra to her painting. She drew the golden cube that served as her Familiar, and Nemesis deposited her back on the balcony. Black tentacles sprouted from the cube, and wrapped around Kendra and Piper in a spiraling embrace.

"Okay, let's get these paintings down," Gideon prompted...and then froze, looking past her. Bella followed his gaze, seeing a door at the other end of the balcony.

Twin shadows had appeared on the marble balcony, extending from under the door. They grew longer as Bella watched, inching toward them.

"Run!" Gideon cried.

And then black cowls rose from the shadows, the twin Reapers emerging from the balcony.

* * *

Gideon backpedaled to the edge of the marble balcony, tossing his magic lantern off of it. Then he leapt backward as the Reapers finished rising from their shadow-forms. He went right off the edge of the balcony, plummeting toward the floor of the tower hundreds of feet below.

He looked up as he fell, seeing Nemesis leap off the balcony after him with her wings spread wide, Bella clutched in the dragon's foot-claws. Nightmare followed right after, its tentacles wrapped around Kendra, Piper, and Thaddeus.

"Gideon!" he heard Bella cry.

His guts leapt into his throat as he entered into free-fall, the air tearing at his clothes. He reached down, pulling out a rolled-up painting from his right thigh-holster.

"Apertus!" he commanded.

The painting unrolled itself, revealing Myko.

Gideon reached in with his stump, hooking it around Myko's collar and yanking the wolf out. He held on to Myko's collar for dear life, looking down.

The floor was only a hundred feet below…and coming up fast.

"Clausus," he commanded, and the painting re-rolled itself. He jammed it into its holster, then grabbed onto Myko's collar with his left hand, swinging his legs over the wolf's back to mount him.

Okay, he told Myko silently. *Remember the Conclave trick?*

He glanced upward, seeing Nemesis and Bella still a good fifty feet above. Nightmare was falling much faster, three of its tentacles extended downward. The Familiar could land and absorb the shock of the impact, bending its legs to make Piper, Kendra, and Thaddeus slow to a safe – if uncomfortable – stop.

He, on the other hand…

Gideon took off his hat, reaching in to pull out a black disc. He threw it down at the rapidly approaching floor, then gripped Myko's flanks tightly between his legs.

Go!

Myko flashed bright silver, and Gideon felt them burst upward! The air howled in his ears as he shot past Nightmare and Nemesis, the paintings all around him a blur. A moment later, Myko's moon-dash ended, and their ascent slowed, then stopped.

Gravity grabbed them, pulling them inexorably downward.

Gideon reached into his chest-painting, drawing out his cane and gripping it as hard as he could, his eyes on the floor far below.

419

The black disc landed in the center of the floor, and Nemesis and Bella landed to one side of it, Nightmare on the other.

"Get back!" he cried, falling toward them with terrible speed. The floor approached rapidly, and he lifted his cane high above his head. "Anulus!" he shouted.

The black disc expanded, creating a large hole in the floor directly beneath him...and he and Myko fell toward it. Gideon brought his cane down as hard as he could right as they passed through, slamming it into the edge of the floor.

And then gravity *shifted*, and he found himself sliding on the floor behind Myko in his Conclave, heading right toward the wall some twenty feet ahead.

Which, conveniently, was heavily padded.

Myko slammed into the wall, and Gideon crashed into Myko, the impact blasting the air out of his lungs. He grunted, hearing Myko yelp in pain as the wolf's ribs crumpled underneath him.

Gideon bounced off, sliding backward across the floor, then coming to a stop.

"Ow," he gasped, rolling onto his belly and pushing himself up to his knees. He felt dizzy with the movement, and closed his eyes, collecting himself. Myko whimpered, scrambling to get to his feet. But one of the wolf's legs was clearly broken.

Sorry old boy, Gideon apologized.

And then Myko burst forward in a ray of silver light, passing right back through the portal of the Conclave.

Gideon got to his feet, feeling his cane vibrating powerfully against his palm. He smiled, then strode toward the portal after Myko.

"Time to kill some Reapers," he declared.

* * *

Bella stood at the edge of the black hole in the floor of the tower, staring into the darkness. Nemesis stood behind her, and Piper, Kendra, Goo, and Grandpa were on the opposite end of the portal.

"Gideon?" Bella called out.

A ray of silver light shot out of the portal, materializing into a large silver wolf. Myko fell to the floor beside the portal, grunting with the impact. Gideon's head popped out of the portal a moment later.

"I could use a hand," he quipped, extending his cane to Piper.

Piper reached down, grabbing the cane and pulling Gideon out of the portal. Then Gideon deactivated it, putting it back in his hat.

"Incoming," Kendra warned, pointing upward. Bella glanced up; there, descending slowly through the air toward them, were the Reapers, their cloaks rippling, their long scythes gleaming in the light of Gideon's lantern, which had landed near the wall. Gideon ran to grab it, tucking his cane into his right armpit.

Then he threw his lantern up into the air, right at the Reapers. "Eruptus!" he cried.

The lantern *exploded* in a burst of eyeball-searing light.

A shockwave burst outward and upward from the lantern, slamming into the Reapers and the paintings on the walls. The Reapers flew backward, one of them vanishing right into a canvas. The other smashed into the wall between two paintings, ricocheting off.

And dozens of paintings fell from the walls, falling right toward Bella and the others.

Gideon flung his hand outward, and his black glove shot off of it, flying upward. Then he ran for the door, flinging it open. Everyone burst through to the room beyond…just as the paintings struck the floor behind them.

Moments later, Gideon's glove returned through the doorway, clutching his lantern…and went right back onto his hand.

"Get back," he warned, handing his lantern to Piper, then holding his cane before him. Myko stood at his side, the great wolf's fur glowing with a soft silver light.

They waited for the remaining Reaper to reappear, but it didn't.

"Bet it ran off," Piper guessed. Gideon said nothing, but stepped through the doorway back into the tower, being careful not to fall into one of the many fallen paintings lying in a heap on the floor. He looked up, his jawline rippling.

"It's gone," he confirmed.

"It's going back to the Collector," Kendra stated. "If we follow it, it'll bring us right to him."

"We need to save these people first," Grandpa countered, gesturing at the heap of paintings.

"And we need to get *you* to safety," Bella reminded Grandpa.

"True," Grandpa conceded. He gave a rueful smirk. "No such thing as battle-Writers. I'm afraid the pen isn't always mightier than the sword."

"We'll store you and the paintings in my Conclave," Gideon decided. He retrieved his black disc, placing it beside the heap of paintings and activating it. "You get in first, and get on the bed, or go in my studio," he instructed Grandpa. "We don't want you to have a live painting fall on you."

"Will do," Grandpa replied. He turned to Bella then, taking a deep breath in. "Well, I suppose this is it then." Bella gave him a weak smile.

"I guess it is," she agreed.

He leaned in, wrapping one arm around her and holding her tight.

"I love you, sweetheart," he murmured.

"Love you Grandpa." She pulled away, brushing a curly strand of hair from her face. "Thanks. For everything."

"You are most very welcome," Grandpa replied. "Your mother would be proud of the woman you're becoming," he added, his eyes turning moist. "But it's hard to imagine anyone being prouder than I."

Bella hugged Grandpa again, kissing him on the cheek. Then they pulled away, and she took a deep breath to collect herself. She turned to Gideon, giving him a nod.

"Let's do this."

Gideon helped lower Grandpa into the painting, waiting a minute or so. Then he began shoving paintings from the pile carefully into the portal. Bella went to his side to help, as did Piper and Kendra. After a few more minutes, every one of the paintings that had fallen — which was most of them — was safely stored away. Bella glanced at Nemesis.

Can you grab the rest?

Nemesis nodded, spreading her wings and flying upward to grab the remaining paintings…at least the ones with Painters stuck in them. The Familiar dropped these into the portal, then landed beside Bella.

"Alright," Gideon stated, facing everyone else. "Ready?"

"Ready when you are," Piper answered. Bella nodded in agreement, but Kendra gave Gideon a look.

"Have an extra Painter's uniform lying around?" she inquired.

"No, but I have paintings," Gideon offered. They went into the Conclave, and soon afterward, Kendra returned, clad in a simple shirt and pants. She'd stuffed small rolled-up canvases in her pockets. It was no Painter's uniform, but given the circumstances, it would have to do.

"Thanks again, Gideon," she stated.

"Ready now?" he inquired. Everyone nodded, and he began the long walk up the tower wall. Nemesis flew Bella up, and with few paintings left on the wall, Nightmare was able to use its long tentacles to climb up to the balcony high above, depositing Piper and Kendra upon it. And Goo simply crawled up the wall to the balcony, being sticky enough to do so.

Kendra led them through the door to a series of hallways beyond, making their way to the tallest tower in the inverted castle. A spiraling staircase led ever upward, bringing them to a small landing. A horizontal bar, like one of the parallel bars a gymnast might swing on, stood there. Kendra leapt up, swinging back and forth until she swung all the way up…and let go, falling *upward* to a landing above.

She looked up at them – or down, or whatever – gesturing at the bar.

Gideon went next, making even quicker work of it than Kendra had, and Piper followed. Bella took one look at the bar, then glanced at Nemesis. The dragon grabbed her shoulders, flying her upward…and then rotating in the air with a sickening lurch, dropping Bella on the platform next to the others.

"Ugh," she grumbled, waiting for a wave of nausea to pass. Myko was last, simply moon-phasing to the spiraling staircase further down from them. Kendra took the lead again, bringing them to the bottom of the stairs far below, where a plain wooden door greeted them.

"This is it," Kendra whispered. "The Collector's office."

Gideon strode up to the door, tucking his cane in his armpit, then grabbing the doorknob. He hesitated, glancing back at Bella.

"You can do this," she reassured. "If you wait until you're ready to do something…"

"I'll never do it," he recited. He smiled, inclining his head. "The student has become the teacher."

"Time to take care of an unintended consequence," Bella declared. "I believe in you, Dad."

"Then I'm as ready as I'll ever be," he replied…and turned the doorknob, opening the door.

Chapter 48

Gideon stepped through the doorway into the Collector's office, Bella, Kendra, Piper, and the three Familiars following behind him. The room was large, with shelves lined with books and artifacts lining the walls to the left and right. Above the shelves were large stained-glass windows, and a domed ceiling rose at least twenty feet above his head. On the far wall was a single door, with a large painting hanging directly above it.

A very familiar painting.

He felt his guts twist, a vision of the same painting standing on its easel in his old studio coming to him. A painting of a boy reaching out to him from under the dark waters of a lake. Of course, the painting of the boy was gone.

But he hadn't gone far.

For there, seated at a large desk in the center of the room, was a man in a white suit, his back to Gideon. A man whose slicked-back hair was half-black, half-white.

"Hello Gideon," the man greeted. Standing up, the man turned to face him. Gideon swallowed, staring at him. At the man who he'd once thought of as his son.

"Collector," he replied coolly.

He'd never seen his son – no, his *creation* – as an adult. The Collector had grown into a fine-looking man, and it pained Gideon to know that this was how his real son would have looked. But something was terribly wrong; the right side of the Collector's face had aged considerably, his skin deeply wrinkled and so thin it was almost translucent. And his right eye was nearly opaque with cataract. He was wearing a bright white suit, a red handkerchief peeking out of his left breast pocket.

"I see you met my wife," Gideon observed. The Collector's lips curled in a little smirk.

"She made quite an impression," he replied.

"She had a tendency to do that," Gideon agreed. He took a deep breath in then, steeling himself. "You didn't have to kill her."

The Collector paused, then nodded.

"You're right," he conceded. "I didn't. But she was protecting Thaddeus, and Thaddeus was a danger to me."

"Only because you attacked him and killed his daughter," Gideon pointed out. "Thaddeus and Lucia had little love for the Pentad after what the Pentad did to them. You could have taken Blackthorne and let them go and they would have let you."

"Perhaps."

"Definitely," Gideon retorted. The Collector raised an eyebrow.

"Are you saying I brought this on myself, Gideon?" he inquired. Gideon grimaced, knowing exactly where this was going.

"I brought you into this world," he replied. "And I daresay I've paid the price."

"And now you've come to take me out," the Collector declared, raising his arms up to either side. "Gideon Myles: the victim, the villain…and now, the hero."

"I'm no hero," Gideon retorted. "I'm just correcting an old mistake."

The Collector chuckled.

"So now I'm your mistake," he murmured, shaking his head. "Did I ask to come into this world, *father*?"

"No."

"Did I ask you to lie to me, to make me believe I was your son?"

"No."

"Did you lie when you said you loved me?"

Gideon paused, then shook his head.

"No," he answered.

"Bullshit," the Collector swore. He tore the red handkerchief from his breast pocket, unfolding it with a flick of his wrist. Black on one side, red on the other, the black side was a portal into a small pocket of space that held Excisus, a glowing silver sword with an edge so sharp it could cut through nearly any substance. A sword – and handkerchief – that Gideon had painted for the Collector himself.

The Collector withdrew Excisus, holding it at his side, point-down.

"I loved you," Gideon stated calmly, ignoring the implied threat. "Even though, deep down inside, I knew you weren't my son."

"You loved the *idea* of me," the Collector retorted. "If Xander had come back to life, you would've sent me right back into my painting!"

"Maybe," Gideon replied. "Maybe not. But I'm going to send you back now."

"Maybe," the Collector retorted. "Maybe not."

Gideon studied the man, eyeing his white suit.

"You're not wearing the black suit I painted for you," he noted. A suit designed to protect his son's painting from nearly any attack, to ensure that he would never die again.

"I'm not," the Collector agreed. He snapped his fingers then, and the door at the other end of the room opened. A woman with short silver hair wearing a silver dress stepped in, followed by a strange, porcelain-skinned humanoid wearing shabby clothes, a bottle clutched in its right hand. And at its side, a sullen-looking boy with slicked-back blond hair.

Wearing a very familiar black suit.

"Simon, this is Gideon, my creator," the Collector introduced.

"And Simon is…?" Gideon inquired.

"My adopted son," the Collector answered. He gave a wry little smirk. "How ironic…a painting with a Painter son, and a Painter with a painted son."

The woman in the silver dress walked to a chair in the rightmost corner of the room, sitting down. Gideon's eyes flicked to her, then back to the Collector.

"There's no need to involve anyone else in this," he reasoned. "Return to your painting peacefully and no one else will get hurt."

"Everyone here has been hurt," the Collector retorted.

"The Painters you trapped are free," Gideon lied. "It's over."

"It's not over until I stop breathing," the Collector shot back, lifting his sword and pointing it at Gideon. "One way or another."

A shadow slid out from under his desk, and a Reaper rose from it, bone-scythe in hand. It levitated beside its master, facing Gideon. The air grew instantly colder, sending the hairs on Gideon's neck on-end.

"Don't do this," Gideon pleaded. The Collector inclined his head at the Reaper.

"Kill them," he ordered.

The Reaper burst forward, swinging its bone-scythe at Gideon!

Gideon swung his cane to block the blow, and the cane discharged its stored energy with the impact, nearly ripping the weapon out of the Reaper's hands and sending it flying.

And at the same time, Myko moon-dashed right into the Reaper.

But the Reaper returned to its shadow-form, vanishing into the floor, and Myko shot past it, slamming into the wall beyond.

"Simon, you and Doppelganger take care of the others," the Collector ordered, striding toward Gideon. "I'll handle Gideon."

The porcelain-skinned humanoid bolted forward, bursting past Gideon, just as the Collector lunged at Gideon, slashing at him with his glowing silver sword.

* * *

Bella saw the Collector lunge at Gideon, and drew Sleep Terror from her chest-painting, whipping it at the man. But the porcelain-skinned creature – the Doppelganger, the Collector had called it – leapt to intercept the blow. Her whip struck the Doppelganger, but its magic had no effect on the thing. It charged at her, raising its bottle to strike.

Nemesis came to the rescue, holding onto Bella from behind and wrapping her wings around Bella protectively. The Doppelganger's bottle went right into one of Nemesis's wing-paintings, and it drew back quickly, clearly surprised.

Behind her, Nightmare – Kendra's familiar – sent a black tentacle outward to wrap around Doppelganger's right arm, yanking it violently to the side. The Doppelganger smashed into the wall, its body shattering…and then promptly re-forming. Piper sprinted toward it, transforming into Vengeance in mid-stride, and rammed it with his massive shoulder.

The Doppelganger's body crumpled...and re-formed again. It whipped its bottle at Piper's temple so hard the bottle shattered.

Piper stumbled to the side, looking dazed.

At the same time, the Collector slashed at Gideon, his lethal sword connecting with Gideon's cane. But instead of cutting right through, the blade stopped instantly, its momentum absorbed by the cane's powerful magic. Gideon counterattacked, ramming the butt of his cane into the Collector's belly.

The Collector grunted, backpedaling quickly...and swung at Gideon's face as he did so. Nemesis was already lunging at the Collector, and whipped her tail, wrapping it around the Collector's free hand and jerking him to the side right before the sword would have cut through Gideon's face.

And Myko moon-dashed right into the Collector's flank, sending the man hurtling toward the wall.

The Doppelganger leapt to intercept the Collector, catching him in mid-air right before he crashed into the wall. Myko finished his moon-dash, rematerializing...and the Doppelganger smashed its bottle right on top the wolf's skull.

Myko yelped, stumbling to the side and looking dazed...and the Collector swung his blade, slicing right through Myko's torso, cutting the wolf in half.

"Myko!" Bella cried in horror.

The wolf glowed bright silver, then dashed away from the Collector, rematerialized at Bella's side...whole once more.

"Gonna need to work together," Piper grumbled, walking back to Bella's side. "How about a little divide and conquer?"

Gideon took a few steps back, joining them as they faced the Collector and the Doppelganger.

"Piper and Kendra, you take Simon and the Doppelganger," Gideon ordered. "Bella, I'll get you as close as I can to the Collector."

"Oh I doubt that," the Collector retorted.

The Reaper materialized from its shadow-form, appearing between them and the Collector, its scythe once again in its hands. The air instantly cooled, goosebumps rising on Bella's arms.

"Oh yeah," Piper muttered. "Forgot about him."

"Nightmare," Kendra prompted. "Go kill the Reaper."

Nightmare sent a black tentacle shooting at the Reaper, wrapping it around the creature's huge scythe and yanking it to the side. But the Reaper merely returned to its shadow-form, reappearing a few feet in front of Bella...and lifted its scythe up to strike.

"Goo!" she cried, even as the deadly weapon plunged toward her.

Goo leapt between them, the scythe plunging into his gelatinous flesh...and stopping there. Goo wrapped himself around the Reaper and its weapon, trapping it inside himself.

But the Reaper merely returned to its shadow-form, passing right through Goo and rematerializing next to the Collector.

"Okay Gideon," Piper grumbled. "How in the hell are we going to fight that thing?"

And then Myko moon-dashed straight into the Reaper, sending it flying backward...right into the Collector's painting.

Trapping them both inside.

"Simon!" the Collector snapped.

The boy rushed toward the Collector's painting, and Nightmare sent a tentacle shooting after him. But the Collector cut that tentacle in half with his glowing sword. Gideon shoved his cane into his chest-painting, then thrust one hand out, his black glove flying forward. It sailed right at Simon, just as the boy reached the painting to pull the Reaper out.

But instead of grabbing Simon, the magical glove grabbed the frame of the painting, yanking it forward...and threatening to trap Simon inside.

Simon dodged out of the way just in time.

Gideon's glove flew right back to Gideon, stopping before its master, the painting still in-hand. Gideon reached into the painting, pulling Myko out...but leaving the Reaper trapped inside.

"The Collector!" he cried, flipping the painting around so its painted side faced the Collector.

Myko took the hint, moon-dashing right into the backside of the painting.

The wolf shot across the room, shoving the painting at the Collector...and trapping him within.

Myko and the painting slammed into the opposite wall, and Myko materialized, stumbling backward from the painting. It landed face-up...and Simon leapt for it, sliding across the floor and reaching into the painting, pulling the Collector out. Then he kicked the painting to the side, and it slid across the floor away from them.

"Nice try," the Collector growled, holding his sword before him. "Playtime's over." He turned to Simon and the Doppelganger. "Kill the woman and the Actor."

"But Gideon," Simon protested.

"Leave Gideon and the girl to me," the Collector ordered.

Simon swallowed, but nodded, glancing at the Doppelganger.

Who sprinted at Piper with frightening speed, lunging at the Actor.

Piper met the Familiar head-on, kicking it right in the belly. His foot smashed through to the Doppelganger's back...but the Doppelganger hardly minded. Piper's leg was effectively trapped...and the Doppelganger grabbed Piper by the head, whirling him around and throwing him bodily toward the open doorway at the opposite end of the room. Piper went right through the doorway, vanishing into the room beyond...

...and Doppelganger and Simon went right after him.

"Piper!" Kendra cried. Nightmare wrapped a tentacle around her waist, carrying her quickly across the room and through the doorway after her husband.

And Miss Savage stood from her chair, walking up to the door to close it...and lock it.

"Thank you Miss Savage," the Collector stated. He turned to Gideon and Bella then. "I believe a little music is in order."

Miss Savage smiled, returning to her chair. She reached up into the air with one hand, drawing it downward...and the bow of a violin appeared in her hand. She set this on her left shoulder, and a violin appeared there.

"Any requests?" she inquired in a smooth, sultry voice.

"Surprise them," the Collector replied.

And then Miss Savage began to play.

* * *

Harsh notes struck Gideon's ears as Miss Savage's bow danced madly over the strings of her violin, the sudden burst of music so jarring it made him stumble backward. Myko cowered, burying his ears in his paws, and Bella cried out, covering her own ears.

431

But the notes climbed higher, screeching with a crazed fury. An onslaught that pierced Gideon's ears, making his eyes water. He dropped to his knees, his head pounding with each vicious strike of Miss Savage's bow across the strings. The Collector strode up to Gideon, his sword poised to strike. He had undoubtedly heard the song before, and had become accustomed to its power.

But Gideon had not. He just knelt there, Bella a few yards behind him, both helpless against the onslaught.

Undead dragons, however, *had* no ears.

Nemesis lunged forward, whipping her tail and striking the Collector across the right side of his face. His head snapped to the side, his thin skin tearing like tissue paper, blood spraying from the wound.

He cursed, turning to face her and raising his sword. But Nemesis jumped upward, flapping her wings forward to send herself flying backward. She landed at Bella's side, the wind from her wings slamming into the Collector, knocking him back a step.

Myko, Gideon cried out silently. *Take her down!*

Myko shot forward as a beam of pure silver light, careening toward Miss Savage.

Who stopped playing the violin…and began to sing.

Stop world
Rest for a while,
Time goes on
But yours is slowing.

And as she sang, time slowed to a crawl.

Gideon watched as Myko moon-dashed toward Miss Savage, beaming toward her inch-by-inch. While his mind moved at normal speed, everything else was painfully slower. His breathing. His heartbeat. Even the speed at which his eyes moved.

He watched in disbelief as Miss Savage calmly stood from her chair at normal speed, continuing to play as she stepped out of the way of the oncoming attack, hooking her chair with one foot and sliding it along with her.

What she was doing was impossible. Inconceivable. *No* one could do it…not even the greatest Musicians in the Pentad.

432

Myko slammed into the wall where she'd been only moments ago, the stone cracking under the impact. He materialized with agonizing slowness, then stumbled backward from the wall.

And Miss Savage eased herself into her chair as if nothing had happened, continuing to sing.

You stop
But Time goes on,
An eternity in every
Second.

Gideon turned his head slowly, watching as the Collector recovered from Nemesis's blow. He was moving slightly faster than everyone else – save for Miss Savage, of course – having apparently desensitized himself somewhat to the song. The Collector ran right for Gideon, raising his sword to strike.

The blade plunged right for Gideon's head...and there was nothing he could do to stop it.

Suddenly wings curled around Gideon from behind, blocking the Collector from view. Gideon waited for the Collector's sword to pierce right through Nemesis's wings and impale him...but nothing happened.

Then he remembered that her wings were painted. The Collector's sword must have plunged through them.

Nemesis retracted her wings violently, throwing the Collector to the side. At the same time, her tail whipped out, lashing him across the right temple...again.

The Collector swore, whipping his sword at her tail as she retracted it. The blade cut right through, amputating the tip of her tail.

Right as Myko moon-dashed into the Collector from behind.

The Collector flew forward with the impact, but as Myko was moving incredibly slowly, the blow had only fraction of the force it otherwise would have had. The Collector dodged out of the way, slashing at Myko's flank as he did so. The blade did no damage – Myko was invincible while he was moon-dashing – and Myko reached the other end of the room, colliding with the wall there in slow-motion.

Then the Collector turned back to Gideon, leaping past Nemesis and thrusting the tip of his sword at Gideon's forehead.

433

Nemesis swung her tail at the Collector's head, and it wrapped around his free arm from behind. She yanked backward, and the Collector's blade veered away from Gideon's head, piercing his right shoulder instead. It sank into his flesh with ease, going right through his shoulder bone and exiting out his back.

The pain was excruciating.

Nemesis pulled the Collector toward herself, the sword yanking free from Gideon's shoulder. The dragon lunged at the Collector's sword-arm, clamping down on it with her powerful jaws. The bones of his forearm crumpled with a horrible *crunch*, blood spurting from between Nemesis's razor-sharp teeth.

The Collector *screamed*.

But instead of sinking to his knees, or giving up, the Collector did something else entirely.

He switched the sword to his left hand, lifting it high in the air, then bringing it down on the dragon's bony neck.

Decapitating her.

Chapter 49

Bella watched in horror as the Collector's sword sliced through her Familiar's neck, cutting through the bone as if it weren't even there. She felt a horrible pain in her own neck, so sudden and agonizing that it threatened to drop her to her knees.

Nemesis's jaws released from the Collector's forearm, her head tumbling to the floor in slow-motion. Her body went rigid for a moment, then collapsed, leaving her headless skeleton lying crumpled on the floor.

And under the power of Miss Savage's terrible song, all Bella could do was watch.

A world
Frozen in Time,
Rest up,
Your moment's coming.

The Collector swayed, clutching his mangled right forearm to his belly. Blood pumped from deep wounds there, spattering on the floor. He turned to Gideon, gripping his sword's hilt so tight that his knuckles turned white.

Bella stared at Nemesis's head, her mind numb. Her legs wobbled, and she fell slowly, feeling her knees strike the floor. She could still feel her dragon's thoughts. The final few seconds of life before oblivion took her.

Look at your enemy, she felt Nemesis order.

Bella turned her head slowly, staring at the Collector. The man had shifted his sword to his left hand, and was striding toward Gideon, his mouth set in a grim line.

No more running.

Gideon raised his cane as the Collector swung his sword, barely managing to block the deadly strike.

Don't think.

Gideon's cane unleashed the energy it had absorbed earlier, and the Collector's sword shot backward.

Do!

Bella looked down, seeing Sleep Terror still clutched in her right hand. She grit her teeth, rising to her feet.

She drew Sleep Terror back, then swung it forward at the back of the Collector's head, watching as the bony whip uncoiled in slow-motion. But the Collector merely dodged to the side, avoiding the strike...and returned his gaze to Gideon, raising his sword again to attack.

And this time, there was no way Gideon would be able to defend himself in time.

Bella reached into her chest-painting. She felt the dull heat of one of the fireballs Gideon had placed within the canvas back before they'd gone through Devil's Pass.

There are bad people out there, Bella. And they'll use your kindness against you.

Bella hesitated, gripping the fireball tightly. She heard a voice inside her head then, Nemesis's final thought.

End him.

Bella cried out, drawing the fireball out of her chest-painting and hurling it at the Collector.

A sudden burst of heat assaulted her as it materialized, shooting forward at incredible speed, even with Miss Savage's song. But somehow the Collector managed to dodge it anyway, lunging to the side.

And the fireball shot right past him, slamming into Miss Savage instead.

Miss Savage shrieked as she and her chair burst into flames, and time returned abruptly to normal.

"No!" the Collector cried, turning away from Gideon and rushing to Miss Savage's aid. He struggled to remove his white suit coat to snuff out the flames, but Miss Savage recovered quickly, her voice filling the room again. A chilling tune that send a shiver down Bella's spine…and turned the air inside the room practically arctic.

The flames around her snuffed out.

"Go Myko!" Gideon cried.

Myko moon-dashed at the Collector and Miss Savage, but materialized halfway across the room, his silver glow dying out early.

"What's wrong?" Bella blurted out.

"He's running out of moonlight," Gideon answered grimly.

Myko bounded toward the enemy anyway, leaping at the Collector. But the Collector dodged out of the way at the last minute, and Myko slammed into the wall behind the man.

And the Collector thrust his sword into Myko's flank, the terrible blade sinking into the wall itself…and pinning poor Myko against it.

Myko *howled*.

Bella burst forward, rushing to the great silver wolf's aid. She went around the Collector's desk – and Gideon vaulted over it, even with his injured shoulder – sprinting at the Collector.

Miss Savage intercepted them, assaulting them with the end of her time-altering song.

Soon Time
Will be with you again,
And give life
To moments.

Time slowed again, even as Bella lashed out with Sleep Terror, aiming for the Miss Savage's head. Bella watched as the skeletal whip unfurled before her, the tip sailing toward the woman. And as the Collector wrapped his fingers around Myko's throat.

And squeezed.

Myko shrieked, the horrible sound cutting off abruptly as his windpipe was forced shut. He flailed frantically, wrapping his big paws around the Collector's arm, his eyes wide with terror. Still the Collector squeezed, harder and harder. So hard his whole hand turned white.

Crack.

Myko's windpipe crumpled.

"No!" Gideon shouted. He rushed at Miss Savage, swinging his cane at her.

Miss Savage dodged Gideon's attack...but not Bella's. Sleep Terror struck her temple in a glancing blow, barely scratching her. But it was still enough for the whip to exert its dark power.

Miss Savage's song cut short, her eyes rolling up into the back of her head. She slumped to the floor, her head bouncing off the hard marble.

Gideon rushed past her, swinging his cane at the Collector. But the Collector yanked his sword out of the wall – and Myko – blocking the blow. Gideon roared, swinging the cane again and again, attacking the Collector viciously.

The Collector stumbled backward, barely managing to fend off Gideon's blows.

Gideon was unrelenting, his face twisted in rage. And the harder each blow struck the Collector's blade, the more powerful the subsequent strike became...until Gideon hit so hard that the Collector's sword flew from his hand. Gideon followed up with an expertly executed blow to the man's right thigh.

The bone snapped in half, and the Collector *screamed.*

He fell flat onto his back, clutching at his ruined leg...and Gideon stood over him, pressing the butt of his cane into the Collector's chest. Gideon's own chest heaved as he glared down at the man, his face beet red.

"You bastard!" he cried, pinning the Collector to the floor.

Bella reached Myko's side, kneeling down before the poor wolf. Myko gasped for air, his eyes wide with terror, a horrible gurgling sound coming from his throat. Blood oozed from his nose and mouth, forming a frothy pool around his snout.

"Gideon!" Bella cried.

Gideon blinked, turning to face them.

"Get him into a painting!" he ordered.

Bella nodded, her eyes going to the Collector's painting. It'd slid to one corner of the room; she got to her feet, running for it.

And the Collector reached out, his glowing sword sliding across the floor and leaping back into his hand. He batted Gideon's cane to the side.

"Miss Savage!" he shouted, "Wake *up!*"

Miss Savage's eyes jerked open.

Bella reached the Collector's painting, grabbing it and hauling it back toward Myko...just as Miss Savage got to her feet. She opened her mouth.

And *shrieked*.

The horrible sound filled the room, piercing Bella's ears. Bella and Gideon – and the Collector – screamed, clutching at their ears in agony.

Bella sank to her knees, her eyes watering as invisible knives plunged into her eardrums, seeming to drill into her very brain.

Miss Savage's scream ended, and she strode up to the Gideon and the Collector. Gideon had also sunk to his knees...and Miss Savage kicked him right between the eyes. Gideon's head snapped back, and he fell backward onto the floor. Blood spurted from his nose, his eyes rolling back in their sockets.

And right next to her, Myko was barely breathing, bloody foam spilling from the corner of his mouth.

Bella gasped, her head still pounding from Miss Savage's shriek. She struggled to get to her feet, but her legs wobbled beneath her, sending her right back onto her butt.

Miss Savage turned to the Collector, kneeling before him. Blood still poured from his right forearm, and his face was terribly pale, his breathing labored.

"Get in the painting my love," she urged, gesturing at the painting beside Bella. "I'll find a way to save you. No matter how long it takes."

"No," he retorted, his jawline rippling.

"But..."

"Take it down," he ordered. "Take it all down."

She stared at him mutely, and he turned to her, lifting his good hand to her cheek. He leaned in, kissing her on the lips, then pulled away.

"I love you," he murmured. She smiled, her silver eyes turning moist.

"I know."

"Why do you love me?" he asked.

"Because I do," she answered, stroking his scalp gently. He smiled.

"That's good enough for me."

"Any requests?" she inquired, a tear dribbling down her cheek.

"One last request," he stated, watching as Gideon and Bella got to their feet. "The End."

Miss Savage swallowed visibly, then bowed.

"As you wish, Collector."

She returned to her charred chair, sitting down to play.

Chapter 50

Piper flew backwards through the doorway of the Collector's office, landing on his back with a *thump* in the waiting room beyond. The impact would have stunned a normal man, but Piper wasn't a normal man. In fact, he wasn't even Piper.

He was Vengeance.

Vengeance sprang to his feet, spotting the Doppelganger rushing through the doorway toward him. It swung its bottle at his head, and he blocked it, grabbing it by the jaw with one massive hand and squeezing.

Its jaw crumpled.

Simon sprinted through the doorway behind the Doppelganger, and Vengeance tossed the Doppelganger aside, lunging at the boy. He kicked the boy's chest, his heel connecting with bone-crunching force.

And felt a force slam into *his* chest with a loud *crack*.

Vengeance flew backward, landing flat on his back. The impact blasted the air from his lungs, making it impossible to breathe. Agony shot through his breastbone, and when he finally was able to draw a breath in, it felt like he was being stabbed in the heart.

He struggled to get to his feet, stumbling backward. Simon stepped leisurely toward him, completely unharmed, his face dark and expressionless.

"You can't hurt me, Actor," the kid said.

Vengeance continued to back away, clutching at his chest. The Doppelganger had already recovered from being attacked, returning to Simon's side.

A thick black tentacle wrapped around the Doppelganger's waist from behind...and Nightmare threw him sideways, so violently that the Doppelganger sailed thirty feet to the right, smashing into the wall.

The creature shattered.

At the same time, Nightmare wrapped another tentacle around Simon's waist. But instead of the Familiar throwing him to the side, *Nightmare* was the one thrown...in the opposite direction. Nightmare careened toward the other wall, but used its other tentacles to soften the blow.

And then Kendra stepped through the door...and it slammed shut behind her.

Piper felt himself changing back to his original form, the room seeming to grow bigger all around him.

"Look kid, I don't have a problem with you," he told Simon, holding out one hand. "We don't want to hurt you. We're here to..."

"Kill the Collector?" Simon interrupted.

"Put him back where he belongs," Piper corrected. "My wife worked for him for over a decade," he continued, gesturing at Kendra. "She did everything he asked. She was loyal to him. And he betrayed her, trapping her in a Painting. And that's exactly what he's going to do to you."

"Wrong," Simon retorted.

"With all due respect, you don't know what you're talking about," Kendra shot back, stepping around him to Piper's side.

"Hey hon," Piper greeted, flashing her a smile.

Green gel squeezed under the door to the Collector's office then, oozing onto the floor behind Simon and the Doppelganger. It was Goo, Bella's creation. Piper resisted the urge to look at Goo, keeping his eyes on Simon.

"Come with us," he urged. "We can help you. You don't know who the Collector is."

Simon's lips curled into a smirk.

"I know who he is," he retorted. "I know his story. The one that made him and the one that *he* made."

"Kid…"

"And your story," Simon interrupted, "…is about to end."

The Doppelganger lifted its bottle, then charged at them!

Or at least it tried to. Goo lunged at it, wrapping a gelatinous tendril around the Doppelganger's legs. The porcelain creature looked down, then raised its bottle, trying to smash it down on Goo. But the bottle merely sank into Goo's translucent flesh…and stuck there.

The Doppelganger went *berserk*.

It thrashed wildly, jerking its bottle free, then struggling to free its legs from Goo. But it was no use. A black mist began to seep from the Doppelganger into Goo, making Goo grow larger.

And larger…and larger.

Still Doppelganger thrashed, becoming more and more violent.

Goo swelled up as he absorbed the thing's fury, doubling in size, then tripling…and quadrupling. But the Doppelganger only struggled more. It started smashing its own leg, breaking through its left shin, then working on its right.

Suddenly it stopped, lifting its gaze to Simon, as if a secret communication had passed between them.

Then it *exploded*.

Pieces of its porcelain body flew outward in all directions, and Piper jumped in front of Kendra, shielding her with his body. The sharp fragments sliced through Piper's skin, opening gaping wounds in his flesh.

Then the pieces converged in front of Piper, the Doppelganger re-forming before him. It raised its bottle above its head, then sent it crashing down on Piper's skull.

A black tentacle shot outward, blocking the blow, then wrapping around the Doppelganger's torso. This time, instead of throwing or crushing the Doppelganger, Nightmare merely lifted it in the air, holding it captive.

Piper grunted, releasing Kendra and facing Simon…just as Goo – now at least ten feet cubed – rose up like a wave in the ocean behind Simon, crashing down on the boy. But Simon reached into his breast pocket, pulling out a small, brown glass orb and throwing it at his own feet.

It shattered…and fragments of glass shot upward, expanding as they did so to form a large, translucent dome around Simon. Goo

443

fell upon it, wrapping himself around the dome, but Simon remained safely within.

Then the fragments of glass making up the dome exploded outward, sending Goo flying upward and backward. Goo slammed into the wall above the door to the Collector's office, and the glass fragments coalesced to form a wall that trapped him against it.

Simon ignored Goo, stepping calmly toward Piper and Kendra.

Nightmare lunged at the boy, wrapping his thick tentacles around Simons legs, belly, and neck, and pinning his arms to his sides. At the same time, Kendra reached into her forearm-painting, grabbing a long silver javelin and launching it at Simon.

It struck the right side of Simon's chest...and vanished.

Piper heard a *thump* to his left, and turned...seeing Kendra stumbling backward, her eyes wide, her mouth agape.

The javelin was embedded in her chest, its cruel tip protruding from her back.

Kendra fell to her knees, clutching at the shaft. A crimson stain spread outward from it, staining her shirt. She fell to her knees, and Piper caught her, staring at her in horror.

"Oh no," he mumbled. "No no no..."

"I told you you can't hurt me," Simon stated, still in Nightmare's clutches. "The Collector's suit does unto others what they would do unto me." Piper turned to him, clutching onto Kendra.

"You bastard!" he shouted. "What have you done?"

"I didn't do anything," Simon retorted.

Kendra tried to speak, but coughed instead, blood gurgling out of her mouth and pouring down her chin.

"Oh god baby," Piper murmured, turning back to her. "Oh god no!" He felt a flash of fear, then anger. Felt the Flow sweep over him. Piper let it take him, the anger turning to rage. His limbs grew, muscles bulging, the room seeming to shrink around him as he metamorphosed.

Into Vengeance.

The floor seemed to tremble under his feet, the wailing of a violin sounding in the distance.

Piper set Kendra down, then lunged at Simon, still bound by Nightmare's tentacles. He punched the kid square in the face...and felt a force smash into his *own* face. Vengeance stumbled backward, blood gushing from his nose.

He *roared*.

Vengeance swung at Simon again and again, each blow striking him instead of the boy. He didn't care, punching and kicking at Simon, ignoring the pain of each attack.

And Simon just stood there, staring back at him with that smug little expression on his face.

Vengeance lunged at Simon, wrapping his huge hands around the boy's scrawny neck...and squeezed. He felt his own throat close, the blood supply to his head cutting off. His vision blackened, and he let go, stumbling backward.

And he felt the Flow leave him, and he became Piper once more.

Piper stood there, beaten and bloodied, staring at Simon. The boy was utterly unharmed...and Kendra was on her hands and knees, a pool of blood growing under her. Piper's shoulders slumped. There was no beating this boy, not when he was wearing the Collector's suit.

"We surrender," he muttered. "Just let us go."

The Doppelganger shattered, its porcelain fragments flying in a straight line at one of the tentacles holding Simon. The razor-sharp pieces cut right through the black flesh, severing the tentacle...and the Doppelganger re-formed beyond it. It repeated the process, severing the rest of the tentacles, and Simon levitated gently down to the floor.

"No," he replied.

The floor quaked suddenly, Miss Savage's desk in the leftmost part of the room vibrating, a glass set atop it tipping over and falling to shatter on the floor. Piper heard the wailing of a violin from beyond the door of the Collector's office again, louder this time. Rapid notes stumbling over each other in a nightmarish song. One that sent a chill down Piper's spine.

A feeling of impending doom came over him, his hackles rising.

The notes swelled, higher and louder, a cacophony of chaos. The castle groaned, a violent shudder running through it. Dust fell from the ceiling, fine cracks appearing in the stone walls.

Simon spun around, rushing toward the door and trying to fling it open. But it was locked.

"Collector!" he cried, pounding on the door.

"Nightmare!" Piper prompted, kneeling down and picking Kendra up in his arms. "Get us out of here!"

The Doppelganger burst into fragments, shooting into the small gap between the door and the floor. Moments later, the door swung open, revealing the Doppelganger standing on the other side.

The wailing of the violin slammed into Piper's consciousness.

Terror gripped him...and the floor shuddered, cracks appearing in the stone. More dust fell from the ceiling, along with hunks of mortar.

The glass wall entrapping Goo shattered, the pieces shrinking and coming together in Simon's hand to re-form the small glass orb. Goo fell to the floor with a *thump*, and Simon left the room, closing the door behind him.

The castle shuddered again, so violently that it nearly threw Piper to his knees. He clutched Kendra to him, spotting a huge crack in the ceiling directly above. It widened, a large chunk of the ceiling breaking free and falling to the floor beside him.

"We gotta get outta here," he urged, carrying her toward the doorway leading out of the waiting room, to the hallway beyond. But the castle quaked again, and the ceiling ahead of them collapsed, huge chunks of stone coming crashing down.

And blocking their only exit.

Piper swore, turning around and making his way back to the door to the Collector's office. He tried the knob, but it was locked.

"Damn it!" he cursed, kicking the door. "Hey! Help!" He kicked the door again, and Kendra gasped, clutching onto the javelin impaling her. "Gideon! Bella! Open the goddamn door!"

Kendra tried to say something, but coughed up clotted blood, each cough making her clutch her chest harder.

"Nightmare, get us out of here," Piper ordered. The Familiar went to the collapsed hallway, lifting pieces of rubble with its tentacles. A small hole appeared above, silver rays of moonlight streaming through.

Yes!

But the castle quaked again, and the floor gave out suddenly under Nightmare. The Familiar vanished below...and the hole in the floor expanded, hunks of the stone giving way only a few feet from where Piper stood. He swore, backing away toward the corner of the room. A small island of the floor remained around Piper and to one side of the door to the Collector's office...where Goo was hanging half-off the edge of the hole.

The ceiling above crumbled, hunks of stone falling into steadily-widening abyss. Directly above Piper, the ceiling sagged, a huge hunk of it threatening to break free.

Goo hoisted himself up onto the small piece of floor, climbing up the walls to what remained of the ceiling. He sent green tendrils out above Piper and Kendra...tendrils that supported the sagging ceiling, preventing it from crashing down on them.

For now.

Kendra gripped the shaft of the javelin tightly, trying to pull it out of herself. Piper gasped in horror.

"Baby, what are you doing?"

"Get it...out," she ordered.

"You'll die," he retorted. She grimaced, trying again, but to no avail.

"Do it," she insisted.

"I can still save us," Piper insisted. The castle quaked again, more of the floor giving way...and then the whole castle seemed to shift.

It was *leaning.*

"And now the castle's tipping over," he realized.

"Can't...save us," Kendra mumbled. Piper hesitated, then glanced up at the ceiling. Goo was the only thing stopping it from collapsing on them...and if this room was collapsing, that meant the main tower above would too. And if the rubble from *that* fell on them...

"Well damn," he muttered.

"Told you...so," she stated with a bloody smirk. She coughed, spitting out another clot. She kicked off her boots then. "Take them," she prompted. "Run down...the walls."

"I'll carry you down with me," Piper said. "We can..."

"My weight will screw it...up," Kendra retorted. "Go. Get out of here."

"I'm not leaving you," Piper insisted.

"I deserve it," Kendra argued. "After everything I...did. The people I betrayed."

"I don't care about any of that," he retorted. "I forgive you."

"I don't forgive myself," she shot back. "Piper, go on without me. It's better...this way."

"No way."

"Do it," Kendra ordered. "Go find…someone else to…torture."

"Babe…"

"She better…be cute," Kendra said, devolving into another fit of coughing. "I want to be jealous when I come back to haunt you."

Piper smiled despite himself.

"You're something else, you know that?"

"Go on," she insisted.

"No."

"*Go*," she pressed, glaring at him. "That's an order."

"Not a chance," Piper replied. He felt the whole castle shift, and it seemed to lean even more to the left. He squatted down, holding Kendra in his arms. "I made a promise, remember?"

"Piper…"

"Where you go, I go," he vowed.

There was a horrible *crack*, and the floor underneath them sank downward a foot. Kendra clutched onto Piper tightly, and he held her close, leaning over to kiss her on the forehead.

"Ready love?" he asked. She shook her head, tearing welling up in her eyes.

"No."

"Yeah, me neither."

And then the world crumbled beneath them, and the castle swallowed them whole.

Chapter 51

Bella stood a few yards from the Collector, Sleep Terror clutched in her right hand. Gideon lay unconscious on the floor, his face bloodied, Nemesis's decapitated body close by. Myko was on his side on the floor by Bella, his throat crushed, struggling for air.

She rushed to Gideon's side...right as Miss Savage – sitting in her chair nearby – drew her bow across her violin, starting a new song. A song that was fast and furious, sending a shudder through Bella. Indeed, the whole castle seemed to shudder, the floor vibrating subtly beneath them.

"Come on Gideon," Bella urged, jostling Gideon's shoulder. But he just stared up at the ceiling. "Wake up!"

"It's over," the Collector growled from where he lay on the floor a few yards away.

"Shut up," Bella retorted, turning to glare at him.

"It's too late," he pressed. "You're all going to die."

Bella stood then, swaying as the castle seemed to shudder again, Miss Savage's song growing louder and more insistent. She took a step toward the Collector, reaching under the neck of her uniform to feel her mother's amulet there. She pulled it out, letting it rest on her upper chest, just above the canvas of her chest-painting. Another step forward, and a bright light began to rise from the Collector's body, streaming into the amulet.

The Collector's eyes widened.

"Collector..." Miss Savage called out from across the room, breaking from her song.

"Play!" he snapped.

Bella paused, then turned back to Gideon, kneeling down and reaching into his chest-painting to retrieve his magical lantern. She tossed it straight up to the ceiling.

"Eruptus!" she cried.

Light exploded from the lantern, sending a shockwave that slammed into the stain-glass windows above the shelves. They shattered, allowing rays of silver light to shine through. Bella caught the lamp as it fell, placing it back in Gideon's chest-painting. Then she glanced at Myko.

His fur glowed ever-so-faintly in the moonlight.

Miss Savage resumed her song, one so haunting that it sent a chill through Bella. The whole castle shuddered, books and artifacts clattering on the shelves around them. Each note threatened to scatter Bella's thoughts, filling her with a sense of impending doom.

Bella grit her teeth against the awful music, turning back to the Collector, still lying on the ground, his right arm and leg ruined. She held her mother's amulet before her, watching as white light appeared around him once again.

"You murdered my mother," she accused, taking another step toward him. "You hunted me and my Grandpa for *ten years*. You tried to kill me!"

He said nothing, just lying there.

"Why?" she demanded. "We never did anything to you!"

"You didn't," he agreed. "He did," he added, pointing at Gideon.

"He never wanted to hurt you," she retorted. The Collector's jawline rippled.

"Do yourself a favor," he replied. "Don't believe a word that man says. He believes every lie that comes out of his mouth."

"You're the murderer," she countered.

"At least I'm honest."

"Well so am I," Bella retorted, taking another step forward, then another. The white light around the Collector brightening, leaping toward the amulet in a steady stream. "You've hurt everyone I love," she accused. "And I'm going to make sure you never do it again."

He stared down at the light rising from his body, swallowing visibly. But he did not back away.

"You Painters and Writers play God," he declared, gripping his sword tightly. "You make us obey you. You *design* us so we have to love you." He shook his head. "It's not right."

"You killed my mother," Bella shot back. "That wasn't right, but you did it anyway."

"She was just like the rest of them," the Collector argued. "She was *worse*."

"You don't know the first thing about my mother," Bella retorted. The Collector gave her a grim smile.

"Neither," he replied, "...do you."

Bella stepped closer to him, even as Miss Savage continued to play. Her violin's notes came faster and faster, a chaotic jumble that somehow fit together, a symphony that shook her to her very soul...and shook the very floor beneath her. She lost her balance, stumbling to the side.

"Gideon never told you about her, did he," the Collector pressed, his eyes going to Gideon, who was still laying on the floor, unconscious. "He never told you what she was."

"Shut up," Bella ordered, catching herself. She took another step forward, and the light coming from the Collector grew brighter. The Collector grimaced in pain, dropping his sword and clutching at his chest.

"You know why?" he pressed. "Because he was ashamed of her, just like he's ashamed of me. And you."

"I said shut up," Bella repeated. More light shot out from him to her amulet, and he cried out in pain, gripping his chest tightly.

"He never told anyone about...you," he gasped. "If his precious Pentad learns that he married a Necromancer and had a child with her, they'll...reject him." He gave a cruel smile. "And if there's anything he cares about more than you, it's his...reputation."

"Shut *up!*" Bella screamed, lunging at him. White light burst from his entire body, shooting forward into her amulet. The heart-shaped ruby glowed bright red, absorbing the Collector's life force. The Collector cried out, collapsing onto the floor, his face twisted with pain.

And as Bella watched, his hair turned gray, then white, his skin thinning and becoming ever more pale. The fine wrinkles in his face deepened rapidly, his flesh drooping from his bones.

451

She swallowed, feeling sick to her stomach. Tears welled up in her eyes, but she did not back away.

"You won't stop," she realized. "So I have to stop you. I have to make sure you never hurt anyone I love, ever again."

Miss Savage slashed at her violin, and it screamed out in wrathful agony. The whole castle shook, books falling from the Collector's shelves, dust raining from the ceiling. Cracks appeared in the floor and the walls, the stone torn apart by Miss Savage's terrible magic.

"Stop," the Collector gasped, his flesh sagging horribly, his eyes sinking into his skull. Bella shook her head, taking a step closer.

"No," she replied. "You won't use my kindness against me. You don't deserve it."

Gideon stirred, waking up...then sitting up. He stared at the Collector, then at Miss Savage...and Bella.

"She's bringing the whole place down!" he realized, scrambling to his feet. The room shuddered, huge cracks forming in the domed ceiling high above. Hunks of stone rained down to the floor, one of them missing Bella by mere feet. She stumbled backward, the white light streaming between her and the Collector winking out.

"Come on," Gideon urged, grabbing Bella's arm and pulling her away from the man. "I'll handle him."

"No," she retorted, resisting him. "He killed Mom! He..."

"Trust me," Gideon insisted. He pushed Bella away gently. "Myko, protect her," he ordered. Then he went to the Collector's side, kneeling down.

The Collector's elderly face was twisted with pain, his right forearm bloodied and broken, his right leg bent at an impossible angle.

"Come to...put me...in my painting?" he gasped. Gideon shook his head.

"No."

"Don't pretend to care about me," the Collector spat. "You never did."

"I'm not pretending anymore," Gideon replied. The Collector glared at him.

"Another one of your...lies."

"You were right," Gideon confessed. "Right about me. Right about how I never truly loved you. How I fooled you – and me – into believing you were Xander."

"How…comforting."

"I'm sorry I didn't let him go," Gideon stated. "I never should have made you."

The Collector smiled grimly.

"Too late."

"I should have kept his memory alive here," Gideon continued, pointing to his heart. "Not in you."

"You can always…make another," the Collector countered. Gideon shook his head.

"No. It's time I let Xander go."

There was a sudden banging on the door nearby, and moments later, fragments of shattered porcelain shot under the door, flying up to form the Doppelganger. The porcelain Familiar opened the door, and Simon stepped through. The boy's eyes widened when he saw the Collector…and Gideon.

"Sir!" he cried, rushing to the Collector's side. Gideon backed away from them, holding his cane out to defend himself. But Simon merely knelt before the Collector, staring down at him in horror.

The Collector reached up with his good hand, grasping Simon's hand. Simon bent down, and the Collector whispered something in his ear.

Simon nodded, then stood, retrieving the Collector's sword. He placed it in the man's left hand. Then he looked up at his Doppelganger…and nodded.

The Doppelganger sprinted toward Bella and Gideon, leaping at them with its bottle held high!

A flash of silver light shot across the room, slamming into the Doppelganger and sending it flying into the wall. It shattered…and none other than Myko materialized nearby, landing on all fours on the floor…perfectly healed.

"Myko!" Bella cried, her heart soaring.

But the pieces of the Doppelganger flew back together, re-forming the powerful Familiar. It lunged at Gideon, and Myko went to intercept, standing between the two and growling at the Doppelganger.

"Let me handle this," Gideon requested. Myko paused, then stepped to one side. The Doppelganger burst toward Gideon, swinging its bottle at his head with frightening speed.

Gideon held up his cane to intercept the blow…and the Doppelganger's arm stopped as the bottle connected with the cane.

In fact, the Familiar's entire *body* stopped, its momentum completely neutralized.

The Doppelganger swung at Gideon again, this time with an overhead chop. Gideon slammed the butt of his staff into the floor, then held up his cane to block again…stopping the Doppelganger's momentum instantly. Again and again it swung, and each time Gideon blocked, then discharged the stored energy into the floor. Such was the magic of his cane that the impacts caused no damage whatsoever to the Doppelganger or its bottle.

Every attack was simply – completely – neutralized.

The Doppelganger went berserk, leaping at Gideon to tackle him. Gideon raised the butt of his cane, tapping it in the chest…and temporarily freezing it in mid-air. Then he tossed one of his thigh-paintings onto the floor below it.

"Apertus!" he commanded.

The Painting unrolled itself…and the Doppelganger fell straight toward its painted surface.

"No!" Simon shouted.

The Doppelganger spontaneously exploded into countless fragments, flying back to Simon's side. The pieces coalesced, re-forming the Familiar.

Gideon tucked his cane into his armpit, thrusting his left hand outward. His glove shot toward the painting on the floor, picking it up and flying it right at Simon…painted-side first.

Simon's eyes widened, and he didn't even have time to react.

But the Doppelganger did.

It grabbed Simon's wrist just as the painting enveloped the boy…and yanked him out of the painting before he was fully trapped. Gideon's glove moved with them, however, sending the painting after them like a heat-seeking missile.

Miss Savage's violin shrieked, a sound so awful that Bella screamed, hunching over and covering her ears. A single note that blasted Gideon's painting away from Simon, and shattered the ceiling and walls. They crumbled, massive stone fragments falling toward all of them.

Simon grabbed Miss Savage, holding up one arm to block a falling piece of rubble. The Doppelganger burst into fragments that flew toward the Collector. But instead of striking him, the fragments *covered* him…and formed a suit of armor around him, so that the Collector was *inside* of it.

And as Simon flew upward into the air, carrying Miss Savage toward a huge hole in the ceiling above, the Doppelganger leapt upward to grab its master's ankle. All four of them disappeared through the hole…just as the room utterly collapsed.

Bella felt the floor shudder under her feet, then start to sink downward, even as a huge section of the ceiling broke free from high above, falling right toward them.

"Gideon!" she cried.

"To me!" Gideon shouted. Bella and Myko rushed to Gideon's side, and he shoved his cane into his chest-painting, then took off his hat, turning it upside-down. He reached inside, throwing something upward.

"Anulus!" he cried…just as the huge hunk of ceiling slammed into them from above.

Chapter 52

Bella screamed, throwing her arms upward...and then felt herself hurtling forward through the air. Her chest slammed into something hard, blasting the air from her lungs. She gasped, scrambling to her feet...and felt a hand on her shoulder shoving her to the left...toward a large bed, which Grandpa just happened to be sleeping in.

The Conclave!

Bella leapt onto the bed, turning around just in time to see an avalanche of boulders blasting through the black portal. Hunks of rock flew across the room, slamming into the wall opposite the portal. More and more rubble came, pouring through the portal until a third of the room was filled with it.

And then, moments later, it was done.

Bella stared at the pile of rubble, then turned to see Gideon and Myko also sitting on the bed. And Grandpa, who'd sat bolt-upright, his eyes wide with shock.

"What the...!" he exclaimed.

"Well, that worked," Gideon declared, dusting off his suit. Myko *wuffed*, licking Gideon's cheek. Then the wolf bounded up to Bella, giving her similar treatment. Bella looked down at herself, checking for injuries, but she seemed intact. Gideon, on the other hand, looked a hot mess. His hair was disheveled, his nose bloodied and his right shoulder covered in dark clots from where the Collector had stabbed him. And as he gave her a relieved smile, it was clear he'd chipped a tooth.

And Myko…well, his injuries had all been moon-dashed away.

"Ran in to a bit of rubble I see," Grandpa noted. "You look terrible, Gideon. Are you all right?"

"Nothing a fresh coat of paint can't fix," Gideon replied, winking at Bella. She smiled back, shuffling up to him and giving him a big hug. He winced.

"Careful with the shoulder," he warned. She eased up a bit.

"Thanks for saving us," she murmured. He squeezed her back.

"Thanks for…you know," he replied. They disengaged, and she lowered her gaze.

"Sorry about your…the Collector."

"I take it you defeated him?" Grandpa guessed. Gideon hesitated, then nodded.

"Bella drained him. He had a protégé…a young boy named Simon. A Painter. Simon managed to take the Collector and escape, but the Collector is as close to death as a man can be without *being* dead. It's only a matter of time now."

"Ah," Grandpa murmured. "I see."

Gideon turned to Bella, looking remarkably guilty.

"Bella, I'm sorry you had to do that," he stated. "That you had to drain the Collector…that you had to be the one to…"

"Kill him?" Bella asked. Gideon nodded.

"I know how you feel about killing," he stated. "But he didn't leave us a choice."

"No," Bella retorted. "I *did* have a choice. And I chose to protect my family."

Gideon hesitated, then gave a sad smile.

"Okay Bella," he replied.

"Gideon, are you alright?" Grandpa inquired. Gideon sighed.

"Letting go of my son was the second most difficult thing I've ever had to do," he admitted.

"What was the most difficult?" Bella asked.

"Forgiving myself," he answered.

She leaned in to hug him again, being careful not to hurt his shoulder. Then she kissed him on the cheek that wasn't bloody.

"You're a great dad," she told him. "Best dad I've ever had, actually."

"How comforting," Gideon grumbled. She laughed, pulling away from him.

"You *are*," she insisted. Then she turned to Grandpa, giving *him* a hug in turn. "You're both the best guys a girl could ask for."

"I daresay we're fond of you too," Grandpa replied with a smile. "You turned out pretty well...especially considering I was the one who raised you."

"Don't be so hard on yourself," Bella retorted. "You did a great job."

"Hmm, well, don't screw it up *too* much," Grandpa told Gideon, punching him playfully on the shoulder. His injured shoulder.

"Ow!" Gideon blurted out, jerking away from Grandpa.

"Oh!" Grandpa exclaimed. "Terribly sorry, old boy."

"Quite all right."

"He was wrong about you, you know," Bella stated, turning to Gideon. He frowned, giving her an inquisitive look. "The Collector. He told me you were...that you weren't a good person."

"Ah," Gideon replied, rubbing his forehead. "Must have been unconscious at the time."

"That woman kicked you in the face."

"I noticed."

"We should get you healed up," Bella prompted. She turned to Grandpa, eyeing his broken wrist. "Both of you."

"Later," he promised. Grandpa cleared his throat then, and they both turned to him.

"Where is Piper?" he asked. "Did he find Kendra?"

Bella and Gideon turned to look at each other, their eyes widening in horror.

"Uh oh," Gideon blurted out. Bella put a hand to her mouth.

"Oh no!" she cried. "They were fighting Simon before..."

"Damn," Gideon swore. "We have to find them!"

"And Goo," Bella agreed.

She jumped off the side of the bed, running toward the portal...and stopped in her tracks. The rubble from the castle had formed a pile some four feet high, completely blocking the path to the trick bookshelf that led to Gideon's closet...and the portal to the Conclave itself. She put her hands on her hips, staring at the mess.

"How are we going to clear *this* up?" she asked.

"Why, the same way we do everything else," Gideon replied, getting off the bed and taking a rolled-up canvas from his thigh-holster. "With art."

* * *

It took a good hour to clear up all the rubble from Gideon's Conclave, using large live canvases to scoop up the rocks one-by-one. Luckily the only boulders that had been able to get through the portal were no bigger than it…and Gideon had a few canvases that were just as large, if not larger, than the portal itself. And even after they cleared the rubble from the floor, more rocks spilled in when they took care of the pile blocking the portal. It took some time before no more rocks came through.

After they were done, it was clear that the Conclave was going to need a lot of repairs. There were dents in the wall opposite the portal, and the floor was pretty well chewed up. Even the bookshelf had sustained some damage.

But the repairs would have to wait; they had a far more pressing mission to attend to.

When they peered out of the portal, they found a narrow tunnel made of rubble leading up to the starry night sky above. They climbed their way out – and Myko moon-dashed out – leaving Grandpa in the Conclave…and found themselves standing atop a veritable mountain of rubble.

The Collector's castle was gone.

All around the perimeter of what remained of the castle were Dragonkin soldiers, some standing on the mountaintop, others flying high above. A few of the latter descended toward Bella and Gideon, landing nearby.

"You are alive, Gideon Myles," one of them said, clearly relieved. "The Creator…?"

"Alive and well," Gideon answered with a weary smile.

"Then you have done well," the soldier declared.

"Not as well as I would have hoped," Gideon confessed. "The Collector escaped, with a boy and a woman. Did you see them?"

"Indeed," the Dragonkin confirmed. "We fought to contain them, but were overpowered." He shook his head. "They are gone, to the Underground."

"Damn," Gideon swore.

"Wait," Bella interjected. "That means Simon can put the Collector in a painting and heal him!"

"The Collector would never allow it," Gideon argued.

"But…"

"Trust me," he insisted. "I know my work."

"Okay," Bella agreed. She turned to the Dragonkin. "We're looking for other survivors. The other man that was with us…his name was Piper."

"We shall aid in your search," the Dragonkin declared. "But thus far we have found no survivors amidst the rubble."

The Dragonkin flew off, and Bella, Gideon, and Myko spent hours searching the ruins for Piper, Kendra, Nightmare, and Goo. But by the time the sun peeked above the horizon, they had no success. Bella was nearly sleepwalking by the time Gideon threw in the towel.

"Bella," he stated, putting a hand on her shoulder. Her eyes snapped open, and she glanced at him wearily. He shook his head mutely.

"We can't stop looking," she protested, pulling away from him. "They're out there somewhere. We have to…"

"Bella, they're gone," Gideon interjected. "Myko can't even find their scent, and he's combed the rubble twice over." He sighed. "If they're here, they're buried under tons of rock. No one could survive that."

"But…"

"I need rest," he interrupted. "And so do you. Myko will keep looking while we sleep…and so will the Dragonkin."

Bella hesitated, then sighed, her shoulders slumping.

"Okay."

With a heavy heart, Bella followed Gideon back to the hole leading to the Conclave. But as Gideon started to lower himself down, she froze.

"Wait," she blurted out.

Gideon stopped, turning to face her.

"What?"

"I feel something," she explained. And she did. A faint *presence*, as if someone were nearby. But somehow far away. It was…strange. She said as much to Gideon.

"That's your Familiar," he realized. Bella blinked.

"She's…?"

"Alive, yes," he confirmed.

"But her head was cut off!"

"Did you feel her thoughts afterward?" he asked.

"Well, yeah. For a while."

"She's undead," Gideon theorized. "Maybe she can't die…not in the traditional sense anyway.

"She's here!" Bella realized, turning in a slow circle. "Over there!" she added, pointing at a spot amongst the mountain of debris a few dozen feet away. She sprinted to it, then circled around, trying to pinpoint Nemesis's exact location. But she couldn't. The sensation was too vague.

"You think she's around here?" Gideon inquired. Bella nodded.

"Somewhere under the rubble," she replied.

"We'll have to start digging tomorrow," Gideon decided. Bella gave him a look.

"We can't just leave her," she retorted.

"She's not going anywhere," he pointed out. She put a hand on her hip, shooting him a murderous glare. "Bella, you're exhausted. *I'm* exhausted. We'll do it after a good rest…I promise."

She sighed, her shoulders slumping.

"Alright."

They went back to the tunnel leading to the Conclave, easing themselves down to the portal. Grandpa was still there on the bed when they arrived, fast asleep. Bella's exhaustion returned with a vengeance, the short burst of adrenaline from realizing Nemesis was still alive suddenly spent.

She slipped in bed beside Grandpa, and within moments she was fast asleep.

* * *

When Bella awoke early that afternoon, she was alone on the bed. The bookshelf opposite the bed had been left rotated open, and she went into the closet, opening the door to Gideon's studio. Gideon was still asleep, using his cloak to float above the floor as he had when they'd traveled to Havenwood what seemed like a year ago. And Grandpa and Myko were nowhere to be found.

Gideon woke at the sound of the door opening, rolling over to squint at Bella.

"Oh," he mumbled, getting up. "Hello Bella."

"Didn't mean to wake you," Bella apologized. "Want me to…?"

"No no," he reassured her, sitting up and rubbing his eyes. "I was actually waiting for you to wake up." He grimaced, touching his shoulder gingerly. "I'm having a hard time sleeping."

"Want me to heal you?" she asked. While she was eager to start digging for Nemesis, Gideon was clearly in pain. He nodded, giving a wry smile.

"Thought you'd never ask."

He pulled off his shirt, then stepped into a canvas Bella placed against the wall. She got to work, mixing her paints, then painting over Gideon's wounds. She fixed his shoulder, then focused on the wounds to his face, being extremely careful to get the details right. When she was done, she pulled Gideon out.

"There," she stated, looking him over. She smiled at him. "Looks good."

He turned around…and she saw the hole in the back of his right shoulder.

"Oh! Right," she blurted out. Ushering him back into the painting, she fixed his back, then pulled him out again.

"Much better," Gideon stated, testing his shoulder out. He smiled at her…and she noticed the chip in his tooth. Back into the painting he went, and this time she finished the job, making him whole once again.

"Where's Grandpa and Myko?" Bella asked. "I still have to fix Grandpa's wrist."

"I already did," Gideon reassured. "Last night, while you were sleeping. He couldn't sleep because of the pain." He frowned then, a faraway look on his face. "Myko says they're searching the wreckage," he answered, his eyes focusing again. "Let's go join them."

They made their way through the portal and up the tunnel to the surface, and were surprised to see a literal army of Dragonkin all around them…far more than before. They'd clearly organized since the night before, and were continuing to search the wreckage. Some were picking through the rubble, while others were helping to clear it. Grandpa was close by, talking to none other than King Draco himself. When Bella and Gideon approached, Grandpa stopped, turning to address them.

"How's it going?" Bella asked.

"Not well," Grandpa admitted. "The Dragonkin suffered significant casualties...over two-thirds of their army is dead or badly wounded."

"Any word on Kendra or Piper?" Gideon inquired. Grandpa shook his head grimly. Gideon sighed, and Bella lowered her gaze, feeling a familiar glumness come over her. She had the sudden urge to go back to bed, to curl up in her blankets and hope that sleep would rescue her from this feeling.

"We did find something," Grandpa offered. Bella lifted her gaze to his, and Grandpa pointed far off in the distance, at a silver wolf sniffing at the rubble. She spotted a hint of green beside Myko, and her heart skipped a beat.

"Goo?" she blurted out.

She broke out into a run, speeding over the rubble. It *was* Goo, crawling over the rubble. Large stones were embedded in his gelatinous body; as she watched, he ejected them into a pile, then crawled into a large hole he and Myko were near, enveloping more of the stones. She reached their side quickly, a huge smile on her face.

"Goo!" she cried.

Goo's surface vibrated excitedly, and he extended a human-sized lump of himself to Bella. She hugged it, then let go, frowning at the two.

"What are you guys doing?" she inquired. And then it hit her. This was where she'd sensed Nemesis earlier! "Did you find her?" she asked excitedly.

Myko *wuffed*, pointing his nose at the hole. It was some ten feet in diameter, and equally deep. Goo crawled all the way down to the bottom, absorbing some stones, then crawling back up to eject them.

He was digging...and doing a rather good job of it.

Myko barreled down the steep slope to the bottom of the hole, slipping and sliding until he reached the bottom. He dug with his forepaws then, sending small hunks of debris flying. Goo joined him, taking more stones and hauling them out. Being far larger now than when she'd first painted him, Goo made quick work of deepening the hole...and soon it was quite clear what Myko had sniffed out.

They were bones, Bella realized. And a very familiar skull.

"Nemesis!" Bella cried.

She burst forward, sliding down the hole on her butt, then running to Myko when she reached the bottom. There, lying amidst the rubble, was her Familiar's skull. Somehow, someway, it was intact!

"Nemesis!" she cried, picking the skull up. Two red lights looked back at her from deep within the dragon's eye-sockets.

Hey there, Nemesis greeted.

"Where's your body?" Bella asked.

Couldn't have gone far.

"Good point," Bella admitted. She turned to Myko. "Can you smell them? Her bones?"

Myko nodded, and he and Goo dug a little further. Sure enough, Nemesis's body *was* nearby.

"How do we…you know," Bella asked. "Put you together?"

I assume you put my head back on my spine.

"Right," Bella replied. She did just that…and a faint red light seemed to bridge the gap for a split-second. With that, Nemesis's body came to life…or rather, un-life…and she spread her wings wide.

That's better.

"I'm so glad you're okay," Bella said, reaching in and hugging Nemesis's neck. She felt a pulse of tenderness from the dragon.

Might want to make me some armor.

"I will," Bella promised.

Make it look awesome.

"*Oh* yeah."

Like, dark and badass. Needs to be epic.

"You can help me paint it," Bella decided. By the emotion Nemesis sent her, the dragon clearly endorsed this plan.

"Ah, congratulations Bella," Gideon stated, walking up to the edge of the hole above and peering down at them. "Hello Nemesis."

Nemesis flapped her wings, flying upward…and grabbed Bella by the shoulders, bringing her right up to Gideon and depositing her beside her father. Myko moon-dashed out, and Goo crawled right up to join them. Bella noticed a few porcelain shards stuck in Goo's goo.

"Is that…?" she asked. Gideon turned to look, and Myko sniffed at Goo just above the shards.

"They're from the Doppelganger," Gideon confirmed. "Better hold on to them, Goo."

"So...what now?" Bella inquired, glancing at Gideon. He smiled.

"How about we go back home?" he answered.

"To Havenwood?"

"To Havenwood," he confirmed.

And, with the Dragonkin army escorting them, that's exactly what they did.

Chapter 53

The long, winding tunnels of the Underground were cast in a deep purple hue, from the strange light peeking from between the seemingly endless series of doors lining the walls. It'd been hours since Simon had entered the magical series of tunnels, following behind Miss Savage, General Bowen, and a few remaining members of the Collector's army. The Doppelganger was right behind her, the Collector carried in his Familiar's arms.

The great man's breathing was terribly shallow, his chest barely rising and falling with each breath.

There was a fork in the tunnels ahead, one leading down and left, the other up and right.

"Left," the Collector rasped.

Miss Savage obeyed his command, taking them down the leftmost tunnel. It wound deeper into the earth, eventually bringing them to a dead-end. A lone door stood at the end of it; this, however, was different than the other doors Simon had seen. It was much larger, with an ornate stone doorframe surrounding it. And, also unlike the other doors, it had a golden keyhole just above the knob.

They stopped before it, and General Bowen glanced at the Collector.

"The key?" he asked.

"Not physical," he explained. He cleared his throat, reciting the following:

"Painted worlds stuck in time,
One world they share,
For a single person's frame of mind
A place called Anywhere."

There was a *click*.

Miss Savage reached for the doorknob, but the Collector stopped her.

"Not yet," he rasped. "Go…after."

"After what?" she asked. He grimaced.

"After I go."

"I can still put you in a painting," Simon offered. "We can find a way to save you."

"Put me down," the Collector requested.

The Doppelganger obeyed, gently lowering the Collector to the rocky floor. Even so, he cried out in pain as he was set down, clutching at his ruined leg. He took a few gulping breaths, then calmed down. Simon knelt before him, gazing at the Collector. His face was pale, his skin slick with sweat. The Collector gazed back at him, raising his left hand to Simon's cheek.

"My boy," he murmured.

Simon swallowed, his vision blurring. He wiped away tears, not saying anything. Afraid that if he did, he would break.

"Take care of her, Simon," the Collector requested. "Take care of each other."

"Sir," Simon blurted out, tears streaming down his cheeks. His voice cracked. "I can still save you, I can…"

"You…" the Collector replied with a smile, "…already have."

Simon's eyebrows furrowed.

"I don't…"

"All my adult life I've hated Painters," the Collector admitted. "I dedicated my life to ending their…tyranny. To make a world where…paintings could be real and Painters would be fiction. Like…me."

"You're real, sir," Simon protested. "You're more real than anyone I've ever met."

467

"I can never be more than what my creator painted me to be," the Collector retorted gently. "But *you*, my boy…you're already more than your father ever imagined you could be."

Simon lowered his gaze, swallowed past a lump in his throat.

"Seek the truth, Simon. In your art, in yourself. In others. The truth will hurt you only once," the Collector declared, tracing one of the scars on Simon's cheek. He reached down then, pulling up Simon's sleeve…and exposing the multitude of scars there. "Running from it will hurt you over and over again."

Simon nodded mutely.

"Lie to your enemies if you must, but never to yourself," the Collector counseled, covering Simon's forearm once again. "And never to her," he added, nodding at Miss Savage.

"Yes sir."

The Collector smiled, patting Simon's cheek gently.

"No one can ever hurt you again," he murmured. "Not with what I've given you."

Simon shook his head, more tears streaming down his cheeks.

"They still hurt me," he said in a near-whisper. He grabbed the Collector's hand, pressing it to his heart.

"Then bring them to justice, Simon," the Collector stated. "Take their power from them, like you took your father's. Not for revenge, but because it's right. Don't be the victim that I was. Be a hero."

"You *are* a hero, sir," Simon replied.

"No."

"You're *my* hero," Simon insisted.

The Collector smiled, closing his eyes and resting his head back on the rocky floor of the tunnel. His hand slipped away from Simon's cheek, falling limply to the ground.

"Sir?"

The Collector opened his eyes, taking a moment to focus on Simon. His breathing was even more shallow now, his breaths coming so seldomly that Simon wondered whether he was breathing at all.

"Don't leave me," Simon pleaded, leaning over and burying his face in the Collector's chest. "Please."

"Remember what I taught you," the Collector pleaded.

Simon nodded mutely.

"I wish…" the Collector murmured.

Simon waited, but he said nothing more, laying there with his eyes closed, his mouth partly open. Seconds passed, and Simon realized that he wasn't breathing.

"Sir?" he asked, shaking the Collector's shoulder gently.

No response.

"Sir!" he nearly shouted, shaking him harder. The Collector's eyes opened, and he smile up at Simon, squeezing Simon's hand.

"Thank you Simon," he whispered.

"For what?"

"For opening my heart."

Simon buried his face in the Collector's chest again, squeezing his eyes shut. He heard the man's heart, felt each beat against his ear. There was an awful rattling sound from deep within the Collector's throat, and his chest rose and fell one last time.

As Simon listened, his heartbeat gradually slowed...then stopped.

And then, surrounded by the only people who had ever truly loved him, the Collector became the very thing that had willed him into existence.

A memory.

Chapter 54

The journey back to Havenwood was refreshingly uneventful. Bella and Gideon went through the Plane of Reflection to the inverted Underground, then enjoyed a short flight back to Dragon's Peak. The Dragonkind dropped them off at the base of the mountain, by the shore of Lake Fenestra. The Everstream flowed into the inverted lake just as it did in the real world – or rather, the original one – sunlight causing the waterfall to sparkle merrily. King Draco bid them goodbye, and promised to send his soldiers through the lake to the original world to help rebuild Havenwood.

After leaping into the lake and returning to the original world, Bella and Gideon got to work, taking all the paintings of the Painters the Collector had collected and drawing them out one-by-one. Most had violated the laws of the Pentad in joining the Collector, and having been betrayed by him, were now wanted criminals without a home.

But Havenwood was a home for those without a home. So it became theirs…and Gideon and Bella became instant heroes.

Having finished the task of freeing hundreds of artists, Bella found herself walking hand-in-hand with Grandpa and Gideon. They strolled up Main Street as it wound up Dragon's Peak, Myko trotting faithfully at Gideon's side. Nemesis, on the other hand, had already flown all the way up to the mouth of the Water Dragon cave, having little patience for walking. Bella found her Familiar's temperament to be quite different than her own, and marveled that she so poorly understood a thing she'd single-handedly created.

That's art, Nemesis told her. *You made me to be like your mother.*

"Funny, I don't remember my mother being such a..." Bella began, then realized Gideon was arching an eyebrow at her. "Uh, sorry," she mumbled.

"You'll get used to it," Gideon reassured.

"I hope not," Grandpa countered, a twinkle in his eye. "I'm dying to know what brought *that* on."

"Was Mom...difficult?" Bella asked. Gideon and Grandpa glanced at each other, then burst out laughing. Which earned them both glares.

"Remember when I told you she was...complicated?" Grandpa asked. Bella nodded.

"She was like a riddle," Gideon piped in. Grandpa nodded.

"One without an answer," he added.

Bella stopped, pulling her hands from theirs, and placing them squarely on her hips.

"Tell me about her."

"Your mother was..." Grandpa began, choosing his words carefully. "A woman at odds with herself." Gideon nodded in agreement.

"That's a good way to put it."

"She was the most heroic villain I ever met," Grandpa continued. "Always drawn so powerfully to darkness, yet desperately yearning for light."

"You're talking in riddles," Bella accused. Grandpa waggled his eyebrows.

"That's what she was."

"Am I *ever* going to get straight answers from you two?" she pressed, feeling rather fed up with them. They glanced at each other, then at her.

"Nope," they said in unison.

Bella threw up her hands in disgust, then stomped up the spiraling path, not bothering to see if they'd follow. Of course, they *did* follow, but only after sharing another laugh at her expense.

Well ha ha, she thought. *Yuck it up.*

They're not wrong, Nemesis notified her.

"Oh yeah?" Bella shot back. "What would *you* know about my mom?"

Well, considering I'm literally some of your repressed memories of her, more than you, her Familiar retorted.

Bella ignored the dragon, focusing on putting one foot in front of the other. Myko trotted up to her side, nudging her with his great big head. His tongue was out, his eyes smiling at her.

"Hey Myko," she murmured, scratching behind his ear. He gave her a big old kiss on the cheek, and she couldn't help but smile. "You always make me feel better, you know that?"

Myko *wuffed*.

"Why can't *you* be like him?" Bella muttered. She felt Nemesis roll her eyes, at least mentally. The dragon didn't have actual eyes to roll, after all. Bella had an evil thought involving a repeat performance of Nemesis losing her head, and Nemesis made it quite clear just how much she cared about Bella's feelings.

"And to think I missed you," she grumbled.

A while later, she made it to the mouth of the Water Dragon cave, making her way with Gideon and Grandpa to her mother's mansion. Animus was quite delighted to see them, swirling about excitedly when they entered the lobby. Gideon gave Grandpa a sly grin.

"Guess you could say she really 'mist' us, eh?"

Grandpa and Bella groaned, and they all went to the living room, flopping onto the couch there. Gideon sighed, staring at the dead fireplace.

"Well then," he stated. "Now what?"

"Pardon?" Grandpa replied.

"We've all spent the last decade being hunted down by a madman," Gideon explained. "Now that he's gone, what do you suggest we do?"

"I suggest," Grandpa replied, "...that we learn how to live."

"I'm on board with that," Bella piped in. "Hey, why don't we go visit the Pentad?"

Grandpa and Gideon exchanged looks.

"That...might not be the best idea," Grandpa replied. "Your father's facing prosecution, and I'm now a wanted criminal."

"What?"

"I published a book on the black market," he reminded her.

"Oh. Right." She frowned. "So my family is full of criminals."

"Including yourself," Gideon piped in. "You painted a Familiar without a license."

"Oh. Well, I guess we're staying here then," Bella decided. The two chuckled, and Bella went to hold Gideon's hand. But it was his right arm, and there was of course no hand to be found. "Hey," she stated. "Want me to give you your right hand back?"

Gideon frowned, staring at his stump.

"I don't know," he mumbled. Grandpa patted him on the shoulder.

"I'd say you've punished yourself quite enough, old boy," he prompted. "You have to forgive yourself if you want to be whole again."

Gideon sighed, lifting his gaze to Bella's. He nodded once.

"All right," he decided. "You've already made me whole again here, and here," he added, pointing to his head, then his heart. "You can give me my hand back."

* * *

Bella did paint Gideon a new hand, and although it took hours to get it right, the results were nothing short of spectacular. His new hand worked as well as the old one had, and upon exiting Bella's canvas, Gideon even got a bit emotional. He hugged Bella – a full hug, for the first time since she could remember, and they shared a laugh…and a cry. Then he got a funny look on his face, staring at her for a long time.

"What?" she asked.

He didn't reply, instead going to the far end of the studio. There was a large painting set against the wall there.

"Help me move this, will you?" he asked. She did so, each grabbing the frame and pulling it to the side…and revealing a door that had been hidden behind it. Gideon twisted the knob, opening it.

A narrow hallway lay beyond, with stairs leading downward.

Bella gave Gideon a questioning look, but he simply stepped out into the hallway, gesturing for her to follow. They went down the stairs, and she found herself in a small foyer adjacent to a living room, the front door to the home directly before them. Gideon opened the door, stepping through, and Bella followed behind him.

And found herself outside.

A grassy field extended outward for a hundred feet ahead, the rotting stump of what must have been a huge tree visible nearby. And beyond the field, a large lake.

Gideon led her past the tree stump, all the way up to the shore of the lake, and stood there gazing at it. The setting sun splashed its red and purple rays over the gently rippling water, a scene so striking that Bella had the sudden urge to paint it.

It was beautiful.

They stood there for a long while, and Bella glanced at Gideon. He stood tall, his shoulders set back proudly. But his eyes were moist.

"This is the lake," Bella realized, turning to look over the placid waters. "This is where it happened…in your Conclave."

Gideon swallowed visibly, then nodded.

"A painting killed my son, and my son's painting killed my wife."

They both stood there for a long while, and Bella wrapped an arm around his waist, pulling him a little closer. He put an arm around *her* waist, and they held each other, neither of them saying a thing for a long time. At last, Gideon stirred.

"I really screwed up," he muttered.

"Yup."

"If I hadn't…" he began, but Bella cut him off.

"But you did," she interrupted. "And it's not okay. It never will be. Mom's dead, you weren't there for me for ten years. And nothing can change that."

Gideon lowered his gaze, looking absolutely miserable.

"It doesn't *have* to be okay," Bella continued. "You made a mistake. A big one. But you can still come back from it." She smiled. "Sometimes the villain deserves to be a hero."

Gideon broke out into a rueful smile.

"Now you sound like your grandfather," he grumbled.

"I learned from the best."

Gideon took a deep, steadying breath in.

"I'm sorry Bella," he apologized. "For being a terrible father."

Bella rested her head on his shoulder, giving him a gentle squeeze.

"You *are* a terrible father," she told him, showing him her right forearm. "A good dad would *never* have let me get this tattoo so young."

He chuckled despite himself, shaking his head.

"Love you Dad."

He smiled a sad smile, squeezing her back. And though he didn't say it back, Bella wasn't offended. He was a Painter, after all. A master storyteller. He didn't need to say he loved her.

He'd already shown it.

* * *

By the time they went back into Gideon's old home, returning through the portal to Mom's house, it was well after sundown. Grandpa, Gideon, and Bella found themselves utterly exhausted. Though the sun had risen and fallen with the usual number of hour in-between, it had easily been the longest day of their lives.

So it was that Gideon bid Bella goodnight, retiring back to his Conclave. Nemesis went "out," whatever that meant, and Bella made her way to her bedroom. Grandpa came soon after, and like old times he laid beside her in bed, on top of her blanket. He spun her a wild tale, one as amazing as any he'd ever told, crafting a masterful story seemingly from thin air.

"How do you do it?" Bella asked when he was done. He rolled onto his side, peering at her through his gold-rimmed glasses.

"Do what?" he inquired.

"Make up such wonderful stories like that."

"Oh, well, I've lived a long life," Grandpa answered, rolling onto his back and staring up at the ceiling. "Nearly a thousand years, Bella. That's a long story."

"Yeah."

"Remember what I said about writing?" he asked. "That it's like being an archaeologist excavating a subterranean tomb, searching for priceless treasures?"

"Pieces of your heart and mind, lost to the ravages of time," Bella recited. Grandpa smiled.

"Well, I find that the more you live, the more stories you'll be able to tell," Grandpa explained. "And not just the years you exist," he added. "You have to *live* to have stories in you. That's where they come from, Bella. From pain and suffering and joy and hope and want and loss."

"Oof," she muttered. "I don't want half of those things."

"You already have them," Grandpa pointed out. "And you'll have more, I'm afraid. That's life. That's *your* story…and it's being written right now, as we speak."

Bella nodded, staring up at the ceiling. She spotted a sudden, faint light shining through her blanket then, and she frowned, pulling it down. Her amulet was there, resting on her chest.

And the heart-shaped ruby was glowing.

She stared at it, watching as it pulsed ever-so-slightly with a crimson light. Almost in time with her heartbeat. She sat up, frowning at it.

"What's this?" she asked, glancing at Grandpa. He sat up as well, staring at the amulet.

"Well I'll be," he murmured.

"Why is it doing that?" she asked.

"I think…I think the Collector must have died," Grandpa guessed. Bella stared at him, then down at the amulet. The ruby wasn't just glowing…it was whole. The crack that had run down its center was gone.

"I don't get it," she admitted. "Why's it glowing?"

"Well, it stole the Collector's life force, didn't it?" Grandpa replied. "Maybe it used it to heal itself."

"Maybe," Bella agreed. They both stared at it for a while longer, then laid back down. "You were right," she murmured.

"You'll have to be more specific," Grandpa replied with a mischievous grin. "I'm right about an awful lot."

"That she was always there to protect me," Bella clarified, ignoring his quip. "Even in…you know."

Grandpa nodded, his smile fading.

"She was quite the woman, Bella," he declared. "And I daresay you're becoming more like her every day."

Bella smiled.

"Thanks Grandpa."

He sat up then, leaning over and kissing her on the cheek, then getting off the bed and walking to the door. He opened it partway, then glanced back at her, his body silhouetted against the light from the hallway beyond.

"I love you sweetheart," he murmured.

"I love you too Grandpa."

He opened the door all the way then, turning to leave the room.

"Grandpa?" she asked. He turned to face her.

476

"Yes?"

"I feel guilty that Mom had to die to save me," she confessed. He smiled.

"Don't," he replied. "Your mother wasn't afraid of death, Bella. She always said that she wanted to die the way she lived."

"How's that?"

"Beautifully," he answered.

And then he closed the door with a soft *click*, leaving Bella alone in the darkness. And yet, within that darkness, a warm, pulsing light shone atop her breastbone, beating in a slow, comforting rhythm.

Beauty in the darkest dark.

Bella gazed at it for a while, then glanced over at her nightstand. She reached out to pull open its small drawer, feeling for a small, folded up piece of paper within. Unfolding it, she read the words on the page, written in perfect penmanship, her eyes going to the last paragraph.

> *Remember that love is something you give, as I gave mine to you. Give it to your art and heal your heart.*

Bella smiled, folding the paper back up, then putting it away. There was a scratching at the door, and she got up, pulling it open. It was Myko, of course. He leapt onto her bed, and she laid down beside him, feeling him curl around her back. His giant paw draped over her side, pulling her close.

She smiled, snuggling against him, and looked down at her amulet one more time, gazing at the steady pulsing of its heart for a moment longer. Then she tucked it under her shirt, closing her eyes.

And then, her broken heart made whole once more, surrounded by the warmth and love of her best four-legged friend, she fell fast asleep.

Epilogue

The innumerable pale, blue and green lights that served as the only illumination in Arx Mortus shone through the window of the cramped, single-room apartment. There were hundreds of rooms just like it in the dark tower that rose high above the city streets, and many more towers. And in each of the tiny rooms, there was a narrow, hard cot. A single window. And nothing else.

The denizens of the Lost Ones.

These wretched souls had stayed too long in the land of the living after their deaths before crossing over to the Plane of Death. Their bodies had decomposed beyond any hope of continuing the existence they'd had in life. Those whose brains had badly rotted still remained retained some memory of who they'd been. But for those poor souls whose bones were all that was left, there was no "self" at all.

No memories. Not even a name. Only a compulsion to act, to carrying out whatever mindless task had been assigned to them by their superiors. And a vague sense of personhood. Such that, had they not been afforded a small place to call their own, they would have been plagued by a profound depression, and not worked at all.

There were tens of thousands of Lost Ones in Arx Mortus, and millions more in the Plane of Death. All servants of Petrusa, Queen of the Dead.

Though the Plane of Death knew no sun, nor the endless cycle of day and night, the memory of these things remained even within the bones of the Lost Ones. They could not sleep, but still they laid in their cots, staring at the ceiling, waiting for sleep to come.

But one of the Lost Ones did not live in the towers of Arx Mortus.

It stayed instead in the palace, the huge castle set upon a great stone platform midway between the floor of the Plane of Death and the great Ceiling of the World above. It existed at the whim of Petrusa herself, following at the Queen's side.

Normally such a thing was not allowed. And indeed, this particular Lost One had been with its brethren in the towers at first. Just another skeleton amongst thousands of others.

It had only two qualities that set it apart from all the others. The first was a circle carved into its forehead, a ring into which molten gold had been carefully poured. Tiny symbols were etched into the ring's surface; runes that few of the living – or the dead – could have deciphered.

And the second were the small strips of flesh covering it on one side. Some muscle between its ribs, a piece of liver magically stuck to the inside of its lower ribcage. A hint of yellow fat deep within one eye-socket.

It was not the presence of these things that was so unique, but rather the fact that they had previously been absent.

And in the Plane of Death, nothing escaped Petrusa's notice. She had eyes everywhere, in the countless sculptures she'd created within her realm over the millennia.

So Petrusa had sent for this Lost One, allowing it in her palace. It became her constant companion, following her mindlessly day after day.

A reminder of Petrusa's failure.

For none who bore the golden ring were supposed to become Lost Ones. That was the promise, that those accepted to Petrusa's service would have their bodies returned to the Plane of Death intact, so they could continue in death as they had in life.

A promise Petrusa had failed to keep…and that was exceedingly rare.

Petrusa eased herself onto her throne, watching as the Lost One shambled to her side.

She felt something beckoning her, the psychic equivalent to a tap on the shoulder. It was the personification of Death, as old as the Plane of Death was.

Shadows from the columns in the throne room moved, converging into one deep shadow on the floor before her. From this rose the great black skull of Death himself.

"CASTLE UNDER HAS FALLEN," he notified her.

"The Collector?" she inquired.

"NEAR DEATH."

Petrusa accepted this. She was not particularly surprised. The Collector had risen to power quickly, becoming a very wealthy – and formidable – player on the world stage. But Gideon Myles was a truly gifted Painter, in a league of his own. The best of several generations. Only one other had approached his level in the last few hundred years.

"Thank you," she replied at last. But Death did not leave, though her statement had clearly been a dismissal. "And?" she inquired.

"HE MAY HAVE VALUE."

"We've followed him most of his life," she stated dismissively. "He has no value to me."

"HE HAS VALUE TO OTHERS."

She considered this.

"Very well," she decided.

Death left her then, vanishing into shadow.

She had no concern that her will would be carried out. The Reapers were denizens of the Plane of Death, after all. They followed whichever master managed to defeat them in battle until that master's death...and the Collector would soon be dead. As such, they would be able to provide a new master with the likely location of the Collector. And Petrusa would ensure that one of her Necromancers became their master.

The Reapers were as much a part of this world as the world itself. A fact that the Collector had not appreciated, for Petrusa had long ago hidden their true nature, concocting a false history for them.

The past was just a memory, after all. And after nearly all who had lived in the past passed away, history could be rewritten with impunity.

It was a shame that the Reapers had not witnessed the Lost One's death...and that the artifact providing its location had mysteriously vanished.

Petrusa sighed, finding her gaze drawn once again to the skeleton standing to her left. To her surprise, it was staring back at her. And that wasn't all.

She drew in a sharp breath, her eyes widening.

The Lost One had changed.

The bare strips of flesh at its chest and flank had blossomed, now flush with rust-colored muscle covered in patches of yellow, marbled fat. One of its arms was so flush with muscle that its bones there were completely covered, long tendons visible as they extended from its forearm to its fingers. The golden ring on its forehead was half-hidden with flesh now.

And a lone eye rested within its socket, staring back at her.

Petrusa resisted the urge to stand from her throne, regarding the Lost One silently for a long, long while. Then she gave it a rare smile.

"Well aren't *you* clever," she murmured.

Made in the USA
Middletown, DE
27 September 2019